SANCTUARY

SANCT

TUARY

CARYN LIX

SIMON PULSE

NEW YORK LONDON TORONTO SYDNEY NEW DELHI

SIMON PULSE

An imprint of Simon & Schuster Children's Publishing Division
1230 Avenue of the Americas, New York, New York 10020
First Simon Pulse hardcover edition July 2018
Text copyright © 2018 by Caryn Swark | Front cover art copyright © 2018 by Jacey
Jacket art on spine, back cover, and flaps copyright © 2018 by Thinkstock
All rights reserved, including the right of reproduction in whole or in part in any form.
SIMON PULSE and colophon are registered trademarks of Simon & Schuster, Inc.
For information about special discounts for bulk purchases, please contact
Simon & Schuster Special Sales at 1-866-506-1949 or business@simonandschuster.com.
The Simon & Schuster Speakers Bureau can bring authors to your live event.
For more information or to book an event contact the Simon & Schuster Speakers Bureau
at 1-866-248-3049 or visit our website at www.simonspeakers.com.
Jacket designed by Sarah Creech | Interior designed by Mike Rosamilia
The text of this book was set in Adobe Garamond Pro.
Manufactured in the United States of America
10 9 8 7 6 5 4 3 2 1
Library of Congress Cataloging-in-Publication Data
Names: Lix, Caryn, author.
Title: Sanctuary / by Caryn Lix.
Description: First Simon Pulse hardcover edition. | New York : Simon Pulse, 2018. | Summary:
"Prison-guard-in-training Kenzie is taken hostage by the superpowered criminals of the Sanctuary
space station—only to have to band together with them when the station is attacked by
mysterious creatures"—Provided by publisher.
Identifiers: LCCN 2017038614 (print) | LCCN 2018007740 (eBook) |
ISBN 9781534405356 (eBook) | ISBN 9781534405332 (hc)
Subjects: | CYAC: Correctional personnel—Fiction. | Supervillains—Fiction. |
Hostages—Fiction. | Science fiction.
Classification: LCC PZ7.1.L5853 (eBook) |
LCC PZ7.1.L5853 San 2018 (print) | DDC [Fic]—dc23
LC record available at https://lccn.loc.gov/2017038614

For my family

SANCTUARY

It drifts, but not aimlessly. With purpose, it drifts.
The signal is prime, and it drifts. Onward, it drifts.
The call comes. The harvesters awaken.
The harvest is ripe.
The signal is ready.
Slowly they unfurl in their tanks,
their sinews finding purchase in the flesh.
They rise.
They wait.
And they drift.

ONE

MY PARENTS WOULD KILL ME IF THEY CAUGHT me reading manga at one in the morning, but I was too keyed up to sleep. I hunched over my tablet, trying to lose myself in the world of *Robo Mecha Dream Girl 5*. Usually I couldn't wait for the latest issue and devoured it in a matter of minutes, only going back later to take it all in and absorb everything I'd missed. Tonight, though, I'd read the same page five times already and I still didn't know what was happening. Yumiko— Robo Mecha Dream Girl herself—was in some sort of breeding facility. What were they breeding? Why? I had no idea.

Yet another thing my parents had managed to mess up with their little announcement.

Five hours ago I thought things were going pretty well—a well-paying part-time job, citizenship in one of the most powerful corporations in the solar system, a family that functioned in its own comfortable routine. And then over dinner came those magic words: "Honey, we need to talk."

I'd turned to *Robo Mecha Dream Girl 5*'s midnight release to distract me, but it wasn't doing the trick. I cleared my tablet's screen. No point trying to read this right now. I had a shift in the morning, anyway, and I needed to—

The shrill of the alarm shot me straight out of my chair. My head smashed against the overhead shelf, and my tablet flew across the room. It shut down in protest, leaving me in a sea of flashing red and blaring alarms.

I thumbed the wall controls and jammed my feet into my boots. The lights came up, revealing I had them on the wrong feet. Swearing, I swapped them and tugged at the laces.

"Kenzie!" Dad's voice boomed from outside.

"Coming," I shouted. I took a second to scrape my curls out of my face and into a ponytail before I slid the door aside.

Dad waited, his hair disheveled. He frowned at the reflective surface of the comm device embedded in his wrist. "I know!" I said, barreling past him. Wasn't it enough that I was never late for a shift? Okay, fine, I was late for everything else. But this one really wasn't my fault—and if it was, I thought Dad's decision to "take a little break" and move into our old house without me and Mom was probably excuse enough.

The klaxon was loud enough to wake the dead, ridiculous since only five guards lived on the entire prison—six if you counted me. You'd think you'd need more people to staff a prison for superpowered teenagers, but not Sanctuary. Not with the power of Omnistellar Concepts and their first-rate AI in charge. A shiver raced through me at the thought of a bunch of superpowered criminals running loose. There was literally no other corporation I'd trust to keep them contained, especially when they happened to live in my basement.

I ran down the deserted corridors with Dad on my heels. We bolted through the living quarters into the larger area of the station that housed medical supplies, airlocks, a common room, and the command center.

The command center was where we found Mom, hands clasped behind her back, not a hair out of place. She was wearing her professional demeanor—no longer my reserved but affectionate mom with her wicked sense of humor, but every inch the station commander. Mom viewed her role of protecting the solar system from the prisoners as a sacred duty, and she demanded nothing less from her crew—including me. Guiltily, I smoothed a hand over my rumpled uniform. Of course I was the only one who looked like she'd just rolled out of bed, and I hadn't even been asleep. No matter how hard I tried to remember to fold my things neatly, I always wound up shoving them into drawers or tossing them in heaps around my room.

"About time," Mom said crisply. I flashed Dad a grin and he shook his head, but a smile played on his lips. Mom, on the other hand, was all business now, as she had to be—if there were any issues with the security systems on Sanctuary, just one of our criminal charges had the power to level the entire station. "Kenzie, pull up the video feed on the prison. Rita and Jonathan are already in position in case of an escape. Colton, back Rita up, and send Jonathan to man the emergency airlocks."

I cringed. Jonathan, Sanctuary's sole medical officer, was the least trained guard on the station. He didn't have the experience to be the first line of defense in the event of a prisoner's escape—that was Dad's job, and he'd already be there if I hadn't made him late. As for the rest of us, Noah and I did our thing on the bridge while Rita stalked around like she owned the place. We'd all been together less than three months, but we were a smoothly oiled team.

Or so I'd thought. Unbidden, my mind returned to that horrible conversation over dinner tonight, when Dad sighed and set his tray aside and my parents dropped their bombshell: Dad had requested a transfer back to Earth. After he finished his training seminar next week, he wasn't coming back to Sanctuary. Oh, they said it wasn't my fault—that it was the long hours and the like. But a lingering doubt made me wonder if I should have seen this coming, if I could have done something to prevent it.

Of course, if this was a genuine prison break, Mom and Dad were the least of my worries, and that meant I needed to keep my wits about me as well as my colleagues kept theirs. Even in a crisis like this one, I felt a surge of pride at being part of Sanctuary, at the trust Omnistellar Concepts placed in my parents—and in me. We had an important job to do, and I wasn't about to let anyone down.

Even if I was a few minutes late.

Dad ran out of the room, squeezing my shoulder as he went. In spite of the tension of the moment, I glanced at Mom, trying to see if there was anything different in the way she looked at him, but she only arched an eyebrow and nodded at my station.

I jogged past her to the row of computer consoles and perched on a stool, then poked at the buttons as if hitting them with enough force would log me in faster. Across from me, Noah, Sanctuary's youngest official guard, wore an expression of agony. "Commander," he called over the klaxon. "Now that we're all in position, permission to mute the alarm?"

Mom hesitated. Muting the alarm technically violated protocol, but how were we supposed to work over its howling? After a second, she gave a terse nod. Noah muttered a *thank you* only I heard, and seconds later the klaxon stopped mid-shriek. Warning lights continued to illuminate us with periodic bursts of red, sending everyone's face into sickly relief.

I logged in and found the feeds Mom requested. Instantly the command center's rear wall dissolved from its normal image of the exterior into an emergency feed, showing us the prison beneath our feet from every angle. By and large things looked normal—or as normal as they got, given that the prison housed catastrophes in human form. "Drill?" I muttered to Noah.

"Of course it's a drill." He flashed me a grin, and again I felt that sense of camaraderie. "The station's top of the line. There's never any real problem."

"*Every* alarm is to be treated as a real problem, Noah." Mom bit off the retort without even turning her head. Noah winced and shot an accusing look my way. He still hadn't gotten used to Mom's bloodhound senses. Me? I'd had seventeen years of practice. I'd mastered the art of the under-your-breath whisper.

I examined the screens more closely. Even if this *was* a drill—and it probably was; Sanctuary scheduled them every few weeks at unpredictable intervals—sometimes the computer did something shocking like open a cellblock or cause a malfunction in life support. Nothing that actually endangered anyone or risked a prisoner's escape, of course—but God help us if we missed it. Omnistellar Concepts hadn't become the undisputed king of universal law enforcement by hiring slackers, and it certainly hadn't earned the right to house the world's most dangerous teenagers with anything less than a fierce adherence to the rules.

The footage didn't show much, although a strange flicker caught my eye. "Unit two reporting," came Dad's voice over the comm link. "All clear through sector five emergency airlock."

"Roger that. Hold your position," Mom snapped.

I tapped the screen to enlarge the flickering video. It looked perfectly normal now. Biting my lip and wondering if I'd internalized more of *Robo Mecha Dream Girl* than I'd realized, I retrieved an interactive map of Sanctuary.

And froze.

"Noah?" I said, my voice shaky. "Could you take a look at this?"

"What?" Noah pretended shock, leaning over my shoulder. "Teen prodigy's not sure of something? Well, color me—" He cursed loud enough to bring Mom to our side.

"Damn!" she said, and I glanced up at her in surprise. Mom never swore on duty. Was this some sort of latent stress from her arguments with Dad? Or was she just worried about the drill? "Colton, Jonathan, Rita! Come in! We've got some sort of malfunction in the door connecting sector five with the server room."

Server rooms existed in each prison sector as an emergency measure, just in case a guard became trapped and needed to connect to the AI. They were all behind firewalls, and you couldn't do much from inside one except access communications and conduct a few other routine operations. Even that much required a lot of codes and specialized knowledge. Still, my breath caught in my throat at the thought of a prisoner with access to our system. Not one of them had a conscience, and they'd stop at nothing to get free.

This was all just a little too involved, a little too freaky, to be a drill. I tossed the map aside, toward Noah's console, so I could go through the video feeds in more detail. None of the cellblocks were open. The prisoners lounged in various poses of irritation and boredom. Some had managed to fall back asleep after the alarms faded. A few had pillows clamped over their heads.

I enlarged the flickering video once again and leaned in to inspect it. I wasn't even sure what I was looking for. The flicker had probably been a product of my imagination running wild at even the *thought* of one of these deadly kids going free.

Except there it went again. "Mom," I said, throwing caution to the wind.

"'Commander' when I'm on duty," she corrected.

I rolled my eyes, making sure she didn't see me. *"Commander,"* I replied. "Something's going on with this vid feed."

Mom leaned over my shoulder, leaving Noah to bark directions to Dad and Rita as they raced toward the server room. "There!" I said, pointing to the flicker again. We both bent closer. The cell was all of five feet square and housed two cots, a toilet, a sink, and a metal desk. An electronic tablet bolted to the desk served as the prisoners' entertainment—Sanctuary's library of music, movies, and books.

A lithe, muscular Chinese boy lounged on one of the cots. He'd tossed his shirt over the desk chair, revealing a series of tattoos inking his left arm and part of his back, and even in our current state of emergency, I couldn't help registering the ripple of muscles along his spine, not to mention the dark hair failing in seemingly impossible geometric spikes over arched cheekbones.

Hey, what can I say? I was still human.

Across from him sprawled one of the biggest prisoners in the cellblock. He lay on his back, staring at the ceiling, occasionally saying something in response to his cellmate. I knew him on sight: Alexei Danshov. I'd looked him up the first time I saw him, certain his sheer mass was a result of the genetic mutations that gave the prisoners unique superpowers. But nope— Danshov's power registered as pyrokinesis. His size was just a freak-of-nature-type bonus, because shooting blasts of flame at people didn't make him dangerous enough.

The screen flickered again, and Danshov moved slightly— a mere tic of his left arm. "Oh my God," I said. My irritation with Mom, my distraction, all vanished in a heartbeat. The oldest trick in the book, and one we would never dream of looking for, one we would never even imagine. "Mom. I mean, Commander. The video's on a loop."

"What?" She lunged forward. "Kenzie, are you sure?"

"I'm *certain!*" I was almost yelling. What if this wasn't a drill after all? What if it was an actual prison break, and Dad and Rita were running into the hands of murderers?

Mom hesitated for a split second before nodding, accepting my judgment. A burst of pride rushed through me as she slapped her hand down to open a channel. "Colton! Rita! Proceed with caution. There's a good chance we have two prisoners on the loose."

Did I imagine the extra strain in her voice? If this wasn't a drill, Dad could be in danger. Separation or not, they'd been together a long time. They had to feel *something* for one another. I searched her expression and she flashed me a quick smile, then squeezed my arm as she turned away.

Rita's voice filled the channel with colorful Spanish swearing. Then my dad, significantly more restrained: "Which prisoners?"

Mom thumbed the mobile unit in its hollowed-out resting place in her wrist, manually calling up the files. "5-B and C. Chang Hu and Alexei Danshov."

More cursing from Rita. "*Danshov?* We're going to need backup."

Mom slammed her hand on the console, making Noah jump. She quickly clenched it into a fist, but not before I caught it trembling. "You're armed. They're not. Watch your backs and you'll be fine."

"Are you kidding me?" I exploded. "Mom, those kids are the most dangerous people in the solar system! They'll—"

Her brows drew together, her jaw tightening in a way that stopped me mid-sentence. "No one understands the stakes better than I do, Kenzie," she said, more gently than I'd expected. "Sit down."

Slowly, I sank onto my stool, my face flaming in embarrassment. Mom was right. The prisoners couldn't use their powers and had no access to weapons. Dad would be fine as long as we followed regulations.

Noah cleared his throat.

"What?" asked Mom.

"Commander, I have movement in the server room."

Mom leveled a finger at me. "Look for other discrepancies in the video feed," she ordered, and transferred her attention to Noah.

Swallowing hard, I retrieved a series of videos and sorted through them, alert for any more blips or flickers. I should have known better than to shout at Mom in the middle of an emergency. My position as a junior guard wasn't exactly stable, and I knew I'd only gotten the job because both of my parents already served on Sanctuary. I had to work to prove myself every moment of every day, and yelling at my CO was hardly the epitome of maturity. The sheer terror of prisoners on the loose had overwhelmed me. I hoped spotting the blip in the video made up for it.

Suddenly, gunfire erupted over the comm link. I shot to my feet, leaving my stomach behind. "Dad!" I cried.

Mom had gone equally pale. "Colton!" she shouted. "Rita! Report!"

"We're here, Commander!" Rita bellowed, making everyone wince. "Someone opened fire on us from the server room."

If I hadn't known Mom so well, I would have missed the slight tremor in her voice when she asked, "Are either of you hurt?"

"We're okay! They didn't get near us."

I closed my eyes in relief, my breath shuddering through

my lips. That first rattle of gunfire and for a moment I'd thought . . .

Noah shook his head. "How in the five hells did they get their hands on weaponry?"

"It doesn't matter how," Mom returned through gritted teeth. "Only that they did. This is no drill, Noah. Kenzie! Find me the auto-turrets in the area."

My fingers flew over the keypad. I paused briefly, cramming another video feed toward Noah's screen, clearing space so that I had room to work. He swore at me under his breath, shoving the security screen to the side, but I didn't care. I'd slipped into the zone. "Something's wrong with the auto-turret in sector five. I think that's what's firing at them." And really, I reminded myself, weapons fire was a good sign. If the prisoners had somehow managed to remove the inhibitors embedded in their necks, they wouldn't bother with guns. They wouldn't need them.

I prodded the system. Something interfered with my ability to link to Sanctuary's defenses. My heart drumming, I scouted a back door, searching for a work-around.

On another screen, I opened the turret's code. I wasn't a programmer, and I couldn't code traditionally, but one of the awesome features on Sanctuary's computer was visual coding, a more pictorial, easier-to-follow version of a program's scripts. Using that, I could access and read most of the station's systems, all but the most complicated. I was already pretty familiar with the visual code for the turrets and I might spot any discrepancies. Sure enough, the computer had highlighted it for me in glowing red, a loop that didn't belong. "I've got it!" I called. "Dad, Rita, hang on!"

So I just needed to delete the offensive loop? It couldn't be that simple. But sure enough, the second I eliminated the loop, the sound of gunfire faded.

"That did it." Relief laced Rita's voice. "Good job, *chica*."

"Get to sector five." Mom's hand trembled with fury, although the rest of her body stayed very still. "Find out what the hell is going on, and if those two are out of their cells, apprehend them. *Do you hear me?*"

"Copy that, Commander," said Dad grimly. "We're on our way."

Mom stared at the screen a moment longer, then shook her head. "*Damn* it," she said. "All right. They need backup. I'm going in, and Noah's coming with me. Kenzie, you're in charge here."

"What?" My head jerked straight up. "Mom, I—"

"It's '*Commander,*' Kenzie. And there's nobody else. Jonathan has to man the airlocks, and Colton and Rita are in combat. You know the stakes. We can't risk those prisoners escaping." She spared me a rare smile, allowing my mother to crack through the commander's facade. "There's not much to do up here except keep an eye on the monitors. If anything happens, call me."

I drew a deep breath. If there really was a prison break, Dad needed her. And . . . well, just maybe this fiasco would be the glue that bound them back together. "Okay," I said. "I'll try to find the prisoners on the video feed."

"I know you will." For a second she looked like she might hug me, but she settled for a smile, a touch of pride in her expression. My own heart swelled in response. I loved my work, loved being a citizen of Omnistellar Concepts—but I loved it even more when I got that uncharacteristic look of approval from my mother.

The door slid shut behind Mom and Noah, enclosing me in the small control chamber by myself, and my pride faded beneath near panic. Red lights continued in periodic bursts through the room. The window behind me showed an endless sea of stars, Earth barely visible in the lower corner. It occurred to me how easily someone could destroy that window, even with its thick glass—at which point I'd be blown into nothingness.

I wasn't used to being in the command center on my own. Mom never left me alone here, and as an underage guard, I didn't have to take night shifts. Not that "night" had much meaning in space, but we kept to an Earth schedule, and I had strict limits on how many shifts I worked and what I was allowed to do.

To be clear, my job description did not include taking command of the entire station during a prison break. That Mom had abandoned me showed her desperation. A coil of hope unwound inside me. What was she afraid of? The possibility of a real prison break—or the possibility of Dad in danger?

I couldn't quite get my head around what was happening. My parents had worked together their entire adult lives. Not even Mom's promotion two years ago that had elevated her to a superior position seemed to bother them, but Dad was never superambitious. He liked his job and it never bothered him to take orders. That worked well because Mom liked to give them. Sure, they'd argued more lately, but I'd assumed . . . what?

Another time, I reminded myself. Mom always said work and the company came first. She'd put a ton of trust in me, and I had to make sure I earned it.

I returned to the task of unraveling the video feed. The cameras would pick up any escaped prisoners somewhere. Impossible not to. Every inch of Sanctuary was under constant surveillance. That meant I had a lot of feeds to browse, but I only focused on cameras in sector 5. I wasn't sure how these two prisoners had managed to escape their cell, much less program a loop into our video feed, but I knew for damn sure they couldn't escape their sector. It was literally impossible. Any attempt would send the station into shutdown, to the point of venting oxygen and killing everyone on board—guards included. It wasn't my favorite thing about Sanctuary, but like everyone else, I accepted the necessity. We simply couldn't risk the prisoners escaping. Their containment came before everything else—even our own lives.

What I was really looking for was another glitch. If they'd somehow managed to get into a server room and loop the video in their own cell, maybe they'd managed it in another area. And if they *had*, I'd know where they were, or at least where they planned to be.

My comm unit sputtered, making me jump, but it was just Rita. "Are you in position, Commander?"

"Affirmative," Mom's voice said over the comm. "Nothing on our end."

"Ours either. Let's get moving. We'll meet you in the middle."

"Copy that. Radio silence until then."

I drew another shaky breath. "Get it together, Kenz," I muttered out loud. "You did not ace every single one of your training camps by panicking in a crisis." The reminder of my past successes steadied me, and I set myself to rooting through video, letting anything not from sector 5 drift aside. I found my parents and tucked their feeds at the top of my screen to keep an eye on them. At least this way, if someone got the jump on them I could shout a warning.

As I sifted through vids, my nerves quickly turned to frustration. Not one flicker, not one bit of movement, that didn't originate from my own people. Was it possible the feed hadn't looped after all? Had I sent Mom on a wild goose chase?

And then, movement did catch my eye. But it wasn't from sector 5.

It was directly outside the command center.

TWO

FOR WHAT FELT LIKE A FULL MINUTE, I DIDN'T breathe. I enlarged the video feed and squinted, and . . . there it was again. A glimmer of *something* at the very edge of the camera's view, barely noticeable to anyone less careful than me.

Right outside the door.

My throat clenched. I searched my memory for the prisoners' power lists. Invisibility? I was almost sure there was a prisoner who could turn invisible. That meant shadows might be my only clue before they found a way in. Or . . . maybe not? Did invisible people cast shadows? Who studied that sort of thing? But I definitely saw something flickering out there. . . .

My heart caught in my throat for another second before I pulled myself together. There were protocols to follow here, damn it, and I wasn't going to be the one who let things fall apart on her watch. Besides, the door to the command center was reinforced and magnetically locked. Unless I opened it from the inside, no one was getting in without the proper codes, powers or not. And the prisoners couldn't access their powers, not without performing some pretty major self-surgery.

Of course, they should also have been vaporized the second they managed to escape the prison, but there were only so many things I could worry about at once.

Keeping a watchful eye on the camera feed from outside the command center and another on the feed showing my parents, I activated my comm link.

Nothing.

I blinked. Comms couldn't be down. I saw Mom talking right now, and Dad nodding in acknowledgment. They were clearly having a conversation. So only command comms short-circuited? How in the name of all that was holy was this even possible?

And that was when it came to me. This whole mess—it really was a drill. Was it a bit intricate, even for Sanctuary's advanced AI? Definitely, but we had been warned when we first came aboard that in addition to the regular drills the computer conducted, several times a year we'd experience a more detailed simulation designed to test our mettle.

Still, that didn't change a thing. First of all, on the off chance I was wrong, I couldn't afford to throw open the door and announce, "Hey, prisoners, come on in!" Second, assuming it *was* a drill, the computer recorded every movement we made, every decision, every action, for later analysis. It was almost as important to follow regulations now as in a real emergency. Every panicked decision, every breach of the rules, reflected negatively on Mom, and of course on me.

And every *positive* action was another feather in my cap, another reason for the other guards to good-naturedly roll their eyes behind my back, another step toward my own eventual command. And if I was *really* lucky, I might even earn a word of praise from my parents.

No pressure or anything. But still, my growing certainty dulled the panic gnawing at my gut. I stared at the monitor until my hand steadied, gave my head a shake, and started pulling up the visual code for the comm system, ignoring the flickers of movement on the hallway feed. As I'd suspected, they increased in frequency the longer I ignored them—Sanctuary's AI, probably, trying to get my attention.

I hesitated for a moment, watching those shadows. This really did seem complicated for a drill. What if I turned my back on them and they turned out to be real? What if they caused damage to the station while I analyzed the code?

I shook off the thought. Real or not, there was only one way to stop them. I pulled up the visual code, trying to keep a wary eye on the shadow screen at the same time. The communications were a lot more complicated than the turrets, full of ifs and thens and ors, but after a few minutes I located the problem. Once again, someone had inserted a faulty loop into the code, blocking my communication with Mom. I copied it before I deleted it; if deleting it didn't solve the problem, I'd paste it back in before anyone noticed. That was the awesome thing about visual coding. You could always save an earlier document, remix to your heart's content, and reload the old version.

Anyway, it turned out I didn't need to mess with reloading, because as soon as I deleted the faulty loop, Mom's voice blasted out of my wrist. "—ing systems. Kenzie, if you don't come in right now, I swear . . ."

"I'm here!" I shouted, wincing at the volume. I grinned in spite of myself at my success. For a moment I considered voicing my concerns about this being a sim, but what was the point? Mom would only scold me for letting that interfere with my doing my job. Bringing my volume under control, I continued, "Sorry, I lost comms for a bit. Someone piggybacked code into the system and locked me out."

"How the hell did they do that?" Rita demanded, her face twisted into a scowl.

Mom glowered, presumably aware of Sanctuary recording every word for later analysis. Before she answered, though, Noah spoke: "Kenzie, why'd they cut you off? Everything okay up there?"

"I don't think so," I replied. "I've got movement on the video feed from outside the command center." Now that I was in communication with the others, I tapped the screen, bringing the outside corridor into sharper relief. "Just shadows so far, but definitely not natural. Someone's there."

"Damn it!" Dad swore. "Kenzie, do not open those doors."

I scowled, catching the slight twitch of Noah's lips. What was I, a child? "Yeah, I know. Doors are locked and will stay that way until we're clear."

On one of my minimized screens, my parents met. They held a brief, hurried consultation off-comm. I hesitated, torn between watching them for any sign of rekindled romance and carrying out my duties in the command center, but my parents were professional as always—Mom could have been talking to Jonathan for all the emotion she showed. Rita positioned herself at the corridor entrance, firearm at the ready. Noah glanced at the camera and winked. An unbidden smile danced across my lips.

"Okay," Mom said. "We look clear down here, so I'm thinking this was a distraction. I'll leave Colton and Noah on guard. Rita and I will check in with Jonathan and make our way to you, Kenz. Hang tight."

Everyone had calmed down in the last few minutes, and I got the sense their thoughts mirrored mine. Sanctuary had messed up in making this sim too unbelievable. Yeah, we'd been shocked when prisoners had escaped their cells, somehow gained server room access, and created a looped video. It was unusual, but not completely unfathomable. But throw in an escape from their actual sector—like I said, Sanctuary knew to blow the airlocks if that happened. And while the server rooms provided access to some of Sanctuary's more basic systems, there

21

was no way to disable a major security backup from anywhere but the command center.

Of course, that sheer unbelievability was enough to give me pause. Why would Sanctuary make a drill this unrealistic? I shook my head. The shadows hadn't done anything. The code was fixed. It *was* a drill, and even if it wasn't, we were going to get to the bottom of it in a heartbeat.

Sure enough, the next few minutes played out quickly. Now convinced the server room was clear, Dad and Noah advanced to the prison, where they confirmed that all prisoners— including Danshov and Hu—remained in their cells. A minute later, Mom and Rita burst into the command center corridor, weapons at the ready and shouting for surrender, and in response, the alarms turned themselves off. The lights returned to normal, and the AI's pleasant voice flooded the PA system. *"This has been a test of the emergency preparedness system of Sanctuary's team. There is no emergency. Please resume your scheduled activities. Debriefing will occur at zero nine hundred hours tomorrow morning. Thank you for your cooperation."*

I groaned. 0900? A glance at my wrist comm told me it was already after three. We'd been dealing with this so-called emergency for two hours now, and adrenaline was coursing through my system. I wouldn't fall asleep any time soon.

Mom's face was a tight mask of fury when she came through the door, but she was too professional to complain. Rita, on the other hand, let loose a slew of enraged comments the second she saw me. "Can you believe this?" she fumed, dropping onto a stool. "Not only does the system drill in the middle of the night, it picks the most impossible scenario it can come up with, one that has us running our butts off all over the station. Of all the ridiculous—"

"Rita," interjected Mom sharply. "If one of those kids ever does escape, we have to be ready to do whatever it takes to stop them. Just one of them could destroy the world as we know it. I think a few hours of lost sleep is a small price to pay to make sure we're ready, don't you?"

Rita inclined her head, taking the rebuke good-naturedly. But I hesitated. Every other drill we'd experienced had been simple—an alarm, a loose wire, a broken camera. They took fifteen minutes to resolve and didn't involve the possibility of escaped murderers. Yes, Sanctuary was supposed to run more involved drills from time to time, and I'd been prepared for that possibility. But I kept coming back to the same question: Why make this one *so* unbelievable, so over the top? "Mom," I said cautiously, "this does seem like an excessive drill. Are we absolutely sure—?"

She held up a hand, cutting me off. Anger rose in my chest, but quickly vanished when I saw the exhaustion on her face. I'd forgotten Mom had been on duty before all of this happened, and had probably only stumbled into bed a few minutes before the alarm. And then, of course, there was everything with Dad. Mom was good at hiding her emotions, but the stress of separation had to take a toll. "We'll review everything in the morning," she said. "In the meantime, I want you all to grab a few hours of sleep."

"I'm on duty," Noah pointed out.

Mom nodded. "I'll take your shift. You can stay if you want to," she added, forestalling his objection, "but I'm going to be up analyzing the data and preparing my report. No point in both of us losing sleep."

Noah glanced over at his screen. "Then I'll take the command center shift you're scheduled for tomorrow. No, don't argue, Commander," he said with a grin, stopping her before she could interrupt. "You can't stay on duty twenty-four hours a day. We need you fresh and alert."

For a moment Mom teetered on the edge of a rebuke, but her face collapsed into a smile. "You're right. Thank you. I'll gratefully accept your offer." Her face recomposed itself into more familiar, stricter lines. "Now, to bed—all of you." She raised an eyebrow in my direction. "Especially you."

Ignoring protocol, I crossed the room and hugged her fiercely. She hesitated a second, then sighed and returned my embrace. "You did a great job," she whispered against my hair. "I know it's been a tough night. I'm proud of you."

I ducked my head to hide my blush, conscious of Rita and Noah watching me in the background. "Mom," I couldn't resist saying, "we are sure this was a drill?"

She pulled back, frowning, and examined my face. "You heard Sanctuary."

"I know. I just . . ."

She hugged me again. "Don't let it get to you. Sanctuary's foolproof. Put your faith in Omnistellar, Kenz. Now get some sleep. Everything will seem clearer in the morning."

When I broke away, Noah's and Rita's smiles were faintly condescending, but not unkind. I resisted the urge to make an obscene gesture in their direction and turned to where Dad beamed at me. "Come on, kiddo. Let me take you home."

I faltered, the events of the night playing through my mind. "I'm kind of amped up, Dad. I'm going to go for a quick walk, burn off some energy. I'll be home in twenty minutes. Promise."

"Promise accepted," he replied. My parents are used to me wandering. I mean, it's a space station. Sure, it's full of murderous teenage criminals, but they're all on the lower levels. It's not like I can get lost or anything's going to happen to me. Back on Earth, on the other hand, I had a curfew of nine p.m. on school nights, ten on weekends. It was ridiculous, and I complained bitterly about it at school—but most of my real friends were other company kids, and they got it. Half of them had similar restrictions.

The thought of my friends made me wince. I'd more or less ignored them since moving to Sanctuary. But it was difficult to keep in touch, between our morning briefings, my assigned studies, and my three-hour shift before dinner. And I'd never been the most social person. I kept to myself a lot, learning about Omnistellar's guidelines and regulations.

Put your faith in Omnistellar, my mom had said. It had been a refrain in my house from the moment I was born. Where other families had prayers or rituals, mine had unwavering loyalty to corporate guidelines. My parents were shining examples of corporate citizens: calm, controlled, competent, responsible. I couldn't let them down by running around like some government kid. Corporate citizenship beat government citizenship hands down, and Omnistellar citizenship beat all the other corporations combined. Omnistellar's people wanted for nothing. A government citizen might starve in the streets, and a lesser corporation might let their workers get by on the bare necessities. I'd always had the best of everything, and my mother made sure I didn't take it for granted.

But as Mom always reminded me, it wasn't enough to inherit my citizenship—I had to earn it. Since Omnistellar Concepts only hired the best and brightest, that meant I had a lot of work to do. My position as a junior guard would help me in the future, but it offered no guarantees. *Put your faith in Omnistellar, but work as hard as you can to deserve its trust.*

So most of my life had been dedicated to the company—to work, to study, to training. Still, there were a few Omnistellar kids I'd always been close to. I used to have weekly chats with another junior guard I'd met at camp a few years back, and we hadn't spoken in over a month. I made a mental note to contact her soon.

I wandered Sanctuary's halls, grateful for the silence after the chaos of the last half hour. A thousand thoughts played through my mind, but I kept coming back to two: my parents splitting up and the drill. Did the drill weigh on their minds too? Had tonight's events had any effect on Mom and Dad? For at least a moment, they'd believed themselves in danger. Maybe, just maybe, that was enough to rekindle some sort of spark?

Thinking of the drill brought a frown to my face. I still couldn't quite convince myself that Sanctuary would come up with such a bizarre, outlandish series of events. I mean, I knew that the others had visually confirmed that all the prisoners were in place—I *knew* that. And there was no way to thwart Sanctuary's AI.

But . . . what if the prisoners had somehow managed to infiltrate the computer? Part of me, maybe the part that couldn't stop Mom and Dad from splitting up or doing whatever the hell else they wanted, itched to be sure. If the prisoners really did engineer an escape, wouldn't this be the perfect time, with all of us exhausted and with our guard down in the wake of the drill?

If only there was some way I could get Sanctuary to discuss the drill . . . But the AI was cold and impersonal and not prone to conversation. I'd just have to take it on trust.

On *faith*.

But then, I'd taken my parents on faith too. I'd seen them as a unit. Maybe not a great one—they'd never been particularly loving or affectionate toward each other—but a unit just the same. A team. Now that team was crumbling. Mom always emphasized structure and routine, but when those things were ripped away, she hadn't really given me the tools to deal with the fallout.

I covered every inch of the station: the empty common room (with Noah's video game console dominating the area—I scooped the VR interface off Rita's favorite couch before she could bury it in cushions again and Noah threw a fit), the storerooms with their perfectly lined crates of food and medical supplies, the exercise room. I hesitated there, tempted by the basketball court. Basketball was one of the few things I'd been involved in at my Earth high school, and the only thing I missed. But shooting hoops by yourself didn't compare to a full-on game, and the solitary pursuit didn't appeal to me now. Maybe Rita would spot me a game in the morning.

Sanctuary stretched around me like a comforting embrace: white, pristine, with steady LED lighting and rounded edges. I didn't miss Earth, or at least not much. There were times when I'd kill for some real sunshine, not the UV rays we were required to sit in front of thirty minutes a day, and I wouldn't mind a dish of actual ice cream. But the noisy bustle of a crowded high school, a busy city street, the constant buzz of traffic and pinging comm devices . . . Give me the gentle hum of an efficient space station any day. And you couldn't beat the view, I reminded myself as I passed a porthole. I leaned against it, staring down at Earth, its lights twinkling so far away. So many lights. Earth was a busy place, with its efficient corporate cities and crime-infested government-controlled zones—unlike Sanctuary. In spite of tonight's commotion, in spite of the prisoners beneath my feet, the station usually lived up to its name.

In some ways, the station was a mirror of Earth. The upper levels were corporate controlled, clean, organized, and safe. The lower levels, like the government-run areas on Earth, were the domain of the criminals. And I belonged firmly upstairs with the other guards and my parents. My parents . . . I sighed, staring at Sanctuary's blank walls like they held some sort of answer. The more I thought about it, the more I realized my parents really had been more like an Omnistellar team than married partners. Their conversations revolved around work. When was the last time I'd seen them do something *fun* together, or discuss anything outside of Omnistellar? Somehow, the thought didn't make me feel any better.

I drifted through corridors until my mind stopped racing and my heartbeat returned to normal, and I was about to turn toward home when I noticed my feet had carried me to the prison entrance.

I glanced at the heavy door, chewing on my bottom lip. Technically, I wasn't supposed to be anywhere near here. I didn't have the authorization, and I sure as hell didn't have the permission of my commanding officer, aka Mom.

But nothing actually stopped me from going through those doors. As a junior guard, I had full access to the entire station— necessary, in case of a real emergency like the one we'd drilled for tonight. And I guess Sanctuary's little stunt was preying on my mind, because I suddenly realized I wasn't going to sleep unless I saw, with my own eyes, Danshov and Hu in their cells.

For the briefest of seconds I contemplated grabbing a stun gun, the image of the shadow on the video feed still fresh in my mind. I rejected that out of hand. The videos would catch me entering the prison, but no one really monitored them unless something went wrong. If I took a stun gun, though, Sanctuary would create an official armaments record, and I'd have to answer a lot of questions when Mom reviewed the logs.

But I didn't need a gun. I trusted Sanctuary. The prisoners were secure. I just . . . needed to see.

I skimmed my thumb over the reader. The keypad turned green, giving me thirty seconds to enter my nine-digit code. I punched it in from memory, and the screen dissolved, showing me a picture of a door opening.

Because even though I'd passed the battery of intellectual, psychological, and physical tests necessary to gain an appointment on Sanctuary, I definitely needed a picture of the door opening to tell me what was about to happen.

The door slid aside in a fairly predictable turn of events, and I stood gazing down the stairs.

Aside from a brief tour the day we arrived on the station, I'd never actually been in the prison levels of Sanctuary. Most contact with prisoners was completely automated. The AI managed feeding and herded the prisoners to their jobs in the manufacturing and data entry rooms within prison boundaries. After, it guided them back to their cells. Sanctuary's skeleton crew made sure nothing broke down and dealt with any recalcitrant prisoners—those who weren't convinced by the turrets lining the walls and the AI's dispassionate voice directing them. Mom came down once a week to do a visual once-over and check in with everyone, and in the case of a medical emergency, Jonathan stepped in. There was no reason for most of us to ever see a prisoner. There was *no* reason—and that was Mom's voice in my head—for me, a junior guard, to *ever* see a prisoner.

But curiosity got the better of me. I'd started here because I needed to confirm the two prisoners were in their cell. Now I wondered: What exactly went on down there? I mean, I'd seen the video feeds, constantly monitoring the cells. The prisoners lived strictly regulated lives, shuffling between their work space, their gym-based physical activity sessions, and their cells.

But what was it *like*?

Now was the time to find out. Mom was distracted and not likely to notice what I was up to. I doubted she'd examine any log from after the drill. That was my mother to a *T*. Right now, she'd be poring over the drill report, analyzing it, trying to catch any potential mistakes before her superiors on Earth so that if they spotted a problem, she'd have a solution ready. I smiled at the thought. If I grew up half the

Omnistellar citizen my parents were, I'd be plenty proud. And part of guarding meant taking risks—listening to your instincts and following your hunches, even if they seemed to go against the grain.

I took a breath and entered the dark stairwell.

Darkness and sound. Sound and darkness.
Alert, but without focus. Direction, not goal.
Heat and motion and pain and anger and
HUNGER, always the hunger, always the drive.
They advance.
They pursue.
They adapt.
They control.
They are, as they are, as they have been.
And in the distance, sanctuary lies in wait.

THREE

ON A SCHEMATIC, SANCTUARY ALWAYS MADE me think of a microphone, a bubble with a cylinder stretching beneath. The prison sectors occupied the bottom five levels of Sanctuary, with the command hub on top. I was heading all the way down.

An air of gloom pervaded the stairwell. In stark contrast to the hall I'd just exited—brightly lit, friendly, with large windows and white walls—this was a narrow set of metal stairs wrapping in on itself into oblivion below. Each level illuminated only when my foot touched the floor, meaning I was constantly descending into pitch darkness. The landings all looked the same: identical doors with bright red numbers marking the sector. A scene from *Robo Mecha Dream Girl 5* flashed through my head. The evil corporate headquarters Yumiko led her mechs through looked just like this. Evil corporations were a common theme in entertainment these days, and I had to admit that the idea of an all-powerful corporation like Omnistellar going rogue was pretty exciting, at least in fiction.

In reality, of course, the corporations did a way better job of managing things than any government ever had. The corporate-controlled cities were safe, civilized, and clean. It was the areas that remained under government control that were cesspools of crime and disarray. When the governments first started selling off entire cities to private corporations, there was an outcry—which lasted all of a month, at which point people in the corporate cities realized how much better off they'd become. Bankrupt governments couldn't provide for their citizens. Corporations could. Still, the idea of the evil corporation kept recurring in fiction, maybe because government citizens always resented corporations for excluding them.

When I hit sector 5, I repeated the actions I'd performed above, scanning my thumb and entering my code. After a moment, the door slid open, and a wave of cold air washed over me. Apparently Sanctuary didn't feel the need to keep the cellblocks at the balmy seventy-two degrees we enjoyed throughout the rest of the station.

I pulled my sweater tighter around me and stepped into the corridor. Dim lights lined the floors, reminding me of emergency lighting on the shuttle that had carried us to Sanctuary. All at once I was on that shuttle again—nervous, excited, twisting my neck to stare as Sanctuary revealed itself above me.

The sleeping prisoners melded with the shadows in their cells, leaving the faces featureless blurs. They were there, though, and lots of them—ten cells, eight holding two prisoners, the rest empty. The boys were in the first half, the girls farther on behind a divider.

It gave me pause. The prisoners weren't used to seeing guards. A teenage girl strolling through their midst, especially one wearing a guard's uniform like me, could cause chaos. But no one seemed awake. No one lifted their head at the sound of the door opening, and I didn't hear whispers or shouts of alarm. So I braced myself and stepped forward.

Instantly, the door slid shut behind me, and my heart leaped into my throat. I looked over my shoulder, and the comforting glow of the screen pad reassured me. There'd be a few more hoops to jump through before I could open the door from this side, but I knew how, having seen Mom do it during the tour. *Calm down, Kenz,* I ordered myself silently. Even if every prisoner in this room woke at once, they were all controlled—locked behind bars and chipped so they couldn't use their powers. As long as I stayed out of reach, the worst they could do was yell at me. I could handle yelling.

I made my way past three cells to where Danshov and Hu stretched out on their respective beds. Danshov had his back to me, his massive body curled in on itself to fit on the cot, and Hu's arm was draped over his face. Their chests rose evenly, as if in sleep.

All at once my errand seemed ridiculous. There they were, right where they were supposed to be. What had I expected? I guess the combination of the late night, the sudden alarm, and Sanctuary's strangely detailed drill had gotten to me. Shaking my head, I retreated toward the exit.

"Hello."

I froze. The voice came from behind me—low and tinged with amusement, not at all the voice of a prisoner woken from a sound sleep. I pivoted to find Hu perched on the edge of his cot, watching me from the shadows. He was still naked from the waist up and was hunched forward with his elbows propped on his thighs. I couldn't make out his expression in the darkness, only the sharp line of his jaw.

Hearing him speak was like hearing a sound in the darkness of an empty room. Somehow I hadn't expected any of the prisoners to acknowledge my presence. "Hi," I said cautiously. What did you say to a prisoner? After three months on Sanctuary, this was my first time actually speaking to one. "I'm sorry, I didn't mean to wake you."

He shifted to his feet in a single fluid motion and crossed the cell. Without quite meaning to, I retreated another step, bringing my back against the wall. Hu draped his arms through the bars, grinning at me. "Oh, I wasn't sleeping," he replied. "None of us are."

I blinked. At the same moment, the other prisoners sat up, then moved to the cell doors, staring at me like I was a creature in a zoo. Their gaze pinned me with an almost physical force. I drew a shaky breath. *They* were the ones in the cages. They could stare all they wanted. At the end of the night, I was the one walking out the door. "Well," I said, "then I'm sorry I woke all of you."

A few of the prisoners laughed, but they didn't sound amused. One girl in particular laughed a little too long and loud, her voice echoing through the shadowed, empty corridors. I glanced nervously in the direction of her cell, but it was too dark to see any of the girls.

When I returned my attention to Hu, his roommate had joined him at the bars. I blinked, surprised someone so big moved so quietly. "Pretty," Danshov acknowledged, looking me over.

From farther down came an annoyed Irish accent: "*Who's pretty?*"

Danshov chuckled. "Easy, Mia mine. Just observing."

An ominous thud reverberated through the cellblock, and Hu grinned at me. "Great. Piss *her* off, why don't you? You sure know how to pick your enemies."

My mom always said I didn't think through the consequences of my actions—usually with a hint of teasing in her voice, but genuine concern underneath. I hated to admit it, but this time, she just might have a point. "All right, I have to go. Good night."

"What's your hurry?" Hu's eyes glittered, and he suddenly became menacing without moving a muscle. "We haven't seen a fresh face in . . . what is it now, Alexei? Two months?"

"'Bout that."

"We get lonely," called someone else, and the prisoners laughed.

I resisted the urge to retreat another step. Sixteen sets of eyes fixed on me with unwavering hatred. Maybe they couldn't hurt me, but the force of their malice was like a wall pushing against me. Whatever lapse in judgment (*your own arrogance*, Mom's voice corrected) had driven me into this room, it was time to go. There was a reason they kept these prisoners isolated. Powers or no, bars or no, they were cruel, physically fit, and dangerous.

Without another word, I headed for the exit. I deliberately kept my pace steady, my eyes fixed on the dim red glow of the door in the distance. The prisoners hooted and shouted as I advanced, but I ignored them. My heart thrummed in my chest, my muscles taut and poised for violence. No matter how many times I chanted the refrain in my head—*they can't hurt you, they can't* hurt *you*—my body refused to listen. I was poised on the precipice of fight or flight, desperate to escape this cage and its cargo of malice.

I'd almost reached the exit when something hit the side of my head. I staggered and leaned against the wall to steady myself. A half-eaten apple rolled away beneath my foot. Actually, I almost tripped on it. The blow hadn't been that hard, but it had been completely unexpected—only shock kept me from crying out. They wouldn't have heard me anyway, because the second the apple connected, the hyenas erupted into howls of laughter, jeers, threats, and taunts.

My control broke.

I bolted for freedom, their shouts echoing off the walls and chasing me onward. I stumbled over my own feet in my haste, smashing my wrist on the ground as I landed. I didn't even stop. In a single motion I pushed myself to my feet and shot for the door.

My fingers trembled so badly it took two tries to scan my thumb and three to enter my code. Then I did a retinal scan and a voiceprint and entered my secondary code. The voiceprint took the longest, because with the prisoners shouting in the background, Sanctuary had trouble picking me out of the mix. At long last the door slid open, and I almost fell through it in relief.

"Hey!" shouted someone behind me.

Every other voice had gone silent.

I hesitated halfway through the door for a moment and then, against my better judgment, turned into the darkness.

I barely made out Hu's form twisted in his cell, his face pressed against the bars. "Come visit us again sometime," he called.

I drew a steadying breath, salvaging what remained of my dignity. "I'm not a big fan of how you treat your guests."

"See you soon," he replied, his voice losing its mocking intonation, making the three simple words a threat.

The laughter rose again, and I fled.

I detoured to the medical bay before I went home, knowing I couldn't let Dad see me smeared with fruit, my hair disheveled and my wrist throbbing. He was probably asleep, but if anyone found out I'd been in the prison, my job would hang in the balance. And even if the crew was willing to lie for me, I couldn't face the derision in their expressions. I liked Sanctuary's guards, and I thought they liked me, but every now and then I caught their rolled eyes, their annoyance when I raced to find the solution to a problem before they did. They never seemed to understand that I wasn't trying to show them up. I just had that much more to prove.

The med bay wasn't much of a walk—Sanctuary was not large, if you didn't count the prison. It was basically a dome divided into four parts: one for the command center; one for work spaces like the medical bay and shuttle dock; one for the kitchen, common room, and gym; and one for living quarters.

You were just as likely to find Jonathan in the med bay as anywhere else, including his own room. Fortunately he wasn't there when I arrived, presumably having gone home to sleep like a sensible person. I wiped the sweat and apple from my face and hair and examined my wrist. I'd twisted it, but I didn't find any real damage—hardly even a twinge when I flexed it.

I sank against the examination table, struggling to catch my breath. This entire errand was beyond stupid. I had only two goals now: to avoid the prison cells like the plague, and to make sure my parents never, *ever* found out about this little exploit.

Against my will, my mind drifted to a memory I'd tried to suppress from three years ago, when we'd been stationed briefly in a government city. The local government had been in the process of selling its land to the company, and Omnistellar asked my mom, who was between assignments, to scout the city in advance of closing the deal. My parents warned me to keep my distance from the other kids, emphasizing that I was an Omnistellar citizen, not some government brat. But I was fourteen, and lonely, and desperate for friends. I'd been invited to a party by a girl at my new school, but my parents absolutely refused to let me go. I'd never seen my mother so furious. "You owe everything to Omnistellar," she seethed. "*We* owe everything to Omnistellar. Without the company, you'd be living in hovels alongside your new friends. I will not watch my only child behave like common government trash."

At the time, I hadn't understood what Mom was so worried about. It was just a party, after all—and while my parents spent their days negotiating the new Omnistellar prison and the corporate city takeover with government representatives, I was stuck with these kids. It couldn't hurt to make friends. So I climbed out the bedroom window, resolutely ignoring my screaming conscience, and made my way through the dark streets to the girl's house.

It turned out that my mom was right. The town kids all got by on the most basic governmental support, without any of the perks that came with citizenship in one of the major world corporations. And they all recognized me on sight as different. My clothes, my attitude, my demeanor—everything set me apart, and I had no desire to fit in with their violence, their drinking, their drugs. I also wasn't in a hurry to inform them that if Omnistellar did take over the city, any of them whose parents didn't get corporate jobs would find themselves kicked out of their homes and sent on their way with a tiny corporate stipend as a buyout. I didn't feel guilty, exactly—it was the way the world worked. But it was awkward hanging out with them, hearing them talk about their hopes for the future if Omnistellar took over. I spent less than an hour at the party before slipping out the back door and heading for home, cursing myself every step of the way.

Every city had a curfew, even the government ones, and it was now well after dark. The streets were quiet. I kept to the alleys to avoid drawing undue attention—curfews are never strictly enforced, but Omnistellar security was moving into this town, and if they picked me up, my parents would die of embarrassment.

It didn't take long to realize I was being followed. I closed my eyes in annoyance and tightened my fingers, tensing and loosening my muscles in preparation for combat. It never crossed my mind to worry—guns were so strictly controlled that no one outside the corporations had them, so the worst I could expect on government land was a pocket knife. I was more than confident in my ability to take on a thug or two.

Still, avoiding conflict was always better, so I put on a burst of speed, rounded a corner—and came face to face with one of the tiniest girls I'd ever seen, a little waif no more than nine years old. I drew up short, startled. She wasn't what I'd expected. "Excuse me," I said, moving to step around her.

She blocked me. I sighed. "Come on," I said. "You don't want to do this."

Her eyes flashed. I took a deep breath—and all the oxygen vanished. I struggled to draw in air, but it felt like someone had closed a hand around my throat. I dropped to my knees, clawing at my throat, spots swimming in front of my eyes. I was vaguely aware of the girl slipping behind me, putting her hands in my pocket. . . .

And then she was gone, leaving me gasping on the ground. I staggered to my feet, feeling in my pockets. The little brat had taken my corporate ID, my omnicard. It wouldn't get her far without my retinal scan and fingerprint, but it was enough to make a few purchases before I reported it stolen—which meant I'd have to explain to my parents how it had gone missing.

That had been my first encounter with a superpowered anomaly, and my last. We didn't see much of them. I knew they existed, but people were apt to think of them as happening somewhere else. There were a lot of anomalies in prison, of course—something about the power seemed to go to people's heads—but the news often mentioned anomalies living in relative obscurity throughout the world. I didn't know any personally, or didn't know that I did. Most people viewed anomalies a little suspiciously, so they tended to lead quiet lives. I was grateful for that. I knew intellectually that most anomalies were probably harmless. But after my encounter with that girl, I couldn't even think of them without my heart skipping a beat.

The little monster who attacked me was more than a thief. She could have killed me easily. Even if there was a way to avoid telling my parents what had happened, I had no choice but to report her to Omnistellar. They never caught her, which meant she was still out there. I wondered how many bodies were now stacked at her feet.

In the end, my parents were more understanding about the whole thing than I had any right to expect. That almost made it worse. For days afterward I woke gasping for air, reliving that moment of sheer helplessness as oxygen drained from my lungs.

One night I awoke from one of those nightmares to find Mom sitting at the foot of my bed, her face lined with exhaustion. "Mom?" I murmured, sitting up.

"Shh." She stroked my hair back from my face and eased me into bed.

"Have I been waking you up?" A wave of guilt suffused me. "Bad enough I snuck out in the first place."

"Kenz." She offered me a rare, genuine smile. "You made a mistake. It happens. But when I think about what that monster could have done to you . . ." Her smile faded, and her fist clenched in the blanket. "Even when you mess up, I'm here for you," she said finally. "Never forget that."

It was the last time we ever discussed the incident, but

after waking up with Mom by my side, the dreams faded, and I gradually stopped thinking about what could have happened that night.

Until now. The helpless feeling I'd had in the prison had been exactly like how I'd felt in that alley, even with the prisoners chipped, without their powers. If one little girl had managed to choke the life out of me without lifting a finger, imagine what that crowd of kids could do with their powers intact.

But their powers weren't intact. I took a deep breath, forcing myself to be calm. Everything was okay. I was human. I was allowed the odd stupid decision. I hadn't done any harm, and the prisoners were safe in their cells.

I took another moment to compose myself, then headed home. The door to our quarters slid open, revealing the dark living room, maybe only half the size of my bedroom back on Earth. Track lighting along the floor illuminated the area—small couch, comfortable rug, bookshelf, and doors leading to my parents' room, my room, and the washroom. No light came from anywhere else. Dad wasn't even awake, which meant my medical detour had been a waste of time. Still, I was glad to avoid his probing and questions. I'd been gone at least double the twenty minutes I'd promised.

I slipped into my bedroom and shed my boots and jacket. My comm device beeped, reminding me to charge it. Groaning at the delay, I climbed out of bed, popped the device out of its metal gap in my left wrist, and connected it to the power outlet.

I ran my fingers over the crevice in my wrist. When I'd first had the device implanted, seeing that metal outline where there once had been flesh was bizarre for a few days. The direct implantation allowed me much more control over the device, though, and it had soon become a part of me. If I'd had it in that alley three years ago, I wouldn't have had to worry about mugging. I could've signaled for help even without air. I would never be without my device again.

Sleep shouldn't be a problem now—my eyes burned with exhaustion, and a huge yawn split my jaw. I climbed between the sheets and dropped my head to the pillow. Darkness enveloped me in its gentle embrace.

Until something occurred to me.

See you soon, Hu had said. Why? What did he mean? He'd only said it to rattle me, I was sure of it. Or almost sure.

But it was enough to keep me awake the rest of the night.

FOUR

THE NEXT MORNING PROMPTLY AT 0900, ALL six guards gathered in the debriefing room off the command center. Mom's uniform was rumpled, her lipstick smudged. The rest of us didn't look much better. Noah was never much use before his morning coffee, which he clutched like a life preserver. Rita continued to sulk over the events of the night before. Only Dad and Jonathan looked completely composed, and I scanned my parents for any sign that last night had had some sort of effect on them. Maybe the moments of fear and stress had made them realize they belonged together. Maybe they'd worked things out.

But no. I realized that Mom had spent most of the night in the command center and Dad had gone straight to bed after the drill. If anything was going to change, it wouldn't be now. They hadn't had a single moment to talk.

"All right, everyone," Mom announced, rubbing her hand over her face. "Here we go."

I sat up straighter in my chair as Mom connected us to the bigwigs on Earth, who proceeded to analyze every second of last night's disaster.

"I'm sure you were surprised by the timing and intricacy of the drill," Colonel Trace said at last, a smile playing on her lips. She'd always had a strange affection for the station's AI. "I must confess that it's our fault. We've asked all Omnistellar AIs to increase security."

Mom's brow furrowed. "Any particular reason?"

"Nothing official, but we always like to be prepared. The fifty-year anniversary of the probes is coming up, and we still don't know where they came from or why they resulted in the anomalies. With that in mind, well . . . as I said."

I frowned. I'd forgotten about the fifty-year anniversary. Why was it on Omnistellar's mind? I suppose they were just being cautious. After all, it was widely accepted that the strange alien probes that appeared almost five decades ago were responsible for the superpowered kids who popped up a generation later, so it made sense they'd want us to be careful. But I couldn't remember any special preparations for any previous anniversaries. What made fifty the magic number?

Before I could ask any questions, Trace pushed on. "Sanctuary has a lot of tricks up her sleeve, but your team performed reasonably well." Her eyebrows tightened. "I can't say we were overly pleased with your decision to leave a seventeen-year-old girl in command of the entire station, of course. . . ."

"Colonel," said Mom briskly, "with all due respect, the auto-turrets had turned on us, and we were struggling to deal with the situation in a—"

"*But,*" Trace cut in sharply, casting Mom a withering look, "we must admit that Kenzie conducted herself with the maturity, insight, and professionalism we expect from an Omnistellar citizen, not to mention a member of the Cord family." For the first time that morning, her gaze found mine, and a smile crossed her lips. "Well done, Kenzie."

"Thank you," I managed, fighting to control the stupid grin spreading across my face. It was almost enough to make me forget Hu's parting shot from the night before.

Trace had more to say, naturally. The postmortem went on so long my eyes grew heavy. Several times I rattled myself awake when my head slumped forward. Across from me, Noah was doing the same. Rita kicked him under the table and he jerked upright, barely stifling an exclamation, and glared at her before returning his attention to the screen. I didn't blame him. Rita kicked *hard*, as I'd learned the other night during mandatory team-building movie night. Apparently she also had issues with people talking during a film or, as she put it, "providing nonstop commentary."

It was almost lunchtime before we finished. Everyone breathed a sigh of relief and sagged in their seats. "Sorry about this," Mom said, "but I need you for a few minutes longer—everyone except Kenzie. You can go work on your school assignments."

I hesitated, torn between insisting on the full involvement due to me as a member of the team and accepting the fact that I actually did have about four hours of homework to cram into the two hours before my shift. Mom arched her eyebrow, and I decided against this fight. I grabbed the hoodie I'd tossed over the back of my chair and exited the briefing room into the command center. I took a moment to enjoy the privacy. This was the station's nerve center, and I rarely spent any time here alone—not counting last night, when I was too panicked to enjoy it. I ran my hand over Mom's black leather chair at her workstation. Did I dare? I glanced over my shoulder at the closed door, then sank into her chair and propped my feet on her console. With a thought, I triggered my comm device, linking to Sanctuary, and gazed at the resulting feeds as they scrolled past me.

This would be mine someday—command of a prison like Sanctuary, or maybe even the big adult prison, Carcerem. I wasn't limited to the prisons, of course. Omnistellar Concepts was the largest, most diverse corporation in the solar system. Still, its prison wing was its most prestigious. Ever since the world's governments had outsourced most of their services, competition to provide those services had been fierce in everything but law enforcement. There, Omnistellar reigned supreme and unquestioned, and I was proud to be part of it. Some of that came from my parents, especially Mom. She was about the most patriotic person I'd ever met, refusing to so much as draw a breath that violated company guidelines, and constantly drilling into my head that Omnistellar's rules and regulations were for more than safety—they were the core of civilization. Case in point: I'd played fast and loose with the guidelines last night by going into the prison, and what had it bought me? A sleepless night and a face full of fruit.

Something thudded in the conference room, and I shot guiltily to my feet. I wasn't doing anything wrong exactly, but it would definitely be embarrassing if the crew caught me acting out my fantasy of command. At that awkward thought, I jogged out the door and headed for the living quarters.

A few minutes later I stretched out on my bed with a tablet, remotely connected to a distance learning center in Edmonton, Alberta. Yumiko winked down at me from her mech suit in the *Robo Mecha Dream Girl 5* poster plastered across the ceiling. I grinned at her affectionately. Yumiko was opposite me in every way: a Japanese citizen, no corporation to call her own, orphaned as an infant, fighting her way through the streets of Nuokyo until she discovered a unique mech piloting ability and took on the evil fictional corporations. Fortunately Mom wasn't really into manga. If she'd realized that element of the story, she probably would have outlawed *RMDG5* the first time I picked it up. Mom only watched Omnistellar-sanctioned news outlets, though, so I'd been able to follow Yumiko since the very first issue. Something about her always spoke to me. Over the years I'd come to think of her as a real person—even as a friend. Oh, I knew it was ridiculous. I wasn't delusional. But sometimes when I couldn't sleep at night, I'd stare up at the ceiling and imagine myself in Yumi's world, piloting mechs and living life on the edge, until I drifted into sleep. Omnistellar provided me with lots of real-world adventures, but they were all strictly controlled. While of course I was extremely grateful for every opportunity I'd had because of Omnistellar, a tiny part of me— the part that had made me sneak out to go to that party three years ago—longed to experience life outside the rigid restrictions of corporation citizenship.

Yumiko gave me the freedom to experience that. I'd even played the *Robo Mecha Dream Girl 5* game, and I was *not* a gamer. But exploring Yumi's world in VR? I actually played the whole thing through seven times, and completed all the side quests besides. I loved every second of it. Noah had tried to get me into some other games after that, but none of them held the same magic. There was just something about her world. Omnistellar wasn't a huge fan of *RMDG5*, since it played on the whole evil corporation thing, but they didn't outright disallow it, so neither did my parents. And as long as they never found out the plot of the story (which, providing it never made its way onto Omnistellar's banned books list, they shouldn't), I would stay safe to enjoy it in peace.

Yumiko's newest exploits summoned from an icon on my tablet, and I was so tempted to lose myself in the mech world of Nuokyo, but duty called. My family might be falling apart, but if I let my homework slide too, I might lose my position on Sanctuary. Whatever happened with Mom and Dad, I wasn't letting go of something I'd fought this hard for. And while Yumiko's world might be an awesome place to visit, this was where I had to live.

Munching on a bag of freeze-dried strawberries, my favorite treat, I tried to focus on the most tedious lecture possible on historical literature, because I would definitely need to identify the characters in some Shakespearean tragedy to effectively guard prisoners on a space station.

It was even harder to concentrate than usual. Trace's mention of the fifty-year anniversary of the probes had caught my attention, and my mind kept drifting to the night before. A shiver raced down my spine as I recalled the way the prisoners had risen in their cells, like wild animals waking in their cages.

Was it possible the same bizarre phenomenon that gave these kids their powers and abilities did something to their minds? That wasn't fair, obviously—there were people on Earth with similar powers who lived perfectly normal lives, many of them never even realizing they had special abilities. Scientists guessed as much as 1 percent of the population might be anomalies. I didn't know any of them, but you heard about them all the time in news reports and history books. Besides, it wasn't like I knew much of anyone. We moved around too much, and I was too busy training to get involved in typical teen pursuits.

But it did seem like the strongest powers manifested in the worst criminals. And if my encounter in the alley hadn't made me buy that theory, last night had convinced me. Their behavior hadn't been human at all. It seemed like they were *stalking* me from behind their bars.

Enough, Kenzie. They can't use *their powers.* The chips embedded in their arms were nearly impossible to remove without a surgical procedure. Tendrils on the inhibition chips literally wound themselves around nerves and pressure points in a prisoner's body. The chips didn't cause any distress unless you messed with them. Removing them without medical supervision and anesthetic, though? I shuddered. Even if the prisoners somehow got their hands on a sharp object, it would be like slicing directly through your body's pain sensors.

The tablet in my lap toned, making me jump. I glanced down and saw it was asking a series of multiple-choice questions about *Othello.* Of course, not having heard a word of the lecture, I didn't have a clue about the answers. I hesitated a moment before closing the video. Just a quick break to go online. I checked my social networking sites—no messages, which probably meant my Earth friends had given up on me. I smiled ruefully. I always said I'd keep in touch, and I always meant to. One of these days I'd manage it.

I skimmed through the highlights of Thursday night's

Knicks game, shaking my head at the disaster of a loss. A superstitious urge made me think that maybe if I managed to catch a game live, my team would have better luck. But the last time I'd tried to watch in the common area, Noah had moaned and complained so loudly I gave up, relinquished the vidscreens to him for his games, and retreated to my quarters to watch in solitude. Watching alone was boring, so before long I was browsing Mecha Dream Girl fanfics instead. I felt more connected to the online Dream Girl fan community than I did to any kids in the real world anyway.

With a sigh, I returned to school. *Othello* beckoned, but I decided to call up an old history lecture instead. It took a few minutes to find the one I wanted, because I hadn't paid much attention to *it* the first time around either. I liked math, computer sciences, and physics. Other than that, school was pretty much a waste of time, all that learning and memorizing of useless dates and facts. Give me a practical training camp any day.

Right now, though, I wanted something specific, and I was sure I'd heard it just a few days ago. Sure enough, I found a history lecture titled "Unit Three, Lesson Seven: The Probes." I skimmed through the introduction until the camera zoomed in on a shot of a sleek black device covered in small spikes. I let the sound come in full.

"*. . . almost fifty years now since the devices appeared,*" said the lecturer, a man with a pleasant and serious British accent. Why did they always give history lectures to people with

British accents? *"Eight of them simultaneously broke atmosphere in various locations around the globe, including one device in Antarctica, which remained undiscovered for nearly a decade. Naturally, people panicked, considering it the first sign of an attack. However, the rudimentary global satellites available at the time confirmed that no further objects remained in Earth's vicinity, although many found that less than comforting given that the same satellites had offered no warning of the devices' approach in the first place. The generally accepted theory accredits these probes to an alien intelligence, as they resemble no technology we've ever seen on Earth. They seemed to emit some sort of signal, which many have interpreted as an attempt at communication. However, Earth's best scientists were unable to make any sense of the message, nor understand the technology behind it."*

I skimmed ahead. The screen view switched to a grainy shot of a young girl with electricity arcing between her fingers, and I slowed it again. *"The next generation, however, began to show signs of the probes' influence. The area's children, dubbed 'anomalies' by the populace, manifested signs of abnormal powers and abilities. Doctors and scientists alike were at a loss to explain these abilities, or what caused them. In fact, to this day, we don't know what specifically caused the reaction. An effort to trace family lines proved futile in many cases, but geneticists had enough success to believe the probes had a direct influence on the birth of those with unusual abilities.*

"At first, no one was sure what to do with the anomalies.

*Although some of them evinced very powerful and dangerous abili-
ties, human rights activists pointed out that to judge each by biology
rather than their individual actions mirrored the worst atrocities
of human history. Eventually authorities registered all anomalies
but accorded them—provided they declared their powers and did
not use them illegally—full freedoms due as government citizens,
although corporations were permitted to enforce their own rules
about offering citizenship to so-called anomalies. Perhaps it was
to be expected that this led to a certain amount of prejudice and
conflict. . . ."*

I ground the video to a halt. I remembered the rest anyway.
When some of the anomalies grew up and confused themselves
with supervillains, Omnistellar, which had long since taken
over most of the world's law enforcement, built two prisons:
Sanctuary, for young offenders, and Carcerem, a work camp on
the moon. Both prisons removed very dangerous people from
the general population and kept the world safe for those with
and without powers. Since Sanctuary's inception a dozen years
ago, almost a hundred prisoners had passed through its cells,
most going on to Carcerem, the adult prison, although a few
were deemed rehabilitated and released into society.

And yes, there was prejudice. There had been throughout
human history. Lots of people believed it was harder to get
corporate citizenship with anomalous powers, and that left
the various world governments, with their minimal funding
and pathetic subsidies, to absorb anomalies. I'd heard rumors

that to become corporate citizens, a lot of anomalies moved to the colonies on Mars and Jupiter's moons: corporate-owned facilities where most people didn't venture because of the harsh living conditions and brutal work schedules. It wasn't fair, and I knew that . . . but given my own encounters with the worst that anomalies had to offer, I understood the need for registration. You couldn't just let superpowered people roam around in secret, because you couldn't guess what they might do.

Reassured, I blanked my tablet. Sanctuary was not only necessary, it was *humane*. It was the best possible way to deal with an impossible situation. And if Omnistellar wanted to increase drills because the fiftieth anniversary of the probes was coming up, well, so what? Let them do it. Whatever Sanctuary threw at me, I'd be ready.

FIVE

MY DAD WAS SCHEDULED TO LEAVE THE NEXT morning for a training exercise on Earth. Jonathan was going to assist him, and Noah was joining them for a week of shore leave. I'd known about that for a while but of course I'd assumed my dad would be coming home, not remaining on Earth and sending someone to take his place. I stayed up late that night, waiting for my parents to call—to say they'd reconsidered, that they'd bonded over the drill, maybe even that thinking of me made them want to give things another try. But they didn't, and the next morning, Dad, Jonathan, and Noah headed for Earth, right on schedule.

Dad hugged me extra tight before boarding the shuttle. Jonathan and Noah hovered in the background, both meticulously avoiding my eyes. "I'll see you soon," Dad promised, squeezing my hand. "And I'll call you the second Omnistellar releases me from the compound."

"Okay," I said, a bit too loudly. I really wanted to return to the illusion that everything was normal. "Enjoy your training thing."

Dad took the hint. He stepped back, nodded, and crossed the room to Mom. The two of them spoke quietly. She clasped her hands behind her back, and he fidgeted with the strap of his bag. They had never been particularly affectionate, but this was painful even for them. I suddenly wondered how much they had in common, really, other than their fierce loyalty to Omnistellar. They'd met at a training camp, and 90 percent of their conversations revolved around work and patriotism. Had I ever heard them discuss music, or movies, or even their favorite food?

It seemed to take forever to launch, but eventually I stood at the window watching the shuttle's small silver mass descend to Earth. I swallowed a sudden lump in my throat, and Mom came up behind me and laid a hand on my shoulder. I layered mine over hers. "Do you think . . . ?" I began, but couldn't quite find a way to finish.

Mom sighed. "I don't know, honey. This has been a long time coming. Your dad and I just lost touch somewhere."

Tears blurred my vision. "Do you hate each other?"

"Kenzie. No. We love each other. It's just . . . sometimes, that's not enough."

Suddenly I became aware of Rita in the background, studiously ignoring us, much more interested in her tablet than anything there could possibly warrant. I cleared my throat and stepped away from Mom. "Is the new schedule ready?" With only three of us on Sanctuary for the next four days, I'd have to pick up the work of a full guard, and we'd all take double shifts.

Mom hesitated. "Yes. Kenzie . . ."

"I'm fine," I said, more sharply than I'd intended. I closed my eyes and forced a smile. This wasn't Mom's fault. I knew that. But she was here, and it would be much too easy to blame her. I lowered my voice. "Let's just get through the next few days, okay? We can talk about it more later." To be honest, there was still a part of me that thought Dad would spend a few days on Earth, miss us—miss *me*—enough to realize the error of his ways, and come home with Jonathan and Noah. Logically I knew that probably wouldn't happen, but until that possibility was ruled out, well . . .

"Okay, honey," said Mom softly. "We'll talk about it later."

I fled from the understanding in her eyes.

Since Sanctuary ran the prison, the company rarely replaced guards on shore leave or external assignments. Sometimes there was even talk of eliminating human guards entirely, but then some sort of emergency would call for human intervention. Three of us were more than capable of running the place, although it made for a grueling schedule.

Usually I hated it when anyone went off station, let alone three at once, but I was grateful for the constant occupation over the next several days. Mom, whether by design or not, covered the night watches, alternating day shifts with Rita. That meant she was effectively never home. Me, I took double my shift, working through the day and rushing to catch up on schoolwork on my breaks. It left me zero time to think about my parents, which was exactly what I needed. On the rare instances when my path crossed Mom's, we treated each other with a polite civility foreign to both of us, but the longer this went on, the harder the pattern was to break. It got to the point where I was counting down the minutes until the shuttle returned from Earth and I knew for sure, one way or another, whether Dad was coming with it.

A lot of my shifts involved busywork and downtime. A few nights before the shuttle was due back, I pulled files on the prisoners in sector 5. They were pretty much what I expected: murderers, thugs, and thieves. I'd never really looked at the prisoners' rap sheets before, and it made for interesting reading, filling up the little empty time I had. As I'd suspected, a lot of them were in for violent crimes—like, just for example, choking someone in an alley. Some were in for smaller things, minor instances of theft that almost seemed too petty to warrant a prison sentence. But in every case, Omnistellar judges had deemed the psychological makeup of the offender, combined with their tremendous power, a danger to society. I spared a moment of gratitude for the company. This was why they existed. They were thorough, careful, ready to do whatever it took to protect society, with far more meticulousness than any judge or jury in the old system. And as Mom constantly reminded me, no one was more dangerous than an uncontrolled anomaly. I could still picture her face when I told her about the girl in the alley: the sheer terror in her eyes, quickly swallowed by her more professional demeanor. That one brief slip, more than anything, convinced me how much danger I'd been in. I still didn't know why that girl let me live, but I didn't want to tempt fate a second time.

For instance, by heading into the prison?

Ironically enough, though, I was probably safer on Sanctuary than on Earth. We knew exactly where our anomalies were here, and their chips prevented them from using their powers. With that in mind, I found the files on my friends from the other night. Their crimes ran the gamut from theft to murder to corporate espionage. Danshov's pyrokinetics had almost leveled a city block. His roommate, Hu of the "see you soon," had incredible speed and a twin sister with some sort of weird ability to fuse with electronics. I also found a Mia Browne, who I suspected was the Irish girl Hu had declared my enemy. Her power was invisibility—and she'd been arrested on multiple charges of terrorism. I blinked at that, realizing that she, for one, would never see the outside of a prison cell again in her life.

Their powers brought to mind old comic books I used to read before I discovered Japanese manga. We had a perfect trio of villains.

Rita came on duty a few minutes later. "Reading prison files?" she asked with a grin.

I flushed, and blanked my screen. "I just got curious."

"We all do. Bit of advice: don't think of them as people."

"What are they, then, animals?" But when I thought back to the other night, that comparison didn't seem too far off.

Still, Rita shook her head. "They're human, obviously. But if you start thinking of them as individuals, things get messy. Consider them a horde. Aside from your mom and maybe Jonathan, none of us has much to do with those kids down there. Our job is to keep them safe from each other and Earth safe from them. That's as far as we need to think. Nothing else matters: not what they've done or who they are. Don't let yourself get bogged down."

She had a point. I nodded, remembering stories my mom read me as a child, cautionary tales of people who befriended anomalies and paid the price. They hadn't been horror stories, of course, and she'd always read them with me cuddled safe in her arms. They were more like modern fairy tales. They were a bit over the top, but I remembered them, so I guess they served their purpose.

As Rita took her place at her console, I debated between finishing some homework or heading to the gym to shoot hoops. Suddenly she straightened up. "What the hell?" she muttered.

Oh God, what now? I jumped to my feet and rushed to her side. "What is it?" *Please* not another drill—not when we were so short-staffed, and right on the heels of the last one. Fiftieth anniversary or not, Sanctuary wouldn't be that cruel, would it?

"A distress signal." She pulled the screen off the console so it hovered in front of our faces. "Looks like a merchant ship. Really weak. If it were a few kilometers in either direction, we wouldn't even see it."

I frowned. Merchant ships traveled between Mars and off-world space stations, sometimes even from the farthest colonies on Jupiter's moons, but we rarely saw them. The approved merchant approach to Earth deliberately avoided any stationary satellites, *especially* Sanctuary. "You'd better contact Omnistellar, right?"

"I'm trying. Something's interfering with our communications."

Warning bells went off in my head. "Another sim?"

"Not necessarily. Even though the distress signal seems weak, it's operating on all frequencies. It might be blocking our comms."

"It's not supposed to do that."

"No, it's not." She caught my expression and shook her head. "You wanna check the code?"

She seemed half-condescending, like she was mocking my instinct to pull code at the least provocation, but I did it anyway, experiencing a strange sense of déjà vu. No flashing red foreign loops were interfering with the comms this time, though. "I don't see anything," I said dubiously, "but . . ."

"Well, we can't abandon them. Call your mom."

My hands shook as I triggered my wrist comm with a thought, not trusting ship comms to wake Mom if she'd fallen asleep. It was probably exactly what Rita had said: a merchant ship distress call, its signal elevated to such a height that it interfered with our signal. But coming on the heels of Dad's departure, Trace's comments about the probes' fiftieth anniversary, and Hu's ominous threat . . . There was something about the situation I didn't like.

In less than a minute, Mom stood over Rita, arms folded, lips pursed, glaring at the distress signal on the screen. Her eyes narrowed to slits as she pondered the situation.

"Commander," Rita prodded. "Regulations state—"

"I know," Mom replied sharply. "Protocol is to contact Earth and, failing that, provide assistance whenever possible. But we also have a responsibility to maintain security on the prison."

"Well," I said slowly, hating myself as I spoke but knowing I couldn't willingly abandon a whole ship full of innocent people, "I guess what it comes down to is, does it really make that much of a difference to have one extra person around? I know protocol says three guards need to stay on the station at all times, but these are unique circumstances. Rita can check out the beacon, then either tow them in or contact Earth for help once she blocks their distress call. You and I can take care of things here."

Rita leveled an accusatory finger in my direction. "I make

all the difference in the world, *chica*," she announced, before grudgingly adding, "but you're not wrong. If there's a full-scale prison break, one gun won't mean the difference between security and disaster."

Mom nodded, her lips still pursed, telltale worry lines creasing her brow. "I know. And we can't abandon a ship in potential danger. I'm just very suspicious of the circumstances." She sighed heavily. "Rita, you're coming off a ten-hour watch. You okay to pilot?"

"I'm always okay." Rita shoved herself to her feet. "I'll get dressed and head out." She hesitated. "I'll have to take the second shuttle. You guys will be on your own here."

Mom slipped her arm around my waist, the first physical contact we'd had in days. I leaned into her, grateful she'd broken our stalemate. "We'll be fine."

Rita grabbed a tablet, already plotting her course. "Shouldn't take me more than a few hours to reach the vessel. If the signal *is* interfering with our comms, I'll probably lose contact with you partway there. Once I hit the merchant vessel, I'll deactivate the emergency signal and get in touch."

"Be careful," Mom advised, and I realized Colonel Trace's comments were on her mind too. "Under no circumstances approach the vessel if it doesn't seem safe. If I order your recall, I want you back here with no questions asked."

"Copy that, Commander." Rita spared me a wink as she ran for the door.

It slid shut behind her, leaving me and Mom truly and completely alone. I hesitated. "So, did you want me to stay on?"

"Head to your room and get some rest," Mom replied. "But leave your comm on. I'll buzz if I need you." She tightened her arm around me.

I hugged her back. "Are you sure? Protocol says . . ."

"I won't leave you out. As soon as something happens, I'll wake you up. But you're coming off shift, and protocol says you're supposed to rest."

She had her command voice back on. My mother had slipped into the background. I nodded, knowing argument was fruitless. Omnistellar Concepts gave us a lot. Citizenship in a corporation, especially one like ours, meant security, freedom, mobility, and better services than for your average person. But it came at a cost. The company demanded utter loyalty in exchange for those privileges. That loyalty had been drilled into me from the moment I was born, and I knew neither my mom nor I would abandon procedure now.

Although I had full intentions of obeying my mother—eventually—I ran to the window near the bay. After a few seconds, the shuttle carrying Rita erupted from the station, hurtling into space. It was eerily similar to watching Dad, Jonathan, and Noah head to Earth a few days ago, and seeing that second shuttle disappear filled me with a sense of foreboding. Mom and I were truly trapped here now, alongside the hundred-odd prisoners.

Rita would be fine, wouldn't she? I shook my head. I was letting everything that had happened lately—Trace's comments, the last drill, my parents, the prisoners—infect my thoughts. The timing was coincidental, but maybe this was another drill? There were plenty of explanations to choose from.

I ran my hand down Sanctuary's wall as Rita receded into the darkness, quickly becoming another prick of light in the velvet sky. We were safe here. Sanctuary was our protection, and it was good at its job. We just had to keep it running, and everything would be fine.

And on that thought, alarms shattered the silence again.

The signal is sent. The waiting is done. And yet there is waiting to endure. And spirit to absorb. And life to harvest.
So few now, and yet so many. So weak, and yet so strong.
They are and they are and they are, and they drift no more.
They have arrived. It is time.
Teeth gnash in the darkness. Malice expands.
It is time.

SIX

AS I TOOK OFF FOR THE COMMAND CENTER,
alarms urging me onward, a security door slid out of the wall
and cut off my retreat. My jaw dropped. I had never seen that
happen before. I hadn't known that *could* happen. "Mom!" I
called, triggering my comm device. My heart thudded against
my rib cage.

Her crisp tone cut through the klaxons. "It's *Commander*,
Kenzie."

That told me everything I needed to know. "You've got to
be kidding me. Not another drill. Not now."

"We treat every alarm as a full-blown emergency, regardless
of the circumstances. Now, I need you in the command center."

"Yeah, great idea," I agreed dryly. "Unfortunately, Sanctuary
locked me out."

"What? Where are you?"

I winced. "Mom, can you turn off the alarms?"

She hesitated. They'd commented on that during the debrief, although as a footnote buried under a lot of *well done*s. To her credit, a second later the klaxons stopped and I could think again. "I'm by the shuttle bay," I said. "I was watching Rita launch."

A moment later, Mom was back, her voice even terser. "I can't contact Rita. Communication is blocked. Kenzie, what do you mean, Sanctuary locked you out?"

"Some sort of blast door." I examined it. I couldn't even find a seam, much less a way through the passage. If I hadn't known better, I would have thought it was another wall. "There's no way past it, Mom—I mean, Commander."

"All right. Grab your XE suit, head into the prison, and use the emergency airlock."

A chill raced through me. "You want me to go *outside*?"

"You've done it before, and I need you in the command center. We're the only two guards on the station." I heard her adjust something in the background. "Cameras show no unusual activity in the sectors. All prisoners are secure in their cells. Still, take it slow. Check before you advance. If anything in the cellblock seems suspicious, lock it down, contact me, and we'll find another route." She hesitated briefly. "If *anything* seems suspicious, Kenzie. I mean it. No one expects you to put your life on the line."

I drew a deep breath. Under normal circumstances, I

didn't mind space walks. I actually kind of enjoyed them. There was something terrifying but awe inspiring about clinging to a station on the edge of nothingness. But this was not a normal circumstance. And the idea of getting anywhere near sector 5, where I'd have to access the emergency airlock, made my knees go weak.

I wouldn't have to go into the sector itself, though, just the prison block. And I could hardly refuse the order. "Okay," I said. "I'll contact you before I evacuate."

"Be careful, honey." Mom's voice caught on the last word—definite breach of protocol, and a sign of how worried she really was. "Contact me as soon as you're in your suit." She signed off, no doubt to deal with one of the other thousand emergencies demanding her attention.

Before I could think too hard about what I was doing, I bolted down the corridor to one of two equipment storage rooms. They held XE suits for each crew member, specially fitted and meticulously maintained. Mine hung on a hook below my name. I didn't put it on, but threw it over my shoulder instead. I'd move faster carrying it.

I half worried, half hoped Sanctuary would lock me out of the prison, but I logged through with the same code and thumb scan I'd used a few nights ago. Once again, I stumbled down the metal staircase, the corridors below illuminating as I advanced. The emergency airlock at the bottom of the stairs, directly outside sector 5, vented the entire stairwell when activated. I had to move quickly. The airlock required Mom's authorization from the command center to blow, which meant I needed to get suited and ready before contacting her.

It shouldn't be a problem. I'd practiced with the XE suit a thousand times, first at camps as a kid, later in junior guard training, and of course during drills on Sanctuary itself—and once even when I wasn't supposed to, late at night with a tempting boy on a station camp. But it would be the first time I'd ever tested a speed prep without anyone to back me up and double-check my seals.

You'll be fine, I promised myself. *You'll tether to the station so you can't get lost. Just keep moving.*

I stumbled over a step, almost dropping my suit but managing to snag it before it went over the edge. After that, I slowed my pace. Speed mattered, but not as much as keeping my suit intact. It wasn't exactly designed to tear easily, but pitching down five flights of metal stairs might test its limits, especially the faceplate.

I reached the bottom without incident. Light flooding the area revealed the airlock, an ominous trap door set into the floor. I dropped my helmet and jumped into the bottom half of the XE suit, effectively immobilizing my legs.

At the same time, something clattered behind me. I jerked up and twisted toward the source of the noise, but the bulky material of my half-worn suit caught around my knees, sending me sprawling on the ground.

Two familiar figures emerged from the shadows.

Danshov and Hu.

My jaw dropped. *"How . . . ?"* I whispered.

They didn't answer, but came at me with identical expressions of grim determination.

"Mom!" I shouted, activating my wrist comm with a thought—thank God for implanted devices. "Mom, I'm at sector five. Two prisoners have escaped! They're—"

Danshov's massive hand clamped over my mouth. I struggled against him, but with my legs tangled in my suit, it was like fighting a brick wall.

"Kenzie!" Mom shouted frantically. "What's going on? Kenzie, come in!"

The terror in her voice gave me new strength, but Danshov's free arm circled my stomach, trapping both arms against my sides. I struggled furiously. My teeth scraped his palm and his grip tightened painfully over my jaw, making me gasp.

In my second of distraction, Hu caught my wrist. He squeezed both sides of the comm device and applied pressure in exactly the right spot. The unit slid out, leaving a metal gap in my wrist. Before I could react, he pressed the power switch. Mom's voice screeched, then faded to nothing.

I screamed into Danshov's hand, working my legs free of the suit. My right foot came loose, and I aimed a kick at Hu's face. He stumbled, hit the wall, and plastered a hand to his nose.

Danshov lifted me right off the ground, shaking me hard. I

kicked my other leg free. After swinging my knees up, I drove both feet back with all my might.

He anticipated the move, twisting aside. I connected with his thigh, a couple inches lower than I'd intended. It drew a grunt from the monster, though. *"Chert voz'mi,"* he grumbled in my ear. "Would you quit it?"

Hu grinned, swiping a hand across his nose to stop the ooze of blood. "Told you she'd be trouble."

"She's trouble, all right. *Now* can I knock her out?"

"That's not necessary." Hu came closer, although he was a lot more cautious about it this time. I channeled the full force of my hatred into my glare, the only weapon they'd left me. He reached into his back pocket to produce a small, jagged piece of metal.

I froze, my body taut against Danshov's. A smear of what could only be blood marred the edge of that metal.

"Right," Hu said, correctly interpreting my posture. "It's not exactly a precision weapon, but it's sharp enough to do some damage. Especially if you're squirming around and we can't control where we're stabbing. You get my drift?"

I glared at him a moment longer, my mind racing, playing the odds. After a moment I bobbed my head.

"Good." Hu glanced at Danshov. "I think you can let go of her now. She knows she's not going anywhere."

Danshov grumbled. "I still think we should knock her out. Quicker and easier."

"Dude, you hang around Mia too much. She's harmless. Let her go."

My feet hit the ground. I slumped forward, shoulders hunched, pretending an injury to my left foot. It was only half pretending—I was pretty sure that whatever Danshov's power chart might say, he was actually made of stone. Nothing else explained the agony caused by kicking him.

"You all right?" Hu asked.

"She's fine," Danshov snapped. "On your feet. Now."

I cringed away, throwing up a hand as if to protect myself. "Okay," I said, allowing a tremor to enter my voice. Not too much of one, a mere hint. I reached for the stair railing as if to steady myself.

Hu and Danshov both moved instinctively to help.

Bracing my arms on the railing, I threw my weight forward, swinging my legs in an arc. I didn't aim at Danshov—he wasn't going down, not from any blow I could deliver. Instead, I drove both knees into Hu's back, sending *him* tumbling into his pal.

And then I bolted.

SEVEN

I COULDN'T OUTRUN THEM, NOT FOR LONG—BUT I didn't have to. I'd knocked them off balance. I only needed to reach the fourth-floor prison cells.

My instinct, obviously, was to run for the exit, but I knew better. If Danshov or Hu caught up to me before I relocked the door, I'd have released them into Sanctuary proper. And while the station could apparently slam down security walls wherever it damn well pleased, that was more than I was willing to risk. Once again, I remembered Mom's momentary panic when she'd learned about the girl in the alley. If I let these monsters loose, who knew what they'd do? They might kill my mom or, worse, find a way to escape the station. And then how many deaths would be on my conscience?

If I made it into the sector-4 cells ahead of them, though, I could trap them in the stairwell. From there I could access the server room on four and restore communication with Mom, who could vent the stairwell, sending both boys into space. I felt a twinge of guilt at that thought but stowed it quickly. As Mom always said, safety and security came first—even at the cost of a prisoner's life. Even at the cost of our own.

Of course, that assumed no sector-4 prisoners were out of *their* cells, but it was a chance I had to take. I didn't want to consider the possibility of rushing into sector 4 only to find every prisoner on the loose. There were only two prisoners in the stairwell, and cellmates at that. Hopefully only one cell was open.

I raced up the stairs three at a time, hauling myself along the railing. Behind me, Hu swore in what I supposed was Mandarin, based on his file. A second later, footsteps clattered behind me.

I slammed my thumb on the scanner. The instant the print cleared, I rattled my code into the keypad. I got through the first three digits before hands caught me from behind and slammed me against the metal door. I cried out—more from shock than actual pain—as air forced its way from my lungs.

Sharp, corded arms surrounded me; a long, lithe body pressed against mine. Hu, not Danshov—which made sense. Danshov was too big to move with that kind of speed. Still, Hu must have blasted off the floor to catch me this quickly. I'd knocked him off balance pretty well, and I was no tortoise myself.

Hu tightened his grip on my wrist, and this time my cry *was* of pain. He brought his lips to my ear and said, in a voice laced with anger, "Enough." He gave me a slight shake. "I'm going to let go of you, but if you attack me again, I *will* let Alexei knock you out. And he won't be gentle about it. You got me?"

My natural stubbornness surged to the surface, but I choked it down. The boys were armed. There were two of them, and they were stronger than me. I'd blown my chance at escape, and they wouldn't fall for another ploy like the one I'd just pulled. Gritting my teeth, I bobbed my head.

Slowly, Hu released me. I turned to face him and pressed my back against the wall as I cradled my injured wrist. He leaned in, seeming to suck the oxygen out of the space. I wished he wasn't so damn attractive—somehow, the clean, angular lines of his face made his malice that much worse. He didn't look nearly as amused as the first time I'd kicked him, at least, so that was something. And if they'd wanted to kill me, they would have done it by now. Another point in my favor.

Still. I didn't have to fake my fear this time when Danshov came up behind him. *He* at least looked the part of the villain, with his square jaw and scarred cheek. I held out my hands in surrender. "Okay," I said. "I'll go with you. I give up."

"Uh-huh." Danshov's eyes narrowed. "Cage, offer's still on the table."

Hu—Cage?—chuckled, his good humor restored. "I think we're okay." He gestured to me. "But I also think you can walk in front of us. Back down the stairs, there's a good girl."

My mother would have recognized the look I shot him, one I'd used to silence countless others in training scenarios. I couldn't stand anyone condescending to me. Fortunately, my anger burned away some of my fear, and I stomped down the stairs without tripping, trembling, or otherwise humiliating myself.

Now I saw what I'd missed before: the door to sector 5 was slightly ajar. I pointed and demanded, *"How?"*

"You'll see soon enough." Danshov prodded my shoulder. "In you go."

I gulped, remembering my last adventure in sector 5. Every muscle in my body strained, itching for me to run. But I had nowhere to go, and no way to flee. If I didn't walk through on my own, they'd make me, and my pride wouldn't allow that. With trembling hands, I stepped through the door.

The prison looked as I remembered it except for one thing: all of the prisoners, without exception, were outside their cells. The doors stood open, the prisoners lining the hall. I froze under the hostility of their glares. Their expressions made it clear: none of them wanted anything so much as to claw the flesh off my face.

Danshov nudged me from behind. "Keep moving."

A girl broke off from the crowd. I recognized her instantly as Hu's twin sister. I would have recognized her even without seeing her file. She didn't look exactly like her brother, but they had the same fluid way of moving, the same sharply defined features. Her hair hung in a loose braid over her shoulder, knotted carefully to keep it secure.

She was also the only person in the room who didn't look like she wanted to hurt me. She took my elbow and guided me gently away from Hu and Danshov. "Come with me," she said.

Her brother leaped between us, and I couldn't help but notice how everyone leaned back, deferring to him. His very presence dominated the room. *"No."*

The girl gasped. "Cage—what happened to your nose?"

"She did. Which is why you're not going anywhere with her. Not alone."

"I need her in the server room." She linked her arm firmly with mine. "She isn't going to hurt me. Are you?"

I faltered. Because the thing was, if I saw an opportunity for escape, I *would* hurt her. She didn't seem like much of a threat. But she was on Sanctuary, so no matter how cheerful and friendly she seemed, she was still a violent criminal. The Hu twins, I recalled from their files, were in for corporate espionage of some kind. At least they hadn't murdered anyone. If Cage was in charge, and that seemed to be the case, maybe I could reason with him.

But not if I hurt his sister.

I'd hesitated too long. Cage nodded. "That's what I thought. I'm coming with you." He gestured around the room, his voice rising. "The rest of you—this isn't a social gathering. You all have jobs to do. Get to it."

The prisoners retreated, muttering under their breaths. Danshov crossed to a pretty girl with iron-straight dark hair who actually hissed at me when we passed. The elusive Mia Browne.

I stayed close to the twins as they led me through the prison. I knew they were dangerous, but neither of them seemed prone to random fits of violence, which was more than I could say for some of the others. At the same time, I glanced around, memorizing the layout—the cells, the cramped entertainment area clearly doubling as a mess hall, the (currently locked) entrances to the gymnasium and the work area.

The server room door stood wide open, and I entered ahead of the twins. They flanked the door behind me, fencing me in. "Listen," I said. "Cage, right? That's what they called you."

He nodded. "This is my sister, Rune."

Not the name on her file either, but I didn't care. I'd call them the king and queen of England if it got them on my side. "Cage and Rune. Got it. I'm Kenzie."

"We know," said Rune. "We've seen your file."

That caught me off guard for a moment, but I refused to be derailed. "Okay. Great. Listen, I've seen your files too, and I know you're both smart people. Too smart to think a plan like this has any chance of success. What's your endgame here? There's no way off this station. There aren't enough shuttles to transport all of you, and both of our shuttles are off station at the moment anyway. Right now the station commander—"

"Your mother," Cage interrupted, his eyes glittering.

I counted to five in my head. How was he so calm in the middle of this bedlam? "Yes, my mother. You only have a few minutes before she vents the entire sector. But if you stop this now—if you convince everyone to return to their cells—we can make this go away. I'll talk to my mom. I can't promise you'll get off with no consequences, but I *can* tell you your cooperation will go a long way toward making things better for you."

"Your mom's not going to vent the sector. Not with you inside."

"She doesn't *know* I'm inside," I lied. The cameras, assuming they were working, would tell her everything she hadn't figured out from our aborted communication.

"She will soon." Rune crossed to the server unit behind me. She took a deep breath, closed her eyes—and plunged her arms elbow deep into the circuitry.

I screamed and scrambled backward into Cage "Take it easy," he said, holding me an arm's length away, presumably in case I attacked again. Smart boy. "She's fine."

She didn't look fine. Rune's head fell back, her eyes rolling into her skull until they were pure white. Her mouth hung open, her jaw working as her body spasmed. "She's electrocuting herself!" I cried.

Cage radiated heat. His hands seared my shoulders right through my sweater, his grip somewhere between restraining and reassuring. "Why would you care if she was?"

I twisted to face him. He didn't release me but let me turn, and I jutted my chin in his direction. "In spite of what you seem to think, I don't take some sort of sadistic pleasure in seeing anomalies suffer. I just don't want you to hurt anyone else."

His expression turned thoughtful, as if he were actually considering my words. "She's bonding with the system," he said at last. "It doesn't hurt her. Trust me."

I snorted my opinion of that, and a near smile touched his lips, although he replaced it so quickly I might have imagined it. A second later, Rune gasped. I turned back to see her tear her arms free of the panel, leaving not the holes I expected but an intact circuit board. She gasped again, resting her hands on her knees as she drew in gulps of air. "Okay," she said. "Cameras are down throughout sector five, but we have communication with the command center whenever we want it. She won't be able to block us."

All at once I became aware of Cage, his hands now relaxed on my arms, his face inches away. I jerked free and stumbled a few steps toward his sister. Realization dawned, slow and insidious. "Your power," I remembered. "But how?"

For the first time, Rune looked openly hostile. She shrugged out of the top half of the jumpsuit the prisoners wore—hers had been unzipped, exposing the white tank top underneath—to reveal a makeshift bandage over her right shoulder. A spot of blood marred it, and Cage growled, pushing me aside. "You reopened the wound. What did I tell you?"

"Hard to take things easy when I'm up to my shoulders in circuitry." She shrugged him off. "I'm okay, Cage."

I could have run—Cage had left me standing in the doorway—but where was I going to go? At least a dozen prisoners waited in the corridor behind us, some of them decidedly more dangerous than the twins. "How did you remove that chip?" I demanded instead.

They spun on me. Cage brandished the jagged piece of steel he'd threatened me with earlier. "I used this," he said coldly. "Alexei knocked my sister out, and I cut the implant out of her shoulder."

I gaped at him. "The computer should have registered the changes in her vital signs."

"It probably did. But she wasn't near death, and the computer doesn't particularly care if we're in pain. Besides, that's why we knocked her out. So her vitals wouldn't race high enough to cause an alarm."

I shivered. I'd never experienced an implant, but I understood the concept of fusing something directly to a person's nerve endings. The idea was to prevent exactly this sort of self-surgery. "She woke up after a few minutes," he continued conversationally. "It got harder after that, but not bad enough to trigger any warnings, apparently."

My brain scrambled to catch up with what I was hearing. "You cut into your sister with a piece of jagged metal? That wound could be infected. She might have tetanus. Brilliant plan."

His expression turned ugly. "We didn't have much choice." He looked like he wanted to say something else, but turned to Rune instead. "Is the computer on our side?"

"More or less." Rune sank against the console, her exhausted expression almost otherworldly in the dim lighting. "I still need a functioning guard code to access some of the systems." She nodded at me. "That's where you come in."

"Absolutely not," I replied flatly. I didn't doubt this pack of monsters could torture the information out of me if they really wanted to, but I didn't have to last long. As soon as Mom realized what had happened, she'd follow protocol and block my code—if she hadn't already.

Cage shrugged, an unreadable expression flickering in his dark eyes. "Well, we don't need your approval. It's just . . . friendlier that way. Let's head to the common room and get started."

Something about his tone set my nerves on edge. Instinctively, I backed away as the twins surged forward. Cage didn't even seem to notice. He caught my arm below the elbow and pulled me alongside him. I spat curses at him in my head, all of my training—not to mention my own natural defiance— rearing its head in outrage. *Stay calm,* I reminded myself. *You've trained for this. Be Yumiko, Mecha Dream Girl.* It wasn't the first time I'd thought this. Whenever I got nervous, I found myself recalling relatable moments from *RMDG5.* Yumiko always said, *Nanakorobi yaoki:* "fall down seven times, get up eight." It was good advice that had pulled me through some tough training situations.

Of course, Yumiko would have had a twelve-foot mech suit to stomp Cage with, but the point held. I drew a steadying breath and swallowed my rage.

Mia and Danshov—*Alexei,* I corrected myself. First names. Familiar terms. I needed to form a bond with these people, get inside their heads, maybe even earn their trust. I'd started on a bad note with my escape attempt, but it had been a necessary first effort. Perhaps the prisoners could even sympathize, given their situation.

Mia and Alexei were waiting on a threadbare sofa next to a vidscreen covered in clear mesh wire. A thin, nervous boy sat nearby, and another perched on a stool. "So," said Mia in her faint Irish accent. "Did you get the code?"

Cage closed his eyes for just a moment as if in pain, and then his features resettled into their characteristic cocky smile. "No. She refused to give it to us."

Mia rolled her eyes. "What a shock. It's not like anyone told you that would happen." Then, without warning, she lunged forward, catching my throat and yanking me from Cage's grasp. I jerked in surprise, jamming both my fists against her arm, but her fingers were like bands of solid steel. "I'll get it out of her."

"Be nice, Mia. You know there's a quicker way."

"Give me the knife. I promise it'll be fast."

Cage shook his head, although he didn't move to detach

her from my throat, where she was quickly cutting off my air supply. I pried at her fingers with my nails and sank them into her wrists as this second anomaly tried to choke the life out of me. Mia at least used her hands, but she didn't even seem to notice my struggles.

"Stand down," Cage ordered, a hint of sharpness entering his voice.

She hesitated a moment longer, her fierce eyes blazing mere inches from my own. At last, she snorted and shoved me aside. I clutched at my neck, gasping for air. I hadn't been in serious danger of choking, but her grip was painful all the same.

Mia sauntered behind Cage, her fingers dancing over his shoulder, and rejoined Alexei, who slid a massive arm around her. Like Rune, they'd shed the top half of their jumpsuits. Mia had knotted hers at the waist.

"Who's going to watch her while we do it?" Alexei asked, nodding in my direction.

Cage shrugged. "I will, at least until it's my turn."

"No. You're the only one who's done this before. You go last."

"It's not an experience I was looking to repeat," he said with a grimace.

"Then it's your lucky day, sport." Mia turned to the tall blond boy on the stool. "I'm happy to cut on you for a while." She produced the knife and wiggled it between her fingers. Cage's eyes grew wide. He patted his pockets, then sighed in resignation as Mia's smirk broadened.

The boy on the stool snorted. "Yeah, I think I'll take my chances with Dr. Cage."

"What's the matter, Matt?" Mia winked. "Don't trust me?"

His silence spoke volumes and was the first sign of sense I'd seen from any of them.

"Better do me first," Alexei said. He stretched out on the couch, which someone had covered with a clean but worn sheet.

"All right. Rune, keep an eye on our guest." Cage glanced at me. "There are prisoners all through those cells. You won't get far if you try to run. And do I need to tell you what will happen if you hurt my sister?"

I brushed aside his concerns, my mind fixated on the scene playing out in front of me. "I don't want to hurt anyone. What are you doing?"

They ignored me. Mia climbed on top of Alexei's legs, extending the piece of metal that passed for a blade. Cage took it from her, and Matt came to the head of the couch and leaned forward, pressing all of his weight onto Alexei's shoulders. He and Cage exchanged speaking glances.

"Ready?" Cage asked Alexei, who grimaced.

"As I'll ever be."

"I'll try to make it quick."

There was a flash of steel and a surge of crimson. I closed my eyes against the truth I'd tried to resist: they were cutting out their chips. That meant they needed their powers for something . . . and the only thing they'd asked for so far was my code.

A chill raced through my body, and my breath caught in my throat. What was going to happen when they asked me a second time with powers to back up their threats?

EIGHT

RUNE GRABBED MY ARM AS CAGE DUG THE knife into Alexei's shoulder. For a moment we weren't enemies, not prisoner and guard, but two girls united by the sight of something horrible. "You might want to look the other way," she said.

But I couldn't—it was like a grisly accident. Alexei sank his teeth into his bottom lip, his muscles quivering with the effort to remain still as Cage rummaged around in his body. "This is where it gets bad," he cautioned.

A second later, Alexei howled in anguish. His massive body bucked, dislodging Matt and almost toppling Mia. Cage flew backward, the knife tumbling from his hand. "Damn it, Cage!" Mia hollered, clamping her legs around Alexei's and heaving her full weight into his chest.

Matt scrambled for Alexei's flailing wrists and pinned them, his limbs trembling with the effort. Cage grabbed the knife, gave it a quick wipe on his blood-stained T-shirt, and plunged it back into Alexei's arm.

With an ear-shattering roar, Alexei heaved again. Cage managed to hang on, but both Mia and Matt went flying. Matt crashed heavily into the wall; Mia rolled on the floor. She shook her head, obviously dizzy from the force of the fall.

I couldn't watch this, not for another second. I didn't care what he'd done, what *any* of them had done. If they were removing that chip, they needed to hurry, because every heartbeat of this was agony to watch. I yanked free of Rune's grip and threw myself over Alexei's right arm, pinning it in place.

The others hesitated again but they weren't in a position to argue. Matt grabbed the other arm and held fast, and Mia clambered over Alexei's legs, her jaw clenched, her eyes narrowed. "Hurry up!" she ordered.

"Yeah, 'cause I'm taking the scenic route," Cage shot back, not even looking at her. He drew a deep breath and plunged the knife in a third time.

I braced for impact, but the violence of Alexei's response still nearly dislodged me. I leaned all my weight into his arm, certain I was going to break his wrist. I didn't even care at this point. He strained against my grasp, and I trembled with effort, sweat dripping into my eyes. How long could this possibly take? I was sure I'd been pinning him for at least five minutes, probably longer. . . .

All at once, Alexei went limp. "It's out," Cage announced, sinking back on his heels in exhaustion.

Alexei moaned. I released his arm, and he dragged his hand over his face, splattering blood as he did so. Mia sank onto his chest and closed her eyes, breathing heavily. Meanwhile, Cage slipped under Alexei's shoulder with a bandage clearly made from someone's torn bedsheet and bound the wound. Matt helped him, and the boys held a hurried consultation, glancing between me and Mia. I sank against the couch, too tired to care what they were talking about.

After a moment Cage nodded and headed for Alexei. To my surprise, Matt joined me on the floor. "Thanks," he said.

I blinked, surprised that he'd even acknowledged me. Well. It was a good first start to building trust. "You're welcome," I replied, and he flashed me a quick, genuine smile that made his eyes sparkle, though his face was still gray.

We all sat a moment, catching our breath. Matt glanced over his shoulder at Cage. "Good job," he said softly.

Cage forced a smile. "I'm not sure that's what I'd call it, but I appreciate the thought. So. Who's next?"

He had to be kidding. As if anyone would volunteer for . . .

"I am," said Mia. She gave Alexei a final squeeze and sat up.

Was she serious? After what I'd just seen, I'd rather volunteer for a full-frontal lobotomy. But she pushed Alexei's legs off the couch and perched there as calmly as if she was about to receive a routine vaccination. A slight tension in her extended arm was the only sign of her discomfort.

Alexei slowly rolled up, shaking his head. "Sorry," he offered.

Cage waved him off. "Hold on to Mia and we'll call it even."

"I don't need anyone to hold me."

"The hell you don't," Alexei replied bluntly, pulling her into his lap and closing his arms around her. "You're tough, Mia mine, but not that tough."

She sighed impatiently and gestured. "Get on with it." Matt moved as if to take her other arm, but a blistering glare from her froze him in place.

"It's all right," Alexei said. "I can handle it."

"I hope so," Cage replied. I hoped so too, because there was no way I was getting near that girl, no matter how much she thrashed. I sank down on the floor again, exhausted.

To my surprise, Matt slumped beside me and shook his head. "Not looking forward to this," he muttered.

I glanced at him out of the corner of my eye. "You don't have to, you know."

He smiled faintly, his gaze fixed on Mia. "And let her have all the fun?"

Mia clenched her fists as Cage made the initial cut, but like Alexei, she didn't make a sound until he found the chip embedded in her arm. Then she screamed and thrashed plenty, but Alexei was true to his word: in spite of his wound, he kept her still enough for Cage to finish much more quickly than before.

Mia shuddered at the chip's removal. She sat a moment, head resting on her hands, before jerking free of Alexei's grasp.

Snatching the chip from Cage's hand, she hurled it to the ground, spat on it, and stomped it beneath her heel, blood trickling down her arm. A diabolical grin crossed her lips—and she disappeared, clothes and all.

"Very dramatic," said Alexei dryly. "Can we bind that arm now?"

Mia rematerialized behind him. "Knock yourself out." She stretched. "God, that feels *good*. Like working a muscle you forgot you had. Who's next?"

"Matt?" Cage gestured.

Matt made a face. "Do I have to sit in Alexei's lap?"

"I will cut you, little man," snarled Mia. The threat lost some of its impact because of the pallor of her face, though.

Mia and Alexei pinned Matt between them, and Cage made short work of his chip too. He took a moment to bind the wound after and said something that made Matt chuckle. In spite of myself, I was impressed at Cage's care of his friends—he might be a criminal, but he obviously wasn't inhuman. That meant there were ways I could reach him.

But then he turned on the boy still hunched in the corner.

The kid's already pale skin went even paler. "I can't," he squeaked. "I . . . I'm sorry. I can't do it."

"Tyler," Cage sighed, "we need you more than anyone."

"We all survived it," Rune pointed out gently. "You will too. It hurts, I'm not going to lie—but not for long. You'll be okay."

The boy shook his head frantically, scrambling to his feet and backpedaling—right into Mia, who caught him by the shoulder and shoved him forward. "Get in there," she snapped. "Or I'll show you pain."

Tyler glanced frantically between Mia and Alexei, who advanced on his left. His gaze took in me, Matt, Rune, and Cage with the knife, and then his eyes rolled back in his head and he collapsed.

"Oh, for God's sake," said Mia, who, instead of catching him, actually stepped aside and let him hit the ground.

"Perfect. Let's work fast," Cage replied. Mia and Alexei restrained Tyler. I prayed he would stay unconscious through the whole thing, but he didn't, waking at the first cut of the knife. The other three, their agony tore me to shreds—but at least they'd signed up voluntarily. Seeing Cage forcibly cut the chip from this poor kid's arm drove home something I'd almost forgotten: I was dealing with ruthless criminals. Seeing them suffer had awakened my compassion, but these were literally some of the most dangerous people in the solar system, and I needed to remember that.

They dumped a sobbing, shivering Tyler on a corner of the couch near where I was perched on the floor. Rune promptly took him in her arms, murmuring softly in his ear. Attention turned to Cage. Mia extended a hand. "Oh, please. Let *me*."

Cage handed her the knife. She arched an eyebrow, and he shrugged. "You've got the nimblest fingers. And you're not going to get distracted by all the blood and screaming." He paused, then smiled. "Also . . . as it happens, I trust you."

Mia made no reply to that, nodding instead to Alexei. "Hold him."

Rune made a strangled sound in her throat as she let go of Tyler, and her fingers closed over my arm—not to restrain me this time, but in search of support. In spite of my resolution of a few moments ago, I reached back and took her hand.

Cage screamed just like the others, and Rune gasped in anguish, the blood draining from her face as she clenched her free hand into a fist at her side. I put my arm around her and held her close, ignoring the pain where her grip seared my wrist. I had four little cousins—children of my dad's sister, the only family we were remotely close to—and Rune was starting to remind me of them. "It's okay," I whispered. "They're almost done."

Sure enough, in spite of her threatening demeanor, Mia was quick and deft with the makeshift surgery. "That's all of us," she said, bandaging the wound on Cage's shoulder. "Tyler, you're up."

Tyler, who couldn't have been more than fourteen years old, shook off his lethargy long enough to glare at Mia. "I really hate you."

She beamed, seeming to take that as a compliment.

Something beeped in the server room. Rune and Cage exchanged a glance, and he turned to Mia. "You okay here?" he asked.

Mia nodded. "I've got this."

Cage glanced at her dubiously, tugging his bandage into place. "All right," he said, with a look in my direction that I couldn't quite interpret. He and Rune ran for the server room. I stared after them, my fingers twitching. Part of me wanted to follow. Sure, Cage had grabbed me and dragged me in here, but given a choice between him, Mia, and Alexei . . .

Tyler and Mia crossed to me, Mia's face settling into an ugly scowl. "Okay," she said. Up close, I could see the sheen of sweat covering her features. "Last chance. You *are* going to give us that code. You want to do it friendly, or do we have to take it?"

I trembled, recoiling against Matt, who'd appeared behind me. "Come on, Kenzie," he said, not unkindly. "Let's make this easy, huh?"

Sinking my teeth into my lip hard enough to taste blood, I shook my head. What was I getting myself into? After what I'd just seen them do to *each other*, who knew what they'd do to *me*?

Alexei snorted at my expression. "Relax. We're not going to hurt you. Doesn't mean you're going to enjoy this, though." He nodded to Tyler.

Tyler sidled up, not meeting my eyes. "Sorry," he muttered.

"For wh—?"

I gasped as something cold rifled through my brain, and I clutched at Matt to remain upright. It didn't *hurt*, exactly, but it wasn't comfortable—like suddenly realizing you had a spike driven through your hand. You stare at it, knowing that it *should* hurt, that it doesn't belong there, but you're in too much shock to register the agony.

No pain followed the spike-in-my-brain sensation, though—just the slimy sense of fingers crawling down my neck, of someone rummaging through my innermost thoughts.

Oh my God. He was inside *my brain.*

I recoiled, frantic to escape the intrusion, but there was nowhere to run even after I shoved Matt aside. Alexei jumped behind me to block my flight. He caught my wrists when I balled my hands into fists, preventing me from attacking Tyler.

The sense of someone in my brain grew. I ground my teeth and closed my eyes, focusing all my attention on the sinister presence. Blackness overwhelmed me, Tyler a blinding flash of light. Without quite knowing what I was doing, I pressed back, straining against his presence in my mind. I remembered they were looking for my code. Unbidden, numbers and letters surged through my head. Desperate, I sang the alphabet song silently, a mental wall of noise to hide the rest.

"Tyler," said Mia sharply. Her voice rattled my concentration, but I tightened my shoulders, clenched my jaw, and braced myself. The physical actions seemed to help, and Tyler slipped back a bit—or I hoped he did.

"I'm trying!" Tyler's voice took on a hysterical edge. "She's . . . *fighting* me, somehow."

That encouraged me, and I pushed back harder. I stood

stock-still. Sweat tickled my brow, but I didn't dare wipe it away. The least movement would disrupt my concentration, and if that happened . . .

Pain rocked through my shoulder. My eyes shot open with a cry, and Mia released the pressure point. I fought to reestablish my hold, but there was no resisting now that my concentration had broken. And then, just as suddenly, Tyler was gone. I sagged in Alexei's arms, furious, my breath coming in short, sharp gasps. My brain felt . . . empty. Pillaged, like an army had swept through, took what it wanted, and left devastation in its wake.

Tyler staggered. "Got it," he muttered, and rattled off my code. At Mia's gesture, he flew for the server room.

I tore free of Alexei's hands and stumbled behind the couch, putting a barrier between us. "What the hell is wrong with you people?" I seethed, forgetting my earlier plan of playing nice.

"What's wrong with *us*?" Mia shouted. She lunged for me, and I dodged around the couch again. I was strong and could take care of myself, but that girl didn't have a bit of compassion in her eyes. I wasn't going to go up against someone as rabid as her, especially with my hands still shaking from Tyler's assault on my head.

Alexei caught her and held her back. "Take it easy, Mia mine."

She punched him in the chest. It looked hard enough to do some damage, but Alexei didn't even change expression, let alone stagger. "Listen," she continued, leveling a finger at my face as she strained against his grip, "*we* are not the ones locking people up in some godforsaken space station for the rest of their lives without so much as a trial!"

I scowled. "I've read your files. Every single one of you had a trial." Besides, give them back their powers and what was the first thing they did? Force their way into someone else's mind. I shuddered, thinking of the damage someone like Tyler could cause out in the world.

"Yeah? If you want to call that farce a *trial,* great. Good on you." She yanked free of Alexei and came at me again.

Cage appeared out of nowhere, catching my arm and tucking me behind him. I grimaced at his back. Great. *Now* he showed up? The sense of betrayal surging through me was completely unreasonable. He was my captor, not my friend. And yet somehow, I'd expected more from him and Rune.

"Alexei, get Mia out of here and calm her the hell down. Kenzie and I have a call to make." Cage glanced at me and gestured toward the server room. The unspoken choice was clear: walk on my own, or have him drag me around some more. All things considered, I'd rather move under my own power. I didn't mind putting some distance between myself and Mia anyway.

The others retreated into the hall, Tyler with another mumbled apology. I spun on Cage. "Was this the plan all along? The second you get your powers back, you use that kid to rip information out of my head?"

He shrugged, but there was a tinge of discomfort in his

expression. "We gave you every chance to tell us on your own."

"So I left you no choice, is that it? And what about Mia? I'm pretty sure she just tried to kill me."

"She wasn't going to kill you. She plays up the attitude."

"Uh-huh," I said, unconvinced. I was still shaking from my encounter with Tyler, and as soon as they were out of sight, Cage took my arm—not to restrain me, but to support me. I wanted to resist, but Tyler's attack had taken a physical toll. My knees were weak, and his grip was steady, almost friendly, as much as I hated that thought.

"Look," he said. His voice was slow, unwilling, as if I was somehow dragging it from his throat. "What just happened, it was . . ."

"Disgusting? Violating? Illegal?"

"Necessary," he replied sharply, glaring at me. "Like I said, we gave you every chance to help us voluntarily."

"Knowing the whole time that I couldn't."

He closed his eyes as if in pain. "Is Omnistellar really that important to you? What would you do for them, huh? Would you die because of rules and regulations?"

Mom's voice answered in my head. She'd always drilled it into me—do whatever you can to protect yourself, but if it ever comes down to you or the company, the company's mission comes first. It *had* to. As Omnistellar citizens, we had a responsibility to the entire solar system. We lived knowing that our deaths might one day be required to keep everyone else safe, though we did everything in our power to keep that day from coming.

So why wouldn't my mouth form the words?

Cage's expression went from challenging to thoughtful, and after a moment, he shook his head. "Well, let's hope it doesn't come to that."

"Let's hope," I agreed dryly, and we set off toward the server room, my brain racing to figure out what had just happened.

Rune awaited us, her fingers phasing in and out of the console. Unlike before, when she'd plunged in all the way to her elbows and set her eyes fluttering like a woman possessed, this was a more casual interaction, like she was petting a small dog. "I've got the cameras ready."

Cage set me in a chair, the only one in the room. "Don't talk unless I tell you to," he said.

I nodded with no intention of obeying. He twirled the chair to face him and leaned forward, trapping me between his arms. "We've spent a long time planning this," he said, his voice low and cold. "I don't want to hurt you, but I'm not going to let you mess it up. You understand?"

I shivered, remembering everything they'd been willing to do so far. "Yeah. I get it."

He nodded, apparently satisfied, and turned me to face the camera.

A second later, Mom's face appeared on the screen. Relief flooded her expression when she saw me. *"Kenzie,"* she cried, dropping her tablet and lunging forward. "Where are you?"

Cage leaned over my shoulder. "Good evening, Commander," he said.

Mom's jaw tightened, and she folded her arms over her chest. "I don't speak to prisoners," she told him.

"You'll speak to me. I have your daughter."

Mom's chin trembled. "Regulations are regulations for a reason. I have nothing to say to you."

All at once the knife was in Cage's hand, resting lightly against my throat. I tensed involuntarily. "You sure about that?" he asked.

"Don't touch my daughter."

"I have no intentions of hurting her. Not if you do what I say."

Agonized indecision played across my mom's face, but I knew what she'd say before she opened her mouth. "I can't let you go, no matter how much you threaten my daughter. As much as I love her, the safety of the solar system comes first."

"If you really do love her, you'll listen to me." He increased the pressure but didn't draw blood. Still, it was enough to make me cringe.

"Kill her and you lose any hope of bargaining," Mom returned sharply. Her eyes locked on mine, pleading with me to understand. She didn't have to worry. I got it. We couldn't let the prisoners escape, and she wasn't wrong: they couldn't kill me, not yet.

"I don't have to kill her to make you both *very* sorry you didn't hear me out."

Mom sucked in a breath. She closed her eyes briefly, and when she opened them, they were resolute. "Kenzie . . . I'm sorry."

And the screen went dark.

NINE

MY HEART WRENCHED AND MY STOMACH
twisted. Shock settled over me like a heavy, prickly blanket. I
stared at my boots, disguising the depth of my hurt. Of course
she couldn't let prisoners loose to murder innocents back on
Earth. I knew that. But she'd just hung up without so much as
attempting to argue. If our positions were reversed, nothing in
the world could stop me from bargaining for her life.

"I don't . . . ," I began, but the words caught in my throat. I
turned my head away, blinking back tears. My hands trembled,
and I laced my fingers together to stop them.

After a second, Cage crouched at my side and laid a hand
on my arm. He stared at it as if he'd surprised himself. "We
expected this," he said at last, raking a hand through his hair.
"Rune's been through everyone's files, and your mom is . . .
fiercely dedicated to the company."

"That's one way to put it," I managed in a semi-normal voice. I shook off his hand and shifted in the chair to face them, shoving my momentary weakness aside. Even as a captive, even without cameras monitoring my every move, I was still a junior guard, and I was going to act like it, damn it. Besides, I couldn't forget that Mom had access to the prisoner files too. Maybe she'd guessed that Cage and Rune weren't killers. Maybe she was playing the odds. Either way, she could hardly just release the entire prison because of a vague threat to her daughter. "What's your plan now?"

Rune shrugged. "We'll wear her down. The longer she goes without hearing from her crew, the more she worries about you. . . ."

I drew myself up, thinking fast. "The sooner she'll vent the prison."

"She can't do that," Cage replied dryly.

Maybe this was my chance. If I could convince them we were in danger, I could help my mom negotiate my release. "You saw her. She cares about me, but not more than she cares about her duty to Omnistellar," I said, putting on a mask of indifference. "If you're counting on me to prevent her from venting this place, think again."

"We're not."

I gaped at them as the reality set in. "You mean she *can't* vent the sector. You control the computer—and you set off the distress signal from the supposed merchant vessel."

Exchanging a glance with her brother, Rune frowned. "Actually . . . I didn't. In fact, I blocked communications between Sanctuary and any outside sources. I have no idea how the merchant signal got through. It must have been seriously strong."

Cage groaned. "Great, you'll get Rune going again. She obsessed about this for hours."

Rune shrugged. "I don't like surprises. Everything went smoothly in the trial run, and . . ."

Trial run? It hit me like a slap in the face. In fact, I felt like slapping *myself* in the face. I settled for dropping my head into my hands. "You orchestrated that drill." Of course. Fifty-year anniversary leading to more advanced drills . . . sure. That drill had *nothing* to do with probes or outside invasions. But we all relied so heavily on Sanctuary's AI that no one thought to question it.

Cage and Rune laughed. Jerks. "I'm pretty proud of it," Rune confessed. "Obviously I made my code a lot easier to catch that time. You did great, by the way."

"Do not praise me," I snapped, my head jerking upright. "How the hell did you do it?"

Rune shrugged. "Cage removed my implant a few days ago."

I jabbed a finger at her. "So you said. But there are cameras everywhere in this station. Someone would have noticed."

Cage swallowed a chuckle. "Kenzie, no way you monitor those cameras twenty-four seven. We took a risk and did it during a break. Everyone collected in the rec room. It was busy and crowded and Alexei kept Rune from making too much noise."

Rune's face paled a bit at the memory. "Afterward, it wasn't too hard to interface with the computer. I have to be in direct contact to do anything big, but I forged enough of a connection to open the server room door without contact, and once I did that, I programmed Sanctuary to run the drill."

"So why all this? Why not just open doors and attack us in our sleep?"

"Sanctuary still has too much control—and so does your mother. There are certain safety features I can't override without physically being in the command center. The airlocks, for one. The station's unfortunate tendency to vent itself if we leave the prison, for another. I need your mom to back down and give me full access."

I smirked, although I saw no humor in the situation. Omnistellar hadn't gotten to the top of its game by allowing prison breaks. Their quest was doomed from the start.

Cage must have read my expression. For a second he looked like he was going to argue, but then he shook his head. "Until then, we have some time to kill," he said. "Rune? How are you coming on the other sectors?"

"Cells are open, but I left everyone locked in their sectors. I didn't think we needed a hundred people mingling in close quarters. We're going to have enough trouble keeping Mia from killing someone as it is."

I raised my eyebrows at Cage, and he grimaced, turning his back on me to face Rune. "Can you make the computer spit out some food?" he asked her.

"Of course I can. We're still limited to what's on the station, so it won't be anything special. But I can probably coax slightly bigger portions."

"Supplies on Sanctuary are limited," I returned angrily. "If you start feeding everyone double portions, we'll run out before a resupply."

Cage grinned. "That won't matter without any prisoners." He glanced at me. "Now, what do I do with you?"

I shrugged, feigning indifference. The prisoners weren't what I'd expected. My mom had always talked about them like they were barely human, animals one step away from chewing through the bars and attacking everyone on the station. My own experience back on Earth hadn't taught me any differently. Cage and Rune seemed normal enough, though. They were full of bluster, especially Cage, but I didn't think he would really hurt me.

But I was still desperately searching for a means of escape. My encounter with Tyler rankled. What other skills did the prisoners camouflage? I remembered a few from my quick hunt through the files, but only those that stood out—names I recognized, particularly startling abilities, anything that seemed like it belonged in the annals of *Robo Mecha Dream Girl 5*. The rest blurred like a page from *Othello*.

Cage folded his arms and tilted his head, studying me with

an uncomfortable level of scrutiny until I finally broke eye contact, transferring my gaze to his scuffed boots. I tensed my muscles and steadied my thoughts. I *really* needed to figure out how to play this. I kept flip-flopping between damsel in distress, helpful friend, and tough Omnistellar guard. Any one of those personas was fine, but not all three in succession. I needed them to trust or fear me, and instead I was irritating them. It was a familiar feeling—the guards on the station always regarded me with something between affection and annoyance. But none of them were quite as volatile as the prisoners.

Well. Rita came close.

"Let's get you fed, anyway," said Rune, breaking free of the computer. "Come on. We'd better get in there before everyone freaks out at the sight of unrestricted food."

Cage groaned, pulling me to my feet by my elbow, and led me along. I didn't resist. For now, my best bet seemed to be making myself as unobtrusive as possible. With a bit of luck, they'd eventually get distracted—whether by Mia's temper or some unpredictable event, bound to happen with this many caged teenage criminals—and I could make a break for the stairwell.

One bright spot: Rune hadn't released the other prisoners from their sectors. The sector-5 crew was more than enough to deal with, but if I escaped, the stairwell would be clear. If I was sneaky enough, I might even have a straight shot to the exit. Of course, all that only worked if I made them forget about me for an extended time.

Could I convince them to give me a jumpsuit like theirs? Among the sea of blue, my black guard's uniform stuck out like a sore thumb.

Hermetically sealed trays had appeared on tables, seemingly out of nowhere. "From underneath," Cage said, noticing my gaze. He nodded at the tables, and when I looked closely, I saw the outline of a door in a tabletop. "Sanctuary pushes them up. We're all monitored to make sure we're eating what we should."

"The AI," I said, bobbing my head. "It's supposed to prevent food theft and hunger strikes."

"That's the theory. Eat too much—or not enough—and the computer locks you in your cell during mealtimes and feeds you individually. If that doesn't work, a guard drags us to medical and inserts a feeding tube."

Matt blocked two younger prisoners, who were running for the table. "Same rules as usual," he said grimly. "Everyone eats from their own tray."

"We know," whined one of the girls, although the look she exchanged with her friend made it clear she'd had something else in mind.

Rune smiled at her. "Don't worry. For once, there's more than enough for everyone." She nudged me toward a table. It was all very friendly, but I noticed the twins kept me wedged between them as we sat on the cold, hard bench. "I pulled an extra tray for you."

The other prisoners filtered in, their excited cries fading

into silence as they caught sight of me. The younger prisoners, most in their early teens, watched me with a mixture of awe and suspicion. From the older kids, I got outright hostility.

Tyler sidled in, caught my eye, and quickly looked away. He scraped his hands through his thin dark hair and chose a seat as far away as possible. "He never really likes using his powers," Rune explained, sliding a tray to her brother and another to me. "For what it's worth, we kind of made him."

A shudder racked my body at the memory of Tyler's mind in mine, like slimy fingers massaging my brain. So they made him. I scowled at her, wondering how that improved things, and tore into my tray, revealing a better quality of food than I'd frankly expected: a steaming bowl of beef stew, a large bun, some kind of gross pickled vegetable, a carton of shelf-stable milk, and an orange. I recognized most of the fare from the guard's canteen. "This your usual food?"

"In smaller portions, yes. It's not fancy, but it gets the job done."

The portions must have been a lot bigger than usual, because the prisoners' voices rose in excitement again. I shrugged. I *was* hungry—I'd come off a six-hour shift without a break before this, and at least a few hours had passed since then. I needed food, and a bit of rest wouldn't hurt either.

Just as I lifted the spoon to my mouth, a voice hissed mere inches from my ear. "So now we're feeding guards? Cute."

I jumped, spilling stew all over my tray. Mia materialized, clearly satisfied with the results. "You . . . ," I seethed.

Alexei strolled into the room behind her. "There you are," he said mildly. "I wish you'd stop disappearing."

"But I *can*, you see," she replied, gliding to the head of the table and snagging a tray. Dropping into the seat across from me, she fixed me with a baleful glare, seeming more interested in intimidating me than eating.

I sighed. "Will you be doing this long?"

Mia shrugged and tore into the seal on her food. "I'm still deciding."

"Eat your dinner." Alexei dropped onto the bench beside her and threw one of his massive arms over her shoulders. Mia tilted her head briefly onto his shoulder before turning her attention to her stew.

An awkward silence settled. Cage glanced at me out of the corner of his eye, his expression impossible to decipher. Our arms brushed as we ate, and it disturbed me to realize how quickly he and Rune had come to seem like my shields, a barrier between me and the rage of the other prisoners. "It's probably not as good as you're used to getting," Cage said at last, a faint tinge of mockery in his voice.

Mia glared at me, and I glared right back. "It's pretty close to what we eat," I replied. "It's a space station. Supplies are limited."

"So the guards aren't as privileged as we thought." Cage's

mockery had intensified. "Limited supplies—almost as bad as a prison cell, huh?"

I set down my spoon and fixed him with a daggerlike stare. "Look, if you want to be a jerk, go ahead. But it's not going to get you out of here any faster."

Cage leaned back, studying me intently. I got the sense I'd caught him off guard, and I pressed my advantage. "We're stuck in here together. Why make things harder than they have to be?"

He laughed in spite of himself. "I don't know what to do about you," he said, half to himself. "You're not what I expected from reading your file."

Neither are you, I almost said, but I caught myself in time. I shrugged instead. "I'm a pretty normal girl, prison guard aside." I deliberately crammed most of a bun into my mouth and rolled my eyes as if it was the best thing I'd ever tasted. "And I get hungry just like you," I added around a mouthful of dry bread.

Cage snorted, and I washed the bun down with milk, hiding a guilty smile. For a second I hadn't been playing him—I'd just been fooling around, and something in him seemed to respond. Maybe that was a strategy I could keep using?

Cage quickly glanced away, turning his attention to Rune, and stirred his stew with a sigh. "What I wouldn't give for a bowl of *niu rou mian,* huh?"

Rune laughed. "Remember that vendor who used to slip us free bowls? It was so good."

"Niu rou mian?" I tried to shape my lips around the unfamiliar sounds.

"Beef noodle soup, essentially," Cage chuckled. "It's good. Once we get out of here, I'll buy you a bowl."

I rolled my eyes. "Somehow I don't think we'll be hanging out when—*if* you get out of here."

He grinned, not missing my slip, and I averted my gaze from what was an entirely too charming twinkle in his eye. "We'll see."

That brought an end to conversation, which was fine with me. I was barely keeping my eyes open. I didn't know how I could possibly want to sleep given the circumstances—a big one being that I was sitting across from someone who would slit my throat as cheerfully as she shoveled stew into her mouth—but with the adrenaline fading, with Mom's dismissal fresh in my mind, exhaustion settled into my bones. I needed to stay strong and alert, and with my more immediate needs met, my body had moved on to the next logical step.

A giant yawn split my face, and I blushed. Rune laughed. "We're all tired. Cage, we should set a watch after we eat and let people get some rest."

"I can watch," said Mia. "I'm not tired."

Cage arched an eyebrow at her. "You sure? We all took a bit of a beating today." He nodded toward the bandage on her shoulder.

"Yeah. I never sleep much anyway." Mia shrugged.

"Although we should dig up a first aid kit or something when we can. The last thing any of us need is blood poisoning."

"I'll sit with you for a few hours," Alexei said, running his hand down her bare arm.

Cage rolled his eyes. "You two know what the phrase 'stand guard' means, right? I know you haven't exactly had a lot of private time lately, but I need you alert."

A spoon slammed into the table like a knife, directly between his third and fourth finger. Cage stared at it in disbelief.

Mia smiled sweetly. "I'm plenty alert," she said, retrieving her spoon. It wasn't metal, just hard plastic, but with the speed she moved, she still could have done some damage. I couldn't believe she hadn't broken it.

"I stand corrected," Cage replied dryly.

Around the room the prisoners drifted toward their cells. "I'll have to tell the computer to reclaim the trays," Rune yawned. "I turned off most of the automated systems. Makes it easier to control what's going on in here, who sees what."

Cage gave her an affectionate hug. "Worry about it tomorrow."

Rune took my hand. "Come on, you can be my roomie for the night."

I nodded, too tired to put up resistance even if I'd wanted to. Cage, on the other hand, shot to his feet and leaped between us. "No. Let her sleep on the couch where Mia and Alexei can keep an eye on her."

"She's not going to hurt me. Are you, Kenzie?"

I shook my head, and this time I meant it. Whatever her past, Rune treated me with respect and kindness. I had no intentions of doing anything to harm her.

Cage studied my face and must have decided he believed me. Reluctantly, he nodded. "Mia can see into your cell from here anyway." He glanced at her. "You'll keep an eye on them?"

Mia's face contorted into a mask of hatred. "Oh, I'll keep several eyes on them. Mine and Lex's."

"All right."

I followed Rune to her cell, very conscious of Mia's gaze burning a hole into my back. For all their threats, most of these kids seemed fairly normal. Mia was the only one who acted like she actually belonged here, or maybe on Carcerem with more hardened criminals. Why the hell did Cage trust her so much?

The thought gave me pause. Had I seriously just questioned whether these kids belonged on Sanctuary? They had been sentenced here by Omnistellar judges after careful trials and consideration. The company had taken care of me from the moment I was born, and after a couple hours in a prison cell I had started doubting them.

I shook aside a wave of guilt. *Nanakorobi yaoki.* Falling down was okay. I just had to get up again.

Rune's actual roommate, a stocky blond girl, hovered in the doorway. "I'm not sharing my room with a *guard*," she spat.

Rune shrugged. "Then you can sleep somewhere else. There

are a few empty cells, or the couches—although Alexei and Mia might not appreciate you breathing down their necks."

The girl gave me another look and stomped off. "Kristin," Rune said. "Not your biggest fan."

"Yeah, I got that."

"Here, you can have her bed."

We faced each other across the cell. "How long have you been in here, Rune?" I kept my voice soft, gentle, thinking back yet again to my prisoner tactic and hostage negotiation classes. Who knew those things would actually come in useful? I'd always assumed they were a waste of my time.

"I'm not sure," she yawned. "A while, I guess."

She looked very small and young, even though I knew she was the same age as her brother. "What do you do all day?" I asked, still trying to build that bond, but also out of genuine curiosity.

"Most days? Um, we get up, we eat, we shower—girls one day, boys the next—and then we take work shifts doing data entry. It's pretty mind-numbing. We have quotas to fill, and if we slack off, the AI starts removing privileges from the entire sector—limiting entertainment time, stuff like that. So everyone stays honest, because if they don't, Mia comes after them."

I grinned in spite of myself. "A fate worse than death."

"Yeah." She yawned again, lying back on her paper-thin pillow. "And then we get a break for lunch, usually two hours of rec time where the gym is open after that, and then another four hours of work, supper, and then . . . Why do you care about any of this, anyway?" She flashed me a disarming grin. "What do you do all day?"

"Me?"

"Yeah. I've been in here so long, I've forgotten what a normal life feels like."

I shifted uncomfortably. "I'm not so sure my life is normal. Honestly, it's more or less the same as yours. Work, a few hours of rec, and food."

"Mmm, but you have the freedom to schedule it, or blow it off. Don't underestimate that." She glanced at me. "You're shivering. Do you want my blanket?"

I blinked. It was cold, but I hadn't noticed when I started shaking. Pulling the thin blanket around my shoulders, I asked, "You're not cold?"

"I'm used to it. You're not."

My heart melted at the intent expression on her face. Was this girl actually trying to give me her blanket? "No. You keep it."

"I'm sorry, Kenzie." Her eyes drifted shut for a moment, then fluttered open. "About the hostage thing, I mean. Cage won't hurt you, I promise."

"No?" I asked, although I'd already suspected as much.

"He was just desperate to get out of here. We all were. When Cage and Mia came up with this plan, well—I guess we didn't really think about you as a person." She sighed. "That sounds terrible, doesn't it?"

Actually, it was pretty much exactly what Rita had said about the prisoners. Quickly, I changed the subject. "Is it always this cold in here?"

"Yes. Worse at night. I should have turned up the heat." Rune yawned again, tossing herself on the bed. "I'll go do it now, I guess . . . ," she mumbled. But she was already asleep.

Just like training camp, I thought ruefully—tumbling into bed too exhausted to move, often without even changing out of our clothes. In other words, the place I spent 90 percent of every summer vacation, and the only place I ever made something approximating friends. I glanced at Rune's sleeping form. Her file said something about corporate espionage. Had she been dragged into it by her brother? It was hard to imagine a judge looking at her and deciding she was a threat, but I didn't have all the facts. How far would she follow Cage? After all, she'd let him lead her into a prison break.

And Cage himself . . . he was another story. I couldn't deny his charisma. I got why the others followed him. He had an easy humor that drew you in, and a playfully devil-may-care attitude that you didn't often see in the real world. You'd expect prison to dampen that sort of approach, but in his case it only seemed to amplify it.

Oh God. I caught myself before that train of thought could derail any further and shook myself back to the present.

Across the cell, Rune shivered slightly. Motivated by something I couldn't identify, I crossed the cell and tucked the blanket over her shoulders. I caught Mia's eye. She shook her head, clearly not buying my concern for the other girl, and watched me like a hawk until I'd stretched out on the cot.

I meant to stay awake and watchful, I really did—but within minutes, I'd fallen asleep.

I jerked awake some time later. The prison was completely silent and mostly dark. A dim light illuminated the common area, where Mia and Alexei were hunched over the table. Their whispered voices carried through the room, although I couldn't make out definite words.

Across from me, Rune murmured in her sleep. She shifted, but didn't wake.

I sat up slowly. Mia and Alexei gave no signs of noticing. I was dressed in black, and shadows cloaked the corridor. This might be my best—my *only*—chance of escape.

Of course, Mia would kill me if she caught me. I couldn't hope to escape without any risks, though. Steeling myself, I slid my feet off the bed. I waited for the cot to creak, but it was surprisingly solid. With agonizing care, I fell into a crouch beside the bed.

Still no sign of alarm.

I crept along the floor, my pulse hammering in my ears. I stayed as close to the wall as I dared. Who knew if the other prisoners were awake? If anyone saw me, they'd raise an alarm— or come after me themselves.

I breathed easier once I moved past the view of the common room. Alexei and Mia continued to talk softly behind me. Almost no light illuminated this area of the hall, and I didn't see movement in any of the cells.

My every instinct screamed to bolt, but I forced myself to creep. My hands spidered along the wall, inch by inch. If someone shouted, I *would* run. Until then, slow and stealthy gave me the greatest chance of success, even if the adrenaline coursing through my system argued otherwise. This wasn't my first rodeo. Two years ago at camp, I'd snuck out of bed in the middle of the night with a boy named Mohammed. We'd circumvented every alarm, stolen a couple XE suits, and gone for a midnight space walk. Afterward, I realized how stupid that was. With no one monitoring us, we could have been hurt or killed in an instant, and if we'd been caught in our little stunt, we'd have been expelled at best, maybe even lost any hope of future employment with Omnistellar. It was one of my rare moments of rebellion, and like my adventure in the alley, it only reinforced in me why company regulations existed, and why I needed to follow them.

This time, the consequences were a little more dire.

I reached the door without incident. At the same moment, Mia's voice carried loud and clear through the hall: "What was that?"

I had no idea what she'd heard, and I wasn't waiting around to find out. The sector door still stood ajar; I slipped through and bolted up the stairs.

The entire stairwell illuminated ahead of me, which was strange and unusual but probably had to do with Rune's tinkering. I didn't hesitate outside sector 4—Rune had released the prisoners, making sector 4 just as dangerous as 5, maybe worse. My only hope lay in reaching the exit before my captors realized I was missing.

I didn't hear pursuit, but who knew what freaky powered kid might chase after me? There might be one who didn't even make sound. I shot up the stairs, catching the railing and yanking myself around corners. I reached the second landing before someone shouted behind me. No problem. It only took seconds to get through the exit—except that Mom had almost certainly blocked my code by now. That was okay. It would only take an extra few seconds to contact her using the ship's comms at the prison exit, and she could open the door from the command center in an instant.

But when I rounded the corner on the top stairwell, I found Cage leaning against the door.

It is time.

The rush rises. Fully awake now, as one and yet separate, united in its goal, their goal, its drive, theirs . . .

Which does not matter.

Which cannot matter.

They are one, and they are coming.

TEN

"HEY, KENZIE," CAGE SAID. HIS HAIR WAS disheveled, his face lined with sleep, his chest bare. But somehow, he'd beaten me to the exit. "Funny, the people you meet."

I stared at him, cursing myself. Of *course*. He'd removed his chip. And his power? "You're the Flash," I said dully, remembering the old comic books I had found in the library during a three-month stint at some random high school. I'd smuggled them onto my tablet and spent most of my lit classes reading them.

Cage snorted, apparently recognizing the reference. "You really thought you were just going to walk out of here?"

I shrugged. Somehow the accusation in his voice left me with the sense he felt betrayed—ridiculous, since we were very clearly on opposite sides here. So why did I feel a twinge of guilt? "I had to try."

"I guess you did," he replied softly. "But you haven't left me a lot of choices here, Kenzie."

Before I could demand to know what that meant, he pushed off the wall, caught my arm, and propelled me down the stairs, ignoring my resistance. Tight muscles corded his arms, and the force of his grip told me I'd have better luck fighting off Alexei.

We met Mia and Alexei at the bottom of the stairs. His face remained impassive as always, but hers twisted in a mask of rage. The second she saw me, she flew at me and slapped me hard across the face.

Cage caught her and shoved her back. She bounced off the wall and came at me again. I yanked against Cage, trying to get my arm free to defend myself, but he pushed me behind him. "Knock it off," he snapped. "Don't blame *her* because *you* weren't paying attention."

She leveled a finger in his direction. "Drop dead, Cage. I was watching for people breaking in, not out."

His neck grew taut. "Which isn't what I asked you to do."

She let loose a string of curses that would have made Rita blush and punched the wall so hard I winced. She must have shattered every bone in her fist.

Alexei sighed, reaching for her, but she shoved him aside and stormed back into sector 5. "Sorry," he said. "I guess we were more tired than we realized."

Cage shook his head. "It's as much my fault as yours. I should have realized we couldn't let her run around loose."

I didn't much like the sound of that, but it wasn't like I could refuse. In a moment reminiscent of our first meeting, Cage marched me into sector 5 with Alexei at our backs. He hauled me past the cells, where most of the prisoners still slumbered.

Rune sat on her bed, tangled in her blanket. "Sorry," she said, although it wasn't clear who she intended the apology for.

Cage turned on her. "Give me control of ten. Now."

"But . . ." She glanced at me. For a moment I thought she might leap to my defense, but she only said, "Okay. Give me a sec."

She darted past us toward the server room, and Cage dragged me to an empty cell at the end of the row. I yanked against him, digging in my heels, but he put on a burst of speed—preternatural speed, the first time I'd seen him do it. It was only a heartbeat, but the force of the movement twisted my feet and sent me plummeting into the enclosure. I would have landed flat on my face if he hadn't been holding my arm; as it was, I gasped in pain as he wrenched my shoulder.

"Wait," I said.

In a blur of movement, he retreated from the cell and slammed the door. The panel beside it sprang to life, and he keyed something in. A second later, the bolt slammed home.

I grabbed the bars and glowered at him. "You want to at least make sure Mia's not hiding in here, waiting to kill me the second you leave?"

"I'm not." Mia materialized behind him, her manner more subdued. She shot me an angry glance and retreated to the common room, where Alexei waited.

Cage didn't move, and I suddenly realized how close we stood. If not for the bars between us, we would have been touching. My breath caught in my throat, but I didn't dare retreat. "You'd better get some sleep," he said. "And for God's sake, would you let *me* get a few hours?"

"You need to stop this while you still can." I forced myself to meet his eyes. "I might be able to help you if you back down now. Take it much further and you're going to get yourself and everyone in this sector—maybe this prison—killed."

"I can't do that. This place . . . you can't understand. It's soul crushing." His lips thinned, his eyes blazing into mine. "We have to get out. If we die trying, well, better than a lifetime of this." He searched my face, and I didn't like the look that settled over his, as if he was seeing far too much. "Actually, maybe you *can* understand."

I shook my head, maybe too quickly. "I've never been in prison."

"Haven't you?" he asked, and unbidden, all the rules and regulations Mom had loaded me down with, the constant obligation to Omnistellar, the responsibilities and pressure to succeed—the things I had always thought gave my life meaning—seemed to take on the edge of burden.

Cage was starting to get inside my head.

"How'd you end up here?" I demanded, desperate to change the subject. "You and your sister don't seem like criminals. Not like Mia."

He tipped his head against the bars. His hair brushed my fingers, but I didn't pull away, staring at him in sudden fascination. I wondered how much time and effort he'd put into planning this escape, how much he was really the mastermind behind it all, and whether the fate of everyone in the sector weighed on him the way my responsibilities as a guard weighed on me. Maybe we really did have more in common than we realized. I drew in a breath, inhaling the scent of his hair and something else that I didn't quite recognize.

His hand slid up the bar until his fist rested under mine, our fingers brushing so lightly I might have imagined it. "Kenzie . . ." He closed his eyes in what looked like exhaustion. "This isn't . . . It was supposed to be easier. You were supposed to be less . . . less *human*."

I laughed in spite of myself. "So were you."

He raised his face to mine. With my neck craned to meet his eyes, our foreheads touched.

And what the hell was I doing? Omnistellar policy was to *pretend* empathy for your captors, not develop some stupid juvenile teenage crush on them. I forced my features into a sympathetic expression and said, "I know you're a good person, Cage. This isn't what you want. Whatever you've done in the past, now you have a chance to make it right." I winced. Even I heard the condescension in my voice. In my attempt to regain control of my emotions, I'd gone overboard.

Sure enough, his eyes flashed, and he took a step back from the bars. "You don't know my story or anyone else's in this pit, and you sure as hell don't get to judge us. Not now, not ever."

I retreated as well, cursing him, cursing myself. "I was just offering friendly advice. The fact is, sooner or later, you're going to be recaptured or killed. If I'm lucky, I won't have to watch."

Cage's eyes narrowed. "Sleep tight," he said, rapping on the bars. "And if you start feeling claustrophobic, remind yourself you only have to put up with it for a few days. Some of us have lived here for years." With that, he turned and stalked away.

I threw myself on the bed, angry tears stinging my eyes. That made, what, three failed escape attempts? So much for the top scores in training. Not to mention the fact that in just a few hours, Cage had me questioning Omnistellar, my obligations, my duty. My parents wouldn't even recognize the sniveling heap I'd become.

That is, if they ever saw me again.

On that cheerful note, I fell asleep.

In what was becoming a pattern, I woke to the sound of sirens. The screaming and swearing of teenagers was a bit less familiar. "Hey!" I shouted, shaking the bars of the cell door. "What's going on?"

Tyler, who was hiding in a nearby corner, hesitated a

second before drawing closer. "We don't know," he said, not meeting my eyes. "The alarms started again. Rune's trying to turn them off."

Hope surged. Mom had regained control of the computer. All I had to do was sit tight and wait for her to free me. . . .

Or vent the entire prison. But she wouldn't do that, would she? Not with me in it. Not at all, I hoped, as the image of Rune—and, for reasons I didn't want to think too hard about, Cage—flashed before my eyes. Whatever these kids hid in their pasts, they didn't deserve to die, not if their rebellion could end without bloodshed.

I swallowed, wiping the doubt off my face as I turned to Tyler. Terror suffused his expression. I still hadn't forgiven him for violating my mind—I shuddered when our eyes met, seeing the darkness of the ability lurking there—but it wasn't like the others left him much choice. Besides, if I got him on my side . . . "Everything's okay," I assured him. "Sanctuary does stuff like this. No one can control it completely. It's a really advanced AI."

"Yeah?" He moved closer. If I'd wanted to, I could have grabbed him, yanked him against the bars, and knocked him out, but why bother? If I took him hostage, I'd only have a handful of superpowered teens call my bluff.

"Yeah," I said, giving him my best smile. I was too exhausted to muster much effort, but it seemed to comfort him. "Don't let it worry you."

Cage appeared in a rush of wind. "Good, Tyler," he said sarcastically. "Why don't you lean against the bars and put your throat in her hands too?"

He blinked, stumbling, and cast me a look as if I'd betrayed him. "Sorry, Cage."

Cage shook his head in disgust. He punched something into the keypad to open the door and beckoned me forward. I folded my arms, glaring at him, but he just shrugged, moving to grab my elbow. Fury lanced through me, and I recoiled. I didn't want his hands on me. "I'll walk," I snapped.

He arched an eyebrow and gestured for me to precede him. "What's going on?" I demanded.

"That's what we need you to tell us."

I shook my head, twisting my face into a scowl. "I'm done helping you."

"I *really* don't have the energy for this," he said, staring at the ceiling as if searching for help. "Or the patience. And by the way, what the hell do you mean, you're done *helping* us? What exactly have you done to help so far?"

I shrugged. "I held Alexei down."

He gave me a considering look. "That's true," he admitted. Was I getting through to him? But after a moment, he shook it off. "Either way, you're coming with me now, if only because you want the damn alarm to shut up as much as I do."

Well, no argument there, but I needed to stop blindly following orders. For a second I was back at my advanced training camp, struggling to keep a straight face as I acted out a hostage negotiation with another girl, who rolled her eyes whenever the instructor turned away. Something must have sunk in, though, because every detail of that lesson burned into my brain. Step one: establish a pattern of bargaining; and step two: build a personal relationship with your captors. I'd already gone a little too far into step two, so time to back up to step one. "I'll come, but you have to tell me how you wound up in prison." I remembered the basics from his file, but it had been light on details.

"*That's* what you want in exchange for helping us?"

I nodded, resisting the urge to grin at his confusion. His mouth moved like he wanted to say something, and then he stopped, fixing me with an appraising stare.

A particularly loud klaxon blared through the room, and a pained look crossed his face. "Can I do it *after* we kill the alarm?"

"Hell yes."

"Then let's go."

We found Matt, Rune, and Mia in the server room. Rune and Matt were arguing about something. Her pixie face flushed with anger, and her hands clenched into fists at her side. "Not if it puts you in danger!" Matt snapped, leveling an accusing finger at her.

Rune stamped her foot. "I heard you the first time! Right now we need—" She caught sight of me and sighed in relief. "Kenzie, thank God. I need your help interpreting some of this information."

"Mine?" I asked dubiously. Even without her abilities, Rune had an instinctive way with computers. I knew precisely enough to realize how little I knew. She was my polar opposite, treating any sort of technology like a child clamoring for her attention.

"It's some kind of security code," she explained. "I assume the guards know them, because they're not listed in any part of the system. Another security feature. And the system won't shut up until we input the appropriate protocol."

Matt rolled his eyes. "The station's just full of surprises. Which is why Rune should keep her hands out of it."

"Yes, we know your opinion," said Cage patiently. "Rune?"

She tugged an image loose from the console, creating a virtual screen, and let it float midair. "I can't shut the alarm off, and I don't think your mom triggered it. I'm getting code 5614. What the hell does that mean?"

I frowned; I'd drawn a blank. Omnistellar literally had hundreds of codes, and I'd memorized all of them at one point, but this one didn't ring a bell. "5614, 5614 . . . ," I said. God, why wouldn't those klaxons *shut up*? "5614 . . ." Suddenly, the memory rushed back to me—a stuffy library on a hot summer day, me surreptitiously watching a table of laughing kids while studying Sanctuary's codes by myself on a nearby couch. They were company kids too, but not Omnistellar—something minor, maybe an accounting firm with fewer rules and regulations. I usually didn't even notice how restrictive my life was compared to other kids', but that day I'd wondered what would happen if I tossed the regulations aside and asked to join them on the trip to the pool they were discussing. The memory became increasingly vivid, right down to the page on my tablet. But . . . "That can't be right. Rune, check it again."

"I *am* checking it," she said patiently. "I'm looking at it right now. Kenzie, what's wrong? What's 5614?"

"It's the code for an external threat. Someone's invading Sanctuary."

It is time.

It is come.

The harvest has begun.

ELEVEN

ALMOST IMMEDIATELY, I CURSED MYSELF AND my mouth. Mom was forever telling me that I needed to think before I spoke, and I'd just proven her right. An external invasion meant only one thing: *Rita*, or maybe even Noah and Jonathan returning early. Rita might have come back and realized something was wrong. It could be Mom, staging a daring rescue and breaching Sanctuary from outside—but no, of course not. That would be against *regulations*.

Or, whispered a tiny, treacherous voice in my head, it might even be Dad. Maybe he'd heard what happened and rushed back. Maybe he'd changed his mind on Earth and returned early.

Either way, I'd probably just given away my own rescue. Well, I'd already screwed up and told them the code. Now I had to play my hand. "We've had reports of attacks in this area," I confessed, lowering my eyes. "We received a security alert last week. With the fiftieth anniversary of the probes coming up, the company's been worried."

"So, alien space pirates?" Matt asked dryly. "That's what you're going with?"

Mia shrugged. "No worries. We can always have Tyler check to see if she's lying." I winced—I had completely forgotten Tyler. Judging from the satisfaction on Mia's face, that was exactly what she'd suspected.

Cage leaned against the wall and shook his head. "I believe her about the code's meaning, if not the . . . alien space pirates." He managed to put just the right touch of sarcasm into his voice to evoke every sneer and condescending chuckle I'd ever faced from older guards, and I scowled. I had *so* not used the phrase "alien space pirates." "Rune, can you stop the alarm now?"

"I can," I said. "If you'll let me."

Everyone stepped aside so quickly it was almost comical. I dropped the appropriate codes into the computer, assuring it I was aware of the situation and dealing with the problem, and the blare faded into blessed silence. "Why didn't my mom stop it sooner?" I wondered out loud. If it was a rescue, why would she let the alarms alert the prisoners?

Rune flushed. "Um, I disabled the alarms throughout the rest of the station. I didn't want to give anyone a heads-up if we triggered something down here." She hesitated. "Kenzie, could the alarm be a malfunction?"

I shrugged helplessly. "A few hours ago I'd have said no. But you've been messing around in the system. Maybe you caused some damage."

Rune rolled her eyes in response, and Matt flexed his shoulders. "Let's assume it's a breach until we know otherwise," he said, and frowned at me. "I don't suppose you can tell where the breach is happening? Or that we can trust you to tell us the truth?"

"I might, but I'd need more computer access. As for telling you the truth, well, like the girl said: you can always check."

They hesitated, and Rune sighed. "What's she going to do, tell her mom she's a prisoner in sector five? She already knows that. Let her take a look."

They all glanced subtly at Cage, which would have been a helpful hint if I hadn't already figured out he was the ringleader in all this. After a moment, he nodded. "Okay. Mia, will you go find Alexei? He was pretty dead to the world when I took over your watch; he might've slept through the alarm. We can check out the problem once Kenzie pinpoints it."

"I'm coming with you," said Matt stubbornly.

Cage grinned at him. "Of course you are. Don't be ridiculous."

I took Rune's place at the computer, tuning out the boys' good-natured ribbing behind me. Taking a deep breath, I ran my hands over the keys, pulling up blocks of code. I searched Sanctuary's systems, looking for something out of place, and if I could get away with it, I was going to send a message to Mom.

Yes, she knew I was a prisoner in 5, but she didn't know the rest. She didn't know they'd cut out their chips, Rune controlled the computer, and they planned to use me as leverage to escape—and she didn't know about the alarm.

It was surprisingly easy, even under Rune's watchful eye. By necessity, I had several screens going. I opened a few more for misdirection, and I moved the text of the message around until I could send it under the guise of trying to connect to the command center. I knew I'd fail to connect—the command center was the one area of Sanctuary with absolutely no remote access—but it looked like a legit effort. I kept my message short and terse, both out of necessity and because I had nothing to say to Mom at the moment. I'd act professionally, get a message to my commanding officer. My *mother* I would deal with later.

That accomplished, I turned my attention to deciphering the alarm and soon found myself frowning at the computer in disbelief. This couldn't be right, could it? "Okay, I've got it," I said slowly, interrupting a whispered conversation behind me. Cage came to gape at the screen, obviously baffled by the code. Rune folded her arms and chewed on her bottom lip, her dark eyes worried. "There's some sort of hull breach in sector four."

"Wait, *what?*" Cage drew up behind me, uncomfortably close. His arm brushed mine as he leaned in, sending an unfamiliar shiver down my spine. I quickly withdrew. "What about the prisoners?"

I shook my head. "I can't say for sure—the computer won't

register their life signs because it shut down all systems to protect itself after the breach." Of course, it also wouldn't register them if they were dead. Inhibitor chips stopped transmitting when life signs terminated. No point going into that little detail. "But I can tell you, even if it's some sort of freak accident— like they blew something up, or an object collided with the station—Sanctuary will seal any breaches in a matter of seconds. Unless they were completely taken off guard and killed in an instant, everyone should be fine."

Cage shook his head, his jaw set. "*Should be* isn't going to work for me."

"What's not working now?" Alexei asked, rolling his shoulders as he entered the room. Mia ducked under his arm, took a disinterested glance at the computer, sniffed at me, and collapsed against the wall, all in a single breath. Behind them, Matt pulled Rune aside and whispered to her. She shook her head, and he sighed, raking his hands through his hair.

"Something's going on in sector four. Kenzie here thinks Sanctuary will take care of the prisoners." The sarcasm dripped from Cage's voice. "But we had the power to release them and we chose not to, so it's our responsibility to make sure they're okay."

It took me only a second to make up my mind. "I'm going with you."

Cage stared at me like I'd suggested he hand me a gun, and Mia actually laughed. "Are you joking? No. You go back to your cell and stay there."

"Why on earth would you want to come?" Matt demanded, seeming genuinely perplexed. "Trust me, no one is going to be happy to see a guard uniform."

"So give me something else to wear."

Mia snorted. "No chance. I like being able to spot you in a crowd."

Of course she did. I glared at her. "Look," I said. "I know the system, I know the layout, and I've got the codes. Unless you're taking Rune with you as backup, you're going to need me if something goes wrong." They didn't seem convinced, and I hesitated. I didn't want to betray Omnistellar, but I also didn't want to see prisoners hurt. Where did my loyalties to the company end and my loyalties to humanity begin? Every nugget of truth I gave them about myself was against company regulations, but if there was a chance I could help, I had to take it. "On top of that, I want to make sure everyone's okay. I have basic first aid training. If anyone is injured, I might be able to treat them."

"Really," said Mia coldly. "You'd help a bunch of lowly prisoners?"

I frowned at her. "People are people. I'll help anyone who needs it." I remembered Rita cautioning me not to think of them as people. Well, screw that. Prisoners or not, anomalies or not, they *were* people, and they were my responsibility. After all, we had medical facilities on the station for a reason. Not even Omnistellar could object to this, right?

Cage held up a hand. "Mia? You got a problem, say so now."

I was sure she would laugh in his face. Instead, she leaned back and scrutinized me. After a while it got uncomfortable, and I glanced at Rune, who shrugged.

Mia shook her head. "No. Bring her along."

My jaw hit the floor. Of all the people I expected to back me up, she was the last. I didn't think her motivations were friendly, either, but I wasn't about to complain since she'd just handed me my goal. Instead, I nodded. Mia just huffed and disappeared.

"Mia," Cage snapped, rolling his eyes. "Grow up. All right. Matt, Alexei—Mia, if you can hear me—meet at the sector entrance in five minutes. Kenzie, come with me."

Alexei, and maybe Mia, filed out of the room, leaving us with Rune and Matt, who resumed their whispered argument. Cage started to say something, but Matt held up a finger without even looking in his direction. Smothering a laugh, Cage beckoned, and I followed him to his cell, where he gestured for me to sit on the opposite bed.

"Okay," he said. "Why are you really coming with us? Because I'm telling you right now, if you're plotting some sort of escape, get it out of your head. The sector four prisoners will tear you apart. They don't know me, and they're not going to listen if I tell them to stand down."

"Maybe I'm telling the truth and I care whether they live or die."

"Uh-huh." He examined me with an intensity that belied the sarcasm in his tone, his lips folded in a thoughtful line.

I examined the empty wrist slot where my comm device should have been. Cage remained completely silent, his gaze burning into me, and words spilled out of me unbidden. "A couple of years ago, I was babysitting my four little cousins. My parents used to send me to my aunt and uncle's lake house for a week each summer. It was nice. Different. Anyway, one day Natalie—she was five—came running down the steps, tripped, and hit her head. There was blood everywhere, and all the other kids were screaming." I swallowed, remembering the surge of panic, the raw terror as I forced my training to kick in. "She was okay, but . . ." But it had scared me. I remembered the screams, the blood on my hands, like it was yesterday. "I don't much like to see children suffer," I settled on at last. "Take that for what it's worth."

"A lot of children suffer on Sanctuary, Kenzie." His voice was so quiet I had to lean in to hear him.

"It's different." Or was it? "They're not being hurt. They're . . . Either way, it's not my turn to answer questions. You promised me answers of my own."

Cage made a face. "Yeah, you did wring that promise out of me, didn't you?" He sank onto the bed and braced his arms on his knees. He'd zipped his jumpsuit to cover the blood splatters on his shirt, but the edge of a tattoo peeked out of his collar. "I don't have time for the long version, though."

"So give me a snapshot." I wasn't letting him off that easy. In a desperate attempt to set my confusion aside, I was reverting to the company's training, making my captors bargain and trust me. By getting Cage's story, I managed both. And maybe I could convince myself that I was sharing bits of my own life with him for the same reasons.

He raked a hand through his hair, leaving it standing on end, and for a moment he didn't look like my enemy—just like a teenage boy, overtired and out of his depth. I glanced away before my brain could go too far with that image. We were on opposite sides of a massive divide, and I needed to keep that clear in my mind.

"Rune and I were born in Taipei. Our mom died when we were babies. Taipei's not a corporate city anymore—all the companies relocated to Hong Kong after the city flooded—so the gangs pretty much rule the street. Our dad belonged to one of them. As soon as we could walk, he put us to work picking pockets. Our powers manifested when we turned eight, and he couldn't have been more excited. He sold our services to every criminal in the Taipei underground and made sure we were too afraid of him to disobey. Before long, someone realized our talents were wasted on street crimes, and they started using us for industrial espionage. After a few years, we got a better offer from a rival gang. Our father was making money. We weren't. So I grabbed Rune, and we snuck away in the dead of night." He grinned at my expression. "That shock you? Our dad saw us as commodities and nothing more, and I guess that's what we were. Eventually, we decided if we were for sale, we might as well reap the profits. We didn't grow up in your perfect world, Kenzie."

My perfect world? I shook my head, thinking of the expression on Dad's face when he left, the fact that my own mother was willing to sacrifice me to her precious regulations. I'd always thought I *did* have the perfect life: citizenship in the best corporation, parents who loved me and lived and breathed company loyalty, which all our schoolbooks said was the epitome of the human condition. But now I was realizing that my family was plenty messed up too. "You got caught?" I asked.

"Rune got caught," he corrected. "She always played the more dangerous role. I can outrun almost any threat, and they kept me on the fringes to protect her. But Rune has to make physical contact with a company's server to penetrate its firewalls, and depending on what she's doing, she isn't always aware of what's going on around her. One night, we took on Omnistellar." He caught the expression on my face and laughed ruefully. "Yeah, your precious company. We didn't know what we were getting into. Their security overwhelmed us. I got away—but when I realized they had my sister, I went back for her. I knocked out a few guards before one of them got clever. He grabbed Rune, put his back against a wall, and held a knife to her throat." He raised his head to fix me in place with his stare. "So I surrendered. And that's our story. Everything you hoped it would be?"

I shook my head, not sure how to answer. I mean, they were criminals. Thieves. And Omnistellar didn't take attacks lightly. But . . . did their crimes warrant a possible life sentence in a floating prison? "How long ago was this?"

He seemed taken aback by the question. "What's the date?" I blinked, but told him. Cage nodded. "I lose track," he explained. "We were thirteen. Almost five years ago."

Five years on Sanctuary, starting when they were thirteen?

But even if I wanted to, I couldn't do anything to help them from in here. I still needed to escape. "Thank you," I said. "For keeping your promise."

Cage frowned, tilting his head and examining me like he'd never seen me before. For a second we faced each other across the tiny cell, tension building between us until it was almost physical. "How much do they tell you about us?"

I blinked. "I have access to your files, but . . ." *Don't think of them as people.*

"Those files are skewed." He held up his hand. "I know, I know. You don't believe me. Not yet. But one day, I think you might."

"That's not very likely," I replied softly. To my surprise, I almost felt sorry at the thought. I *wanted* to believe him, this dark-eyed boy with his wicked smile.

"You're not at all what I expected."

"You said that before."

"Well, it's true. I didn't know many corporate citizens back in

Taipei, but we grew up seeing them as the enemy. And you, with your glowing commendations and perfect test scores . . . I figured you'd be a brainwashed drone parroting corporate policy." He leaned forward, draping his hands between his knees and looking up at me. "That's not the case."

I bristled at the suggestion that Omnistellar might have brainwashed me. Yes, my family followed the rules closely. But we had good cause for that. The rules existed for exactly this sort of situation—to protect me from people like Cage and his crew. I owed the company *everything*. "What's your excuse for Mia?" I demanded, thinking back to her crimes. "Multiple charges of terrorism. Did you know that?"

"Mia was set up," he replied bluntly. "And that's all I'm going to say. It's not my story to tell." He reached out, and for a second I thought he was going to take my hand. For a second I thought I'd let him. Then he seemed to shake off the impulse. "We'd better get moving. Remember what I said, Kenzie—no one in sector four is going to be happy to see you. If you value your head, you'll stick right beside me. Because if the prisoners in four don't get you . . ."

". . . Mia will," I said dryly. "I get it."

He flashed me a grin. I looked away quickly. I didn't like it when humor transformed his face. It did something to him— made him simultaneously less threatening and more likable, and I needed to maintain my vision of him as the enemy in order to plan my escape. "Let's go," he said.

We met Alexei and Tyler at the door. Rune and Matt stood behind them. "Mia?" Cage called. "You there? *Ow*," he added. He spun, and glared into the emptiness as he rubbed his arm. "I'll take that as a yes."

Alexei beamed. "She's mad at you."

"I can tell." Cage dragged his hand over his face. "Fine, stay invisible. Just don't get lost."

Rune stepped forward. "I still can't get any cameras in four. I don't like this."

"*There's* a shock. You're usually so happy when I put myself in danger."

"Ha. Ha." Rune poked him in the shoulder. "You have your knife?"

"If Mia hasn't pickpocketed me again, then, yes." He glanced around suspiciously but produced the small chunk of metal to show his twin.

Rune nodded. "Please be careful."

He pulled her into a one-armed hug, avoiding the wound on her shoulder, and dropped an affectionate kiss on her forehead. "I will be. I have pretty solid backup." He nodded to the two boys and, presumably, Mia. I noticed I wasn't included in their number.

"I'll look after him," Matt promised.

Rune gave him a grateful smile and half stepped toward him, then caught herself with a glance at her brother. Cage only smiled and shook his head, but Rune still blushed. "I know you will," she said.

We followed Cage into the corridor. I jumped at every sound, not knowing where Mia was or what she was doing. I didn't know how the others stood it. They seemed completely unperturbed. They couldn't be used to it, because none of them could use powers during their captivity. Either years in prison had messed with their instincts, or they trusted Mia a lot more than I thought wise.

She was set up, Cage had said. Was it even remotely possible? Could Omnistellar have made a mistake? They were only human, after all. I'd been raised to think of the company as infallible, but of course that wasn't true. There were miles of regulations and red tape to prevent exactly this type of error, but . . . it *was* possible.

I processed that as we climbed the staircase, the lights flickering on as we went. "My mom will have changed my code," I reminded them as we climbed. "Can Rune open sector four?"

Matt shook his head. "Your code works. Rune blocked your mother," he said, a tinge of pride in his voice. "There's not much she can't do once she's in contact with the system."

Cage glanced over his shoulder, an amused expression on his face. "How long are you two going to keep this up?"

Matt turned beet red. "I don't know what you're talking about."

"Uh-huh."

"Keep walking, tough guy."

I shook my head, focusing on what was important: my codes would still function. I filed that information away for future reference.

Cage paused outside sector 4. "Now we see if we can trust you," he said, gesturing to the door.

Anger knifed inside me. I swallowed it down. He had no more reason to trust me than I had to trust him, after all—but what did he think I planned to do? I mean, I could trigger a lockout with three incorrect codes, but they'd catch me in the act. And besides, I'd meant what I said: I wanted to help anyone in 4 who might need it. So I plugged in my correct code, and the door slid open.

A burst of cold air swept over us, alongside a strange, almost familiar smell. Not a single sound came from inside the sector.

We all froze, staring into the dimly illuminated corridor. It was a mirror image of 5, lined with empty cells. We couldn't see very far inside, but there were no shouts of welcome or anger, no enraged teenagers rushing us. "Trap?" asked Alexei, very softly.

Mia materialized directly behind me, and everyone jumped. "Damn it, Mia. . . ," Cage ground out between his teeth.

She leaned against the door, peering in. "Let me go first. I'll scout and report back."

"No," said Alexei immediately. "It might be dangerous. We'll go together."

Mia glanced over her shoulder. "It's a lot safer for me than you. And you guys are seriously the loudest people I've ever met. Just wait here."

She vanished again, and Cage threw up his hands. "Well, it's not like she's leaving us much of a choice," he said in response to Alexei's scowl. "Matt?"

Matt frowned, shaking his head. "I sense . . . *someone*. Someone's alive."

"Someone better be alive," Alexei snarled.

Matt rolled his eyes. "Not Mia. I mean, yes, Mia. But I feel other living things in there. I'm not getting it as clearly as I usually do." His shoulders slumped in frustration. "Sorry, Cage."

Cage clapped him on the arm, and the boys exchanged a look I couldn't read. "Don't worry about it. We'll wait for Mia."

I tried to remember Matt's file but drew a total blank. "What exactly can you do?" I asked, not really expecting an answer.

He surprised me with a wink. "Sense life," he replied. "Human life, mostly. Sometimes I can tell when animals are around, but it's more muddled. Most of the time I can tell you exactly how many people are in a room when I'm this close. Heightened emotions mess me up, though. That's probably what's happening here."

He didn't sound sure, but I didn't push, and neither did anyone else.

We stood in the corridor outside the door in total silence.

Sanctuary's gentle hum surrounded us, but for the first time, it didn't seem familiar or comforting. The corridor was *cold*— a natural response, I supposed, if there'd been some kind of hull breach and Sanctuary hadn't compensated for the change in temperature. Maybe something caused equipment damage? Still, this didn't feel right. It looked less and less like a rescue attempt.

A shiver raced through me, and Cage took a step forward, raising a hand as if to put his arm around me. He thought better of it and touched my shoulder instead. I blinked. Maybe my attempt to connect with him was working. Why didn't that thought bring me more satisfaction?

"You okay?" Cage asked quietly.

He still radiated heat. I resisted the urge to lean into him and nodded. "Just cold," I lied. Something was wrong here, and I knew it. So did the boys, judging by the set of their jaws. Alexei in particular held himself as rigid as a statue. He really did care for Mia. I abandoned any attempt to understand that emotion.

For the first time, we heard Mia before we saw her. Her footsteps echoed through the hall at a dead run. She rematerialized a couple of feet in front of us, stumbled through the doorway, and collapsed against the wall. "They're gone," she said. "All of them. Just . . . vanished."

TWELVE

"WHAT DO YOU MEAN?" CAGE DEMANDED. "What did you see?" The door slid shut behind Mia, but no one seemed to notice; everyone was fixated on Mia's drawn face.

Mia shook her head. She was clearly shaken, and that scared me more than anything. I got the sense it took a lot to ruffle Mia's feathers. "There's definitely a hull breach in the server room," she gasped. "Which explains why it's so cold, why the cameras are down. There's life support, but that's about it. The prison sealed the breach, but you can see right through it into space."

"What about the prisoners?" Matt demanded.

Her old impatience flickered through her agitation. "I told you. They're gone."

This time I shook my head. "That's impossible. There is no way they all got blown out of a hull breach before Sanctuary sealed it. Not unless every single one of them was clustered around the server wall before it ruptured."

She spun on me with such ferocity I retreated a step. "Then that's what happened. I don't know if you noticed, but there aren't exactly a lot of hiding spots in a prison. If they were there, I would've seen them."

Matt smacked his hand into the wall. "Mia, I sensed life. I still do."

"I did not miss anything. I'm telling you right now, the place is empty. I even pounded on the gym door. It was locked, I'll give you that. So maybe they're huddling in there refusing to open up, but otherwise, those prisoners are gone."

We stared at each other. "No," I said again. "No, that's *not possible*. The breach seals in under three seconds. There's not enough *time*."

Something clattered inside sector 4, and all five of us jumped, retreating a few steps. Cage grabbed my arm, and I caught his wrist, both of us clinging to each other in pure terror. After a second we realized what we'd done and jerked apart, flushing.

Fortunately, no one else seemed to notice.

Mia squared off against Cage, fists clenched. "Give me the knife."

"Yeah, no." Cage produced the knife himself. He swallowed. "This is ridiculous. Kenzie, open the door again and get out of the way."

I stared at him. "Are you serious?"

"Just do it. Please."

I suppose I should have been glad they were so determined to get themselves killed since it would make my escape easier. To my confusion, I was not. Maybe I was getting sucked into their world, but I didn't care. "Whatever happened, there's no precedent for it. Going inside might be dangerous."

A pained expression crossed Cage's face. "Please."

"No."

He stared at me, and I felt like I could see his mind working. "Tyler . . . ," he said, slowly and softly, almost to himself. I winced. Of course Tyler could pull this second code from my mind. I wouldn't let him—I'd give it to them first. I opened my mouth to say so.

But then Cage closed his eyes, as if exhausted. "Lex, go get Rune."

My jaw dropped. I had expected him to ask for Tyler, not to bring his sister into possible danger. What was going on? What had changed his mind?

Alexei must have wondered the same thing because his eyebrow shot up. "Really?"

Cage's eyes flew open, and he fixed his cellmate with a furious glare. "She's not setting one foot in this horror show, but I'm getting inside. And if Kenzie won't do it, Rune's the only one who can."

"Cage," said Matt sharply.

The two boys exchanged speaking looks, seeming to have some sort of silent conversation. After a moment, Matt nodded and stepped aside.

Obviously Matt trusted Cage not to let any harm come to Rune. Cage's love for his sister was so obvious, almost painful in its intensity. Kind of like how I'd thought Mom loved me. If Cage placed Rune in danger—however minor, however temporary—would she face the same aching betrayal gnawing at my own heart?

I pivoted, scanned my thumb, and punched in my code. The door slid open again, revealing the same dark, ominous cold.

Cage gulped audibly. "Wait for me here," he ordered, and slipped inside.

Mia swore and vanished.

The rest of us exchanged glances and followed. Cage glowered over his shoulder. "Not one of you can follow orders, can you?"

Alexei shrugged. "I think I missed the meeting putting you in charge."

We found everything pretty much as Mia had described right up until we gathered outside the gym entrance. Sure enough, when Cage tried the keypad, he found the door locked. "Kenzie?" he asked.

I rubbed my fingers together to warm them and examined the screen. The keypad was meant for emergency override situations and didn't require a lot of effort to operate, since there wasn't much damage the prisoners could cause in the gym. It only took a scan of my thumb to get the door open.

Lights flooded the room at our movement. I remembered the gym from my tour—a series of treadmills, rowing machines, exercise bikes, and hanging bars for resistance exercises. Even a miniature basketball court and a few balls, I noticed ruefully. No free weights or anything prisoners could use to hurt themselves or someone else, but plenty of space for them to burn off energy.

At first I thought the room was empty, but something caught my eye. "Cage," I murmured, and he nodded.

The two of us advanced on the exercise bike in the far corner, leaving Matt and Alexei in the doorway. Without consultation, we circled around, approaching from opposite directions. Cage moved with fluid ease, mirroring my motion as if we'd spent years training together, and for a moment I felt a connection to him, like he was another guard, not a prisoner.

A young girl, no more than eleven, huddled against the wall, knees drawn to her chest, arms wrapped around her legs. She didn't look up at the sound of our approach, only hugged herself more tightly.

I gestured to Cage to hang back and crouched beside her. He grimaced and made a slashing motion across his throat, then indicated my guard's uniform. I hesitated. This little girl was obviously scared, and I didn't want to make it worse. On the other hand, I trusted my ability to play nice more than I trusted his. I scowled and shook my head, waving him aside. "Hey," I said softly. "Are you all right?"

The girl moaned into her folded arms. Carefully, I laid a hand on her shoulder. She tensed but didn't pull away. "Hey," I said again. "My name's Kenzie. I'm here to help you." She still didn't move, so I brushed her blond hair back from her face, but it was no good. She'd folded in on herself too tightly.

Someone brushed past me—Mia. Oh God, just what we needed. "Hi," she said, her voice surprisingly calm. "I'm guessing something pretty scary happened in here, huh?"

The girl made some sort of noise. It might have been acquiescence or simply clearing her throat, but either way, it was more than I'd managed to coax from her. I backed off a few steps to give Mia more room. "Yeah," she continued, as if she hadn't noticed the girl speaking. She settled against the wall beside her, shot both me and Cage a dirty look, and flapped her hands, urging us away. "I came here to see what happened. I did it invisible. Did you know I could make myself invisible? It's my power."

Cage drew up beside me, and for the first time, his presence seemed friendly. "So, uh . . . Mia," he said.

"Yeah. Who'd have guessed?"

"Girl's just full of surprises," he whispered with a grin.

I blinked, startled, and gave him a smile before I could stop myself. But that was good. It was what I was supposed to be doing, building a connection. So why was I starting to feel guilty about the idea?

The child turned her head, revealing a tearstained face. "How'd you use your power?" she managed, in a soft accent similar to Alexei's.

"Oh, that?" Mia shrugged, twisting to reveal her left shoulder. "I chopped the chip out of my arm."

"For God's sake, Mia," Cage muttered.

Not so surprising after all, I thought.

But the girl seemed more intrigued than repulsed. "Didn't that hurt? It hurts when you poke it."

"Hell yes, it hurt. But I'm tough. I can handle it." She leaned in conspiratorially and said, "Maybe even tough enough to protect you from whatever happened here."

The girl's face crumpled, and she shook her head. Mia quickly switched tactics. "What's your power?"

That caught the girl's attention. "I used to fly," she said wistfully. "But I went into an area I wasn't supposed to, and . . . they put me here."

What? She was a child. What the hell area had she flown into to land herself on Sanctuary? There had to be more to the story. Omnistellar didn't lock kids up and throw away the key over an innocent mistake.

"I know the feeling." Mia smiled. The expression transformed her face, softening her features and bringing light to her eyes. "My name's Mia. Will you tell me yours?"

"Anya." It was barely a sound, a breath of a name on a gust of air.

"Okay, Anya. I want to take you out of here. Is that okay?"

Her head flew up, hope lighting her expression. "Out of the prison?"

"Not quite. Not yet. But I can take you to sector five with me. There are people down there—nice people. People like us."

Anya sighed, her body sinking in on itself. "It won't matter," she said. But she nodded.

Mia and Cage exchanged glances, but Mia didn't push the girl further, just caught her under the elbow and helped her to her feet. Anya walked like she was in a trance as Mia led her through the prison. "Mia," Cage murmured under his breath, "we need to know what happened here."

"Not now," she snapped, urging Anya to walk faster.

I fell into step with Matt. "Is she the life you sensed?" I asked.

He frowned. "I don't . . . Yes. Yes. She must have been."

"You don't sound very sure," Cage pointed out.

Matt shrugged helplessly. "It didn't feel like anything I'd ever sensed before. But like I said, emotional turmoil messes with my abilities. And she's pretty tumultuous."

"Can you sense life now?"

He paused, closing his eyes, then sighed. "Just the six of us. The weird feeling is gone. It must have been . . . I don't know. Maybe I'm rusty."

"Maybe," said Alexei dubiously. "And maybe we should block the doors behind us."

From ahead of us, Anya screamed. We ran the last few yards down the corridor and found her clinging to Mia. "The door shut automatically," Mia explained, stroking the girl's hair. "Kenzie?"

I hesitated. For once I was in a good position to bargain. They couldn't get out of here without me. As far as I knew, they couldn't communicate with Rune. I finally had something they wanted, something they couldn't get without my cooperation.

But on the other hand, if they waited here long enough, Rune would probably come looking. Until then, I'd be trapped with them in the weird, creepy mausoleum that sector 4 had become—and they wouldn't be happy. No one had hurt me yet, not really. Would they if I stood between them and their exit?

On top of that, Anya had started to cry.

"Kenzie," said Cage sharply. Everyone except Anya turned angry, mistrustful expressions in my direction.

I winced. My hesitation may have cost me any trust I'd built with them. "Sorry," I said, searching for an excuse. "I was just . . . thinking. Let me get the door."

Impossible to tell if my hasty attempt at damage control did any good. It seemed to take forever to enter my codes, Anya's sobs punctuating the silence. My hands trembled, but I managed to enter everything correctly the first time.

We rushed into the corridor. Without waiting for the rest of us, Mia took Anya down the stairs. "Can you close this door any faster?" Cage asked me.

With only a swipe of my thumb, the door slammed shut. We stood staring at it a moment. "All right," he said. "Let's see if we can find out what happened here."

By the time we returned to sector 5, Rune had coaxed the computer into providing a glass of milk and a plate of cookies I recognized as coming from Jonathan's private stores. I gave a fleeting thought to my own private stash: freeze-dried strawberries, Oreos, and three remaining bottles of soda—probably more than the prisoners had seen in years.

Anya curled up on the couch, munching away without seeming to taste anything. Mia and Rune sat nearby, talking to her quietly. "Who knew?" said Matt dryly. "Mia has a mothering instinct."

"Mia *had* a little sister," Alexei replied, so sharply that everyone shut up. I didn't miss his use of the past tense, and judging by their expressions, neither did the others. "If you value your tongue, I wouldn't mention it."

Rune caught our eyes and slid over. "She won't tell us anything," she said. She brushed against Matt as she passed, making him beam and earning a quickly hidden smirk from her brother. "Every time we mention sector four, she clams up. Come see if the rest of you can make any progress?"

Anya glanced at me with interest as we approached. "Is she a guard?"

"Yes," said Cage before anyone else could answer. "But she's a friendly guard. She helped us escape, remember?" The look he shot me warned me to play along. He needn't have bothered. I wasn't about to get mean with a traumatized child.

"That's right," I said, crouching and arranging my features into the non-threatening look I reserved for unavoidable social situations. "I'm a guard, and I'm here to help."

For the first time, Anya seemed hopeful. "Can you kill it?" she whispered.

It? I raised my eyes, startled, in time to see Cage take an involuntary step backward. "Maybe," I hurried to answer. "But I need more information first. You're the only one who's seen . . . it, and I need your help." She dropped her gaze to her plate, and I clasped her hand. "Hey," I said. "I know you're scared. But right now, I need you to be very brave and tell me what happened." Instinctively, I glanced at Mia for approval. She gave me a half nod.

Anya tilted her head. "If I help you," she said, "will you get me out of here? I want to go home."

I hesitated. I couldn't promise her that. Even if I wanted to, I didn't have the authority. Cage offered no help, narrowing his eyes and folding his arms.

"Honestly, Anya," I said, "I don't know." The words echoed my own thoughts and feelings, the growing inner turmoil about

Omnistellar in general and Sanctuary in particular. I stuck to the truth as I continued. "But I want to help, and I can't unless you tell me what happened. I promise I'll do whatever I can to make things better."

She seemed to think about it for a minute before nodding. "All right. I'll tell you. It was . . ." Her voice lowered dramatically. "It was a monster," she whispered.

THIRTEEN

MATT GROANED AUDIBLY AND TURNED AWAY. The rest of us glared at him and he shut up, luckily before Anya heard him. Rune folded her arms over her chest, tapping her foot, and he spread his hands in apology. "What kind of monster?" I asked.

Anya hesitated, and Rune brought her a refill of milk. The girl's answering smile broke my heart. The brutality of sticking this little girl in a prison away from her friends and family with only a bunch of teenage delinquents to look after her—it all struck me at once. She received one fifteen-minute video chat a month with her parents, if she had any, and wouldn't see them again until she turned eighteen, or possibly ever. She didn't even see the guards. Instead, her needs were met by a cold and impersonal artificial intelligence. And why? *I flew over the wrong place,* she'd said. What did that mean, exactly? Without access to her file, I couldn't know.

Omnistellar *had* to have a reason. Right?

"How old are you, Anya?" I asked suddenly.

She swallowed a gulp of milk. "Ten."

Ten. God. My oldest cousin was ten, and I'd watched her grow up. How would I feel if it were her locked away? And how long had Anya been on Sanctuary? I pushed my own fears and worries about the company away and forced my face into a smile, hoping it didn't look too grotesque. "All right. I'm going to try to help, but I need to know about the . . . monster."

Anya nodded but still didn't say anything. After a moment, Alexei came over. I glanced up in alarm—I didn't think a guy whose shoulders filled the doorway was the best choice to calm a frightened child. But he ignored me, folded himself down to a surprisingly compact size, and said, *"Ty govoriš' po-rússki, Anya?"*

Her head shot up, her eyes flying open. *"Da,"* she whispered.

Alexei nodded, and spoke to her in what I assumed was rapid-fire Russian. She seemed much more willing to talk to him in her native language than in the English everyone on Earth learned before they finished preschool, so I backed off to join the others. Matt glanced at me sheepishly. "Sorry," he muttered. "I shouldn't have laughed. Just . . . a monster, you know?"

I blinked. He'd directed his apology to me? "Don't worry about it."

Rune laid her hand on his arm in a clear gesture of forgiveness, and after a moment he slid his hand over hers, shifting a step closer to her. I glanced away, a smile playing on my lips.

"Good job," Cage said. I tried to ignore the warmth suffusing me at the praise. I had definitely been in this prison too long.

But I could still play along, so I gave him a nod and whispered, "Thanks."

He seemed startled, as if he'd expected me to refuse his advance, but then he flashed me a grin so warm and genuine it pulled an answering smile from me—a real one, not the manipulation I'd flashed him a moment before. As if he could tell the difference, his gaze softened. I returned my attention to Anya and Alexei, fighting to bring my suddenly racing heartbeat back under control.

After a few minutes in their own private world, Alexei said something that made Anya laugh. He ruffled her blond curls, stood, and nodded at Cage to follow. Without waiting to be told, I tagged along. So did Mia and Matt, while Rune rushed to Anya's side.

We crammed into Alexei and Cage's cell. "I took a guess from her accent," Alexei explained before anyone said anything.

Cage shook his head. "Glad you did, man. She opened right up."

"Yes, well, I'm not sure it helped. She says that after we opened the cell doors yesterday, no one knew what to do, so they stood around arguing about what might happen and what to do next. She was farthest away, hiding in her cell. She thought the open doors might be a trick, and she was afraid to get in trouble. Suddenly, she was slammed against the bars and couldn't breathe—the hull breach, I assume. The breach lasted way longer than a couple of seconds, by the way."

I shook my head. "Impossible. Ask Rune—it's protocol. The breach seals in seconds. It probably just *felt* like a lot longer."

"I don't think so. Not from the way she described it."

Cage pursed his lips. "Kenzie, can you think of any situation where it would take longer to seal the breach?"

I started to say no but hesitated. "Well, if a person blocks the breach, Sanctuary won't seal it as long as it detects life signs. But no one could stand there blocking the breach. And why would they?"

"I don't know, but it gives us something to think about."

"Anyway, the breach did seal eventually," Alexei continued, "and she heard screaming. She wanted to hide under her cot, but she was scared she'd get trapped in her cell, so she snuck along the corridor. Then . . ." He paused, making a face. "She says a monster dragged one of the prisoners into the server room."

Everyone shifted uncomfortably. "So we're back to the monster," said Matt dryly.

Mia shrugged. "Maybe it was a guard. We hardly ever see them, and when we do, it usually means trouble. The younger prisoners might think they're monsters." She glared at me as she said it.

"It wasn't a guard," I said crossly, "and you know that. The only ones on the station are me and my mom, and she sure isn't knocking holes in the station. Maybe one of the other prisoners had the same bright idea as you, and their power made them into a monster."

"No, it wasn't a guard," Alexei broke in, ignoring my suggestion. "She described it as a four-legged creature with a tail and big teeth." He grinned. "Even in dim light, I'm not sure Kenzie fits the bill."

"Thanks for that," I said, but I had to fight the urge to laugh in return. It was the first sign of warmth I'd seen from him directed toward anyone but Mia and Anya.

Cage sighed, rubbing his temples. Red rimmed his eyes, standing out against the shadows underneath. How much sleep had he gotten recently, what with planning his brilliant prison break and all? Particularly last night—he'd been awake when I'd gone to sleep, awake to foil my escape attempt, and awake when I got up. "I'm not buying the monster thing. But . . . something isn't right. Where are all the prisoners from sector four? It might be worth our time to explore the rest of the prison."

"Not unarmed," said Mia flatly. "I don't know what Anya saw, but something happened in four. On the off chance someone is out there, we need weapons."

"It took us three months to carve that pathetic excuse for a knife," Matt reminded her.

"I know. I'm hoping Kenzie here can help us expedite the situation."

They looked to me, and I froze. We didn't keep a lot of weapons on the station, but we had some. Stun guns and the like. Only the two most senior officers carried guns. The rest of us rarely interacted with prisoners, so we didn't need them. Now these prisoners wanted me to lead them out of the prison and arm them. I couldn't do it.

But at the same time, Mia had a point. I didn't really think Anya had seen a four-legged monster, but I did know something strange had happened in sector 4. Whatever it was, it might be a lot more dangerous than the sector-5 prisoners. "Sanctuary," I said slowly.

"Come again?"

I swallowed. Saying even this much was grounds for landing in the prison myself. Hey, at least they had basketball. I could form a team. "If I tell you, how do I know you won't turn the station on me—or my mom?"

Cage watched me for a long moment, as if weighing his words. When he spoke, his tone was cautious and measured. "If someone's on this station, they haven't made any attempt to rescue you or contact you. That means you're in as much danger as we are. We've got to be in this together." He inspected me with an almost intimidating level of scrutiny. "For what it's worth, I give you my word. Anything you tell me right now won't be used against you later on."

"What about my mom?"

After a moment, he nodded. "Her either."

"She has no reason to trust us," Matt objected. And then, when Mia sneered at him, "Well, sorry, but it's true."

It was. And yet . . . I looked to Cage, who shrugged, his expression carefully neutral. "Swear on your sister's life?" I asked.

He nodded without hesitation. "I swear, Kenzie."

My mom was going to kill me. "We don't keep a lot of weapons on board because Sanctuary itself is armed. It has turrets, sleep gas, all kinds of stuff. If Rune can access the weapons systems . . . I mean, there's a life signs scanner too. We can see if this thing really exists without even leaving the sector."

Matt nodded slowly. "Not a bad idea," he said.

"Better than stomping around the prison in search of something out of my nightmares," Cage agreed. "Kenzie, let's go talk to Rune."

We found her in the server room. She nodded as we explained our plan. "I'll try," she said. "But, Cage, I don't like this. I mean, monsters? Are we seriously hunting for monsters?"

He laughed, and hugged her, swinging her around over her protests. "You're not scared of things that go bump in the night, are you, *meimei*?"

She scowled and pushed him off. "I'm younger than you by exactly eight minutes, Cage. Get a grip."

We both snickered, and even Rune grinned, although she ducked her head so her hair hid the expression. "Here's another question," she said with a glance at me. "Are we abandoning the other plan in favor of this monster hunt? Because if not, we're behind schedule."

Cage groaned. "No. We can't afford to." He shot me an apologetic look. "We need to videoconference with your mom again."

"She'll have blocked communications."

"Um, hello?" Rune wiggled her fingers in the direction of the circuit board. "I think I can handle any block your mom comes up with. Your code still functions, doesn't it?"

Cage sagged against the wall. "We need her to think you're in danger, Kenzie. I know you're not going to want to play along."

In an instant, all the camaraderie of the last few minutes vanished.

"You're right," I said coldly. "I'm not." Once again, I'd almost forgotten—in the shared danger, in my sympathy for Anya—that these were criminals staging a jailbreak and I was their hostage. Now it was like someone had flipped a switch on our relationship. We were right back to where we started the day before, facing off across the room.

Rune rummaged on a shelf and produced a sealed packet of ketchup. "Best we could do for fake blood," she explained. "But it ought to hold up to the cameras."

"It doesn't matter. I'm not going to sit here while you make me look like a beaten wreck, and I'm certainly not going to lie to my mother. The second you activate that camera, I'll tell her the truth." My insides twisted at the words. After all, hadn't Mom abandoned me? Why was I working so hard to help Omnistellar?

But she didn't know any better, I reminded myself. A few hours with these kids had convinced me that they weren't the danger Omnistellar believed, but as far as my mom knew, they were cold-blooded, murderous monsters, and if she released them to save me, she might be sentencing hundreds of others to death. "You'll have to do your little film session without me," I finished, relieved to hear steel—not uncertainty—in my voice.

Cage rose, a good six inches taller than me, corded muscles on his arms standing out beneath his jumpsuit. He assumed an intimidating expression. "Kenzie, I don't want to hurt you, but . . ."

I laughed in his face. "You've already played that card too many times. I'm calling your bluff. You're not going to hurt me." I walked right up to him, until our toes touched. "Go ahead," I invited, angling my head. "Hit me."

For a moment, he just scowled at me. Then he swore loudly in Mandarin and walked right out of the room. I dropped to the chair, smug and a touch relieved. I'd been *almost* certain Cage wouldn't hurt me, but a lingering doubt had remained until he backed down.

Mia, on the other hand . . . I really hoped that wasn't where his mind went. Cage wasn't a big enough coward to ask her to do what he couldn't, was he?

"You know," said Rune softly, "Cage and I didn't do anything to deserve imprisonment three thousand kilometers above the Earth's surface. And some of the kids here have done even less."

"Like Anya?" I asked, curiosity getting the better of me. "Did you look at her file?"

Rune nodded. "She's a corporate citizen, do you know that? Her family lives on one of the Jupiter colonies and works for Apexi Mining. Anya was born there, but her family decided a mining colony wasn't the best place to raise a child, so they relinquished their citizenship, went back to Earth, and took up citizenship with the Russian government."

I blinked. "Why would anyone *ever* give up corporate citizenship for government?"

Rune sighed patiently. "Because they didn't want her to work in the mines, Kenzie. Have you ever been to the Jupiter colonies? They're not much better than a prison themselves."

"No—wait, have you?"

"Once," she said slowly. "Running a mission for . . . well, never mind. This is about Anya. A few weeks after they returned to Earth, her family ran out of food and money, and you know what government subsidies are like. She went on a flight in search of more, and it took her over contested airspace. It caused a huge commotion. Omnistellar launched a missile at her, and another corporation, Silver Sun Maltech, I think, thought it was launched at *their* jets, at which point a bunch of other companies got involved." She shook her head. "It was a disaster, no doubt about it. But the kid was *nine*. She was just trying to help her family. Now she's on Sanctuary with no hope of review until she turns eighteen, and then she's got a fifty-fifty chance of going to a mining labor camp on the moon for the rest of her life, which is pretty much the ultimate irony at this point. Does that seem fair to you, Kenzie? Is it a system you're proud to be part of?" Her voice caught in her throat. She clenched her hands into fists and made a visible effort to hold back her anger.

My own heart stuttered in sympathy. I resisted the urge to reach out to her, reminding myself that we weren't on the same side. "You know it's not. But you *are* still criminals. Lots of you—Cage and you included—have committed real crimes. I sympathize with your circumstances, but you're still thieves."

"What chance did we have?" Rune demanded. "Kenzie, you grew up a corporate citizen. An *Omnistellar* citizen. Did you ever have to worry about where your food was coming from? Where you'd sleep at night? What would happen to you if you got sick? Cage and I lived with those fears *every day of our lives*. And if a corporation wouldn't take care of us, a gang would. I wonder how long your principles would last if you were wandering the streets of a corporation-abandoned city."

I'd never thought about that before, and it gave me pause. Hesitantly, I took a step toward Rune. "I . . ." My voice trailed off. What could I say? Rune was right. I'd grown up in total security—*luxury*, really—all thanks to Omnistellar. And while I'd never doubted my good fortune, I'd rarely spared a thought for the unfairness of the situation. What made me so special? Why was I more deserving of corporate citizenship than someone like Rune? "Being down here with you guys has opened my eyes, okay? And once I get out, I'm going to do everything I can to help you. I promise."

Rune laughed, but there was a touch of hysteria in the sound. "You can help us right now, Kenzie, if you want to."

I shook my head in frantic denial. Part of me wanted to help her, it really did. But I couldn't just betray my company, not to mention my mother. Rune's description of life outside the corporations reminded me exactly how much I owed to Omnistellar and made it clearer why my mom reacted the way she did. We really wouldn't have anything without Omnistellar. The corporation, as usual, knew best. "It's not that I don't believe you," I tried to explain. "Rune, you're obviously not dangerous. I don't know why the judges thought you were, and it's bullshit you wound up in here. But I can't just betray everything I've ever believed in!"

"Yeah, we know," said Cage behind me, making me jump. He grabbed me by the shoulder and shoved me down. Before I had a chance to react, he'd tied my left wrist to the chair with a torn strip of cloth. I lunged for freedom, but Rune flew out of nowhere, pinning my other arm. Cage tied it, too.

I glared at them, a faint tinge of fear encroaching on me. Had I overestimated Cage? Or *underestimated* his desperation to get himself and his sister out of here?

"Get that look off your face," he said sharply. "Remember, you've got me pegged. I'm not going to hurt you. But"—he moved behind me, and I craned my neck to follow his movements—"I'm also not letting you give us away." His hand clenched over my jaw, forcing my mouth open. He shoved something inside and knotted a cloth around my head, effectively gagging me.

I made an inarticulate sound of fury. Cage came around to face me, frowning thoughtfully, like an artist examining a masterpiece. "I don't think we need the theatrics. She's a mess, and she looks ready to kill us. What do you think?"

Rune scowled, refusing to meet my eyes. "I just want this over with."

"Okay. Establish the link." Cage glanced at me. "And dim the lights."

I screamed at him through the gag, tearing at the cloths around my wrists. Cage knew what he was doing. The bonds didn't hurt, but I also wasn't going anywhere without a couple of hours to work on them.

I closed my eyes and forced myself still. Thrashing around screaming only worked in their favor. They wanted Mom to think they were hurting me. I would stay calm and collected, like I was lounging in my favorite armchair in the common area, chai in my cup and manga in my lap. *Nanakorobi yaoki.* I'd lost track of how many times I'd fallen already.

Mom's face appeared on screen, and my eyes widened in shock. Strands of hair framed her face, her bloodshot eyes and sallow cheeks. Her hands trembled around her coffee mug, and she had the jittery appearance of someone who'd had way too much caffeine. Was all of this her terror for me? Or was it the stress of the situation taking its toll? I ducked my head, embarrassed by my moment of weakness. I couldn't believe I'd even considered betraying the company, betraying *her*.

"How did you—?" she began.

"We have our ways," interrupted Cage. "More importantly, let's talk about your daughter."

He'd positioned me wisely. I glanced at our own video feed in the bottom corner, and the combination of low lights and the angle of the camera made me seem frail and pale. My hair was tangled, and a mark showed on my cheek where Mia had slapped me. I looked, in short, like they'd smacked me around and left me starved in a cell, and that fear was reflected in Mom's eyes.

Still, she stuck to her guns. "There's nothing to discuss," she said coldly. I gaped at her in disbelief. Where was Mom, and who was this hard stranger standing in her place? "What you don't understand, Mr. Hu, is that while I'm on this station, I'm a commander first and a mother second. I will not negotiate your freedom for the safety of my . . ." She coughed. "Of a junior guard." She glanced at a console to her right. "I will, however, discuss terms in return for you restoring my communications with Earth."

Cage snorted. "Not likely. We all know how that ends— with reinforcements blowing out the prison."

"No, that's how your current course ends. You may have taken over the prison, but there's no way you've breached Sanctuary's controls deeply enough to reach our central security system. I control that airlock, and you're not leaving me any other choice."

Cage glanced at me and his voice softened, a strangely sympathetic expression on his face. "Your daughter's here, Commander. I'm sure you wouldn't blow the airlock knowing it would cost her her life."

I waited for Mom's denial.

It didn't come. I raised my eyes to the screen, shock tearing at my insides. She was bluffing. *She was bluffing.* She *had* to be.

Mom dropped her head in her hands, her coffee forgotten on its stand. "If you make me do this," she said, her voice breaking on the last word, "I will hunt down every prisoner on this station. If the airlock doesn't get them, I will. *You will be responsible for a hundred deaths, Mr. Hu, including your own.* Do you understand me?"

"And you'll be responsible for your daughter's. That's cold, Commander. Whatever we've done to wind up in this hellhole of a prison, none of us murdered our own children." His tone verged on cruel, but out of sight of the camera, he laid a steadying hand on my back. I ignored him. My entire attention fixated on my mother, and I waited for her response. She wouldn't do this. She *couldn't.* I was her *daughter.* She was bluffing. She was . . .

"You can't manipulate me, Mr. Hu. One last chance," she whispered, her voice barely audible. "Please. Let's discuss terms."

Cage folded his arms, leaving a hollow feeling on my back where his hand had lain. "No."

Mom's gaze drifted in my direction. "They're dangerous," she managed, her skin ashen. "If this goes on any longer, if they manage to break free, they could kill hundreds of people back on Earth. I . . . I can't let that happen."

I made a strangled sound of protest, of denial. The prisoners had the *potential* to be dangerous, no arguing that. But from what I'd seen over the last day, Omnistellar was wrong. If they managed to escape, they were more likely to go into hiding than on some murderous rampage across the planet. But I couldn't tell her that through the gag.

Mom looked helpless in the face of my silence. "I know you understand," she said, closing her eyes and drawing a shaky breath. "We owe our loyalty to the planet, Kenzie—to Omnistellar. We have to protect the many before the few. I love you, sweetheart. I really do, and I'm s-s-sorry." She heaved a sob. "So sorry."

I screamed through my gag, but Mom had looked away. Her face grim, her jaw set, she pulled up a screen and pressed the button.

FOURTEEN

NOTHING HAPPENED.

My heart hammered in my ears and I tasted bile at the back of my throat. Had Mom been bluffing? But no, she looked as shocked as me, her eyes wide in terror. "You . . ," she gasped.

Cage's jawline went rigid. "I didn't think you'd actually do it," he said, his casual tone belying the tension in his arms. "Blow the airlock with your daughter inside."

"You can't have reached central security. You can't."

"We control the entire AI, Commander. We blocked your access to the airlock before we did anything else." A grim smile touched his lips. "Rune is truly amazing once she gets going. If you read our files more closely, you would have known that. But then, we aren't really people to you, are we? Just animals to be fed and monitored. So why would you bother?"

I swallowed what felt like a golf ball as the world swam

around me, and I squeezed my eyes shut against the tears, willing myself to stay strong. My own mother tried to kill me. Me, and every prisoner on the station. Oh, I knew the policy. *Procedure.* Sanctuary's criminals were too dangerous to be allowed to run free.

But I was her daughter. And she had been willing to let me die alongside them. Not just *let* me die but actively *kill* me. Her own *daughter*.

I opened my eyes to see Cage peeling off the top of his jumpsuit, revealing the bandaged wound on his left shoulder. "You know what this is?" he asked conversationally.

Mom studiously avoided my eyes. She was visibly shaken, her hands trembling as she folded them in her lap and focused all her attention on Cage. "I'm sure that hurt a great deal," she said. How could she sound so calm? How could she not feel my anguish—my *fury*—at her betrayal?

"So that answers your question about how we hacked your comms," Cage continued, as if she hadn't spoken. "Among other things. Here's what I want you to do, Commander Cord. Check out our files—*all* of our files—and see what we can do without those bloody chips in our arms. Then think about what we're doing to your daughter and what we're going to do to you, once we get through that door. And I'm telling you now, we *will* get through." He nodded to Rune, and she moved to cut the comm.

Something scuffled behind Mom, and her head jerked up.

"Wait!" I cried, the gag muffling my voice. But even without my intervention, Cage and Rune had both frozen.

"What was that?" Mom demanded.

"Mom, don't!" I shouted involuntarily, but of course the gag garbled the warning. I shook the arms of the chair, pleading with my eyes for Cage to step in.

He hesitated half a second before saying, "Commander Cord—wait."

Mom leveled her commanding stare at the camera. "I don't take orders from you, boy."

"We think someone else is on the station. Commander, *please*, stop!"

But she didn't listen. She drew her pistol from her waist and stalked off camera.

A second later, her scream shattered the quiet.

I shrieked into the gag. *"Commander!"* Cage shouted, grabbing the console and leaning forward. "Commander Cord! Are you there?"

Silence. Then a low, slithering hiss followed by a thud and a whoosh, like something was being dragged across the floor.

Then . . . nothing.

I shook the chair, almost capsizing it, choking on my gag. Cage and Rune raced to my side and untied me. The second my arms came free, I ripped off the gag and ran to the camera. "Mom!" I shouted, craning my neck as if I might be able to see past the camera's lens. *"Mom!"*

After a long moment with nothing but Sanctuary humming in the background, I braced my fists against the console, my head hanging low, hair falling around my face. I closed my eyes and struggled to breathe normally, to control my temper.

It was a lost cause. "You son of a bitch!" I screamed, spinning on Cage and landing a solid punch that sent his head snapping back and his body reeling into the wall. I drove my knee into his gut, and he doubled over.

"Kenzie!" Rune yelled. *"Stop!"*

Rage choked any response. I swung at him again, but this time he caught my fist and yanked me off balance. He whirled behind me, pinning me between him and the wall. I pushed off with all my strength, almost dislodging him, but he wrapped his arms around me, trapping my hands at my side.

I screamed again, twisting in his grasp. "Kenzie!" he shouted in my ear.

"What's going on?"

Alexei's voice cut through my fervor, and I dropped my head to the wall. I stared straight ahead, my gaze focused on a smudge in the gray metal, my chest heaving with barely controlled sobs.

Voices rose in a swell of noise, none of the words making sense. After a while, they quieted, and footsteps receded. Cage turned with me still in his arms and pulled me to the floor. I landed half in his lap, my head on his shoulder. His grip relaxed in stages, as if he was afraid I'd go after him again. He needn't have worried. I'd expended all my energy in that first attack, and only fear remained—blind, consuming terror for my mother.

Slowly, his grip turned from restraining me to holding me, one hand on my back, the other on my head. I clutched the front of his shirt and hid my face in his shoulder, biting my tongue until I saw stars so that the pain chased away the humiliating urge to cry. I couldn't let myself lose control. Now more than ever, I had to hold to my self-discipline.

And, I reminded myself, I didn't know what had happened. I didn't have any facts at all. I had to believe my mom was okay.

Slowly, my breathing returned to normal, but I lingered, postponing the moment I'd have to face Cage again. He didn't seem angry and didn't really have any right to be—yeah, I'd attacked him, but he'd taken me hostage and tied me up, so I figured we were about even on that score. Still, I'd been trying to maintain my composure, remain the tough, together guard, and here I was huddled in his arms like a frightened child.

But when at last I lifted my head, I found no judgment in Cage's expression. He stroked my hair back from my face and brushed his thumbs over my cheeks, wiping away ghosts of unshed tears. "I'm sorry, Kenzie," he said quietly.

I nodded. "But you're not going to let me go check on her."

He hesitated. "I will, but only if . . ."

"Only if I take you with me." I laughed, a short, angry bark. Anger surged in my chest again. I closed my eyes, drawing deep breaths.

"At this point, it's as much for your safety as anything else," he replied. "I wouldn't let *anyone* out there alone."

What difference did it make? There were no shuttles on Sanctuary, and no way to escape the station. Sooner or later, Rita or the other guards would return, but until then, we were on our own. And I had to know what had happened to Mom. "All right," I whispered. Near-hysterical laughter bubbled out of me. "Happy now? You got what you wanted. I'll take you out of the prison."

His hands stilled on my hair. The guard inside me screamed my name, told me to get off the dangerous prisoner, to put some space between us. I didn't know what kept me huddled against him. Stockholm syndrome? Or something a little more insidious?

Nothing made sense anymore. Something horrible had happened to my mom seconds after she tried to kill me. I was alone on the station with criminals who might not be criminals, wondering if the corporation I'd trusted all my life might not be as noble as I'd always believed. And, oh yeah, someone— or according to Anya, some*thing*—was apparently stalking Sanctuary's inhabitants.

Maybe it was no wonder I was clinging to Cage like a child.

He sighed. "I don't . . ."

"What?" I tipped my head back and our eyes met, danger-ously close. He searched my expression, and his own softened, bringing his exhaustion into sharper focus. Still, the hand stroking my hair was strong and controlled. Everything about Cage was controlled, I realized, from the way he managed his power to the way he led the other prisoners. Strangely enough, he was a lot like me: struggling to prove himself in circumstances he hadn't created, desperate to live up to the expectations of others. It was why I'd always identified so strongly with Mecha Dream Girl, and now that same compulsion drew me to Cage.

Rune's words echoed in my head. If I'd been born in a noncorporate city and Cage a citizen of Omnistellar, would our places be reversed right now? I reached out a tentative hand and slid it over his arm, his shoulder, his neck. His hand tightened against the back of my head.

The position abruptly became far too intimate. I grew aware of his body cushioning mine, and I scrambled to my feet. Instantly, I felt cold and bereft, like I'd been abandoned—which was stupid, since I was the one who'd ended the embrace. To hide my consternation, I crossed to the screen and resumed searching for any sign of Mom. The camera showed an empty view of the command center. "Where'd everyone else go?" I asked, my voice almost normal.

"Let's find out." He regarded me. "Actually, why don't you take a few minutes in the cell to clean up while I talk to them first?"

Great. That gave me a pretty good idea what I looked like. I'd made a fool of myself in front of Cage, but I'd hoped to retain at least a bit of dignity in front of the others. I nodded and let him lead me out of the server room. Once we hit the common area, every eye turned to us, but I kept walking. Cage shifted positions subtly, half hiding me, and for a moment I let him. I tucked myself behind him and drew my strength from his hand against my back, and just for one damn second, I didn't let myself think. It was maybe the most freeing experience of my life.

Fortunately, it seemed like all of the prisoners had gathered in the common area, so I didn't meet anyone on my way to Cell 10. After Cage left me there to join the others, I quickly used the toilet, praying no one would come along. It was another glimpse into the prisoners' lives—not even privacy for that basic function, since they all shared cells. Afterward, I washed my face with cold water, smoothing my hair into place as best I could. Without a mirror to check, I just hoped I looked presentable.

I hesitated a second longer, realizing I was completely alone. I might sneak past the common room and . . . what? Cage had a point: right now, there was safety in numbers. Besides, I wasn't even sure I wanted to escape anymore. I wasn't sure of anything.

He must have given orders, because although I got a few curious glances as I returned, most prisoners kept their eyes fixed on him. They hadn't managed much in the way of weapons aside from some metal rods, black and twisted at both ends. I remembered Alexei was pyrokinetic. Had he sat there melting through prison bars? He looked tired enough that it was a possibility, slumped on the couch with Mia behind him, her hands on his shoulders. I wondered how they'd wound up together. I pictured asking Mia and had to smother a grin. Good to know I could still laugh at something, I supposed. Unbidden, the look on Mom's face when she pushed that button skittered through my mind, killing any inappropriate humor. I bundled all that emotion—fear and betrayal and anger and confusion—into a little ball and swallowed it down to deal with later.

The prisoners scrutinized me, less hateful and more frightened than the first time I walked through their midst—not of me, but of the general strangeness. They parted as I came to Cage's side. He and Rune stood at the front of the room, and Cage slid a hand onto the small of my back when I drew near, as if to steady me. This time I didn't even consider resisting the gesture. I even leaned into him. Part of me knew I should pull away, but we were so far beyond that now.

"So that's it," he said. "Kenzie's going to take us into the station proper, and we'll figure out what's going on. I need a small group of volunteers. The rest of you stay here and wait for us to come back. Take care of each other."

A long moment of silence greeted this pronouncement, after which Kristin, Rune's cellmate, spoke up. "So you're looking for volunteers to go hunt for a potential murderer with a few metal pipes to defend yourselves. Is that it?"

Cage shrugged. "I'm not going to sugarcoat it. That's it."

She spat on the ground. "This is ridiculous. I thought this plan was dumb when you first came up with it, but I figured, hey, any chance of escape. But now? This has gone so far off the rails we—"

Mia slapped her metal bar into the palm of her hand so loudly everyone winced on her behalf. "I'll volunteer," she said, crossing to Cage's side. Without a word, Alexei rose and followed.

Matt muttered something under his breath, but when he spoke, his voice was steady and calm. "I'm in."

"And me," said Rune.

Slowly, Tyler raised his hand. "Me," he whispered. I shot him a surprised glance, but he was fixated on Cage, his jaw trembling in determination.

The other prisoners stared at their feet. Even Kristin seemed reluctant to speak.

Cage nodded. "That's more than enough. The rest of you head to the cells for now. Don't worry," he added, raising his hands at their grumbles. "We're not locking anyone in. We just need to get organized. That'll be easiest if we have some space."

The prisoners filed out of the room, until only the seven of us remained. Tyler cleared his throat. "I thought you might need me," he said. "Because maybe I can sense the . . . the monster's thoughts or something. But if you don't want me to . . ."

"No," said Cage. "We'll gratefully take your help. And don't worry. We'll keep you safe. But let's avoid the word 'monster' for now, huh? We only have the word of a frightened kid for that, and I'd rather not create a panic." He took Rune's hand. "Also, you're not coming."

Her eyes narrowed dangerously. It was the first time I'd seen Rune angry. "The hell I'm not."

"You can't. You have to be here in case something goes wrong with the system. The last thing we need is Sanctuary reestablishing control and venting the prison airlocks or something. I need you on the system. Maybe you can even get Sanctuary's weapons functioning and keep them from targeting us." He squeezed her hand. "Please, *meimei*."

"What'd I tell you about that?" she muttered, but she broke eye contact and nodded.

"Thanks."

Matt frowned. "You're leaving her here all alone?"

"I'm hardly alone," Rune pointed out. "You're in more danger than I am."

"I know, I just . . ." Matt stared at the tops of his shoes, scuffing them on the floor. "Maybe I should stay with you. Just in case."

I caught Cage smothering a grin. "If you think it's necessary."

"No," Rune replied firmly. "I appreciate the thought, but I'll be fine. Cage needs you more than I do." She hesitated. "Take care of him for me."

Matt raised his head, his expression gentle. "You know I will."

"Matt?" Cage asked. "Is your power working right now, even with all the heightened emotions?"

"I think so. Of course, I know everyone in the sector, which is nice."

Rune pushed him teasingly. "It doesn't matter if your power's working. You're always nice."

"Oh God," Mia grumbled under her breath. "Can we please get out of here before this gets any more sickeningly sweet?"

Cage chuckled. "We'll stop in at the other three prison sectors, just to check on the situation. Kenzie will take us through the prison door into the station proper. We'll scout weapons, access the command center, and figure out what happened to her mother. From there, we'll be in touch."

Rune hugged him fiercely. "Be careful," she said. Then, to my surprise, she hugged me, too. "Be careful," she repeated. "And you take care of my brother too, okay?"

"I will," I promised.

She retreated to stand by the server room and caught Cage's eye. "We'll be fine."

"Don't open that door unless you're sure it's us."

"We won't."

Cage nodded. "Let's go."

We faced one more obstacle in the corridor: Anya, wrapped in a thin blanket, her face pale and drawn. "I don't want you to go," she whispered. "Why can't you stay here?"

Alexei picked her up like a toddler. "We have to get out of

here, *kotyonok*. It's the only way to keep us all safe." He set her down behind us, dropping to place his hands on her shoulders and look her in the eyes. *"Ya vernus. Ya obeshchayu."*

She glanced at Mia, who gave her another one of those rare smiles that transformed her face. "You go find Rune and stay with her, okay?"

"Okay," said the girl softly. "Don't forget. You promised you'd come back."

"I always keep my promises," Alexei assured her.

She scampered down the hall, and with her went our last excuse. I looked to our crew: Mia with her sharp mask of indifference, Alexei hovering behind her as always, Cage's tired but determined expression, Matt's thoughtful eyes, Tyler's trembling legs. I was about to unleash this group on the station, and it would cost me my job, my future, and maybe even my freedom.

So why couldn't I bring myself to care?

FIFTEEN

IT FELT LIKE SANCTUARY HAD TURNED AGAINST me. Now the soft hum of its mechanics seemed ominous as we proceeded up the stairs, our feet clanging against metal. Within a few seconds, Mia disappeared. That, at least, was par for the course.

I opened the door to sector 3 and found it empty. No hull breach this time. Simply . . . silence. We walked through in search of survivors, but there was no Anya here, no one hiding in the gym or beneath a console in the server room. Even without conversation, it didn't take an anomaly to sense the emotional turmoil: Cage's growing tension, Alexei's taut muscles, Tyler's naked fear. A few times Matt whispered something to Cage, who shook his head in response. The two boys drew nearer together, outdistancing the others, and I wondered how close they really were. Alexei and Cage were clearly good friends, but Cage and Matt had an easy trust of each other that made me think they'd known each other much longer. As I watched, Cage chuckled and draped his hand on Matt's shoulder. Matt shoved him aside, grinning, a forced smile that didn't quite manage to dissipate the tension.

A forced smile instead of asking what we were all thinking: Where *was* everyone?

Cage took a moment to contact Rune, who confirmed what we already suspected: no life signs throughout the sectors.

We found the same situation in one and two.

The mood grew steadily grimmer as we progressed through the levels. "Why?" Tyler whispered as we emerged from sector 1. "Sectors one through four, but not five. Why?"

No one had an answer, although one occurred to me: maybe something entered in sector 4 and worked its way up.

Until now, we'd all stuck to human terminology. *Someone* else was on the station with us. But Anya had not described a some*one*. She'd described a some*thing*. *Four legs,* she'd said. *A tail.* Had a particularly vicious poodle found its way into sector 4? Or . . . or was it finally time to consider another possibility?

Humanity once wallowed in the blissful view that we were alone in the universe. The probes' arrival half a century earlier had shattered that thinking. But since then, we'd had no contact with aliens of any kind. We'd explored the solar system, colonized the moon, Mars, and some of the moons around Jupiter, set up space stations and interplanetary corporations—

all without a hint of life from outside our boundaries.

In the fifty years since the probes, we'd come to think of them as a one-time encounter with creatures we'd never truly meet. But Colonel Trace's debriefing after the drill echoed in my mind. Sure, now I realized that Rune had engineered the whole thing. Trace, though, seemed to suspect increased security from the Omnistellar AI as the fifty-year anniversary of the probes approached. Why? What did she know that I didn't?

Aliens?

If they were hostile, if they wanted us dead, why send us a device that gave powers we could use against them? I glanced around at the others, wondering what would happen if I voiced my fears out loud.

Don't get ahead of yourself, answered Tyler in my head.

I screamed. So did just about everyone else, jerking to attention, weapons brandished. As they realized nothing was attacking us, they gaped at me in disbelief.

I fumbled for words, pointing at Tyler. "He . . ."

Cage groaned. "Tyler, stay out of people's heads!"

The boy had the decency to flush. "You think really loud. I didn't mean to listen. You were, like, *projecting* or something."

A crack resounded through the corridor, and Tyler jolted forward. Mia materialized. "You do that again and I'll kick you down these stairs. You follow me?"

"Yes!" he yelped, hands clamped around his face as he cringed away from her. "I'm sorry!"

"It's okay," I said quickly, my brain reeling because *Mia*, of all people, had leaped to my defense. It was hard to gauge the seriousness of her threats, though, and I didn't want to risk her actually murdering him. I wasn't thrilled to find Tyler prowling around my brain again, but this time seemed different—less invasive, more like brushing against someone in a crowd. "He just startled me. Let's keep moving."

And *not* talk about aliens. Tyler's objection—nervous, skinny little Tyler keeping his head when I was losing mine—made me more embarrassed than ever about my suspicions.

Of course, I'd been suspicious about the drill in the first place, and I'd turned out to be right about that. . . .

I shook my head. If *Tyler* didn't think aliens were a possibility, I could just imagine trying to convince the others. And I wasn't convinced myself. Anya *wasn't* thinking clearly. I didn't know what she'd seen. But there was someone who would be able to give us a much more complete view of what was going on, and that was my mother.

Assuming she was still alive.

I clamped down on that thought before it could go any further, fighting down a sick twist of betrayal and grief. Mom was alive. She *was*. I just had to find her.

We reached the top level, and I hesitated, staring at the door. This was my last possible second to back out, and seventeen years of training echoed in my head: the company first and always.

Mia popped into existence. "Hurry up," she snapped.

I glared at her. "I'm not sure you get what's happening here. After I open this door, I'll have broken every law, every oath I took when I became a guard. My future will be ruined, and worse, I'll have committed treason, which I'm pretty sure carries a life sentence. So do you mind if I take one freaking minute to think about what I'm doing?"

"For what it's worth, you can say we forced you," Cage said quietly. "None of us would deny it, whatever happens. We appreciate what you're doing."

"It won't make any difference. You heard my mom. No matter what you do to me, my job is to resist and stand my ground. After this, my life is over." I scowled at each of them in turn, and even Mia shut up. Shaking my head, I spun toward the console and began the long series of scans and codes necessary to unlock the door.

The exit slid open with ease, and I shivered and led them into the station proper. As soon as the door closed behind us, Mia vanished. "That girl really likes to be invisible," I muttered. Her constant disappearances were starting to wear on my nerves.

Alexei shrugged. "It works to our advantage. She scouts ahead, warns us of danger."

"Yeah, except I'm the one who knows the way."

Another shrug. Tyler, Matt, and Cage, presumably sensing my mood, lingered behind me. I led them through the corridor to a weapons locker and went through the same rigmarole with my code. Inside we found two stun guns and a collapsible baton, not exactly a wealth of weaponry. I holstered one of the stun guns and gave Cage the other, and Matt took the baton. Alexei and Mia seemed content with their makeshift pipes, and Tyler clearly hoped to never wield a weapon in his life.

Cage caught up to me as we stalked through the halls. "Calm down," he said under his breath.

"Why should I?"

"Because if there *is* someone on this station, we need to take it slow and make sure we don't wander into their arms. *That's* why." He grabbed me and pulled me back. I tensed, but there was nothing dangerous in his expression—on the contrary, it was a little too understanding. "I know you're upset, but take a second, okay? We're not going to do your mother any good if we get ourselves killed before we find her." He hesitated. "Have you given any thought to what you're going to say when we *do* find her?"

I shook my head, suddenly very tired, but I noticed and appreciated that "when." "Mom turned her back on me. She was willing to kill me to stop you from escaping. I'm not going to let her die, but I don't have any illusions about her protecting me from Omnistellar if I play dumb. So I won't betray you, if that's what you're asking. I told you, the second I opened that door, I threw my lot in with yours." Cage reached out like he wanted to touch my face, but he dropped his hand with a glance at our audience. My skin tingled as if he'd made contact, and I shook my head. "Okay, you're right. I'll take a few deep breaths or something."

This time he did touch me, squeezing my arm. "We'll do everything we can for your mother," he said. "Promise."

I believed him. He hadn't lied to me yet—except when he told me he was going to hurt me, and I was willing to let that slide for obvious reasons—and my exhausted mind couldn't cope with any more stratagems or tricks. Besides, I didn't have much choice about trusting him. I really had thrown myself in with this ragtag band of prisoners. My allegiances switched when Mom betrayed me. It just took my brain a few hours to catch up.

Maybe it had even started before that, I realized—the moment I started talking to them. Rita had been right. Thinking of the prisoners as people wasn't just a bad idea. It was dangerous.

Matt nudged my shoulder as we progressed through the corridors to where the blast wall had descended. I'd completely forgotten about it, and it was gone now—part of Rune's plan, I suspected, to shepherd me into the prison. "We appreciate what you're doing," he told me.

I swallowed a lump of bitterness. "Are you a corporate citizen, Matt?"

"Me?" He laughed. "Hell no. American citizen through and through. My family lives on a farm in Nebraska. Totally without corporate sponsorship. Last time I talked to them, they were debating selling the land and moving to the city. It might not be corporate, but at least there are jobs there. The farm just doesn't produce like it used to."

"They're still talking about that?" asked Cage softly.

Matt sighed. "I know. I told them what you said, that anything was better than a government city. But they don't listen to me much these days, you know? Kind of the black sheep of the family."

The two boys fell into quiet conversation, and I tuned them out. Everything they'd just said made it clear: they couldn't understand my dilemma.

We pressed on toward the command center. A quick glance in the shuttle bay told me Rita had not returned. We were still trapped on Sanctuary.

About fifty feet from the command center, a scuffling reached my ears, soft and almost indiscernible. I threw up a hand, stopping the others. "You hear that?" I whispered.

The sound stopped at once, throwing fear over me like a bucket of cold water. I'd barely even spoken. It—whatever *it* was—couldn't have heard me, could it?

"What is it?" Cage murmured.

I shook my head, drawing my stun gun and making sure I disengaged the safety. I beckoned the others forward and led them down the hall at a crouch. Where the hell was Mia? Part of me wanted to call Alexei, let him take the lead and block for us. But I knew the way, and more importantly, I was the guard around here. Omnistellar might have abandoned me, but its lessons still informed my core. Like it or not, this was my job. More than that, it was who I was.

We rounded the corner but nothing was there, only the empty expanse of hall leading me on. Had the noise been my imagination? I wouldn't be surprised. By now, even Sanctuary's soft hums and thumps made me jump.

Tyler bounced on the soles of his feet. "What was it? What did you hear?"

"Nothing," I said, ignoring the looks the others were exchanging. *Think I'm imagining things if you want. I don't care.* I just needed to get to the command center, find Mom, and make sure she was okay. Then I could deal with everything else.

I holstered the gun, scanned my thumb for entrance, and shouldered through the door before it even finished opening. A quick scan of the room told me what I'd already suspected: my mother wasn't there. Even though I'd known that would be the case, my heart plummeted into my boots, and I closed my eyes, taking a moment to compose myself.

Mom was okay. She *was*. I just had to find her.

The others entered in silent awe. This was their holy grail, the place they'd wanted to reach so badly that they'd concocted this ridiculous scheme. I hoped it was worth it.

While they milled about in confusion, I settled into my station and called cameras on one screen, comms on another. "Rune, are you there?"

She answered so quickly that she must have been sitting in

the server room waiting. "Kenzie! Is everyone okay?"

"We're fine. I only have minimal camera access here. Is that your doing?"

"Yes. Hang on a second." Something released in the code, and full camera functionality leaped to life. "I still can't get the station's defenses working, though. They seem designed to target our chips, and I can't work around it."

Disappointing, but not surprising. "It's okay. Thanks, Rune. Let's see what I can do on my end." I set to work on the system, telling the cameras to scan for movement. One by one, lenses came to life, most of them in sector 5, a few in the command center. The prisoners gathered behind me, buffeting me with their nervous energy.

Suddenly, something streaked past one of the cameras, too quickly to see what it was. We all tensed. "You saw that?" Tyler squeaked.

"We saw it," I said grimly, refocusing the screen. "That was near the medical bay, not too far from here."

Another camera flickered as something rushed by. "Where's that?" Mia demanded.

I swallowed. "Corridor between here and medical."

Another camera. Another step closer to the command center. It erased any doubt.

Whatever it was, it was heading this way.

And fast.

SIXTEEN

MY HEARTBEAT ECHOED IN MY EARS AS THE thing drew steadily closer. Camera after camera flickered with movement. My fingers flew over the keyboard, searching for manual control of Sanctuary's defenses. As soon as I pulled them up in one area, a screen flickered somewhere else. And then, all at once, the movement stopped.

"Where is it?" Tyler gasped. He clutched my arm tightly enough to leave bruises. "Where?"

"Matt?" Stress laced Cage's tone, but he managed to make the word both command and question.

Matt fumbled, his breathing shaky. "I can't sense anything—nothing at all. Either it's totally jacked up on something, or . . ."

Or it's not human.

Mia slammed her hand down on a console. "This is ridiculous. It's an *anomaly*, you guys. Cage would register the same way on a security screen."

"I would sense Cage," Matt retorted.

"Like you said, not if he was jacked up. It's . . . a prisoner. Someone got out of the sectors, got into something, got . . ." Mia's voice trailed off as she stared at the screen.

Got out of the sectors? Without me? Without setting off any alarms? I suppose it was possible, depending on their powers. But . . . "We don't keep hallucinogenic drugs on Sanctuary," I said softly, still searching for signs of movement. "And the drugs we do have are pretty secure."

We stared for another minute, but nothing moved any further. At last I gestured toward the screens. "Well, whatever it is, it's somewhere between us and the medical bay." I swallowed hard. "Also, the cameras aren't detecting any other movement outside the prison. Not any of the prisoners from sectors one through four, and not my mom."

"Tyler," said Cage slowly, "can you get into its head?"

Tyler half whimpered, caught himself, and answered in a fairly steady voice, "I've been trying. I can't find anything to grab onto. Just you guys."

"Maybe it's out of range?"

"Maybe. But I can reach pretty far. I should at least be able to get a feel for anyone on this floor. I've never just drawn a blank like this before."

Which meant he didn't sense my mother, either. I took a

deep breath. That didn't mean anything. She could be unconscious, or on a lower level. She might even be outside. Wherever she was, she was out of Tyler's range. That was all.

Another silence had fallen, this one darker, colder. Alexei drew a step closer to Mia, and she stood on her toes to whisper something in his ear. Tyler, Matt, and Cage looked to me like they wanted answers, but I had nothing to offer. What exactly were we dealing with?

As usual, Cage broke the silence. "Then I guess we either wait here and see what happens, or we keep moving."

I laughed, the sound sharp and bitter even to my own ears. "Moving *where*? There's no sign of Mom, not anywhere. No clues as to what—*who*—this might be, or what they want." I waved my arm around. Not a drop of blood, not a single sign of Mom besides a half-empty mug of cold coffee on her console. I resisted the urge to hurl that coffee at the wall. Where *was* she?

"That thing started in medical, which makes it as good a spot as any to look for survivors. Maybe it . . . took them there, for some reason. I don't know. But I think it's a better plan than sitting here."

He had a point. If Mom was on this station, I had to find her, and that meant I had to get moving.

"Except for one thing," said Tyler, his voice high and on the edge of hysteria. "Whatever's out there, it's between us and medical. And I think that makes sitting here a *very* good plan."

"Tyler," I said gently, "whatever attacked my mother

walked right into the command center to do it. We're not any safer here than anywhere else."

He closed his eyes and moaned.

"Are you freaking kidding me with this?" Mia demanded. "*Whatever?* I'm telling you, this is a prisoner, someone with incredibly strong powers. I don't know how they got out of the sectors, but they did." She rolled her eyes and cracked her neck. "Fine. You children wait here. I'll go scout things out."

Cage shrugged. "Actually, that's not a bad idea. Mia can move more quietly by herself, and obviously she won't be seen."

Alexei scowled, opening his mouth to object, but Mia stifled him with a glare. "Good," she said. "It's settled."

We opened the door and waited. No sound of anything in the distance, but that didn't mean it had gone. Mia shook out her muscles like an athlete preparing for a race and disappeared. We listened to the sound of her footfalls—soft, but not entirely silent—as she advanced.

A few seconds later, her scream echoed through the hall.

I broke into a run and rounded the corner in a burst of wind—Cage zipping past me, and then stopping so abruptly that I crashed into him. He reached back to steady me, and I pushed into the corridor.

Mia lay slumped on the ground in a pool of blood. My heart caught in my throat, and I stepped toward her.

Something lunged from the alcove. At the edge of my vision, a blur of gray and shadow rushed toward me. It smashed into me, throwing me into the wall. My head smacked the doorway and I collapsed, the world lurching.

I straightened, trying to focus on what had attacked me. Something—a tail?—whipped around the corner.

Alexei released a choked cry, something between a yelp and a sob, and ran to Mia's side, Cage a step behind. I shook my head, feeling for blood and finding none. A bit unsteadily, I joined the boys. "Come on, Lex," Cage was saying, tugging futilely at his shoulder. "Let me see her."

Together we managed to move Alexei aside. Matt and Tyler raced up to us, skidding to a halt at the sight of us crouched on the floor. Their demands for information barely penetrated the haze around us where Alexei knelt staring at Mia, tears streaming down his cheeks, his hands clenched into fists. It was jarring, his normally implacable demeanor dissolving into near hysteria.

"She's got a pulse," I announced.

Cage peeled back the torn corners of her jumpsuit to get a better look at the wound on her stomach, hissed, and folded them over her again. "We have to get her to medical," he said. "*Alexei!* Snap out of it. I need you to carry her."

Alexei shook his head, seeming to emerge from a trance. He lifted her with infinite care, cradling her in his arms. Without waiting to see if anyone followed, I set off at a dead run.

"Kenzie!" Cage shouted after me. "Damn it, Kenz, slow down! We don't know where that thing is!"

I heard him, but I couldn't make myself stop. I kept seeing Mia, stretched out on the floor with blood soaking through her clothing . . . and then, superimposed over her face, my mom's. . . .

I reached medical without incident. I'm not a doctor, but with a staff as small as ours, everyone is familiar with every system, and we all possessed first aid certifications. My driving need to excel at everything had made me a little more attentive to Jonathan's instructions than the other guards, but I'd hated every moment of it. Even talking about blood gave me the shivers.

Only action kept me from collapsing on the floor at the thought. Clearing the medical table with a sweep of my arm— Jonathan had left a smattering of personal belongings when he packed—I scanned my thumb to access the medical closet.

I arranged things we might need—rubbing alcohol, gloves, scissors, thread, a needle, tweezers—on a tray as the others raced into the room. Alexei laid Mia on the table, while Tyler and Matt hovered near the door.

Cage rushed to my side and pivoted on Matt and Tyler. "Look for it!"

Matt gestured helplessly. "Dude, *how*? I can't sense it!"

"I don't need you to sense it! I just need a few seconds' warning if it's going to burst through that door!" Matt opened his mouth to argue, and Cage closed his eyes, visibly composing himself. "Matt. I don't have anyone else to rely on here."

Matt hesitated, then pointed accusingly at Cage. "I should

have walked away the first time you offered me contraband. You know that, right?"

Cage grinned. "Thanks, buddy." As Matt retreated to the corridor, Cage drew so close that his arm brushed mine and dropped his voice to a whisper. "Any idea what you're doing?"

"Some," I whispered back. "Now explain to me how the hell you smuggled contraband onto a space station."

His eyebrow quirked in surprise, and he half laughed. "I didn't, obviously. We're talking pieces of food I managed to pocket from dinner, or little items swiped from the workroom. Matt exaggerates."

The scanner gave a loud beep, and I quickly silenced it. "I just pushed the wrong button," I snapped in response to his look. "I can work the medical scanner and I know first aid. You?"

"Some street experience. I can stitch her up if I have to, although I'd rather she not wake up in the middle of it."

We exchanged worried glances, but there was no sense delaying. Cage eased Alexei out of our way while I loaded the medical scanner. I dragged the cart to the table, positioning it over Mia's face. Then I logged on and set it up the way Jonathan had shown me. The scanner ran the length of Mia's body with agonizing slowness. At last, we had a three-dimensional look at the wound on her abdomen. The computer found signs of injury on the back of her head, too, meaning she'd probably hit it on her way down.

I breathed a sigh of relief as the scanner spit out her vital signs, which looked steadier than I'd dared hope. But the wound itself . . . "There's something inside her," I said to Cage, gesturing at the misshapen lump on the screen.

He nodded. "We need to get it out. Do you have any anesthetic? Anything to keep her under?"

"Nothing I know how to use. Too much might kill her, and I don't know the dosage."

"So no messing with that." We both stared grimly at the wound. "Well," said Cage dryly. "You want to do the honors?"

My stomach roiled at the thought. "You're the one who spent all day digging chips out of people. I'll assist."

"Great. Thanks for that."

I shook off my reluctance. Mia could regain consciousness at any moment. I wasn't sure how she would respond if she woke to find us digging around inside her.

I sterilized my hands and put on gloves, and I made Cage do the same. We were going to do this *much* cleaner than they'd done in the prison. I cut away the section of shirt and jumpsuit blocking her wound. Bile rose in my throat at the sight—there was a reason I never considered entering the medical corps, and a reason I was making Cage do the cutting, although I wasn't about to tell him that. Forcing my reaction down, I took a deep breath and cleaned the area with alcohol. It was a lot less gruesome once I cleared away the blood, but also a lot more disturbing: two deep, jagged tears right across her abdomen. "They look like claw marks," I whispered.

Cage cast a worried glance at the others. Alexei was the only one in earshot, and he was too busy pacing to hear. "Yeah, they do." He drew in a shaky breath and grabbed the scalpel. "At least I have more to work with than a makeshift chunk of metal this time."

"What do you want me to do?"

"Can you find a light?"

I ran back to the medical locker, returned with a penlight, and angled it at the wound. Cage winced as he slipped the forceps into her flesh. He rummaged around, one eye on the 3-D display, and in a matter of seconds he'd retrieved a long, furrowed *claw*.

We stared at it. There was no seeing that as anything *but* a claw. It was about an inch in length, black, and curved. "Oh God," I whispered. "What *are* those things?"

"I wish I knew."

What had they been planning to do with Mia if we hadn't shown up? And what were they going to do with my mother?

Another thought occurred to me. "Do they bleed? Cage, if she got its blood inside her . . . Who knows what diseases or parasites they carry."

He cast another glance at Alexei. "Let's cross that bridge when we come to it. I'm going to stitch her up."

Cage's hands shook so badly it took him three tries to thread the needle. "I hate doing this," he said under his breath. He grimaced, examining Mia's side. "Can you hold the wound?"

"Yes," I said, but it took all my willpower not to look away when he started sewing. As the only actual authority figure in the group, I probably should have taken responsibility for this. I didn't care. Blood always made my insides churn. The sight of needle piercing flesh sent my stomach plummeting into my feet, then roller-coastering into my chest. I focused on Mia's pale, sharp ribs, taking deep breaths to steady my hands.

Cage finished with Mia, and the wound looked about as pretty as he'd promised. It had stopped bleeding, though. I cleaned it once more for good measure. Cage called Alexei over to lift Mia while I wrapped bandages around her midsection. Alexei cradled her like a child, his big blue eyes fixed on her face. "Why isn't she waking up?" he demanded.

"I think she's in shock," I told him. "The wound wasn't deep. She hit her head, but not hard. She'll be okay, Alexei."

He nodded, smoothing her hair back from her face. Matt and Tyler joined us, but unlike Alexei, they weren't looking at Mia. They were both staring at the claw Cage had deposited on the tray. "What the hell is that?" Matt asked, his voice very soft.

"It was stuck in the wound," I replied honestly.

Matt drew a hand over his face. "All right," he said. "I guess we can put a line through the idea that we're dealing with an escaped prisoner."

"Yeah? What was your first clue?" Tyler sounded on the verge of hysterics. "The *tail*?"

"Dude, calm down." Matt laid a restraining hand on Tyler's arm.

"Don't tell me to calm down! This is a nightmare! What is that thing? Where did it come from?"

Alexei turned from Mia to slam a hand over Tyler's mouth. "Listen to me," he growled. "If that thing hears you and comes back here . . . Mia's helpless. She can't move. She can't fight. She can't run. Do you want to be responsible for her death? More to the point, do you want *me* holding you responsible for her death?"

Tyler paled. For a moment I thought he'd faint again. Then Matt stepped between the boys, gently prying Tyler loose from Alexei's grip. "All right, Lex. I think he gets the idea." He eased Tyler to a nearby chair, rolling his eyes at Cage.

Cage grinned in response. "Cellmates," he explained to me. "Matt's used to dealing with Tyler. Lex, can you move Mia to the bed?"

Alexei nodded, gathering her in his arms.

"Why?" I asked.

Cage gestured at the table. "Hop up."

"What? No."

"Kenzie, I'm not blind. You hit your head hard, and I want to make sure you're okay."

"We don't have time. I have to find my mom."

"I know, but we need to give Mia a few minutes to recover. Let me check for a head injury while we wait, okay?"

I hesitated a second longer, but he wasn't wrong, and it didn't hurt to check it out. "All right," I said. I pulled the scanner over and gave Cage a crash course in its operation. Then I took Mia's place on the examination table.

Cage keyed in the right buttons, and the scanner passed my head, starting its descent. He leaned over me as it made its painstaking progress. "So," he said. "Did you see it?"

"Yeah." Our arms were inches apart. I glanced into his eyes and found I couldn't quite look away, even though I was laying bare every inch of fear and weakness inside me. "Maybe. I mean, I did see something that looked like a tail."

He closed his eyes, his head drooping in exhaustion, bringing his face within inches of mine. "I guess there goes any hope Anya was just imagining things," he murmured.

I sucked in a gasp of air through a suddenly tight throat. Worry lines creased Cage's forehead, accentuating the sharp lines of his eyebrows. "Yeah," I managed, as his warmth surrounded me. This must be what people were talking about when they said someone "took my breath away."

I was losing my goddamn mind. I struggled to compose myself, but drawing in a steadying breath just bathed me in his scent, his warmth.

Maybe my head injury was worse than I thought.

The scanner beeped, signaling its finish. Cage raised his

head, flashed me a wry smile, and pulled it toward him as I heaved myself to a sitting position, still trembling a bit from the proximity.

His smile quickly changed to a frown. "That can't be right," he said.

Panic flashed through me. "What?" I demanded. "What can't be right?"

"I don't know. Hang on." He twisted the display, coincidentally shielding it from me.

I choked on a wave of panic. "Cage!"

"Just give me a second."

"I'm not giving you anything!" I grabbed for the display, which he swung out of my reach. Red-hot fury shot steel through my spine, and I stiffened, bringing my breathing under control. "Cage, you have exactly three seconds to tell me what's going on, and then I start throwing punches."

He checked the display one more time and shook his head. "I . . . I don't know how to tell you this. Kenzie . . . you have a chip."

SEVENTEEN

FOR A MOMENT I JUST STARED AT HIM. MY LIPS worked, but no sound came out. I felt every gaze burning into me, like I was the guest of honor at some kind of horror convention.

A *chip*? Like a prisoner? It made no sense. None. "How?" I managed at last, my voice verging on hysterical. By now all of the boys were crowded around the scanner, gaping like *I* was the alien. "How can I have a chip?"

"If you don't know, the only person who might be able to find out is Rune." Without waiting for my permission, he stalked to the panel and activated it with a sweep of his hand. "You there, *meimei*?" In a few sentences, he explained the situation.

By then I'd recovered enough to ask, in an almost normal voice, "Rune. What the hell is going on?"

Rune's voice answered, hollow and disconnected through

the comm unit. "I don't know. Part of your file requires high-security clearance. I'm trying to access it now, but it's seriously guarded. The system's fighting me at every step. I'm going to need to get off the comms and give it my full attention. I'll let you know what I learn."

I shot to my feet and paced back and forth, shaking off any attempt to placate me. I had a chip. *I* did, like a prisoner. "Run the scan again."

"Kenzie, you know that won't—"

I grabbed his sleeve, yanking his face down to mine. *"Run the scan again,"* I seethed. The world swam in front of me, and I groped for the table and got back into position. With a sigh, Cage reset the scanner and slid it over my head.

There was no intimate brush of his arm this time. He stood back, waiting, as I ground my teeth and clenched my fists through the scanner's interminable progress. "Well?" I snapped, when at last it completed its journey.

Cage turned the screen toward me in response. I grabbed it, nearly wrenching it off its hinges in my rush to see for myself. Sure enough, there it was: a little white blip in my arm, right where the prisoners' chips rested. "It's something else," I protested weakly, searching my memory. "I broke my arm when I was five. It must be a bone fragment or—or *something*."

"Kenzie, it's not a bone fragment." Cage pulled up the accompanying text on the scanner. I gaped at it in disbelief. Serial number. Coding.

He was right. It was a chip.

"How did it get there?" I demanded. "When?" I clawed at my arm as if I could physically remove it. "I want it out." I could *feel* it under my skin, a foreign presence as much an intruder as the creatures on Sanctuary. How long had it been there? How had I never noticed? "I want it out."

Cage grabbed my wrist, preventing me from actually tearing my skin. "Absolutely not."

I turned on him, my stomach heaving into my chest. "Excuse me? Everyone in this room gets to cut out their chips, including you, but mine has to stay?"

"It's not like that," Matt said, glancing at Cage for support. "When your powers first manifest, they're sometimes hard to control. If you do have powers and you've never used them before, who knows what will happen if we yank that chip out of you?"

"On top of which, I'm kind of tired of people screaming in pain while I cut into them," added Cage.

"Oh!" I shouted, ignoring Tyler's attempts to hush me. "Well, if you're tired, I guess that's all right, then!"

"What's all the yelling about?" came Mia's weak voice.

"Mia!" Alexei shot to her side. "Don't sit up. Don't—"

"Get off me, Lex." Mia swung unsteadily to her feet, almost collapsing. Alexei threw an arm around her waist, helping her hobble to where we were gathered. She sagged against the table and examined her abdomen. "That looks like Cage's work."

"It was a team effort," said Cage, ducking behind me. I glared at him, swallowing down the sarcasm itching to escape my throat. Not the time.

Mia poked at her wound and winced. "Yeah, maybe don't do that," I snapped, too staggered to be afraid of her.

Matt offered a wry smile. "As for the yelling, it turns out Kenzie has a chip in her arm. She wants it out, and we're explaining why that's a bad idea."

I opened my mouth to release the surge of arguments battling for supremacy on my tongue, but to my shock, Mia interjected. "How is that any of your business?"

"What?" Cage's jaw dropped. "If I'm the one who has to do the cutting, it *is* my business."

Mia shrugged. "Then let me do it." I glanced at Mia's shaking hands and bit my lip, but she pushed on. "It's Kenzie's body and Kenzie's chip, and if she doesn't want it—especially if someone stuck it in without her knowledge or permission—she has as much right to get rid of it as we did."

Cage swung and kicked the wall, making everyone jump. "When did I become the official surgeon around here? And don't you think we have more important things to worry about right now?"

"Kenzie's power might tip the scales in our favor. We don't know." Mia closed her eyes, obviously in pain. "And no one said it had to be you. I already told you, I'll do it if I have to."

I faced Cage, my chin jutting out in defiance. This chip

had to go. Wherever it came from, whatever it hid, I wanted it out. Yeah, I'd rather have Cage's hands—experienced and not shaking from pain—handle the procedure. But I'd take Mia if he made me.

Cage groaned. "You can't scream," he said, leveling an accusing finger at me. "Not if there's any chance that thing will hear us."

"I won't scream."

"You will," said Matt grimly. "You're underestimating how bad this is going to be."

"I'll help," Alexei volunteered.

"Let's get this over with, then."

"Mia, please lie down." Alexei took her arm and urged her toward the bed. "I need to focus on Kenzie, and I can't do that if I'm worried about you."

"Well, maybe just for a minute." She hesitated, glancing at the claw on the tray. "So that . . . *thing* was inside me, huh?" She smiled thinly. "All right. It's definitely not an escaped prisoner. I was wrong."

"Mark the calendar," said Cage dryly. "Mia admitted a mistake."

It was a sign of Mia's exhaustion that she didn't reply, just let Alexei half carry her back to the bed. I grabbed a bottle of painkillers off the tray. "Hey, Alexei," I said, tossing them in his direction. He barely even glanced up, snatching them out of the air, and handed them to Mia.

Cage slammed something on the table. "Wow," I said. "What happened to 'keep it quiet'?"

He shook his head in frustration. "Are you sure you don't have any anesthetic? Something that'll numb the pain?"

"I'm not going to start injecting random medication into myself without knowing what it does."

"Kenzie, I get how you're feeling, I really do. When they put that chip in my arm, I scratched at it for days. But it's not hurting you, and removing it *will* hurt you, and beyond that, the results could be . . . dangerous. It's better to wait. I know people in Taipei, people with medical training and . . ." He looked into my eyes and shook his head. "I'm not going to talk you out of this, am I?"

"No. Whatever's going on with me, I need to know now."

"Fine." He sighed. "I'll try to be quick."

Alexei returned and hopped on the medical table, scooting back to make room for me. I ignored my stomach, which was trying to claw its way into my mouth, and let him pull me up to sit between his legs. "Sterilize," I ordered Cage.

He nodded and scrubbed the forceps with alcohol wipes.

Alexei closed his arms around me, not tightly. Not yet. "I may have to cover your mouth."

I nodded. I didn't trust my voice. Now that I wasn't arguing with Cage, I doubted myself. Why was I putting myself through this? Was I still just angry at my parents—about their separation, about Mom abandoning me? They had to have known about the chip. There was no way it had gotten into me without my parents' involvement. So not only had Mom tried to kill me, she had somehow, at some point, chipped me.

Did that mean I had a power? Was I an anomaly? I refused to go another minute in the dark. That chip blocked something essentially *me*. Just a few days ago, my world had been this straightforward, clear-cut place. Now, I wasn't sure of anything anymore. My mom had been willing to kill me, Omnistellar had sentenced a child to prison for flying, and the anomalies were far more human than I'd been led to believe. Nothing made sense anymore. This, at least, I could resolve.

Cage wiped my arm with alcohol, taking longer than strictly necessary. "Last chance to change your mind."

I shook my head, surprised to find myself steady and firm— at least on the surface, which meant that the illusion would last as long as Tyler didn't go prying into my mind.

"All right." Cage closed his eyes as if steeling himself.

"You've got this," said Alexei. "You've done it half a dozen times, and with much less equipment."

"Uh-huh." He wiped his hand over his face, analyzing me with an inscrutable expression. "Sorry, Kenz."

I nodded and looked away. Pain I could handle, but the sight of Cage's trembling hand, the scalpel slicing into my flesh . . .

I sucked in my breath at the first cut but managed to stay otherwise silent. Alexei's grip tightened over my wrist as my hands clenched into involuntary fists. I ground my teeth together, wincing as Cage prodded the corners of the wound. "Okay," he said. "This is the part that's going to hurt."

He inserted the forceps and I gasped at the sharp sting. I twisted my head into Alexei's shoulder, locking my hand over his.

A second later, agony like I'd never known tore through my arm. A scream escaped my lips but Alexei was ready, clamping a hand over my mouth while his other arm wrapped around my elbows, pinning me against him. I jerked involuntarily, every instinct working to wrench my arm free of his grasp. Excruciating pain assaulted me, like a hot poker through my flesh. I screamed again as the torment crested, black surging at the corners of my vision. . . .

The agony retreated, leaving me trembling, my stomach churning. I slumped in Alexei's arms, struggling to maintain consciousness. I was dimly aware of a new pain in my arm, a burn with pricks of more intense sensation. Alexei removed his hand from my mouth. He winced, rubbing at the imprint of his fingers in my flesh. "Sorry," he said.

His touch was surprisingly gentle for someone so big and powerful. I nodded and leaned against him, exhausted. A somewhat hysterical giggle bubbled up inside me. Just yesterday, I'd thought he was a monster. Now he was holding me, supporting me, and I had volunteered to have Cage cut me open. The difference a few hours—and a total upheaval of your world—could make.

I glanced over to find Cage snipping the string; he'd

dropped a few stitches in my arm. "How come we didn't get stitches?" Mia demanded from across the room.

Cage ignored her, wrapping a bandage around my shoulder.

"She's right. You should all clean and rebandage your wounds," I said, surprised at the shakiness of my voice. I glanced at Alexei over my shoulder. He still had his arms wrapped firmly around me. "You can let go now."

He nodded. "In a minute."

Cage finished with my arm. He removed his gloves, cleaned his hands, and pressed what looked like a small white bean into my palm. "There you go."

"Thank you," I said. I held it to the light. It was so innocuous looking. . . . I slipped it into my pocket and slid off the table. Cage caught and steadied me. "Thank you," I repeated, this time to Alexei. He nodded, already on his way to Mia's side.

I looked at Cage expectantly. "So . . . what do I do?"

He frowned. "I don't really know. I mean, for most of us, the power just sort of . . . shows up."

Tyler was slumped against the wall, hiding from the sight of blood—and maybe from my pain. I hadn't considered whether his powers would make him suffer alongside me. Now he eased to his feet, carefully avoiding the gore-spattered medical tray. "For me, I started hearing everyone's voices in my head all at once," he said. "I was in the fourth grade. They thought I was having a nervous breakdown." He laughed shakily. "So did I. It took me years to get it under control."

"How did you?" I asked.

Tyler flashed me a guilty grin. "Mom was a cardsharp. She figured she could use my power, so we spent days, weeks, practicing. I learned that focusing on one person blocked all the background noise. From there it got easier. We went through every casino on Mars before I got caught."

"You're from the colonies?" I asked, surprised. There were almost three million people living on Mars and Jupiter's moons, so I guess I shouldn't have been shocked. I'd never met anyone actually born there before, though. Jupiter's moons were mostly mines, but Mars was a little more advanced, and often even attracted tourists with its gambling, flashing lights, and relaxed laws. "Were you with Mars Mining?"

He smiled sadly. "Corporate citizens don't usually wind up on Sanctuary, Kenzie. I'm from a mining family, but we were Mars citizens."

I supposed he was right—corporations would provide better legal assistance to their citizens than any national or planetary government. Even Anya hadn't been arrested until her family renounced their corporate citizenship.

Tyler's story unnerved me. I didn't relish the thought of a million minds crashing in on me all at once. "Something should be happening by now, right?"

Cage shrugged. "Not necessarily. We don't know what your power is, or even that you have one. It might show up when we least expect it."

I paced back and forth, nervous energy having driven me to movement. "Why would someone chip me if I didn't have a power?"

"Kenzie, I don't know. None of this makes any sense."

I searched inside myself, looking for something that felt different but coming up blank. I couldn't be an anomaly, could I? But if not, then why would I have a chip I didn't know about? Did my parents know? They must. It would have come up on medical scans.

A cold hand closed around my chest, and I felt the physical weight of every eye on me. I forced myself to stop pacing, to lean against the wall and steady myself.

"We should get out of here," interjected Matt nervously. "Get back to the prison. Rune can take a look at Kenzie's file, and we can make an escape plan. Because the longer we stay . . ."

As if timed by some evil force of nature, an unholy scream split the room, sending all of us crashing to our knees.

EIGHTEEN

I CRINGED, HANDS PLASTERED OVER MY EARS. "Is that it?" Tyler cried. "Is that the monster?"

"Time to go," said Cage as the shriek faded, leaving us with ringing ears and pounding hearts. "Matt?"

He shook his head, frantic. "I don't know! I told you, I can't sense it!" His face twisted in concentration. "I'm maybe getting *something*, but I can't tell you where."

"Not helping!"

Mia staggered over, Alexei behind her, his face twisted in a scowl. She pointed at him. "Stop trying to carry me! I'm fine. Listen, I'm pretty sure that thing is blind."

I shook my head, struggling with the abrupt shift in topic. "What?"

"Obviously it didn't see me before it attacked. I assume it heard me. But *I* got a pretty good look at *it*. Its eyes were milky white, like cataracts. It didn't even turn my way before it lunged."

Blind. "It's possible," I said.

"But let's not bet our lives on it," Cage replied sharply. "In fact, let's try not to encounter it at all. Everyone stay here—I'm going to check the hall."

"Alone?" I demanded.

"Let me," said Mia at the same time.

Cage gaped at her. "You think you're going to move quieter than me with that wound in your stomach? *Faster* than me?" He softened his voice. "Listen, I know waiting around drives you up the wall, and you've been my right hand since we started planning this disaster. But for now, I need you to stay put."

Mia scowled but nodded, and now Matt spoke up. "*She's* your right hand? And here I thought Alexei and I backed you up against every challenge."

"We don't have time for this right now!" Cage managed to nearly explode without raising his voice above a whisper. He brought himself under control with visible effort, squaring off against Matt. "I'm going. You're staying. We can talk about it later."

His face twisted in annoyance, Matt looked away. But when Cage made for the door, I followed. He spun on me, eyes flashing. "No."

"I'm not your dog, and you can't tell me what to do." I glared at him. "Get moving."

For a moment he looked like he might argue, but then he shook his head in disgust. We both drew stun guns, flicked the safeties off, and stepped into the hall.

Sanctuary's empty corridors stretched in either direction. "Coast clear?" I whispered.

"Let's check a little farther. Tyler's slow at his best, and Mia's going to have trouble running. I can't carry them both."

We crept onward. Sanctuary's familiar corridors seemed ominous now, their bright, whitewashed sterility more like an oddly threatening hospital than the home I'd come to love.

We peered around the corner, and there it was.

It had its back to us, its legs bent like reverse knees, its body glistening in spite of Sanctuary's dry air. Its skin—pale and fleshy, but mottled with black—clung across its body, so taut I made out each individual rib. The row of spikes along its backbone and its pronged toes gave it a reptilian appearance, but the way it stood made me think of something more human. It craned its neck, listening maybe, or . . . thinking.

The creature reared up, doing something with its three-pronged hand. I couldn't see its face, but its broad back hunched in the hall, blocking our escape. No way to sneak past it, that much was clear.

Cage and I had frozen in horror. Now I gathered myself and caught his attention, beckoning him.

We withdrew around the corner just as the shriek sounded again—from somewhere behind us.

Oh my God. Another one.

An answering scream echoed nearby, sending me and Cage involuntarily to the ground, hands clamped over our ears. Seconds later, another creature tore through the hall, coming so close the wind of its passing ruffled my hair. It didn't even seem to notice us, lending credence to Mia's blindness theory. I had the briefest glimpse of its face—a narrow, skeletal visage with huge white eyes and a single curved fang.

Cage and I retreated without so much as a look to confirm our plans, hugging the walls. Around the corner, a series of hisses and growls chased us. Talking? Communicating? I didn't want to find out.

We almost reached the med bay before Cage's foot struck the wall. The soft reverberation echoed down the hall.

The hissing stopped.

Our eyes met, and Cage gestured frantically. I scrambled into the med bay, Cage on my heels. We slid the door shut behind us and I engaged the lock.

"Scratch escape," Cage whispered to the others at the rear of the room. "They're outside."

"They?" Mia challenged.

"At least two, maybe more. I think you're right about the blindness. One ran right past us without seeming to notice."

"So how are we supposed to get back to the prison?" Tyler demanded, his voice shrill and hysterical.

And loud.

Too loud.

Matt lunged for him and clamped his hand over his mouth. The rest of us pivoted to stare at the door.

All sound ceased. Then came a long dragging noise—the creature's tail sliding behind it?

I looked from the door to the prisoners, all of them panicked, their eyes wide, their breathing fast, and I closed my eyes. *Hello, superpower? If you're in there, this is an* excellent *time to make yourself known.*

Nothing. Figured.

But superpower or not, this was my responsibility. *They* were my responsibility.

I wiped my sweaty palms on my pant leg and tightened my grip on the stun gun. "I'll draw them off," I whispered. "You guys head for the prison."

A hushed chorus of *"What?"* and *"No!"* met my pronouncement.

I held up my hands. "I know the station. I can get away." Maybe. But if I couldn't help Mom, I could at least help the prisoners. Mia couldn't keep up with us if we had to run, and I had my doubts about Tyler, too. And if another creature showed up? Trying to outrun *three* of those things? Now that I knew what we were up against, I needed to find Mom now more than ever. I wasn't ready to retreat just yet. "I'll meet you back at the prison. Go as soon as I lead them off."

Before anyone had time to argue, I set out for the door, but quickly realized that Cage was right behind me. "You didn't let me go alone," he said when I opened my mouth, "and I'm not letting you. Besides, I got us into this. It's my responsibility."

I didn't have time to fight with him about who was responsible for who. Every second we were stuck in here was another second for the creatures to find us. "Let's go."

We took positions on either side of the door. Our eyes met, and Cage nodded. I thumbed the switch, and the door slid open.

The creatures weren't as close as we'd feared. But as soon as we moved, one of them screamed.

"Follow me!" I shouted, and bolted in the opposite direction of the prison.

Cage trailed me by seconds, and behind him, the creatures. They were *fast*. I'd planned to run for the supply room, where a maintenance hatch connected to the living quarters, but we weren't going to make it.

Suddenly, Cage grabbed my elbow and hoisted me off my feet and into his arms. "Hold on!" he shouted. I barely had time to react before he broke into a superhuman run, the force of his speed throwing me against his chest. I buried my face, hiding from the wind tearing exposed skin.

But Cage was running blindly, and he couldn't keep it up forever. We had to hide. "Right!" I shouted. Cage followed my order, pivoting into the living quarters and setting me on the ground.

"Where to?" he demanded, glancing behind us, still clutching my arm. We'd outdistanced the creatures, but we could hear their claws scrabbling for purchase nearby.

Instinctively, I charged into my own living quarters. I grabbed Cage's hand and yanked him into my bedroom, then dove under the bed, pulling him with me. *"Don't. Move."*

The bed wasn't much more than a capsule, and Cage landed almost on top of me. He wedged me in further, blocking me from sight with his own body. I started to protest, but at that second the outer door hissed open.

We froze. Cage's arms came around me, pulling me against him. I tensed in shock. Cage had touched me often enough, a hand on my arm or my back, but he'd never held me like this. There was a protective quality to his hold, as if he could somehow keep me safe if he just made me small enough.

I didn't even think about arguing. I tangled my hands in his shirt and squeezed my eyes shut. Whatever the creatures did to their victims, I didn't want to see it coming.

This close, Cage's breath ghosted my skin, his every tremble ricocheting through me. His arms clenched almost painfully around me, as if he could make me disappear. He smelled of sweat and antiseptic and something else, something more appealing that I couldn't quite place, and his body had a lean hardness I'd never felt before, not even in the other guards I'd fumbled against in dark corners and closets.

Another slide. Their claws clicked across my bedroom

floor. One of them gave a quick chirping sound, and the other responded with a huff. Cage's arms shuddered with the effort of silence.

His chest encompassed my entire range of vision, but I sensed them stalking closer, listening with predatory senses, sniffing as they scented the air. Did they smell us? If they could scent blood, the fresh wound on my arm and the spilled blood on Cage's shirt would draw them like a magnet. I hadn't even considered that, and now it was too late.

I held my breath and felt the catch in his chest as he did the same. We kept perfectly silent, as still as another piece of furniture.

One of the creatures snorted. Their footsteps receded across the floor, and the door hissed shut behind them.

I allowed myself a small, measured breath. A moment later, the softer sound of the outside door of our quarters followed.

I still didn't dare move. Cage relaxed his grip, although he continued to hold me. We stayed under the bed—pristine and spotless thanks to Sanctuary's vigilance, not at all the disaster of dust bunnies and graphic novels you'd find under my bed in our house on Earth—huddled together, neither of us willing to risk action.

"I think they're gone," I whispered at last.

Cage nodded, his jaw set.

I pressed gently against his chest. Part of me wanted to stay right here, safe and hidden beneath the bed. But we had to throw them off our track, discover what these things were, what they wanted. And I *had* to find Mom. "Cage," I said.

He closed his eyes, pressing his jaw against the top of my forehead. "This is on me," he said.

"What?"

"This whole stupid escape, it's something Mia and I put together one day. But she was just talking. The actual planning? That was me."

"Your escape didn't summon those creatures." I pulled back so he had no choice but to look at me, both our faces shadowed in darkness. "They were coming either way. You can't hold yourself responsible for any of this."

"If it wasn't for me, everyone would have been locked in their cells. Maybe the creatures would have run right past them."

"Or maybe they would have sat there, trapped and terrified, while the creatures tore the cells apart and . . . did whatever they do." I couldn't let myself believe everyone was dead. Mom was not dead. And that meant the other prisoners might be alive too. "We can't know."

He looked like he was going to argue but couldn't quite come up with the words. The lines of his forehead relaxed as he allowed, "You have a point."

I squeezed him. "Then let's get out from under the bed."

He hesitated almost imperceptibly before releasing me and sliding away. He reached back, and I let him help me up, although I didn't really need the assistance. Something had shifted in our relationship, and I wasn't sure when. Was it when he'd agreed to help me search for Mom? When he'd cut the chip out of my arm? Or maybe just now, hidden beneath the bed?

Cage. Hu. A thief. A gang member. A prisoner who'd taken me hostage, blackmailed my mother. I called on every memory of his arrogance, his threats, his taunts. None of it seemed to matter.

I was in a hell of a lot of trouble.

NINETEEN

WE CREPT TO THE EXIT AND LISTENED. I strained for any sound in the outside corridor but came up empty. I felt like we'd abandoned a layer of safety in leaving the bedroom—I didn't know if the creatures had *thumbs* per se, but they certainly seemed able to operate the keypads opening the doors, and so far none of Sanctuary's security had presented a barrier. "Let's give them a few minutes," I said at last. I didn't want to waste time, but blundering into the creatures in the corridor wouldn't help my mother. We were better off waiting, giving them time to move away, and then resuming our search in earnest.

Cage nodded. He shifted uncomfortably, taking in the room's clean lines, the painting of a forest over the white leather couch. "So. This is where you live, huh?"

"Yeah." My voice sounded flat to my own ears. In the

chaos of the last few hours, I'd almost managed to forget what happened last time my whole family gathered in this room. *Honey, we need to talk.* "We should get away from the door. Let's go back in my room—we can hide under the bed again if we have to."

But once we were in my room again, I saw how small it was. It seemed even smaller with Cage inside, pacing like a restless animal. "Do you want a clean shirt?" I asked suddenly. "I think Dad left a few. They'd probably fit you."

"Left?" he asked.

I winced. "Um, yeah. My parents are . . . well, it doesn't matter. You're covered in blood."

Sure enough, I found a few of the plain black T-shirts Dad wore under his uniform in the closet he shared with Mom. I grabbed one and returned to find Cage sitting shirtless on my bed, his jumpsuit folded over his waist, hunched over with his head in his hands. I hesitated in the doorway, staring at the tight cording of muscles on his arms—and the scars riddling his back.

He straightened up and half smiled. "Thanks," he said, reaching for the shirt. He shrugged into it and knotted his jumpsuit sleeves around his waist the way Mia always did. "You want to sit down?"

I sank onto the bed beside him. It wasn't a very big bed, and our arms almost touched. "What does your tattoo mean?" I asked when the silence became too heavy to bear.

"Which one?"

I nodded to the Chinese characters on his arm. He smiled, softer and more real than his usual broad grin. "It's Rune's name," he explained. "Her Chinese name, I mean. Not 'Rune.'"

"You have a Chinese name too, right? What is it?" I asked. I'd read it in the file but forgotten it. He'd only ever been Hu to me, and now Cage.

"Chang. We don't use them, though. No one does in Taipei, at least not where we grew up. You go by your street name." He nodded over his shoulder. "The dragon on my back, that's the gang we worked with. Rune has a matching one. We have snakes on our left legs from the first gang."

"Do you have any more?"

"A bird in a cage beneath my shoulder. Rune used to say I reminded her of a caged tiger. It's how I got my name." His lips quirked in amusement. "I made it a bird to dodge expectations. How about you? Any tattoos?"

I barked a laugh, stifling the sound with a worried glance at the door. No inhuman howl answered me, though, so I must not have been too loud. "Yeah, I don't think my parents would approve. The company doesn't love tattoos either."

"You've been with Omnistellar Concepts your whole life?"

I shrugged. "I was born into the company. My parents are really patriotic, especially Mom." My throat caught on her name, but it was helping to talk like this—normally, like we were friends having coffee, not until-recently enemies running for their lives. "My earliest memory is of my mother telling me how lucky I was to be part of a corp like Omnistellar. Every time we walked by a hovel in some city, she'd point it out and remind me how much we owed the company. And Omnistellar always taught us that anomalies were dangerous—so dangerous they had to be contained at any cost." Was I trying to justify the way we'd treated him, all of the prisoners? Maybe. Maybe even to myself. "I went to Omnistellar summer camps, clubs, schools. . . . All I've ever known is the company."

"Kind of like a gang."

"Hardly," I said, enough of the guard left inside me to recoil at the suggestion.

Cage grinned, spreading his hands. "Seriously. What would your guard tattoo have been?"

"A serial number, probably." Although part of me had always wanted one, maybe a symbol of strength. That was a secret I'd take to my grave, though.

Cage chuckled. "Sorry." He hesitated a minute before repeating, "Kenzie, I *am* sorry."

"For what?"

He stared at me in disbelief. "Are you kidding? For taking you hostage. For threatening you. For letting Mia hit you. And then there's this. . . ." His hand ghosted over the bandage on my arm, his jaw tightening in distaste.

I caught his hand between both of mine, held it a moment, and then let it go, forcing a smile. "I asked you to do that."

"Not for the rest, though."

I glanced away, uncomfortable with the conversation's direction. He was right, after all—he *had* taken me hostage, and he'd planned to use me to escape. But now that I knew the prisoners on a personal level, everything muddled in my mind. I was starting to understand why Omnistellar forbade contact with inmates except under the most dire circumstances, and I wasn't sure I liked the reasons. "You didn't hurt me," I pointed out. "And you weren't going to."

"No, I wasn't." He scrubbed at his temple. "I'm glad you figured that out. I was getting pretty sick of playing the bad guy."

His left hand remained on his lap where I'd dropped it, only inches from mine. My fingers were pale beside his darker skin, his warmth radiating through me even from a distance. I searched for a topic of conversation, anything that would distract me from our current situation. "Mia and Alexei," I said suddenly.

"What about them?"

"Alexei seems relatively calm. More or less stable. How'd he wind up with Mia?"

Cage shrugged. "I don't know the whole story. They were arrested together. Alexei was never exactly forthcoming with the details." He frowned, biting the corner of his lip. "You know, I never really thought about it. They were just a pair. Mia and Alexei."

"It's not a big deal."

"But now I'm curious!" he said in frustration.

I laughed in spite of myself. "You and Mia seem close."

"You jealous?"

I scowled and pulled back from him a split second before I caught the teasing glimmer in his eyes. "Oh, very funny. Besides, it seems like Matt's the one who's jealous."

Cage groaned loudly. "He does not like Mia. And he likes to be in charge. He was willing to follow me, but he doesn't like her tossing out orders."

"Matt seems all right," I said cautiously.

"Oh, he's more than all right. He's one of the best friends you can have: loyal, solid, and always ready to have your back. But he's not a risk taker, you know? For that, you go to Mia." He tipped back suddenly, flopping on my bed and stretching out his arm, wiggling his fingers in invitation. "Speaking of risks?"

I laughed in spite of myself and leaned back, curling against his shoulder, solid and real beneath my head, though my mom's voice screamed at me to get up and retreat. But I wanted this, a moment of normalcy in the midst of chaos.

He gestured at the poster on the ceiling. *"Robo Mecha Dream Girl?"*

My eyes flew open. "You know it?"

"I've read it. It's pretty good, but I'm more of a *Warriors of Silver* guy myself."

"Oh, come on. *Warriors of Silver* hasn't produced anything good in years. I mean, yeah, it wasn't bad back when it was all about the training camp, but now that they're fighting aliens every other week . . ." My voice trailed off. "Well," I said dryly, "maybe that's not as unrealistic as I thought."

Cage groaned, dragging his free hand across his face. "Let's just stay here," he suggested. "We can go to sleep, and maybe when we wake up, all of this will have gone away."

And just for a moment, I was tempted. Here in my bedroom, where I'd been safe and happy, I could pretend there wasn't a bleeding spot on my arm where a chip had been yanked out, that my parents still loved me and each other, and that there weren't some kind of alien beasts stalking the station.

But of course we couldn't do that. Because my mom wasn't in the next room joking with my dad. I didn't know where she was. "We can't stay here," I said softly, as much to myself as Cage. "I have to find my mom and make sure the others got back to the prison okay."

His expression collapsed, and I had a second of bitter regret for breaking in on his tranquility. But he nodded. "Rune's going to be freaking out. I don't suppose you know a shortcut."

I did, actually—the one I'd originally intended for us to take. If we reached the storeroom, a maintenance hatch led to the hall near the command center. Once there, we could at least talk to Rune and decide on our next step.

But as I opened my mouth to tell him, an alien's high-pitched scream cut me off, a triumphant roar as it closed in on its prey. And right on its heels came another, this one full of terror and all too human.

TWENTY

"WAIT!" CAGE CRIED AS I LUNGED FOR THE
outer door. "Kenzie, we don't know what's out there! Slow
down!"

I spun on him. "That was a human scream! What if it's my
mother? One of the other kids?"

"I'm not saying don't go. I'm saying take a minute to think."

I bit my lip until I tasted blood, bringing my racing heart
under control. Drawing my stun gun, I gestured for Cage to
stand opposite me. I steadied my grip on the gun and thumbed
the door control. As it slid open, I lunged to the side and plastered myself against the inner wall, holding my breath and waiting for something to attack.

Nothing happened. I made myself count to three before
catching Cage's eye. We nodded at one another, and I slipped
into the corridor.

"Which way?" he whispered.

Gunshots rattled through the station—actual gunfire. My heart stuttered. Only two people on Sanctuary carried real guns: Mom and Rita.

I broke into a run, ignoring Cage's whispered command, already thumbing the trigger on my stun gun. Another scream rose in the air, and then choked off abruptly.

I skidded around the corner to find the creature hunched over a limp body. "Mom!" I roared.

The creature pivoted, howling so shrilly I dropped to the ground and instinctively covered my ears. Somehow my training held and I didn't lose my grip on the gun. In a single movement, I swung it up, aimed, and fired.

Electricity arced, blasting through the air. I wasn't screwing around—I had that thing set on full force, enough to fry a human being. The creature reared back, howling again. This time I was prepared for the sound and managed to keep my feet.

The creature staggered, shook off the blast, and snarled at me, its front claws pulled into menacing hooks. I fumbled with my gun, readying another charge. At the same moment, Cage appeared behind me, took one look at the situation, and let off a shot of his own.

The second blast of electricity set off another scream, and the creature fled down the corridor. I barely saw it move. I wasn't sure even *Cage* could outrun these things for long.

I noticed all this in the blink of an eye, and then I threw

myself down, grabbing the fallen body and rolling it over. "Mom?" I cried frantically. "Mom!"

But it wasn't Mom.

It was Rita.

I stared at her in disbelief, and Cage swore softly. "I thought she was off station," he said.

"I thought so too." I glanced at him over my shoulder. "You're sure Rune didn't engineer that distress call?"

"No, just the interference." His gaze followed the path the creature had taken, and his eyes widened as he caught my implication. "You aren't saying . . . ?"

I scrambled at Rita's throat and found a thready, stuttering pulse. "We can ask her when she wakes up."

Cage knelt and placed a hand under Rita's shoulders, then lifted experimentally. "I can carry her," he said. "If you think it's okay to move her."

"Anything's better than leaving her here. Let's get to medical." I scanned the hall for Rita's gun but didn't see it anywhere. Strange—I'd definitely heard shots.

Unless . . . The creature hadn't *taken* the gun, had it? My mind recoiled from the possibility.

Cage holstered his weapon and staggered to his feet, grunting under Rita's weight. Blood seeped through a torn corner of her uniform. "Why didn't we find blood in the prison sectors?" I whispered.

Cage shook his head, as baffled as me. I led us through the

hall, leaning around each corner braced for action, stun gun held ready. Those things didn't like electricity. That was something. On the other hand, two full blasts had barely frightened the creature, let alone harmed it. My hand grew slick around the gun. *Keep it together.*

We entered the med bay as the comm system crackled to life. "Cage?" came Rune's semi-hysterical voice. "Cage, are you there?"

I lunged for the comm before she could alert the creatures, guilt suffusing me. How long had she been calling for us, frantically scanning station comms? There were no cameras in crew living quarters. She'd have lost sight of us when we left medical. "Rune, we're here. We're okay."

"Oh, thank God." Her voice cracked, and even over the comm I could tell she was crying. "I couldn't find you anywhere. The others got back a while ago and said those *things* were chasing you. I thought . . ."

Cage carefully set Rita on the bed, then came over, rolling his shoulders. "I'm here, *meimei*," he said, bending over the console. His arm brushed mine, and in spite of the situation, it sent a pleasant rush through me. His face softened as he spoke to his sister. "You all right down there?"

"Everyone returned safely. Mia doesn't look great, but she says she's fine." Rune hesitated. "Kenzie, I got into your file. I'll patch it through to your console, and you can take a look when you have time."

"Thanks," I said. For the moment, my file was the least of my worries.

"We found one of the guards," Cage told her, glancing over his shoulder at Rita.

"Which one?"

"Rita," I said. "Mom's still missing."

"Rita . . . Hernandez?" Rune's voice shot up an octave. "The one who went to check out the distress beacon?"

"Yeah."

"Cage." Rune clearly struggled to control her excitement. "That means she returned the shuttle. It means we have a way off this station."

For a moment we stared at each other. Somehow we'd missed that little detail. If Rita was back, so was her shuttle. We had an escape.

"Okay," I said, hope blossoming in my chest even as I reined it in. "This isn't over. We need to help Rita, and then we need to get everyone to the shuttle bay. And I'm not sure where the hell we're going to go."

"Off this station is good enough for me," Cage replied grimly.

I glanced at Rita and thumbed the mute switch on the comm. "Cage . . . when she wakes up, chances are she's not going to be happy to see you. And even if she comes around, if we go to Earth . . . it's not an escape. They'll arrest us before we leave the shuttle."

"Yeah, well, I've got a few cards up my sleeve yet. Anyway . . ." He shrugged. "Prison sucks, but it's better than being eaten by space monsters."

"Fair enough." I reactivated the comm. "Rune, lock the place down. Don't let anyone in except us. I don't know how those things are traveling, but you might want to block off air vents, too."

"All right." Rune's voice went distant for a minute, and I heard her talking to someone in the background. Then: "People are asking a lot of questions here, Cage. What do I tell them?"

Our eyes met. "Tell them . . . ," said Cage slowly, "tell them everything's going according to plan and we'll be back soon. Keep them calm. And make sure Alexei's standing behind you when you do it. Don't let him talk. Just tell him to look scary."

Rune laughed. "Got it. See you soon, *gege*."

Cage shook his head as we disconnected. "She's good and scared."

"How can you tell?" I mean, of course she was. But still.

"She called me *gege*. It means—"

I nodded. "'Big brother.' And?"

His eyebrows shot up. "How'd you know that?"

I wrinkled my nose. How *did* I know that? "I must have heard it somewhere."

He nodded absently. "Anyway, she never calls me that. She hates it when I remind her I've got eight minutes on her."

I forced a smile and turned my attention to Rita. Her life

signs were fairly stable or I wouldn't have left her side for a second. Knowing she was stable, though, made it no easier to face the blood and gore. I crossed to her and stroked her hair back from her face, a lump welling in my throat. Cage followed me, groaning. "Please don't make me do any more stitches."

"No promises." I examined the wound on Rita's stomach. It looked a lot like Mia's, and almost certainly *would* require stitches. I didn't mention that to Cage quite yet.

The sight of Rita, even crumpled and bleeding, brought the world into a semblance of order. She was strong and confident and, most importantly, an authority figure. If I got her back on her feet, I knew she could help me find Mom. "She's lost a lot of blood. See her jacket?"

"Well, we don't exactly have the resources for a transfusion. Let's slap some bandages on her and hope for the best."

I shot a look in his direction. I didn't like the flatness in his tone—as if he realized that for him and his friends, the best-case scenario was one where Rita never woke at all. From a mercenary perspective, his reasoning made sense. But I wasn't a mercenary. My fingers trembling, I grabbed Rita's arm as if I could physically pull her to life. Rita, more than anyone, treated me like a friend, maybe even a sister. When the other guards rolled their eyes— *Kenzie has all the answers again, what a shock*—she only smiled and winked. Convenient or not, she was coming through this alive.

Besides, if Rita could survive those things . . . well, so could my mom.

We worked in silence, straining our ears for the click of claws on tile or the shrill scream heralding the aliens' appearance. I catalogued the creatures in my head, their reptilian skin, the cataracts over their eyes. We'd seen three. Were there more?

At last we finished with the worst of Rita's injuries, having bandaged and bound her until she was half mummy. I breathed a sigh of relief, dropping a kiss on her forehead, something I would never dare when she woke.

We hovered over her, me squeezing her hand, Cage carefully working stitches through her more superficial wounds, muttering under his breath in Mandarin. After a few minutes it became obvious she wasn't waking up any time soon. I glanced over my shoulder, drawn to the file Rune had sent, but held by my obligation to Rita.

"Go," said Cage.

I started. "What?"

He flashed me that devious grin and went to flip his hair out of his face, but stopped with a wince at the sight of blood smearing his gloved hand. "You're itching to read that file, and you're not helping Rita by standing here."

I hesitated a second longer, but Cage was right. There was nothing else I could do to help, and if that file held clues to the chip in my arm . . . I nodded. "Thanks. Let me know the second she wakes up, okay?"

"I will."

The first file contained familiar stuff. My place of birth, camps and trainings I'd attended, aptitude scores and intelligence tests. Most of my scores fell on the high edge of normal—good stuff, not remarkable. I didn't have any illusions about why I'd scored the junior guard position on Sanctuary; it had more to do with my parents than my spectacular skill set. Still, I worked ten times harder than everyone else, and that counted for something too. Nepotism might have set me apart from the crowd, but it hadn't earned me my place.

Another file lurked beneath the standard stuff, though, this one labeled CONFIDENTIAL: OMNISTELLAR CONCEPTS EYES ONLY. I cast a quick glance at Cage, who was hunched over Rita with an expression of concentration on his face, slid open the file, and found a medical report.

Subject admitted for initial tests following suspicions of parents. Demonstrating unreasonable alacrity in language acquisition. Not necessarily sign of powers, possibly high intelligence. However, combined with family proximity to region of incident, warrants investigation.

Subject Kenzie Elaine Cord, admitted for testing on second birthday. Removed from parental custody following proper channels of investigation.

I paused. There it was, in black and white. Removed from parental custody . . . proper channels.

In other words, Mom and Dad turned me in. Why? To protect me? Or because company regulations demanded it?

Day 3:

Subject is a cheerful child with few tears. Has called for mother and father several times but is easily soothed by other adults. Previous days spent observing and acclimatizing her to the facility. Testing begins in earnest tomorrow.

Day 4:

Initial medical testing reveals high probability of genetic anomalies, although exact forms remain unclear. However, such testing is not conclusive and is known to produce false results. More thorough testing is required to confirm anomaly.

Day 6:

Subject became violently angry today, demanding to return home. Nurses were unable to calm her as previously. Child revealed herself to be surprisingly verbose for a toddler. At one point, paused in her rage to turn to the nurse and say, "I insist you return me to my parents." Lends further credence to anomaly theory, although again, may simply indicate advanced development or intelligence. Tantrum allowed to play itself out. Eventually subject fell asleep on floor and was moved to her bed.

I paused again, wiping my hand over my face. Where had my parents been through all of this? Obviously I'd missed them—cried for them. And they'd been where? Nearby, watching me on a monitor, their hearts breaking? Or curled up at home with a mug of coffee?

Day 7:

In effort to eliminate theories of advanced intelligence, spent today on a battery of IQ tests. Subject displayed normal or near-normal results in all areas (slightly advanced in logical and spatial reasoning). No results seem to indicate genius levels of intelligence or even abnormally advanced IQ. Further credence lent to anomaly theory.

Day 10:

Subject is definitely anomalous.

Today had the simple but expedient idea of bringing in speakers of another language. Parents of subject assure us she has never been exposed to any language but English. After two hours spent with M. Lebleu, however, subject was speaking French near fluently (with appropriate adjustments for age and development). Someone found an intern who spoke some Japanese. Within a slightly longer time (allowing for adjustment to difference in grammatical structures between Japanese and English not present in French?) subject was also speaking conversationally with intern.

This level of language acquisition is unprecedented in the human population. It is this researcher's conclusion that subject is definitely anomalous. Recommend immediate chipping. Should parents be unwilling to comply, subject should be transported to foster home for observation and potential incarceration.

I stared at the screen, seeing it but not fully understanding. "Cage?" I said. "Can you come here a minute?"

"What's up?" He sank into a chair beside me and took a good look at my face. "You okay?"

"Yeah. But . . . can you speak Mandarin to me?"

His eyebrows shot up. "What do you want me to say?"

"Anything. It doesn't matter. I just want to hear you speak it for a while."

Cage stared at me, then shrugged. He transferred his gaze to the ceiling as if considering. After a moment, he began to talk.

I closed my eyes, letting the soft, rushed sounds of the language wash over me. It was relaxing in a way, his voice shaping his speech like a melody. And it was reassuring in another, because I didn't understand a word. Even without my chip, I had no powers. My parents did chip me. Somehow, they believed I had a power. But they were wrong. Maybe it was nothing more than a . . . a talent.

Still—my parents had me *chipped*. Everything inside me rebelled at the thought. Anger choked my common sense, urging me to rant, to rave, to scream until the walls shook. Sure, they may have had their reasons. Maybe they were afraid for me . . . but why? And even if they were, why keep it a secret so many years? Didn't they think I deserved to know the truth about myself? Were they *ever* planning to tell me?

I clenched my hands into fists on my lap, breathing through my nose, bringing a truly Mia-level temper tantrum under control. This wasn't the place to scream and cry—not with aliens lurking around every corner. Besides, no matter what my parents had done, they were still my parents. They did love me, right? Maybe they really *were* afraid for me . . . but if so many people lived peaceful lives with powers, why did my parents think I'd be any different?

Of course . . . I had never met anyone with an ability, not counting that girl in the alley. I just took my parents' word for it that they existed. I took *Omnistellar's* word for it. I read the history books and swallowed the tale and never stopped to ask questions.

The last word in the file leaped out in my memory. "Incarceration." Had Omnistellar actually considered imprisoning a two-year-old for no crime but speaking languages? I'd already come to suspect the company had secrets, but this . . . In that moment, everything I thought I'd known about the company to which I'd dedicated my life turned upside down. I ground my nails into my palms in an effort to steady myself. The pieces fell into place.

Omnistellar weren't the good guys.

And that meant I wasn't either.

". . . There were lanterns," Cage said quietly, his gaze fixed on lights overhead. "I remember that above everything, those lanterns. Red and yellow and gold, the most beautiful things I'd ever seen. I stood and stared at them, transfixed, as the crowds surged around us. Fireworks and noise and laughter were so alien to us, to anything we'd seen. Rune was scared of all the people. She pressed against me and tried to get me to run back to our father's hotel. But I didn't move. But I wanted to join the celebration, the music and the food and the dance. I didn't realize then, maybe *couldn't* realize, how far that world existed from ours."

"Why?" I asked, getting caught in the tail end of his story, welcoming the distraction from my own nightmarish thoughts. "It sounds beautiful."

Cage had been leaning back, staring at the ceiling as he talked. Now he straightened to fix me with a hard, piercing stare.

"What?" I asked.

"When did you learn Mandarin?"

I started. Now that he said it, I heard it. I'd thought he switched back to English, but he didn't. Even now, he spoke Mandarin: *Nǐ shén me shí hòu xué pǔtōnghuà?*

I tried to answer him, searching for the sounds, but they slipped away. I reverted to English. "Did I speak Mandarin?"

"You did. Perfectly, more or less."

I stiffened. "More or less?"

He grinned. "You mimicked my lazy accent. Kenzie, what's going on?"

I shook my head. How the hell did I explain what I'd learned? "You better read this," I said, sliding the tablet toward him. I staggered to my feet and crossed to Rita, my hands shaking. I'd spoken Mandarin? I couldn't do it now. I closed my eyes and gritted my teeth, looking for words and not finding them.

I ran my hand over Rita's hair, her fierce face relaxed as

though sleeping. I'd heard her curse in Spanish many times without understanding what her words actually meant—but I'd had a chip, I reminded myself bitterly. Even if I had some sort of power, I would never have known.

I glanced at her face and met her eyes. "Rita!" I cried.

At the same moment, she swung to a seated position, snatched the stun gun from my holster, and aimed it directly at Cage.

TWENTY-ONE

"WHOA!" I SHOUTED, LEAPING BETWEEN THEM.
Rita, surprisingly strong for someone who'd just come out of
what looked like a coma, grabbed my arm and shoved me aside,
then slid unsteadily to her feet.

"Get your hands in the air!" she barked.

Cage rolled his shoulders, his back to us. His fingers
twitched, as if he was considering reaching for his own weapon.
"Stop it!" I shouted. "Rita, he's not dangerous!"

Rita shot me a furious look. "*Chica*, are you out of your
mind? This is an escaped freaking felon. I don't know what's
going on around here, but—"

"That's right," Cage interrupted. "You don't." He glanced
at me and said something in Mandarin. I almost caught it, but
it was frustratingly out of reach. I shook my head at him and he
half shrugged, a smile touching his lips.

He vanished. Rita pivoted, fury in her expression. Cage appeared behind her, caught her wrist, and twisted. The gun clattered to the ground, and he kicked it away. Another blink and he was across the room, both weapons in hand, one aimed at Rita.

"Now," Cage continued pleasantly, "why don't you sit down so we can talk about this?"

Rita trembled with rage. She turned toward me, seeking help or an explanation, I don't know which, and all I could do was shake my head. Her eyes narrowed, and I knew I'd lost her trust. That, more than anything, tore at me. If Rita could stare at me with such betrayal in her eyes, what would I see in my mom's expression if—*when*—I found her? And what would she see in mine? For a moment I let myself revel in that possibility. My mom had been willing to kill me. Let her feel that pain for a moment, that burn of treachery.

But wasn't I doing the exact same thing right now, to Rita? My mom had her reasons. They might seem flimsy to me, but I knew her, knew the all-encompassing fire of her patriotism, the depth of her convictions. Until recently, I'd shared them. If she really believed that by sacrificing me, she would save thousands of others . . .

We could talk about it when I found her. For the first time, a glimmer of hope entered my soul. If I could convince Rita—admittedly, a big if—that would go a long way toward swaying my mother. With Rita at my back, she couldn't blame my conversion on youth or Stockholm syndrome or anything else.

Of course, Rita didn't exactly look ready to listen. With no other choice, she climbed onto the bed, her quivering limbs revealing how much effort her actions had cost her. I fumbled among the medications on the counter, popped open the bottle of painkillers, but when I approached her with them she shot me a murderous look. I suddenly suspected that Rita would get along well with Mia.

"You saw what attacked you?" I asked without preamble. There was no point explaining that the prisoners weren't the monsters we'd assumed they were. Rita might play at insubordination, but she was Omnistellar through and through; if I tried to spring everything on her at once, her reaction would be the same as mine had been, only multiplied tenfold. And I couldn't predict her reaction if I told her the contents of my file, my newfound revelation that Omnistellar was on the wrong side of just about everything. My only hope lay in convincing her we had no choice but to work together. With a bit of luck, she'd follow the same path that I had, slowly coming to know the anomalies for who they really were.

Rita faltered at that. "I saw . . . something."

"What happened when you chased down the distress beacon?"

"I'm not sure I'm the one who should be answering questions right now," she snapped, glaring at me. "What the hell's going on around here, Kenzie? Where's your mother?"

"That's a good question," I said, ignoring how my stomach

plummeted at the mention of Mom. I was equal parts worried about and furious at her, and I was desperate to find her so I could let the fury take over. "We don't know. The things that attacked you, we think they might have gotten her, too."

Rita's expression softened a bit. "You okay, kiddo?"

"I'm fine." I nodded at Cage. "And so are the prisoners from sector five, but we don't know what happened to the rest. This isn't about guards and prisoners anymore, Rita. It's about survival."

Cage registered what I was trying to do and lowered his stun gun, although he continued to hold it at his side, his finger on the trigger. I didn't miss that and knew Rita wouldn't either.

She glanced between us, her eyes working feverishly. After a moment, she nodded. "Put down your gun, kid," she said. "I'm not going to hurt you. Not until we figure out what's wrong with this station."

Cage laughed, the sound utterly lacking humor. "Great. I'll watch my back afterward, then." He tucked the stun gun into his waistband next to the other. He might not be pointing it at her, but he didn't return one to *me*, either.

Sliding to her feet, Rita accepted a handful of painkillers and a glass of water. "The distress beacon was a decoy," she said. "I got there and found some sort of device. The pulse it gave off temporarily blasted my entire shuttle. Fortunately I was wearing an XE suit, because the pulse wiped out power, life support, and gravity. Took me hours to repair everything, and by then I was frantic. I figured someone lured us out of the prison to stage a jailbreak. When I still couldn't contact Sanctuary, I assumed the worst."

"Well, you were half right." Cage was back to his arrogant, devil-may-care attitude, not exactly designed to win friends and influence people. "There was a jailbreak, but we didn't draw you away. I'm guessing that was *them*."

Rita scowled. "They don't seem smart enough. More like animals."

"I don't know," I said dubiously. "They had to come from somewhere. They lured you off the ship, and they seem like they're communicating. Just because they *look* like animals doesn't mean they think like them. They might be smarter than we realize."

"Safer to assume they are," Rita agreed with a shrug.

And just as she finished, one of the creatures burst through a ceiling panel. It hit the ground with splayed limbs, landing in a crouch.

We all froze in shocked disbelief, and that probably saved our lives. The creature raised its head at a peculiar angle, sniffing. A long, dark tongue slithered out from between its jaws, tasting the air like a snake.

"Don't move," Cage snarled at Rita, his voice barely audible. "Don't make a sound."

The thing's head swiveled in his direction. It screeched and lunged, but Cage was already gone, reappearing on the other side of the room. He teetered and caught the wall, then stood stock-still.

The creature howled. It spun and sank its claws into the console. Sparks flew, but they didn't seem to faze the monster in the least; the tiny jolts of electricity were nothing like the staggering power of a full blast from a stun gun.

A shrill scream answered from nearby. I trembled, desperate to keep still. Could they hear my pounding heart?

Another creature charged through the door. It tilted its head, obviously listening, and let loose a quick, short screech. The other answered in kind.

And then a *third* dropped through the ceiling.

I gasped. All three heads perked, and I clenched my teeth, forcing myself silent.

The creatures moved toward me in a loose triangle. I wanted to close my eyes against them, but I willed myself to keep them open as the monsters crept steadily nearer. They spread out, searching the room, their claws fumbling in the air, their tongues working, their ears twitching.

Cage caught my gaze and shook his head, telling me to stay still. As if I had much choice in the matter. I reached for my stun gun—but no, Cage had it. Not much good against three of the things anyway.

The creatures targeted me, twitching and hissing. Fortunately, I stood in a corner, not within easy reach of their grasping claws. But they were going to find me. They searched methodically now, not at all like the animals Rita had theorized. They drew closer and closer. I trembled, scanning the area for something, *anything*, to use as a weapon.

One of the creatures drew so close the rush of its breath washed over me, rancid and sour. Drool slid from its mouth, puddling on the floor. Its jaw clicked, and its head cocked to catch any sound.

This time I did close my eyes. I would have screamed if I hadn't.

Something hit hard against my side. I was straining so much to stay silent that I didn't make a sound even then, just let out a gasp, bracing myself for claws tearing my flesh.

Instead arms clamped around me. A familiar burst of air struck me as Cage swept me off my feet and blasted right out of the medical bay. He deposited me in the hall. I stumbled and caught his arm, and he held my elbows to steady me. "Rita," I said.

He nodded. "I'll go back for—"

An alien scream echoed through the hall. A moment later, Rita's scream followed.

We charged to the door. Rita crouched on the bed, a scalpel in one hand. Blood oozed from a fresh wound on her shoulder. The creatures surrounded her. "Get out of here!" she shouted.

Cage hesitated. "Can you reach her?" I demanded.

One of the creatures sprang at us. Cage grabbed me and dashed twenty feet down the hall. He barely had time to get my feet off the ground, and his grip bruised my arm as he hauled me against him. Behind us, the alien lunged at the spot where we'd stood seconds before, roaring in rage.

Rita screamed again in the distance.

The beast pivoted toward us, even though we hadn't made a sound. "They're catching on," Cage said. "We need to get out of here."

"But Rita!"

"We can't help her if we're dead!"

The creature lunged. Once again, Cage snatched me and bolted, but this time he didn't stop. I twisted in his grasp, fighting to return to Rita, but the rush of wind against my face prevented me from even speaking, much less escaping his arms. He continued until we reached the prison entrance, where he put me on the ground, afterward doubling over and gasping for breath.

"Rita," I choked out, panic suffusing my voice. "We just *left* her!"

Cage sagged against the wall, breathing too hard to answer. Obviously the run had winded him, but I wasn't exactly brimming with sympathy. "We have to go back!" I shouted, charging in the other direction.

Before I'd gone two steps, Cage caught my arm, swung me around, and held me in place. He stared at me like I'd suggested a friendly walk outside. "Kenzie, there was *nothing* we could have done to help her. *Nothing*."

"Yeah," I said, my anger brimming. "And it's in no way convenient for you that the person most likely to arrest you after we escape this mess is out of the picture?"

He jerked upright at that and towered over me with an expression of raw fury on his face. "What exactly are you suggesting?"

"I think you know."

He shook his head, his face twisted into a snarl. "I guess I shouldn't expect any less from an Omnistellar guard."

"What's that supposed to mean?"

"It means your training is showing. Assume all prisoners are soulless husks, anomalies without a conscience." He grabbed my arm again, not gently as he had in my bedroom, or in panic to save my life, but with the roughness he'd shown when he first took me hostage. "Come on. We have to check on the others."

I yanked free of his grasp. "Give me my gun."

"Are you kidding?" Something flickered in his eyes, as if my mistrust hurt him as much as it enraged him, but it vanished in a heartbeat. He pulled my gun out of his waistband and shoved it into my hand. "There. Happy now? Let's go."

I followed him into the stairwell. How had things gotten so messed up? Half an hour ago, this boy clutched me against him as if he'd give his life to protect me. Now the tension rolled between us like we hated each other. And the betrayal I'd seen in his face mirrored what I'd sensed from Rita. I didn't fit anywhere anymore—not with Omnistellar and not with the prisoners. I was an anomaly without a friend, a guard without a company, a daughter without a mother—or at least, a daughter whose mother believed so fiercely in Omnistellar's lies and manipulations that she was willing to sacrifice her own child.

My throat itched to take back my words. Reeling from leaving Rita behind, I'd lashed out at Cage, basically accusing him of murder. But he couldn't have gone back for her, not without getting one of us killed.

Hot tears pressed against my eyelids. Rita was almost certainly dead. Those things would rip her apart and . . . what? What did they do to their victims? I wasn't sure I wanted to find out. Images of Rita's torn body assailed me, and I fought them off, my vision swimming. *Rita was dead.* What about Mom? I had to keep believing she was alive, had to fight for the hope that I would find her. If I stopped, well . . .

A sob threatened to tear from my throat as we hit the bottom of the staircase, but I turned it into a muffled cough. Cage muttered a Mandarin curse and took an awkward step in my direction. "Kenzie," he said. After a moment, he reached out and laid a hesitant hand on my arm. I stared at it, then covered his hand with my own.

"I'm sorry," I said, still staring at his fingers. They flexed against the sleeve of my uniform. "I didn't mean . . . I know you didn't want to leave her."

"No, I didn't." He pulled me toward him, slowly, almost experimentally. When I didn't resist, he gave me a quick hug.

For a moment I inhaled his scent, drawing comfort from his warmth, and then he stepped back, although his hands lingered on my shoulders. "And we won't leave your mom, not if there's any chance to save her. I promise."

I nodded. "At least you got a useful power out of the deal," I grumbled, taking a step back and straightening my spine. I couldn't afford to fall apart, not now, not yet. "What the hell use are languages?"

"Probably a lot in day-to-day life. Not so much when fighting killer space monsters." He cocked his head and grinned down at me.

I smiled in spite of myself. "Sorry. I'm okay now."

"Don't apologize." He stared at me another second and words seemed to form on his lips. I waited with bated breath, but whatever he'd been about to say slipped away like a half-felt dream. "Let's go talk to my sister."

I nodded, glancing over my shoulder. No cries. No clacking of claws on the stairs. Maybe they hadn't registered another sector below 4. If we were lucky, we had some time to plan before they found us.

And if we were really lucky, none of us would get killed along the way.

TWENTY-TWO

THE INSTANT THE DOOR SLID ASIDE, SHOUTING echoed through the stairwell. Cage closed his eyes and thumped his head against the doorframe. "It never stops," he said. "Just for one second, I'd like it to stop." And he disappeared in a burst of wind.

I charged up only a few seconds behind him and found the source of the commotion in the common area. It didn't take long to figure out what was going on. Mia stood on a table, blood seeping through the bandage beneath her torn shirt. Behind her, Alexei tugged at her pant leg, his face twisted in frustration. Matt and Rune hovered in the server room entrance, Cage at their side talking furiously to his sister.

What looked like everyone in sector 5 gathered in front of Mia. Kristin stood at the front, her face mottled red and white. I spotted Tyler slumped on a couch in the corner, clearly hoping no one would notice him.

"Enough!" Mia's voice cut through the noise. "I swear to God, if you people don't shut the hell up I'm going to . . ."

"You're going to what?" Kristin snarled. "I think we've all had enough of you and Cage running this show, thanks very much. Where has it gotten us?"

Mia's hands clenched into fists, but at the same moment, Cage leaped onto the table beside her. "You're right!" he called, spreading his hands. That quieted the crowd, although the murmur of unrest remained. "You've been very patient. Give me a second and I'll explain everything."

The kids surged forward, their anger coursing, but Cage deliberately turned his back, talking quietly to Mia, and the crowd didn't revolt. I threaded my way through them, making for Rune. Halfway there, a foot caught my ankle, almost sending me plummeting. Years of training kicked in. I leaped over the foot, pivoting to face my assailant.

I met a sea of incredibly hostile faces. My resolve wavered. Whether or not these prisoners were actually guilty of crimes, some of them had spent years confined on Sanctuary. None of them had much love for guards, and even the kindest among them couldn't help but view me with suspicion. I had no way to explain to them my newfound mistrust of the company. I reached for my stun gun, and the tension rolling off the crowd became a tangible presence.

Suddenly, Tyler appeared at my side. "Just keep moving," he said nervously, taking my elbow and backing up, half sheltering behind me. Still, the crowd parted, letting us through.

We reached the table, and I leaned against it, my breath unsteady. Cage glanced down at me, eyebrow raised. "Everything okay?"

"Yup." I nodded my gratitude at Tyler and then headed for Rune and Matt.

"Are you all right?" Rune whispered, grabbing my hand. "God, Kenzie . . . When I found that file, I didn't know what to think." She glanced at me sideways and flushed. "I didn't mean to read it. I got it open, and the next thing I knew I was half done. I stopped as soon as I realized."

So Rune knew everything. "It's okay," I said. "Thanks for digging it up." The calmness of my tone impressed even me.

Above us, Cage gently but inexorably guided Mia into Alexei's waiting arms. "Yes, I know," he said. "And don't get me wrong, I appreciate you holding off the revolution. But you're on your last legs. Please. Let me finish this."

Mia hesitated, but Alexei got his big hands on her, and the argument ended as he swung her to the floor. She half sagged against him, as if she'd burned through the last of her energy ranting at the crowd. "You're bleeding, Mia mine," Alexei murmured. "Let's go take a look." It was a mark of how much her wound hurt that she nodded and let him guide her toward the cells.

Cage reached a hand back to me. "I need you," he said.

Rune and Matt both tensed beside me. I arched an eyebrow and folded my arms, refusing to join him on the table. "Are you kidding? I don't think they're in the mood to listen to a guard."

He crouched and caught the zipper of my hoodie, then tugged me toward him. The knuckles of his hand brushed my neck as he unzipped my sweater. He slid it down my shoulder, his touch leaving tiny sparks in its wake. I shivered visibly, but if Cage noticed, he didn't say anything. Instead, with infinite care, he turned over my arm to reveal the bandage where he'd extracted my chip. "They will be once they see that."

I hesitated. Cage was asking me to throw off the last vestiges of my old identity, to completely and irrevocably shift from Kenzie the guard to Kenzie the anomaly, the freak—the prisoner.

Was that a step I wanted to take? After reading my file, I'd realized that Omnistellar wasn't the beacon of civilization it claimed to be. I knew I'd already sacrificed my citizenship with them, and probably in any corporation. But if I threw in with the prisoners, who did that make me? I would have committed the ultimate treason, and there would be nothing left of the person I knew.

Of course, in the eyes of the law, I'd pretty much done that already. And I didn't have time to waste with Kristin and her pals tripping me whenever I walked by. Besides, Omnistellar had threatened me with imprisonment when I was a mere child. They'd drilled my mother until she was willing to kill me rather than betray them. I grabbed Cage's hand, and he caught my elbow, then lifted me onto the table without jostling my injuries.

The murmur from the crowd became a growl.

He raised his hand, positioning me in front of him so they couldn't miss the bandage on my arm. "Enough," he said. "She's one of us."

That stopped them, all right. I didn't exactly sense a wave of warmth and acceptance, though—more like tentative confusion. I took advantage of the lull to chime in. "It's true. I didn't know it myself until an hour ago, but I had a chip in my arm, just like you. And now . . . well, now I don't."

"More importantly," Cage called, stalking up beside me, "we aren't alone on this station. I know rumor has it other prison sectors are empty, the prisoners are missing. Well, that rumor's true. Some of you have talked to Anya there." He nodded to where she sat huddled against the wall, one of the older girls beside her. "And you may have dismissed her story as hallucinations, the result of trauma. I know I did."

He faltered, and I covered. "But it isn't. It's true. There's something on this station—more than one, actually. And if there's a better word to describe it than 'monster,' I haven't found it."

Stunned silence met that announcement. Kristin recovered her voice first. "Right. There's a scary monster running around the station, so we all have to stay here. What'd you do? Drug Cage so he'd hallucinate? Use a VR sim? Because I'm not buying this *monster* for a minute."

"You think we all hallucinated?" Matt called from the background. Rune caught his arm and tried to tug him back, but he gently pushed her aside and jumped onto the table beside Cage. The two boys bumped fists without even looking, and Matt continued: "Because I saw it too, and let me tell you, it was a pretty damn vivid 'hallucination.'"

Kristin snorted. "So if these things are so vicious, how come you're all still standing?"

"Are we?"

I spun. Mia was back, leaning against the wall, Alexei behind her. He met Cage's gaze and shrugged helplessly.

Mia pulled her shirt over her head, leaving her in a plain white bra and catching the interest of most of the room. Their attention shifted quickly, though, when she unwound her bandages to reveal the gaping claw marks scoring her abdomen. Cage's hasty and messy stitches had done nothing to make the wound less horrifying.

A collective gasp went up, and Mia hopped onto a chair, wincing at the movement. "Take a long look," she invited. "That creature did this in about three seconds. Cage and Kenzie scared it off, or it would have gored me." She reached into a pocket and produced the claw. She must have grabbed it off the medical tray when I wasn't looking. "Does that look like a bloody hallucination to you?"

A murmur went up at the sight. Mia swayed but caught herself. Alexei leaped forward and steadied her from behind, and she swatted his hand away. "If you really think this is some elaborate scam, all I have to say is, don't expect me to save you from your own stupidity." She stared straight at Kristin when she said it, holding her head high until the other girl backed down.

Mia's dramatic display accomplished what Cage and I hadn't, and a frightened hush fell over the crowd. A scowling Alexei helped Mia off the chair and back into her shirt.

One of the other kids piped up. "You knew these . . . these *things* were on the station and you just left us here?"

"We *didn't* know before," Cage replied. "Besides, you were as safe here as anywhere—safer, frankly. My guess is that they came in through sector four and worked their way up, not realizing we were right beneath their feet. But they will. I guarantee it. They're smarter than they look, and they're not here to make friends. But I can give you one bit of good news: we have a way off this station."

This time, a thrill of excitement laced the crowd's nervous fear. I couldn't blame them—after years in prison, some of them probably for no crime other than existing, the possibility of escape overshadowed the threat of aliens.

"Look, you have to be quiet!" I shouted. It was kind of contradictory, but it worked. Their voices dropped. "So far, we've been lucky. But we don't think those things can see, which means they hunt by sound. You get what I'm saying? The quieter we stay, the less likely they are to notice us. And trust me, you *don't* want them to notice us."

Silence fell, and Cage seized the opportunity. "There's a shuttle. It won't carry us all in one go, and Kenzie's the only one who knows how to operate it." I blinked—I hadn't told him I could pilot. But of course, he read it in my file. I wondered how many of my skills factored into their original plan. If Mom had backed down, would I have become their pilot?

"What do you need from us, Cage?" called a boy at the back of the room.

Cage cast him a grateful look. "Quiet," he said. "Quiet and patience. We need to leave you here one more time while we check on the shuttle. Then we'll transport as many of you as we can to . . ." His face blanked, but he barely missed a beat, finishing smoothly, "To safety before we return for the rest."

Cage glanced at me, then at the crowd. He pulled me more tightly against him, his grip burning my goose-bumped flesh, giving me his warmth, his security—and making his allegiance clear to the prisoners. "Thank you," he said to them, his voice softer. They leaned in to listen. "I know this hasn't gone according to plan, and I know I've asked a lot from all of you. I'm asking for just a bit more. I swear to you: I'll get you to safety or die trying."

He got an appreciative murmur as he turned back toward the server room, jumped from the table, and held out his hand. I understood he was offering a show of solidarity more than physical assistance, and I slid my fingers through his, stepping down to join him. With a grin, he extended his other hand to

Matt, who chuckled and accepted the offer. His laugh seemed to lighten the mood in the room, and it was like a physical veil of tension lifted from the crowd at our backs.

Cage nodded at Rune, and they set off for the server room. He still had my hand, so apparently I was going with them. I noticed he wasn't squeezing Matt's fingers any longer.

We entered the cramped space, which didn't get any bigger when Tyler, Matt, Mia, and Alexei shoved in behind us.

Cage kicked the door closed. He ran his fingers through his hair, leaving it standing on end. "Thanks, Mia," he said. "If you hadn't stepped in . . ."

"They're all fired up," she said, slumping against a console and closing her eyes. A second later she shook her head and fixed everyone with a furious glare, like we'd somehow been spying on her moment of weakness.

"You can't blame them," Rune said. She glanced at Matt and frowned. "Everyone's scared. Cage, Kenzie . . . do you really have a way off this station?"

Cage smiled at her affectionately. "Would I lie about that, *meimei*?"

"Probably. Yes."

"We have a way, but it's not going to be easy," I interjected. "It'll take at least two trips." *And I don't know where we're going.* Back to Earth, I supposed. It wasn't a great option, but as Cage said, it was better than being eaten by space monsters. "I need to reach the shuttle and see if it's fueled and intact—Rita didn't exactly have time to tell me before . . ." My voice caught in my throat, and Cage steadied me with a hand on my elbow. The others exchanged mystified glances, but I didn't feel like going over the details at the moment, so I said, "Anyway, we should get going. The sooner, the better." *And once I get you to safety, I'm going to find Mom,* I added silently. But I wasn't sure how Mia would respond to that, so I kept it to myself.

Cage nodded. "The creatures don't seem to like electricity. I think we should leave one of the stun guns, and you and I can take the other."

I didn't love the idea of us only having one gun, but I got it—otherwise, we left everyone unprotected. "Great. You can leave yours," I said.

Cage grinned, checked the safety, and passed it to Alexei. "You know how to use it?"

"*I* do," Mia snapped.

"Yeah, but I'd rather give it to someone not in danger of passing out at any second. No offense."

Alexei nodded. "Mia's the crack shot, but I'll handle it."

"Oh, will you?" Mia twisted to glare at him, and froze with a grimace of pain. Instantly, Alexei was at her side, supporting her. She folded into his arms and rested against his shoulder, her eyes closed and her teeth sunk into her bottom lip so far I was surprised she didn't draw blood. "Okay," she ground out at last. "I get your point."

"Good," said Cage dryly. "Maybe now you'll sit the hell

down before you tear your stitches. Rune, I'll need you on the computer. Have you had any luck scanning for those things?"

She shook her head. "They don't register as alive. The bioscanner is useless."

"What about the station's defenses? The turrets?" I asked.

"I can activate them, but without the chips to target, they're . . . imprecise. They spray bullets everywhere. The way those things move, I'd probably hit one of you before a creature."

I racked my brain for anything to make this job a little less . . . what was the word?

Oh yeah. *Impossible.*

Then I remembered. "Where's my comm unit?"

Cage blinked. "Your what?"

"My comm unit. You popped it out of my wrist when we first met." I indicated the empty slot where it should rest. "Give me that, and we can talk to Rune from anywhere on Sanctuary."

"Good thinking," he said, then reached into his pocket and produced the slim metal circle. He tossed it to me, and I slid it into place. The familiar click sent a rush of peace through me—I'd worn the comm so long I felt empty without it. A quick check of my battery revealed a half charge remaining, more than enough to finish the job. Unread messages scrolled past my eyes: three from Dad, one from Noah . . . and twelve from Mom. A quick glance at the time told me they'd all been sent in the hour after I went missing. Swallowing the lump in my throat, I set them aside.

"One more thing," I said. "Matt . . . would you come with us? You at least got a sense of where they were and when they were nearby."

Rune reached for him, then checked herself. "Yes," she said, although she didn't sound convinced. "That's a good idea. You can keep them safe."

Matt shook his head dubiously. "I can try," he said. "I didn't sense much of anything before, though, so I don't know how much use I'll be."

"Even if you can't find the creatures, maybe you can help us locate the rest of the prisoners." *Or my mother.*

Cage caught my eye and nodded, following my train of thought. "I'd appreciate having you nearby," he said to Matt, meeting the other boy's eyes.

Matt smiled, the lines on his forehead softening, and the tension that had appeared between them back in the med facility faded away. "Whatever I can do to help," he agreed.

"Just like always," Cage chuckled.

"Sounds like a plan." Mia rubbed her hand across the back of her neck. "And if you lot get yourselves killed? What then?"

"I can pilot the shuttle," Rune volunteered timidly. "At least, I can access the operator's manual. I might even be able to interact with the controls directly."

Cage nodded. "Good. We'll—"

Rune's voice sharpened. "I wasn't finished. I was going to say that I could probably figure it out, but I won't have to, because you *are* coming back, *gege*. And Matt with you."

"Thanks," I said dryly.

Rune punched me in the shoulder with surprising strength. My eyes widened, my fists clenching instinctively, but before I could react, she threw an arm around me in half a hug. "You're *all* coming back. That's an order. You hear me?"

"Yes, ma'am." Cage pulled her out of my arms and into his own for long enough to drop a kiss on top of her head. "Stay with Mia and Alexei. Tyler, you too. We'll be back soon." He glanced at me. "No point putting it off. You ready?"

I nodded. "Let's go. We'll—"

"Wait," said Matt, his face screwed up in concentration.

Something thudded overhead.

The entire group froze, staring at the ceiling panels. "Matt?" whispered Cage, barely audible.

He shook his head, backing Rune toward the console. At the same moment, the panel shattered on the ground, and one of the creatures dropped into the room.

TWENTY-THREE

THE ALIEN SNIFFED THE AIR, ITS JAW WORKING furiously. There was no way to avoid it in this tiny, cramped space, no matter how still and quiet we stayed. If it reached out, its claws would graze Rune's shoulder.

Cage could escape and take one of us with him. But the rest . . . What good was invisibility or the ability to understand freaking Mandarin against a space monster?

So far the creature wasn't moving—because it was *listening*. Waiting for us to make the first move?

I slid my hand to my waistband and nudged the holster of my stun gun aside with agonizing slowness, sliding my fingers around the trigger and easing it into my hand. Alexei caught my eye and shook his head.

Alexei. Of course. His power.

Fire.

If electricity bothered them, fire might too. The only problem was that Rune, Cage, Matt, and I stood directly in his path.

Rune had caught the glance too. She gestured at the consoles, her meaning clear: Fry the electronics, and who knows what kind of damage you'll do? It was a valid concern. If we damaged Sanctuary badly enough, it might block me from launching the shuttle.

There was some kind of frantic unspoken conversation going on in the room, the tension palpable, and still the creature hadn't moved. The next thing we knew, its neck craned upward. It bent its powerful hind legs and launched itself into the ceiling.

I was the first to recover my composure. My eyes glued to the hole where the ceiling panel had been, I backed toward the door but bumped into Alexei, who automatically steadied me, then tucked me behind him and gestured the others forward. No one argued, not even Mia—if that thing burst through the ceiling, we needed Alexei front and center. If it came to a choice between saving the electronics and saving myself, I knew which way I leaned.

We reached the main area without incident, and Alexei slid the door shut behind us. "Well," said Cage dryly, "I think our respite is over."

"But it left," Rune pointed out. "Why would it leave if it knew we were here? We were quiet. Maybe it didn't hear us. Maybe it was just checking the room and—"

"They don't just check things," I said. "Trust me." I couldn't explain why the creature hadn't attacked. Maybe it went for reinforcements. But whatever the reason, it spelled trouble. "Cage, we need to move everyone out of sector five. I don't know what that was, but I don't like it."

He nodded in agreement. "But move *where*?"

"Sector four," said Mia, her arms folded over her chest.

"Four? You mean where all of this started?"

"That's exactly what I mean. If they came in through four—breached the hull and did whatever they did to the prisoners—they're less likely to check it a second time. We move everyone up there and keep them quiet. That'll be the hard part." She shook her head, then brightened. "Unless we leave Kristin behind."

"Mia," Rune reproached softly.

She shrugged. "Fine. If she gets too loud, I'll knock her out."

"I have another idea," said Rune hesitantly. "But you're not going to like it."

"Well, that's a ringing endorsement." Cage sagged against the wall, running his hands through his hair again. "I haven't liked much of anything that's happened today, *meimei*, so let's hear it."

Rune shrugged. "I can activate emergency lockdown."

"No." Mia leveled an accusing finger in her direction. "Not a chance in hell."

"What's emergency lockdown?" I demanded. I'd thought I knew everything about Sanctuary. Apparently not.

"Emergency lockdown," Matt replied grimly, "is when the

prison electrifies the floors. Anyone seated on their cot is safe. The rest of the prison becomes one huge electrical conduit. It's not a strong enough jolt to kill you, but if you get stuck there, with electricity coursing through you, well . . ."

"So the floors are completely electrified," I said. "And that means if the creatures burst through the ceiling . . ."

"They get zapped," finished Rune. "Yes. The only catch is that none of *us* can leave our cots."

"What about you?"

Another shrug. "I'll be okay if I bond deeply enough with the system." She caught my look of confusion and elaborated. "I can skim the surface, or I can go deep. You've seen me do both. If I totally immerse myself in Sanctuary's AI, I can control almost anything—including which rooms the lockdown affects. I'll just leave the server room out of it."

"Yeah, great—unless the creature drops in there," Cage pointed out. "Which is exactly what it did a few seconds ago."

Rune frowned. "True. Well. We can drag one of the cots up to the console."

"If you're trying to avoid contact with the floor, couldn't you sit on the chair and fold your legs up?" I offered.

"I think the cots are made of a specific material, or contain a signal to block the jolt. Mia tried staying on the couch in the rec area one time and almost got herself killed."

Mia grimaced. "Not my brightest moment, but I wanted to see if it would work. Fortunately it was only a drill. Over in seconds, not that it felt like it. I got burned so badly they had to call an actual human to take a look at me." I hadn't seen anything about that in her file. My expression must have reflected my horror, because she rolled her eyes and continued: "I spent a couple days in bed and I was none the worse for wear. Which doesn't distract me from what an incredibly stupid idea this is." She ticked off points on her fingers. "One, we'll all be completely helpless. If one of those things lands on a cot instead of the floor, it'll eat us alive while everyone else watches. Two, as we just saw, they can jump from the floor to the ceiling. What'll stop them from doing that as soon as they get the first jolt?"

"At least they won't be—"

"*Three*, they're smarter than they look. They'll hear us shuffling around on our cots and realize they're not electrified. The next thing we know, they'll land on top of us."

"I can end the lockdown if that happens—"

"*Four*," Mia interrupted, glaring at Rune, "what if one of them lands behind you and gets in a good swipe before the electricity kicks in? We could be stuck in lockdown mode— completely trapped with no way to end it while they pick us off one by one."

We all exchanged helpless looks. Mia wasn't exactly wrong. But still . . . "I think it's the best chance you have of protecting yourselves," I said. "If you drag a cot into the server room for Rune, and maybe one nearby for Alexei so he can target as wide an area as possible—"

Mia kicked the wall so hard something snapped. Rune and Matt sucked in gasps of air, and Alexei grumbled in Russian. He reached for her hand, but she shoved him away. "So that's it?" she demanded, her voice rising to a dangerous level. "After all this, we're going to walk back into our cells and *voluntarily imprison ourselves again*? This time with a couple of bloody space monsters running around?"

"Mia, please be quiet," Rune whispered, with a panicked glance at the ceiling.

We'd drawn attention from other areas of the prison too. Other prisoners were glancing at us from beneath lowered lids, reluctant to stare outright but obviously curious. Mia closed her eyes, visibly bringing herself under control, then stalked off toward the cells. "Do what you want," she tossed over her shoulder.

Rune took a step in pursuit, her face a picture of misery. "Mia, where are you going?"

"Back to my cell," she said. "The same one I've lived in every day for the past three years."

"I didn't mean . . ."

"We know you didn't." Cage hugged Rune tightly. "And this plan puts you in as much danger as anyone. But without it, we're leaving you here defenseless. . . ." He glanced at Alexei. "Well, more or less."

Alexei nodded. "We'll get everyone up to sector four, and I'll move cots for me, for Rune, and for Mia."

"Mia?"

"I won't leave her alone. And she'll do better in the common area than a cell." Alexei glanced at me. "Mia is not a fan of enclosed spaces. Prison has been . . . difficult for her."

I winced, the accusation in his tone grating against me. But Sanctuary wasn't my design, and I couldn't keep taking responsibility for everything that happened here. I straightened my back and met his eyes. "Then you'd better get ready."

It only took a few minutes to put Rune's plan into motion. The other prisoners weren't much happier about the idea of huddling in cells than Mia, but they more readily accepted the necessity. Before long, everyone shuffled up to sector 4—after Cage, Matt, and I checked to make sure no aliens lurked there, waiting—and took up residence in the cells. "I think we're ready," Cage said. "Where's Matt?"

I shrugged. "Last time I saw him, he was ducking into the server room with Rune."

Cage groaned. "Of all the times . . . Matt!"

"I'm right here." Matt rounded the corner, Rune on his heels, a smile playing on her lips.

She gave everyone a quick hug, even me. "Stay with Alexei," Cage reminded her.

Rune rolled her eyes. *"Hǎo, gege."*

He flicked her cheek affectionately and she snapped at his fingers like a puppy. They exchanged grins, but hers lasted a moment longer when her gaze landed on Matt. "Quiet," he whispered, pointing at me as we slid into step behind Cage.

I assumed a look of innocence. "I didn't say a word."

"Uh-huh." But he was smiling too.

Smiles didn't last long after we entered the corridor. We took the steps as quickly and quietly as possible. "Matt?" Cage asked every few seconds, and Matt responded with a frustrated "I don't know! Nothing? Nothing. I think." Every exchange set my heart thrumming a bit faster, my hands trembling on the stair rail.

My mind raced. I had to get everyone off this station, and I had to do it fast. But Mom was still somewhere on board. Not to mention all of the missing prisoners. Where the hell were they? This wasn't exactly a big place. Not counting the prison levels, which we'd already explored, you could loop the station in five minutes.

A ceiling panel caught my eye. Movement?

No. My imagination.

The creatures weren't skulking around in the air vents. They wouldn't fit well, and their weird backward-flexing legs weren't made for crawling. But they definitely used the ceilings to travel between levels. Reinforced steel crisscrossed the ceiling panels in the prison levels, but that didn't mean much to creatures whose claws could rip through Sanctuary's hull. Was it possible they used the vents or the empty space between the drop ceilings and next floor above as some sort of . . . storage?

Oh God. The image rising in my mind made my stomach

clench. I stopped and leaned against the wall for support, and Cage caught my shoulders. "Kenz. You okay?"

I nodded, then told them what I suspected.

Both boys stared suspiciously at the ceiling. "How the hell do we find out?" Cage muttered. "Matt? Anything?"

Matt closed his eyes, his forehead wrinkling with effort. "Nothing," he said at last. "But . . . Kenzie . . . I don't know how to say this. I've been searching for signs of life since we left the prison level and I haven't found any. Us, of course, and I'm vaguely aware of everyone back in four. Otherwise, it's just that weird feeling I sometimes get when *they're* around. Nothing else."

"It doesn't matter," I replied, more sharply than I'd intended. "You said yourself there's a ton of things that interfere with your abilities. Emotional turmoil, right? I bet Mom's feeling pretty messed up at the moment. And that's if she's even conscious." He nodded but didn't meet my eyes, and somehow that made me angrier than anything in the last few hours. "She's *alive*, Matt. And I'm not leaving this station until I find her." As I said it, I realized the words were true. Part of me wanted Mom to suffer for betraying me—not at the aliens' claws, of course, but to know the same agony of learning someone you loved was no longer on your side. But I couldn't afford to be petty where her life was concerned. However Mom betrayed me, I was different from her. I made my own choices, and one of those choices was not to leave her behind.

And yet . . . there were fifteen people down in four. *They* were alive, and I didn't know how much longer they'd stay that way. Without me to pilot the shuttle, probably not long. And that made them, first and foremost, my responsibility.

And not because I was an Omnistellar guard. Not because I was like them, an anomaly. Just because I was me. I might have fallen down seven times, but I would get up eight. "I know there's a chance she's . . ." I trailed off, unable to get the word out. "But I won't believe that until I have to. You don't have to worry. You guys are my priority right now, getting you off Sanctuary. But after . . . I'm coming back to find Mom."

Cage nodded. "I'll be with you," he promised.

No. He wouldn't. I wasn't taking anyone else into danger once I got them off the station. But I didn't need to tell him just yet. Instead I turned and hugged him, a full-on rib-cracking embrace. For a second Cage hesitated, and then his arms came around me, pulling me against him. "Thanks," I said.

Matt coughed loudly. "Should I go around the corner?" he asked. "Give you guys some space?"

I smothered a totally inappropriate grin, broke free, and swiped my thumb to unlock the prison door. From there it was only a few hundred feet to the shuttle bay.

Breathing a sigh of relief, I jogged forward. The shuttle bay had one of the only doors on Sanctuary with a window to allow someone to witness the docking procedure and give visual confirmation when it was safe to enter. The console showed a secure airlock, and inside I saw Rita's shuttle cleanly—if hastily—docked in the bay. "That's it," I said. "Everything looks good. Let me run a quick check on the shuttle and we can collect the first load."

I reached for the door panel, but something stopped me from scanning my thumb. Movement from the corner of my eye? I hesitated.

"Kenzie?" Cage asked.

"Yeah, I . . . Hang on a sec." I leaned against the door, peering through the window, examining every corner of the shuttle dock.

And suddenly one of the creatures stared back at me.

TWENTY-FOUR

IT THREW ITSELF AGAINST THE WINDOW inches from my face. I screamed, recoiling, and the creature roared in response. If it hadn't been aware of me before, it sure as hell was now. "How'd it get in there?" I shouted, grappling for Cage's hand. He squeezed in return, steadying me.

"The same way it gets anywhere," Matt replied.

I shook my head frantically. "Not the shuttle bay. That's a potentially sealed airlock. There are no maintenance hatches or ceiling panels, and it's on its own ventilation system. If it just clawed its way inside like in sector four, we'd see the damage. I don't see any holes in the walls, do you? So where did it come from?"

The creature howled, the thick door diminishing its screams. It pounded on the glass. The three of us flinched away, but that glass could withstand a botched shuttle entry. It easily held up to the monster's pounding. I had no doubt that the aliens could breach a normal window, but the specially formulated glass was a different story. Without somewhere for its claws to find purchase, they skidded against it.

All at once, the alien seemed to give up. It retreated, its tongue snaking from its mouth, dabbing at its fangs. I couldn't hear, but it looked like it might have hissed.

We charged for the window. Of course Cage got there first, but I elbowed my way in front of him. The creature stalked to the shuttle. For a being without sight, it moved with unerring accuracy.

My heart caught in my throat when it raked its claws lightly over the shuttle's hull, almost a caress. "No," I whispered.

Cage shook his head. "There's no way it can break through a shuttle hull," he said. "Can it?"

"It got onto Sanctuary somehow," Matt pointed out. "I'm guessing through that hole in four. So if it can smash through Sanctuary's hull? Yeah, I'm guessing the shuttle won't cause much of a problem."

Helpless, we watched the creature press against the shuttle, experimentally probing the hull's strength.

It turned and stared at us with its unseeing eyes, and for the first time I became aware of a keen, malevolent intelligence lurking there. It cleared any lingering doubts: these were *not* animals. They thought and planned and strategized—maybe as much as we did.

Maybe more.

Without looking away, the creature poked the shuttle with a long-clawed finger.

"How did it know we were here?" Matt whispered.

"It might have heard us approach," I replied. "After which my screaming probably clued it in."

The creature slashed viciously at the shuttle. I winced at the screech of rending metal, even though no sound actually escaped the bay. "Cage," I said desperately.

He clutched at the doorframe, his knuckles white, and shook his head. I turned to Matt, but I could tell he didn't have any more ideas than I did. Could I get the door open and shoot it with the stun gun? Would I have time? Or would it attack, dodging my shot, and destroy everyone in the blink of an eye? If it had been just me, I might have risked it, but with everyone depending on me—not to mention Mom—I held back

The creature ripped into the shuttle. This time great gaps appeared in the hull. Tears flooded my eyes, blinding me. That shuttle would never fly again. The aliens had well and truly trapped us.

Cage took my elbow in one hand, Matt's in the other, and pulled us in the opposite direction. "Come on," he murmured. "Let's get out of here before that thing finishes with the shuttle and rips through the door."

I closed my eyes and let him lead me away. He was right, of

course—but still, deserting the shuttle bay felt like abandoning our only hope.

"What do we do now?" Matt whispered.

"Command center," I replied, forcing my voice steady. "It's the only place I might accomplish something." I glanced at Cage. "We have no choice now but to contact Earth. You know that, right? Whatever's waiting for you, it can't be worse than what's here."

Matt snorted. "What's waiting for *us*? Kenzie, have you taken a look at your arm lately? You chopped out your chip just like everyone else. Don't kid yourself: the company will know what that bandage means. If we go to prison, you come with us."

I'd known violating Omnistellar regulations would get me fired, ruin my future, and I'd given lip service to the idea of prison. But I hadn't seriously considered this before. Matt was right. I was a company traitor, a vile and ungrateful turncoat destined for a sentence on a penal colony.

Was that what my parents wanted to protect me from when they sent me away and dumped a chip in my arm? Would I ever get the chance to ask them?

I shook my head. The two boys stared at me, Matt with a hint of challenge, Cage with pity. I didn't know which was worse. "It doesn't matter," I said, surprised at my firmness. But then, I'd given up on Omnistellar a while ago. Now more than ever, I really was Robo Mecha Dream Girl. "Either way, we can't stay here. The shuttles are gone, and those things are all over the station. We have to contact Earth, which means we have to get to the command center." For good measure, I smacked Cage in the chest. "And stop looking at me like that."

He broke into his more characteristic grin. "All right," he said. "Let's get moving. Matt . . ."

Matt shook his head, his jaw set in frustration. "I'll come with you, but I'm useless. I didn't sense that creature until it popped up in the window. Apparently my abilities are limited to humans."

"You sensed something in the prison," I pointed out.

"Okay, fine. My abilities are limited to humans, with a rare glimmer of a split-second warning included for aliens. Still not useful."

"You're too hard on yourself," Cage said with surprising gentleness. Matt scowled, clearly unhappy, but he acknowledged Cage with a nod.

"Well, you can help just the same," I pointed out. "Look for human life signs. Look for the other prisoners." *Look for my mom.* I didn't say it, but it hovered on my tongue, a bitter tang begging to be spit out.

Cage heard it and slid his hand against the small of my back. Matt only sighed.

Keeping our steps light and careful, we ran in the direction of the command center.

Amazingly, we arrived without another alien encounter.

How did they actually hunt? We often spotted the creatures alone, but it seemed like every time we encountered one, another lurked in the shadows. Did they hunt as partners—in teams?

How many aliens were on this station?

Mom's congealing coffee still sat by the command chair. Hard to believe it was less than twenty-four hours since I'd been taken captive. I swallowed the lump in my throat, focusing on the computers. When Sanctuary went into lockdown, the shutters slid over all the windows. High on my list of priorities: get them up. If more creatures hovered outside, searching for ways to blow holes in our hull, I wanted to see them. I didn't know what we could actually *do* about them if we did see them—Sanctuary's weapons all aimed inward—but I hated working blind.

First things first, though: I connected to Rune in the prison. Everything was fine, according to her, but her voice carried an edge of strain. By the tight cording of muscles on Cage's arms, I could tell he caught it too, but he kept his response light. "She's okay," I said after I disconnected.

"I know." He rubbed his hand across his forehead, easing the lines there. "I want her off this station. I want *everyone* off this station."

"I'm right there with you," I agreed, pulling up the next screen. I'd asked Rune to drop any shielding she maintained on the system, so that I had full control of Sanctuary again, not that it did much good. I could track the prisoners who hadn't removed their chips, but the aliens hadn't been helpful enough to install any in themselves before invading my home. And according to Sanctuary, the only prisoners remaining on the station huddled in sector 4.

Without Rune's intrusion, I should have had full communications access, but I didn't. I got the exact same interference when I tried to call Earth now as I did when Rita and I picked up what we thought was a distress call yesterday. "It's not Rune," I said out loud.

"What?"

I shook my head. "It's not Rune interrupting our comms."

Matt leaned against the wall, his lips pursed. "She also didn't manufacture the signal your friend investigated. Something else is going on."

I stared at the screen for a long moment. Next logical step: get the shutters up. But something inside me argued against it. Right now, my imagination filled in terrifying details about what lurked outside. What if the reality was worse?

Setting my jaw, I plugged in the code to reset the system after an alert triggered the lockdown. The lights in the command center flickered briefly, and the motors in the window shutters roared to life. As an afterthought, I killed the primary lights in the command center—not that the aliens could see in, even if they floated right outside, but it made me feel better. Safer. More hidden.

I wasn't sure what I expected. The normal expanse of space, with Earth majestic below? A sea of space monsters converging on Sanctuary? Maybe even the lifeless bodies of the prisoners drifting forever in space?

Inch by agonizing inch, the shutters slid up. My mood must have spread because Matt and Cage halted their conversation and came to stand by my side. Tension rolled off us, suffusing the air.

Outside, stars speckled the sky, more brilliant than ever with the command center lights dimmed. As I'd predicted, we were angled the right way to see Earth stretched below us. But neither of those sights drew our eyes.

It was the massive ship stationed between us and the planet that caught our attention.

TWENTY-FIVE

CAGE CHOKED ON HIS OWN BREATH, AND MATT surreptitiously made the sign of the cross. I closed my eyes in defeat. The ship was huge, easily three times the size of Sanctuary. "How did Rita miss this?" I said hollowly, and then answered my own question. "The same way they disabled our sensors and lured us off the station. They blocked her sensors. They damaged her shuttle. She was flying blind." I wondered if the alien got into the shuttle bay by hitching a ride on Rita's shuttle without her knowledge. It would explain how it entered a sealed room.

Cage shivered. "If they see us as a . . ." He swallowed, hard, obviously forcing himself to go on. "As a *food source*, it was like a buffet table lined up and waiting to happen. They lured you off the station, blocked your comms, and got close enough to gain entrance without you noticing."

I shook my head. "But *why*? They're too strong. They had to know we couldn't stand against them. Why not just storm the station and kill us? Why the games?"

"I'm not an alien shrink, Kenz. I'm guessing, same as you."

I shot him a glare, but he was frustrated, not condescending. And so was I. Who knew how many of them lurked in the ship outside? Their technology—their thinking—existed completely beyond my comprehension.

Take the ship. While our ships tended to be sleek metal bearing fresh coats of paint, this looked like it was made of black blocky plastic. It resembled nothing so much as something my little cousins built out of LEGOs, aerodynamics be damned. I couldn't conceive of a ship like that breaking planetary atmosphere.

"We're screwed," said Matt, eloquently summing up the situation.

I didn't want to agree with him. But we had no shuttles. No way off this ship. No way to contact Earth. No way to kill the aliens.

No way to do anything but die slowly at their claws.

Matt sank into a chair and dropped his head into his hands. Cage paced to the other side of the command center and hunched over a console, his arms held so tight his shoulder blades knifed under his shirt. And I stared dumbly through the window.

Where the hell had these things come from? What did they want?

Or, more terrifying: Did they want *anything at all?* Maybe they came to kill us, and didn't care about anything else—just planned to destroy us and take the planet. Maybe the probes all those years ago were nothing more than a way to scan our world for life, and if they found any, to bring the aliens.

How could we stop them?

And if we didn't stop them, what would they do next? Once they worked their way through Sanctuary, would they turn their sights to Earth? With no way for us to communicate with the planet, Dad might be its only hope. When he couldn't reach Sanctuary, couldn't reach *me*, hopefully he'd return with reinforcements, warn Earth, and save his own life.

Or get himself killed as the aliens started their destruction of the planet.

I gritted my teeth and stared at a corner of the room. No. I couldn't let that happen. Even if I couldn't save Sanctuary, there had to be a way to save Earth. But what could I do? We had no comms. No shuttle. No hope.

As if he'd read my mind, Matt asked softly, "Doesn't this station have an escape pod or anything?"

"Sure," I said. "It'll hold one person, and you can't launch unless you've triggered the self-destruct system." The boys stared at me blankly, and I laughed. "Omnistellar doesn't encourage leaving your post. If you're launching the escape pod, it's because things are so spectacularly messed up that only one guard survived, and they're coming home to report to central command."

Funny how that had seemed perfectly reasonable before.

It was an option, I supposed. Maybe the only one left. We could record a message explaining the situation and put someone—probably Anya—in the pod, activate the self-destruct, and launch.

And then what? The aliens almost certainly had weapons on that monstrosity of a ship. It was better than no chance at all, but it probably meant sentencing Anya to a terrifying death on her own, and Earth would be no safer at all. And of course, there was the fact that everyone on Sanctuary would die in a fiery explosion.

And then, all at once, it came to me. We *might* have a way to stop the aliens from targeting Earth.

But it was an awful, terrible idea. One I probably wouldn't survive.

My voice caught in my throat. Once I spoke, I'd be committed to this ridiculous plan. My brain knew what to do, but my body shut down, going into full denial.

Matt arched an eyebrow in my direction. "Kenzie?" he asked.

I realized I was leaning forward in my chair, gaze fixed on the ship outside, jaw locked so tightly it sent waves of pain radiating down my neck. "Okay," I managed. "Okay. So there's no way off this station, no way that doesn't involve killing everyone we leave behind. But there might be a way to save Earth."

"What?" Both boys shot to their feet, staring at me like I'd lost my mind.

"How?" Cage asked.

"The same way I planned to reach my mother after you guys trapped me by the prison." I nodded at the alien ship. "I go outside."

Stunned silence greeted my announcement. "Go *where?*" Cage demanded after several seconds.

"The alien ship. Where else?" They both started talking at once, and I held up my hands to deflect them. "Look, I'm not thrilled about it either. But it's that or sit around and wait for death. If we stay here, we die anyway, and Earth might die with us. If I go over to the alien ship, I can . . . I don't know. Find a way to sabotage it, maybe."

"And almost certainly get yourself killed," Cage snapped.

I winced. That was a possibility I'd been willfully ignoring. "There is that," I allowed, forcing myself to confront the idea. But in every manga I'd ever read, every fantasy I'd ever imagined, the odds had been worse than zero that the hero would survive, and yet somehow they always did. Maybe I'd manage to channel some of their luck. "I'm not quite as happy with how I've lived my life up to this point as I used to be," I said at last. "I'm not looking to die, but if I can save everyone on Earth, well . . . I'm willing to take the chance."

Matt shook his head. "This is the worst idea in a series of bad ideas. Starting with this entire escape plan," he added, glaring at Cage.

"Hey, my escape plan didn't invite aliens onto the station."

"That doesn't make it smart."

I got to my feet, but they didn't even seem to notice, continuing to argue over my head. I stomped my foot and stepped forward, backing them down as I fixed my attention on Cage. "I agree with Matt. Your plan was stupid. What's wrong with mine?"

His eyebrows shot up to his hairline. "Where should I start? For one thing, you don't even know if you can get *on* that ship. They tore a hole in our hull to gain access, remember? We don't know how they board. We don't even know if they need *oxygen*, which means they might not have airlocks. And if you *do* get on board, what then? There might be hundreds of the things. So you'll, what, tiptoe around and hope they don't notice you?"

"I didn't say it was a perfect plan, but it's the only one I've got. If you have a better idea, I'd love to hear it."

Cage's face twisted in what I was coming to recognize as resignation—albeit that special brand of Cage resignation, reserved for the most difficult decisions. I made things easy for him. "I don't need your permission. I'm going to the alien ship, and you can't stop me."

I really hoped he didn't call me on that. Cage was stronger than me, and he was sure as hell faster. He could absolutely stop me if he wanted to. I was just banking that he *wouldn't*.

"All right," he said at last. "But I'm going with you."

I rolled my eyes and his expression turned dangerous. "Sorry," I said. "But have you ever been in zero g before?"

"Actually, I have. Some of the operations we ran in Taipei were zero g. It's a common security feature with the bigger corps." He leveled me with a challenging stare. "Any other assumptions you want to make?"

Arguments taunted the tip of my tongue, but I bit them off. I read the resolve in his eyes; Cage wasn't letting me go on my own any more than I would have let him. We had enough XE suits—Cage would fit in Dad's easily enough. His speed would definitely come in handy, and I wasn't ashamed to admit I wanted the backup. I relented. "Okay. We'll go together. Just make sure Rune knows it wasn't my idea."

Matt nodded. "I'm no use to you, so I'll stay here. What can I do to help from the command center?"

"Stay in touch with Rune," Cage directed. "And hopefully with us. Let us know if anything changes. And don't get dead."

It was pretty simple as directives went. Matt almost smiled. "Can you show me how this stuff works?"

I ran a quick program, unlocking all of Sanctuary's systems in blatant defiance of security protocols. At this point, I almost gloried in the feeling of disobedience. "Everything's pretty straightforward and user friendly," I said, pulling up the most important things—primarily security and communications. "My personal comm unit should keep working unless something blocks the signal, and the XE suits each have their own. You can keep in constant contact with us. If we don't come back . . ." I hesitated. "Remember the escape pod?" I walked him through the steps to activate the self-destruct and launch the pod. It was a mark of how much I'd come to trust the prisoners that I gave him these directions. After all, Matt could just escape himself if he was willing to sacrifice the others. But somehow I knew he wouldn't.

Particularly with Rune back in the prison.

Sure enough, Matt scowled and shook his head. "I won't be doing that."

"If we don't come back, it'll be your only chance to save Earth. Stick Anya in there. Give her a chance. Send a message with her."

He hesitated a moment longer, then nodded, clearly unhappy. "And . . ." I hesitated before unholstering the stun gun at my side. "You'd better take this."

He raised an eyebrow, making no move to accept it. "I think you'll need it more than I will."

Somewhat guiltily, I started to return it to my side. He was right, but leaving him here defenseless felt wrong.

"With the kind of numbers we'll probably face on that ship, a single stun gun won't make a difference," Cage replied. "We're relying on speed and stealth, not weapons, and we can't leave you defenseless. Take the gun."

"Station defenses," I said suddenly. I leaned past Matt and pulled up the commands for the turrets in the hallway. A few minutes of fiddling with the code gave me control.

"Didn't Rune say those things would just spray bullets around?"

"Yes, but if there's anyone in that hallway other than you guys, I don't think sprayed bullets are going to be your problem. Use the turrets. Shoot anything that moves."

"Yeah? What if it's your mother?"

I winced at the thought but managed to keep my voice steady. "Then you'll sense her before you pull the trigger, right?"

Matt's hands shook pretty badly as he adjusted the gun controls, and the fear in his face seemed almost as bad as when he'd seen the creatures. I glanced at Cage. Was Matt going to be okay? The ashen pallor of his face made me question leaving him here at all, let alone giving him control of something as deadly as a station turret.

Cage slapped Matt on the shoulder hard enough to make me flinch. "You'll be fine," he said. "Just don't kill anything you recognize."

Somehow, the display of bravado seemed to steady Matt. He rolled his eyes, then pulled the code screen off the console and set it to the side, within easy reach. To my surprise, he stepped forward and hugged me, a quick, awkward embrace I barely had time to return. "Watch yourself," he muttered.

"You too," I said.

Cage nodded at me. "All right. So we get to these XE suits, wherever they are, without meeting the creatures, make our way to their ship, find a way on board, and then . . . ?"

"I haven't figured that part out yet." To be honest, I wasn't even sure we'd get that far. My only hope, the one line of reasoning I clutched like a lifeline, was that since the aliens didn't seem to walk through walls, there had to be a physical way on and off their ship. All we had to do was find it.

I led Cage out of the command center with a glance at Matt, who was hunched over the console, one finger twitching toward the turret controls. "Is he okay?"

"Yeah. He's uncomfortable around guns of any kind. When he was younger, someone shot up his school trying to weed out anomalies." Cage kept his expression carefully blank, his gaze on the far wall.

I blinked. "I didn't hear about that."

"You wouldn't," he replied dryly. "They keep anything involving anomalies quiet. You probably heard about the shooting, though, just not the cause. Nebraska. About six years ago."

I racked my memory. I did remember hearing about a school shooting, but not specific details. School shootings were rare enough to make big news, but I'd been pretty young at the time. "Will he be okay?" I repeated. Cage's new information did nothing to lessen my concerns.

"He's fine. I've known him quite a few years now, and he'll pull it together. He always does. Now, where are we headed?"

Good question. Most of the XE suits hung in the shuttle bay, but if the creature was trapped there? "Let's go through the initial airlock," I said at last. "We keep two suits there for sure." Not *my* suit, the one fitted to me, the one I'd practiced in. But really, an XE suit was an XE suit: a slightly bulky, uncomfort-able monstrosity that kept you alive in a vacuum.

This was actually happening. We were going outside, crossing a nightmare of deep space in hopes of breaching an alien ship. Cage tossed me a grin, and my own lips quirked in response. We might be foolish. We might even be going to our deaths.

But at least we were doing it together.

TWENTY-SIX

WE REACHED THE PRIMARY AIRLOCK WITHOUT incident, aside from the fact I almost chewed through the insides of my cheeks. My stomach hurt, my shoulders ached, even my jaw throbbed. Every rustle in the ceiling, every shudder through the station, sent us diving to the ground, where we crouched for several tension-filled seconds before resuming our trek. A few times I almost cracked and asked Cage to pick me up and whip us to our destination. But that might draw the aliens' attention, and besides, my pride wouldn't allow it. It was one thing if he grabbed me and whisked me off in an emergency; asking him to carry me around for convenience was another matter.

Cage stayed uncharacteristically quiet, probably as engaged in watching for movement as me. Or maybe he hated my plan too much to speak. I wouldn't blame him. I kind of hated my plan too, but what choice did I have? I still didn't know what had happened to Mom, and I'd lost Rita already. I wasn't going to lose Dad—not to mention my entire planet—too.

Upon reaching the airlock, we slowed as if by mutual design. I signaled Cage to wait on the other side of the door. He complied, and I tucked myself against the wall. If the creatures were in there, they'd hear the door, no question. I could only keep perfectly still and hope they charged by, giving us a precious few seconds to slip inside and close the door behind us. My fingers clenched convulsively around the stun gun. I didn't know if it would do much good against more than one alien, but at least it was something.

I scanned my thumb to open the inner airlock.

The door slid open with agonizing slowness. I held my breath, not moving a muscle, poised to respond if something crept, or burst, or lumbered through the opening. Across from me, Cage met my gaze with a steadiness belied by the tic at his throat, his fists clenched as he too poised for action—although without a weapon, he was even less prepared than I was.

Nothing happened.

I raised my eyebrow in question, and he nodded. I pointed to myself, to him, to the door—a *let me go first* gesture. Again Cage nodded.

Still, it took a moment to make my feet move. Conscious of Cage's eyes on me as much as anything else, I forced myself into the airlock.

It was empty—as empty as when I'd arrived on Sanctuary

three months ago. On my left were two lockers that I knew held XE suits and some emergency supplies. A computer console, a first aid kit, and a collapsible ladder occupied the area to my right.

I breathed a sigh of relief. We should be safe for the time being. This was a sealed room in case of some sort of airlock disaster; the only way in was through the doors.

Just like the shuttle bay. But I shook that thought aside. However the aliens got in there, it couldn't have been quiet. We should at least have advance warning if they decided to make an appearance.

Cage sagged in relief. "I hate this," he growled as the door slid shut, closing us in. "I hate not knowing where they are. I hate that they could drop on Rune at any second. I hate that I can't protect her—that I can't protect anyone."

"I know." I holstered the gun and opened a locker, then pulled down a helmet and pressed it into his hands. "So let's see if there's a way to stop them on their own ship."

He nodded, placed the helmet aside, and reached into the locker for the larger of the two suits. I watched the muscles in his arm tense, every tendon standing out in sharp relief, and I realized this might be the last time I saw him outside an XE suit. At any second, an alien might burst through that door and eat me alive. If we made it off the station and by some miracle actually got onto the ship, we would probably be killed before we came up with a way to destroy it. If I wanted to take a chance, I'd better do it now.

So I kissed him.

I snagged his arm, turned him to face me, and leaned in, catching his lips with my own. For a moment he stayed frozen against me, his entire body rigid. Then he took my shoulders and, very gently, pushed me away.

I recoiled, my face flaming. "Sorry," I muttered. "We'd better get moving."

"Kenzie, wait."

"It's fine," I said, frantic to forestall any explanation. I fumbled in a locker for the other XE suit and yanked it free of its moorings. It tangled on a hook, and I yanked at it until it wrenched free and clattered to the floor. Swearing, I dropped to my knees and hauled it the rest of the way out of the locker. Anything to keep my hands busy. "We won't even mention it. Let's just . . ."

"Kenzie, *wait*." He pulled me to my feet and spun me to face him. I stared at his chest. Dad's T-shirt was a little too small on him. "I didn't mean . . ." He ground his teeth in frustration. "Look, I'd have to be stupid not to be attracted to you. You get that, right?"

"Right," I said, anger surging in my chest. It gave me the courage to meet his eyes. "Because that's how boys *usually* respond to girls they're attracted to."

"It is if they're not sure the girl's really into them."

I gaped at him, and only barely managed to avoid shouting. "Cage, I *kissed* you. That's a pretty clear indication where

I come from. Not sure how it works in prison. Should I have punched you in the face or something?"

The corners of his lips quirked. "Sounds more like Mia's style than yours. No, it's not that. It's only . . . We barely know each other. I took you hostage and then we all got tossed into this stupid survival situation. Add in finding out about the chip in your arm, and . . ." He shrugged. "I don't want you to do anything you'll regret."

"Oh, shut up."

His eyes shot wide open. "Excuse me?"

"You heard me." I shook my head, relaxing in his grip. "I'm a big girl, Cage. I'm responsible for my own decisions. You're right, it's been a rough night—for both of us. It doesn't mean I don't know how I feel. I might not be an underground street criminal, but I'm not some naive little girl who's going to fall for the first bad boy who crosses her path. So if you're rejecting me out of some misplaced macho protective impulse, you can shove it. I know what I want. If you don't want it, well, that's another story. But don't stand there patronizing me like I'm some sort of princess who needs you to take care of her."

The last words had barely left my mouth before he shoved me against the wall, his mouth crashing down on mine. I grabbed his shoulders, pulling him closer, and his arms encircled me. One hand tangled in my hair; the other snaked around the small of my back, hauling me more tightly against him.

The kiss was fire and lightning arcing through me, my

skin burning and singed wherever he touched. I tugged at his shoulders, desperate to erase any distance between us, and he responded with a growl, pressing me more tightly against the wall. I gasped for air, turning my head aside. His lips fell to my neck, my shoulder, overwhelming my common sense.

I'd kissed plenty of boys—starting with another trainee the summer I was thirteen, and most recently my boyfriend on Earth, who I'd broken up with when we moved to Sanctuary. None of those kisses compared to this. They had been halting, nervous things, pleasant in their way but lacking the spark I'd been promised.

Kissing Cage struck a match to a fire waiting in my soul. I clamped my hands in his hair and pulled. He obliged, pressing his mouth to mine.

I didn't know how long it was before we finally broke apart, our breath mingling in short, frantic gasps. He tipped his head against mine, searching my eyes, his hand still tangled in my hair, an arm around my waist. I clung to his shoulders. We kept each other upright, afloat.

"I . . ." I licked my lips anxiously. "I guess that answers any question about who's attracted to who, huh?"

Cage laughed, the rumble making his chest vibrate against mine. "You are unbelievable."

"Am I? Why?"

"Well, for one, you're kissing me with aliens running around trying to eat us." He dropped a kiss on my forehead, lighter and softer than before, but it triggered the flame all the same. "For another, you're managing to crack jokes when I can barely think straight." Another kiss—this one on the bridge of my nose—and two more on my closed eyes. "Not to mention everything else I've seen you do in the last twenty-four hours. Yeah, Kenzie. 'Unbelievable' is definitely the word."

He drew me in again, and I wanted it, I did—so much I had to summon every ounce of my willpower to stop him. "Cage. We can't do this now."

He laughed again. "You started it."

"True." I brushed my fingers over his cheeks, admiring the way amusement lit up his eyes. "But those things aren't going to get bored and go away. If we have any hope of stopping them, we need to get moving."

Cage made a face, his breathing a little unsteady, and dropped his lips to mine, kissing me once more, thoroughly enough to make me question my resolve. "That sounds like an argument for continuing to me."

What the hell. If this was my last kiss, I meant to enjoy it. I grabbed the collar of his shirt, yanking him closer.

Something clattered in the distance. We froze, our faces inches apart, the spell broken. As much as I wanted this, I couldn't risk Earth's destruction because I was busy kissing a boy. "I was right the first time," I told him.

Cage closed his eyes in resignation and nodded. "Okay. Let's put more clothes *on*. That seems like a logical next step."

I grinned in spite of myself as Cage returned his attention to his XE suit. I stepped into its partner, then sealed patches and connected tubes, leaving my gloves for last. As always, a vague claustrophobia pulled at the edges of my senses when I sealed the helmet over my head, and as always, I fought it resolutely.

This thing with Cage—it was moving fast, most likely too fast. And he was right: a big part of what I was feeling was probably adrenaline and fear and just a need to remind myself I was alive. But I also hadn't imagined his kindness, his resolve, his spirit. Something in Cage called to me, and I really hoped I was going to get the chance to explore that something before my life ended in a flash of screams and claws.

My helmet display sprang to life, immediately running an autocheck and confirming that everything was, as Rita liked to say, copacetic. I glanced over to find Cage a few steps behind me, not quite as deft at sealing himself inside the XE suit, but capable. Hopefully that indicated enough experience in zero g for him not to become a liability outside.

I turned on my comm unit as soon as his suit lit up, indicating that he'd activated his own. "We have really limited thrusters," I told him. "You know how to use them?"

He nodded. "It's a different system, but it's pretty standard. I can figure it out." He looked at the display readout and frowned. "You aren't kidding when you say 'limited.'"

"It's not a jetpack."

"I'm used to more propulsion."

"Get unused to it." I stalked over and caught his elbows, meeting his eyes through his faceplate. "These suits are not designed for travel; they're for short emergency jaunts between shuttle and station, or to conduct exterior repairs. We need to drift as much as possible. Only use small bursts when absolutely necessary." I scrutinized him for another minute, then cursed under my breath. "We'd better tether together."

Cage scowled at me. "I'm not stupid, Kenzie. I know this isn't a joyride."

"I didn't mean that," I said, struggling to keep my voice patient. We needed to get moving before the aliens stumbled across us. "I'll just feel better knowing we're secured. That way if something does happen—if there's a malfunction, or one of us runs out of juice—we aren't totally screwed." I was only half lying. The chances of something going wrong with an XE suit were one in a thousand, but I didn't relish the idea of plummeting into Earth's atmosphere unprotected, or worse yet, drifting aimlessly until I suffocated.

I didn't wait for his agreement. I found a tether in the top of the locker and affixed it to the slot in my own suit before stretching it to Cage. He made a face at me but allowed me to fasten us together. "Okay," I said. "Let's do this."

I punched in my code, then set the computer to let us evacuate manually, and we plodded through the airlock door and sealed it in our wake. I always hated the few minutes of standing around while the airlock depressurized, although it was a great double check on your suit—any signs of trouble, and Sanctuary immediately repressurized the room. Still, I never quite trusted the system enough to relax. Cage and I stood shoulder to shoulder in the cramped area, my heart drumming in my ears, the expanse of space visible outside the porthole—and the weird, blocky alien ship marring it like a black hole. It was strange, being so close to him after the last few minutes and yet completely unable to touch him, to even see his face, with his helmet turned away from me.

"Depressurization achieved," announced Sanctuary in its pleasantly androgynous tone. "Airlock procedure complete in five . . . four . . . three . . . two . . . one . . ."

With a hiss, the door slid open. We jerked against the release, our magnetic boots keeping us stable. All other noise instantly faded into nothing, swallowed by the vacuum of space. My system monitor continued a steady, reassuring hum in my ears, and Cage's breath echoed over our active comms. But other than that, it was the stillest, most silent silence you'd ever hear—the utter absence of sound.

I wanted to take Cage's hand, but the bulky gloves prevented me. XE suits have come a long way since the days when they were made out of dryer tubing, but they're not the sleek armor you see in vids. I settled for coiling the tether around my arm, keeping us connected as we stepped to the doorway and pushed off into space.

That push propelled us toward the ship, albeit at an agonizing pace. As we approached, the ship grew rapidly, swallowing the entire Earth in its shadow. I risked a glance back. Sanctuary seemed small and helpless in the distance. A powerful longing welled in my heart for the time a few days before when Sanctuary was home to me, to my parents—when I knew my parents loved me and my future was secure. Now, nothing made sense anymore.

I returned my attention forward. We were on a collision course, but not fast enough to bother using the thrusters. We brushed against the ship. Its blocky surface provided plenty of handholds, and we clung there like bugs on a windshield.

I closed my eyes, settling myself. Part one was accomplished. Part two would be a lot more difficult. If we couldn't get onto this ship, we'd have to risk sending one person in the escape pod. I wasn't excited about that conversation. If Cage hated *this* idea, he'd really hate that one. Besides, frankly, if I was going to die, I'd rather do it trying to save Earth than huddling in Sanctuary, listening to the station count down the seconds to my death. Of course, dying wasn't exactly my Plan A either. "Well, we're here," I said, forcing brightness into my tone. "Now it's just a matter of finding a way in." *And*, I added silently, *saving our thrusters in case this is a useless endeavor.* Hitting the ship had been like hitting the side of a house. If we couldn't get into the alien ship and had to return, on the other hand, hitting the tiny door in Sanctuary's hull would take a lot more precision.

"Great," said Cage. He looked vaguely green.

I examined him with concern. "I thought you said you'd done this before."

"I have. I didn't say I *liked* it, though."

Terrific. "Don't puke," I commanded. "It's not fun."

"Yeah. I know."

From experience. He left it unsaid, but I heard it in his voice. Fan-freaking-tastic. "Do *not* puke," I repeated, as if the authority in my voice could calm his stomach. Cage only nodded. That would have to do. "Go as far as the tether allows and look for anything resembling a hatch."

Cage was clumsier in zero g than me, but he got himself moving in the right direction. I was confident enough to turn away and begin my own exploration.

It was futile. The ship looked even more like LEGOs up close: smooth, shiny, plastic, the shades of black not all uniform now that I was crawling over them. But LEGOs had visible seams. The ship's exterior was sleek and unmarred. It did have strange protuberances at odd angles, making it easy to climb along the ship's surface without using our thrusters. Any one of them could hide an entrance, I supposed, but I didn't know enough about alien technology to spot them. I didn't even see any windows. I guess blind aliens didn't need them.

The cord stretched taut between us, and I made my way back to Cage. He shook his head needlessly, and we crawled up the ship to start our search again.

We covered half the ship's surface before I began to despair.

Our oxygen was okay—we'd been out here thirty minutes, which left us at least ninety before we'd have to recharge. But all the oxygen in the world didn't help if we couldn't find a way onto the ship.

Something caught my eye, a tiny difference in one of the knobs lining the ship's hull? I pulled closer, reaching the end of my tether. "Cage," I said. "Come this way a bit, would you?"

"You find something?" he asked. The tension on the line went slack, and I crept forward.

"I don't know. Maybe." I tilted my head, scrutinizing the knob.

And then I had it. "Here!" I exclaimed as Cage hovered behind me.

He leaned past me as best he could in the bulky XE suit. "It looks like . . . claws?"

I nodded. There was an indentation in the knob, far too narrow for my gloved fingers. I fumbled through the tool kit at my waist and drew out a flat-head screwdriver. Other tools bobbed alongside my face, tethered to my kit, and I batted them away impatiently, then angled my screwdriver—a miniature for use in emergency repairs—into the slot. If it wasn't strong enough, we'd have to go back to Sanctuary for more appropriate tools. Hopefully not far, maybe not even beyond the airlock, but before I went to all that trouble . . .

I slid the flat edge under the knob and tugged. The screwdriver gave slightly beneath my hand. I glanced at Cage and shrugged. I wasn't strong enough to break the screwdriver off in the lock. If worse came to worst and I bent it, well, who cared? I shoved all of my weight behind the handle.

It gave way suddenly, the black plastic of the knob sliding like mercury into itself, remolding. The knob became a hole big enough to put my fist through, and continued to expand faster and faster, until it opened beneath my feet, leaving us staring into a pool of gaping darkness below.

I guess we'd found our way in.

TWENTY-SEVEN

I LANDED HEAVILY IN THE DARK. MY TEETH rattled and I froze, torn between risking my light and stumbling around blind. Cage settled behind me, and I made up my mind. These things couldn't see. It was our one, maybe our only, advantage.

I activated the light on my helmet and turned to Cage, who flinched at the sudden brightness. After angling the beam down, I showed him how to access the control panel on his wrist. He figured it out quickly, and soon his light joined mine, giving us our first real look at the enemy stronghold.

I don't know what I expected—walls dripping with blood, maybe, or some sort of horrifying nest. What I got was more of what I'd seen on the outside: slick black surfaces, these lacking the protrusions of the ship's exterior. We stood in an empty circular room with another strange doorknob on the wall. An airlock?

Behind us, the fluid door melded shut. Panicked, I angled my light upward, to find another claw-shaped indentation on its underside. I breathed a sigh of relief. It hadn't even occurred to me to wonder what the hell we'd do if we found ourselves trapped on the alien ship.

I checked the readings on my display. The oxygen steadily increased with the door closing, like atmosphere returning on Sanctuary. Maybe the creatures needed air after all. Maybe they reached Sanctuary in some sort of shuttle or space suit and cut through the hull after. Or maybe they could survive without air longer than us—but not indefinitely.

I watched my monitor with bated breath. If we couldn't breathe in here, we'd have to stomp around in loud, clunky XE suits, limited to ninety minutes of air. If we *could* . . .

Sure enough, within moments the air pressure and oxygen concentration in the room reached something approximating human normal. My sensors actually registered a little *more* oxygen in the air than Sanctuary allowed, and slightly lower gravity. But everything fell within human requirements.

Cage's gaze followed mine. "What do you think?" he murmured, quirking an eyebrow.

I shrugged. "It looks breathable." But what if it was a trick? Or some sort of sensor malfunction? What if we removed our helmets and found ourselves in a totally toxic atmosphere? "Maybe we should . . ."

I cut myself off when Cage reached up and twisted his helmet. "Wait!" I cried, grabbing at his hands.

He lifted it off, then tilted his head and sniffed the air. "I don't *feel* dead," he announced.

I closed my eyes at a rush of relief. "I hate you," I managed to say, and ignored his answering chuckle. I yanked off my gloves before going for my own helmet. A familiar rush of oxygenated air met my lungs. If there *was* a trick here, it was well hidden.

We stripped off our XE suits and were then faced with the somewhat problematic issue of what to do with them. If the aliens stumbled across them, they'd know we were here. Even if they didn't find us, they could tear our suits to shreds, leaving us no way to get back to Sanctuary. This could very quickly turn into a suicide mission.

Panic hit me in a rush as the reality of the situation set in. I'd talked a good game back on Sanctuary, secure and safe in the bright lights of the command center. But now, in murky darkness with maybe hundreds of those creatures lurking around every corner?

Cage reached out, his touch steadying me. "You okay?"

I swallowed. "Yeah, I'm fine." And more profoundly grateful than I could say to have him with me. I'd wanted to go alone. But it wouldn't have protected Cage to leave him behind, and I wasn't sure I could have managed this without him.

XE suits, I reminded myself. What to do with them? We

lacked a lot of convenient hiding places. In the end, we shoved them into a corner where no one was likely to trip over them. I took the screwdriver, a backup—the flat-head from Cage's tool belt—and a penlight, leaving the rest of my tools in a heap. I clutched the screwdriver in my left hand and settled the comforting weight of the stun gun in my right. It was an emergency measure only, since I was pretty sure the sound of it firing would alert any creatures on the ship. But I was glad to have it just the same.

I took a deep breath. "Into the belly of the beast," I muttered.

Cage grinned. "God, I hope not."

I laughed in spite of myself, a nervous giggle I quickly squelched. I reactivated my wrist comm. "Matt, it's Kenzie. Do you read?"

His voice crackled to life in my ear. "I'm here. Rune's online too." Oh, great. Of course he'd told Rune. I just hoped she didn't blame me. "Where are you? We lost sight of you a while ago."

"We're inside the ship."

"No way." That was Rune, disbelief and fear making her shriller than usual. "You're seriously in the ship? How'd you do it?"

"How about later?" Cage asked gently. "We're a bit busy right now."

"*You're busy?*" Her scream made me clap a hand to my ear;

it was as if she'd flipped a switch, going from scientist to siren. "Are you kidding me, *you're busy*? What were you *thinking*?"

I winced. "Rune, I know you're worried. But if you keep shouting at us, I'll have to mute you."

There was a long silence while she mulled that over, and when she came back, she was more subdued. "You guys know you're going to get yourself killed, right? And for what?"

"To save the planet," I replied, more sarcastically than I'd intended. "Rune, we had to try. And for what it's worth, we aren't intending to die."

She sighed heavily. "I know. I know. I know that. I just . . ."

"Love you too, *meimei*," Cage said gently. "You okay over there?"

"We're all right. I still have us on emergency lockdown. Mia hates it. She swears at me from the next room every few minutes."

"She'll do that. If you're lucky, her voice will give out after a while."

"I don't really mind. Lets me know she's alive, you know?" Rune hesitated. "Please be careful, *gege*. I get what you're doing, but I want you to come back."

"I know. We'll do our best."

I wonder what she'd say if she realized my secondary plan involved blowing us all to smithereens. "Keep us posted," I said. "We're going to go silent and have a look around."

"Don't stumble into an alien nest," Matt replied.

"Copy that." I cut the connection, leaving our comms connected on low volume in case they needed to contact us. I didn't know how we'd help if they encountered trouble, but I couldn't bring myself to mute Sanctuary entirely. "Okay. Where do we start?"

Cage shrugged. "This was your plan. You tell me."

"With this door, I guess." I knelt beside it and worked the screwdriver into the slot in the door. Once again, I hit the right spot and the door flowed open like liquid, reforming itself into a space big enough for us to walk through—*more* than big enough, reminding me once again we weren't anyplace meant for humans.

We exited into a dark, curving corridor. Only my penlight illuminated the slick walls, everything as dark and still as space itself. We were at a serious disadvantage here, one only a good pair of night-vision goggles would have fixed. "I don't suppose anyone on Sanctuary can see in the dark?"

"Not that I'm aware of," Cage replied, his voice barely audible. "We should keep the noise to a minimum."

I accepted the mild rebuke. I was mostly babbling to comfort myself. But a human voice on an alien ship could only lead to trouble. If the aliens heard us shuffling around, well, they might assume it was one of them. If they heard us whispering . . .

Speaking of aliens, though, I didn't see any. I beamed my light around, reminding myself not to scream if I suddenly hit a pair of sightless eyes and angry teeth, but I found only a strange triangular crevice in the ground. I gestured to Cage, who knelt beside it. He glanced at me, shrugged, and slipped inside. The ground came to his shoulders, and I aimed the light at his feet. As near as I could tell, there was nothing there: just more black plastic. It wasn't really plastic, of course—you couldn't make a spaceship out of plastic—but I didn't have a better word to describe it.

Cage gestured for the light. Reluctantly, I passed it over. While he explored the crevice, I crouched in the dark, gnawing on my fingernail until I realized what I was doing and folded my hands into fists, clutching the stun gun so tightly its edge dug into my palm.

A minute later he hoisted himself out of the hole. He shrugged, as mystified as me. "Let's put the XE suits in here," he suggested. "I'm not thrilled about keeping them in the airlock. They'll be more out of the way, less chance of discovery."

I nodded, and we retrieved the suits and stashed them in the crevice by the door. Then we followed the curving corridor.

About ten feet later, we discovered another hole. We continued along the corridor, seeing holes in the floor at regular intervals, until we found ourselves back at the airlock entrance. We'd gone in a complete circle without meeting a single alien or seeing anything of interest.

"This adventure sucks," I muttered.

Cage laughed softly. "You'd prefer slavering beasts?"

I almost would. The constant tension was getting to

me. "I'd prefer a big red button labeled 'self-destruct' and a twenty-minute countdown that gave us enough time to get off the ship."

"Well, in the meantime, let's circle again and check the outer wall," he murmured. "Look for more doors."

We set off, this time focusing the light on the walls. Sure enough, halfway around the circle I found another knob. Cage wedged the screwdriver into the slot while I held the light, and the door slid open. Emboldened by our success so far, we weren't as quiet or careful entering the next area. I illuminated a room similar to the one we'd just left: rounded walls, shiny black surfaces. The only difference was that instead of crevices in the floor, raised black platforms dotted the area.

I approached one of them and gave it a once-over. The sides were made of familiar black plastic, but the top was clear. Inside, one of the creatures drifted an inch below the surface.

My scream rose unbidden in my throat. I jammed my forearm into my mouth, strangling the sound, and staggered back. The gun and light slipped from my hands and clattered across the floor, and my heart kicked off a rhythm to match. I cringed against the wall, tensed for a creature to explode to life at the commotion.

Nothing happened. After a moment Cage focused the penlight on me. I blinked against the illumination, and he aimed it down. "Kenz," he whispered, barely audible. His fingers stroked my arm, pried it loose from my mouth. "You okay?"

I nodded, closing my eyes and forcing myself to breathe through my nose. *How stupid can you get?* I reproached myself sharply. "They're in there," I murmured, pointing.

Cage got to his feet. I grabbed his elbow and pull myself up along with him, careful about how I placed my feet. *They can't see. Stay quiet and you're safe.* Just the same, I paused to scoop my stun gun from the floor, then held it steady. Dropping it at the first sign of trouble had been a fantastic move—definitely what they taught us to do at camp when facing a dangerous opponent. I tightened my grip on the handle, determined not to lose it again no matter what jumped out at me.

Together, we peered over the . . . whatever it was. It came to Cage's waist, a little higher on me. The creature continued to drift. I couldn't tell if it was sleeping—its eyes were wide open, but it was immersed in some sort of liquid and didn't respond to us or the noise we made.

We stared at it for a long time. It didn't look even a bit less harmless in repose. Its claws glistened in the liquid, its jaws were drawn back, exposing razor-sharp teeth, and its milky-white eyes stared sightlessly into mine.

After an excruciating pause, we backed away. Cage's hand trembled on the light and I steadied it with my own. Together, we angled it down the corridor, revealing an endless sea of the things—at least seven or eight were in sight, with more stretching around the curve. "Do you think they all . . . ?" he asked.

"Let's find out." I braced myself and peered into the next chamber. Sure enough, another alien reposed there, unmoving and unseeing. Same with the next chamber, and the next. "At least they seem to be sleeping," I pointed out softly.

"Yeah, for how long?"

With that cheery thought, we pressed on. We had to walk halfway around the circle to find another door. This room seemed a lot larger than its predecessor. I was starting to get a sense the ship was arranged in a series of concentric circles.

Sure enough, when we finally found an exit, it led to a larger area—the walls hardly seemed to curve at all. In the first section we'd entered, it was obvious we were in a circular room; here, if I hadn't known better I'd have thought the hall stretched straight in either direction.

This corridor held more chambers, and once again, each of them housed one of the sightless, staring aliens. "How many do you think there are?" I whispered, scrutinizing the sea of creatures.

"At least fifty, maybe a hundred," Cage replied, his voice unsteady. "That's just in these two areas. We might find more. And someone must be awake to run the ship."

That was a thought I'd tried to avoid. Still, this was better than I had any right to hope for. If the creatures were all asleep, if the only ones awake were over on Sanctuary—plus maybe one or two here to keep the ship moving—well, then we had a chance. We could explore the ship and find a way to destroy it, or at least a way to contact Earth. It wasn't much, but it was more than we'd had before.

We continued on, weaving through the monsters. Cage's hand fumbled against mine and grabbed hold. I wasn't sure if he wanted reassurance or if he was keeping me close in case he had to run; either way, I didn't argue. I threaded my fingers through his and held tight.

This time we walked for what felt like forever before we found an exit, but I wasn't sure if that was because there weren't any or because pod after pod of alien creatures kept us distracted. At any rate, we'd almost returned to the beginning before Cage's light glinted off a knob on the wall. I inserted the screwdriver and stepped back, stun gun raised and at the ready. We'd gotten more cautious with our advance since discovering the creatures.

Surprisingly, though, this doorway led into an apparent storage room: a small chamber lined with metal boxes. Each box had a series of raised figures—like braille? Did the aliens read? Did they even have a language? I traced my fingers over the characters. Something about them seemed familiar, but I couldn't quite place it. "You ever seen anything like this?" I asked Cage.

He leaned closer but shook his head. My imagination, I supposed. It certainly had enough to work with in this house of horrors.

We found another door leading to another chamber. This time we progressed straight through, opening the door on the far wall.

And finally, we found ourselves somewhere useful.

Or at least, someplace different. We were in a large room, maybe double the size of Sanctuary's command center. Blocky shapes lined the walls, emitting a very faint light, not even enough to see by without the penlight. We drew closer, poised at any moment for an attack.

More raised shapes lined the tops of the blocks. The glow came from beneath them, an almost incidental hint of illumination. Cage crept onward, but I stopped to examine the console. When I touched a screen, the whole thing went flat. The lights swirled beneath the black surface, then pressed against the screen, rising into a series of symbols. It was like self-forming braille letters in an alien language. We couldn't communicate with them or even understand them, but these creatures were intelligent. They had purpose.

I sure wished I knew what it was.

"Cage," I whispered. "Bring the light back here."

He reappeared at my side, then directed the beam of light to follow my dancing fingers. "What is it?"

"I'm not sure, but I think . . ." I swallowed, taking in the general layout of the room. "I think these could be computers of some sort. Cage, this might be their command center."

He leaned forward, interested. "Can you make anything of it?"

I squinted at the symbols and ran my fingers over them. They shifted, becoming something else, and after only a few seconds I gave it up. "No."

"Well, let's look around, anyway. Maybe we'll find your big red self-destruct button."

I snorted and set off in one direction, letting him take the light in the other. The console's illumination didn't provide enough light to see by, but it did break the utter darkness and let me explore the space. Predictably, I found nothing but more consoles.

A door slid open with a soft hiss, and I jogged to Cage's side. He'd used the spare screwdriver to open an exit. "Don't wander off by yourself," I snapped, fear making me angry.

He turned on me, annoyance written plainly across his face, but caught himself before he spoke. "Sorry," he murmured, running a hand through his hair in what I was coming to recognize as a nervous gesture. "I found a door and thought I'd try it. I wasn't planning on leaving without you."

I wanted to spend more time on the consoles, but they weren't doing us much good at the moment. Better to explore the whole ship, see what we were up against, and return if need be. "I almost wish we'd run into one of the creatures just so we'd know where they are," I whispered to Cage as we shone our light into the next area. After the brief repose, the pitch black seemed even darker. "They're here somewhere. They can't all be napping."

"I know." He stepped through the door, and I followed.

This was the first area we'd entered that wasn't a smooth-walled circle. There were actual corners here—jagged black edges to the walls. It reminded me of the outside of the ship, and I suspected we'd reached the final layer, the outer edge. Cage aimed the penlight at the wall, and I frowned. Something hung near the top. "Are those . . . ?"

Cage stepped closer, his nostrils flaring in alarm. "They look like . . . manacles?"

They did look like manacles. A set of metal straps hanging from chains—adjustable, but even at their largest, far too small to hold the creatures.

"Don't jump to conclusions," I said, more to myself than him. "Let's check things out." We picked a direction at random and set off to our left, rounding a corner.

Cage illuminated something against the wall. It took me a second to figure out what I was looking at, but when I got it, I almost screamed. I jammed both hands over my mouth, stifling the sound, managing to keep a grip on the stun gun even as I pressed it against my cheek.

"Kenz!" Cage caught my arm. "What did you . . . ?"

His voice trailed off as his light caught a dangling foot—definitely human, wearing a heavy combat boot. Slowly, he raised the light, tracing a leg, a belt, the curve of a breast, until his light came to rest on her face.

Rita.

TWENTY-EIGHT

HER EYES WERE CLOSED, AND HER ARMS were manacled above her head. She dangled from the ceiling, coated in some sort of clear, sticky liquid—was it the same junk the aliens slumbered in? "Rita?" I asked, my voice shaky. I reached a trembling hand for hers.

Cage's hand clamped over my wrist, arresting my approach. "We don't know what that liquid is or what it does."

"I can't just leave her here!" I cast my gaze around, searching for a solution. "Gloves. The gloves from the XE suits. We can go back for them."

He hesitated. "All right. I'll go. Wait here."

I started to argue, but he vanished before I formed the words.

I advanced on Rita, fumbling in the darkness, tempted to ignore Cage's directive. My fingers found the place where the manacles bit into her wrists, making my own arms swell in sympathy. Drawing closer, I strained to catch her breathing, but no sound penetrated the heavy haze of silence.

Cage was gone less than two minutes, more than long enough for the silence and creepiness of the ship to get to me. I jumped a mile at the blast of wind heralding his return and damn near shot him in my panic. "The suits were right where we left them," he said, dropping both pairs of interior gloves—thin, cloth affairs—and one pair of bulky XE gloves at my feet. He didn't seem to notice that I hastily holstered my weapon, blood surging to my cheeks at the thought of what I'd almost done. "Everything seems normal. I stopped to examine the cuffs we saw before. There's a slot along the back that feels like the claw spaces on the doors. I think if I jam the screwdriver in there, the cuffs will release."

"Let's give it a shot." I pulled on both the inner and outer gloves. "If I hold her, can you get her down?"

"Not sure I can reach." Cage stood on his toes, his hands encased in thin cloth gloves of his own, and shook his head. "Hang on a sec."

He disappeared again in another burst of wind, this one carrying the unpleasant, almost astringent scent of the liquid coating Rita. Seconds later he reappeared with one of the metal boxes from the supply room, and he climbed on top of it. "Okay, I can reach now. You got her?"

I braced my hands on Rita's waist. "Yeah."

"Try not to get any of that fluid on yourself."

"I know, Cage. Hurry up."

He twisted at an awkward angle as he jimmied the cuffs. Rita came loose with a *pop*, and she sagged against me. I tried to shift her toward the wall, but she slumped forward, coating my shoulder with slimy, disgusting goop. I shuddered as it oozed over my neck, dripping past the collar of my sweater.

Cage leaped off the box and grabbed her arms, pulling her off me. Together we laid her down. "Well," I said in disgust, running my finger over the slime on my shoulder, "if this stuff is dangerous, I guess we're about to find out."

"Not our best-laid plan," he agreed, groping along her wrist in search of a pulse. His lips drew tight and I knew what he was going to say before he spoke.

"No." I shed both pairs of gloves and pressed along Rita's throat. Her skin was cool to the touch. I dug my fingers into her skin, waiting for that telltale flutter meaning her heart still beat.

Nothing.

I sagged against the wall, pressing my hands to my closed eyes until I saw flashes of light. Gently, Cage pried them down. "Please don't get that junk in your eyes."

I nodded, reluctantly acknowledging the wisdom of his advice, and fixed my gaze on Rita. "I knew she was dead," I whispered, half to myself. "I knew that."

"Just because she's dead doesn't mean your mom is."

Fury surged in my throat, but I quickly choked it down. It

wasn't Cage's fault. He didn't know how things operated when you were in a corporation together, when you worked on such a small space as Sanctuary. "It's not just that. It's Rita. She's . . ." I swallowed, searching for words and breath and space. "It's Rita," I finished helplessly.

"Oh," he replied softly, his hands gentle on my wrists. "Oh. Kenzie, I'm sorry."

"I know." I forced myself to take a breath, then another. Cage angled the light away from her face, but somehow I could still feel Rita's empty gaze. She was the most full-of-life person I'd ever known, always ready with a quip or a grin, never seeming to have a moment of exhaustion or self-doubt or fear. And yet here she lay, covered in some sort of alien slime, her limbs cold and stiff. Once again my heart clawed its way into my throat, and once again I fought it down, drawing deep breaths until the haze in front of my face cleared.

"What is this stuff, anyway?" I demanded to distract myself, wiping the goop off my gloves against the wall.

"I don't know," Cage replied, but his tone gave him away.

I narrowed my eyes. "You have a theory, though."

"I don't . . ." He met my gaze and frowned. "Okay, fine. It might be some sort of . . . preservative."

"Preservative." The word caught in my throat as his meaning took hold. "*Preservative?* Like they're going to eat her and they want to keep her *fresh?* Are you kidding me?"

He winced. "Now you see why I didn't want to say anything."

I inspected Rita for damage, but I didn't see any signs of recent violence, any clue to what killed her. In fact, I didn't see *any* signs of violence. Her earlier wounds had healed.

And more importantly, if *Rita* was here . . . I stared into the corridor's murky depths. "Mom," I whispered.

Cage nodded. "Let's go."

I pulled Rita against the wall and wiped away as much of the gunk on her face as I could. "I'm so sorry, Rita," I whispered. As an afterthought, I folded her hands around the small golden crucifix she wore around her neck. I hesitated, not wanting to leave her, but if Mom was somewhere on this ship . . .

I couldn't help Rita now. I could only try to help Mom—not to mention the kids back on Sanctuary and Earth itself. I squeezed Rita's hand one last time and let Cage tug me to my feet.

We rounded a corner and stopped short. Our dim light illuminated the horror stretching in front of us: bodies as far as the eye could see, each one glistening with the bizarre liquid. "Oh my God," I gasped. "Are they all dead?"

Cage swore softly. "They're all ours." He directed the light, revealing the uniform each wore—the same jumpsuit as his. The same one worn by all Sanctuary prisoners. "These are the missing kids."

"Mom," I said. I snatched the penlight from his hand and took off, shining the light into every face I passed. Behind me, Cage called something, but I didn't pause to listen.

I made it past at least three dozen bodies before I found her.

My mother drooped against the wall like all the others, and I lunged for her, scrambling to reach the cuffs. "Cage!" I cried, mindless now of my volume. "Cage, I need help!"

He was at my side in an instant, absorbed the situation in another. Before I blinked, he vanished again, then reappeared with the box and scrambled up to pop her free of the cuffs.

We caught her and lowered her to the ground. The flickering light illuminated her in glimpses and flashes. Her neat ponytail had come loose and her hair clung to her face in damp clumps, surrounding pale skin and drawn lips. My fingers slid over her cold, slick flesh as I stretched her out on the ship's floor. For a moment, I froze, terrified to confirm my suspicion. Then, gathering up all the strength I had left, I fumbled for her neck.

And felt nothing.

I let out a sob that told Cage everything he needed to know. "Let me see," he said, pushing past. I clenched my hands into fists on my knees. This couldn't be happening. This couldn't be real. Whatever was between us—whatever caused my parents to chip me, whatever made her choose Sanctuary over me when Cage threatened my life—she was still my mother. And she couldn't die like this. Not here. Not now.

And not without giving me answers.

Cage sat back on his heels, not meeting my eyes. "Kenzie . . ."

"No."

"Kenzie, I'm sorry."

"No." I bent over her lifeless form, shaking her viciously. "Mom. Mom!"

"Kenzie."

"Mom!" I slapped her face, gently at first but then with increasing strength. Her head lolled to the side, her eyes sliding open, staring unseeing into space, covered by milky-white cataracts—exactly like the aliens'.

I cried out, recoiling. "Her eyes," I gasped.

Cage lifted me and tucked me against the wall. "Stay here," he ordered. "I'll take a look."

I sagged, shock settling into every crevice of my being. Finding Rita had twisted my stomach, sent pain stabbing through my heart—but Mom, my mom . . . and her *eyes.* What were the creatures doing to her? If Cage was right, if they planned to *eat* her, why would her eyes have gone white? None of it made any sense.

Cage returned, angling the light away, leaving me the comfort of darkness. He didn't say anything but put his arms around me and pulled me into his chest. I leaned against him, staring blankly into the darkness, trying to process a new reality where Mom was dead, where Rita was dead, where Dad was gone. Where it was just me, alone and without my family, abandoned by my corporation, in a world where murder by aliens was not only a possible but a likely way to die.

"Kenzie." Cage's voice seemed to come from a long distance, as if he was on the other side of a tunnel. I barely registered his arms around me. "Kenzie, please move. Say something."

I shook myself, attempting to claw out of the well I'd fallen into, but I couldn't blink, couldn't move my gaze from the blocky wall across the corridor. Cage didn't say anything else, just held me and stroked my hair. We sat in the midst of death on this alien monstrosity, and we were silent, and still. Why was I silent? Why wasn't I crying, or screaming, or swearing? Why couldn't I feel anything? My heart seemed as cold and dead as my . . .

The pain surged through me like a lance, starting in my stomach and piercing straight through to the top of my head. I closed my eyes against it, choking on agony, clutching Cage's arm as the only lifeline left.

Mom was dead. My mom. Mom with her teasing smiles and stern patriotism and gentle hugs and willingness to kill me. She was gone. I'd never get to ask her any of the questions burning inside me, never get to find out what had really been going through her mind when she pushed that button. All I wanted to do was shove Cage away, lie down on the ground, and sleep. Forget everything, forget everyone, and sleep until I woke up and all of this was a dream.

But I couldn't do that, could I? Even if Omnistellar had betrayed me, the training remained seared deep into my soul— and that training said there were people depending on me back on Sanctuary, on Earth. Dad, for one. And Rune, and Alexei, and Matt, and even Mia. I owed it to them to keep going. And after, well . . . I couldn't think that far yet.

I went through the training exercises one at a time. Listen to your breath. Become aware of your hands. Name a smell (the astringent stench of—no, no, no, *Cage*, focus on *that*). Blink twice.

My heartbeat returned to normal, the grief sliding into its prison. I pulled away from Cage experimentally and found I could sit under my own power. "Her eyes," I managed. It was less than I'd meant to say, but the words seemed reasonably calm.

Cage hesitated. "Kenzie, are you okay? You're . . ."

"Her eyes," I repeated with more force. I refused to look at my mother lying on the floor. Instead, I pulled my stun gun free and busied myself with checking that the safety was off. "Did you see them?"

"Yeah," he replied softly. "And that's not all. Her . . . teeth. They're longer, sharper. Same with her nails."

"What?" I pulled back to stare at him in disbelief. "I need to see."

"Kenz, I'm not sure that's such a—"

"What would you do if it were Rune?" I demanded.

Cage hesitated a moment longer. "All right." We crept to her side, and I realized that he'd done for Mom what I'd done for Rita, wiped her face clean of as much liquid as possible, folded her hands

I ran my fingers over Mom's face. From this angle, she could have been sleeping. I forced myself to examine her, keeping my body taut, my expression dispassionate. Still, I squeezed her hands before checking her nails. Cage directed the light for me and sure enough, her nails extended a solid half inch past her fingers, curving in clawlike formations, darker at the tips. I folded them over her chest and spread her lips. There too I found things exactly as Cage described them: all of her teeth longer, sharper. Her incisors in particular had reached the vampire stage.

"What's going on here?" I whispered. "All of these people . . . what are they doing to them?"

"I don't know." Did I imagine the slight hesitation in his words? "But, Kenzie, I'm sorry—so sorry about Rita and your mom."

I stared at Mom a moment longer, then unholstered her sidearm. I ejected the magazine, verified it was loaded, and shoved it back into place. "What?" I demanded as Cage watched me, his expression inscrutable. "The stun guns aren't stopping those things. Maybe a bullet will."

"Your mother had a gun," he reminded me softly. "So did Rita."

And we didn't even know where Rita's was. But right now, I didn't care. I tucked the pistol into place in my uniform holster, my expression daring Cage to challenge me. He didn't. I passed him my stun gun as a reward, and he accepted it, his face still carefully neutral.

Finding Mom made me realize what a waste of time this trip had been. We still had no way to destroy the ship, nothing to help us communicate with Earth. Just a panel of stupid symbols that meant nothing. We'd have been better off staying on Sanctuary and releasing the escape pod. At least that was still an option. So far we'd seen no aliens here, which meant we could probably head back to Sanctuary easily enough. Maybe the pod stood a chance of getting to Earth after all. We could send Anya away, save her life—only for her to be instantly arrested and re-imprisoned, but still—and warn everyone back on Earth what waited in orbit.

If we failed . . . well, I didn't even want to imagine that possibility. The creatures had torn through Sanctuary with almost no effort, even once we had our powers. Sure, guns might faze them, but if no one on Earth saw them coming . . .

No. I wasn't going there. We *would* find a way to warn Earth. I didn't care whose life it cost at this point. I might fall down seven times, but I was getting up eight.

Cage's thoughts must have mirrored mine, because he dropped against the wall, resting his chin on his folded arms. I focused on smoothing Mom's hair into place, arranging her in a more restful pose. My penlight played over the ink on Cage's arm, the Chinese characters he'd told me represented Rune's name. I traced them with my fingers, stroking the delicate shapes, and he inclined his head, watching me with dark, steady eyes.

Lin.

I blinked.

I could *read* them. Of course—my power. If it worked for spoken languages, why not written?

At that thought, I paused, my heart stuttering.

Why not written?

"I need another look at those computers," I said, jumping to my feet.

Cage glanced up at me. "Why?"

"I'll explain later. Come on." Voicing the hope felt like tempting fate. But if I was right—if I had even a chance of deciphering the alien language—it might change everything.

I faltered, glancing at Mom. . . . No. I had to focus on saving everyone else. If I let myself think about Mom, even for a minute, if I let myself feel the wrenching grief welling inside me, I'd collapse and *never* get up. Gritting my teeth, I set off at a run.

At that moment, one of the bodies twitched on the wall. I skidded to a halt so fast Cage smacked into me, and we both stumbled. "Did you see that?" I whispered, angling the light at the body, now hanging limp.

"See what?"

I stared into the shadows. It was a girl, my age or a bit younger, with long black hair and brown skin slicked with sweat. She remained absolutely still, hanging limp. "Nothing," I said at last. "Nothing. My imagination."

At that second, the girl's eyes flew open, revealing milky-white, unseeing depths.

"Help," she croaked, and her voice came out in a horrible rasp—a clash between an alien's shrill cry and a human girl's sob. "Somebody . . . please. Help me."

TWENTY-NINE

SCREAMING, WE RECOILED, COLLIDING WITH
the wall. Cage erupted into a string of furious Mandarin, and
my ankle twisted, almost capsizing me. "She's alive," Cage whispered unnecessarily.

The girl spoke again, her voice stronger but still with that
horrible shrill edge. "Who's there? Please . . . help me. . . ."

"Hang on," I managed at last. "We'll get you down." I
turned to Cage, but he was already moving, grabbing the box
and scrambling up to pop the girl's cuffs. She collapsed against
my arms, and her knees gave way the second her feet hit the
ground. I staggered under the sudden load, and Cage leaped to
help me. The crushing weight relaxed as he shared the burden.
For a moment I flashed back to Rita's body landing the same
way, to Mom's.

Together, we laid her on the floor, then wiped fluid from

her skin. I seized the opportunity to examine her hands. Sure enough, her nails had elongated like my mother's, and maybe even more so. There was a strange, mottled pattern on her skin—something I *hadn't* noticed on Mom. "Are you okay?" I asked stupidly. I rested her head on my lap and pressed her hand with my own. "What's your name?"

"Imani," she murmured, closing her eyes. "It's so dark. I can't see."

I exchanged glances with Cage. How much should we tell her? "You're okay," I lied. "We're going to get you out of here." *Just like I did for Mom and Rita.* I squelched that inner voice and forced myself to focus on the person I *could* help. "Are you hurt?"

"So thirsty," she whispered. "Water?"

I hadn't seen water anywhere on this ship. Cage shrugged. "I'll go look," he said. "I can't search in the dark, though."

I really didn't want to be alone in utter blackness with this poor girl and the lifeless—or not?—bodies, but I could hardly begrudge him the light.

Cage retreated at a normal speed, the light bobbing along. I stared after it, memorizing its impression in case I never saw light again. He rounded the corner and vanished, leaving me in sudden, total darkness.

Imani's fingers trembled around mine, and I adjusted my grip to avoid her nails. "It's going to be okay," I repeated. "Cage will find water. Just hold on."

She didn't try to reply. I wasn't even sure she was conscious.

We huddled together in a sea of shadows. I'd never seen absolute darkness before; there'd always been ambient light from the stars, or from a computer console, or from passing vehicles back on Earth. When I first reached Sanctuary, I'd remarked on its silent darkness at night. But even then, there'd been the whir of machinery, lights from my charging comm device.

My mind created noise—the other prisoners waking, moaning, thrashing in their bonds. What would I do if that happened? I couldn't help them, not on my own, not in the dark. My hand tightened involuntarily around Imani's, and she responded in kind, reassuring me that she, at least, was still with me. The darkness, the silence, left too much to my imagination, which kept forcing pictures of Mom's lifeless face to the surface. I ground my teeth, directing my thoughts elsewhere.

"For someone with super speed, he sure takes his sweet time," I muttered, mostly to hear my own voice.

To my surprise, Imani answered. "Chip . . ," she said.

It took me a minute to figure out what she meant. "Oh, the inhibitor chips. He cut his out."

A choking sound escaped her, and I realized she was laughing. "Dumbest thing . . ."

"Kind of, yeah." I fumbled for her forehead in the darkness and smoothed her hair back from her face. Her skin burned my hand, a shock of heat. Rita and Mom hadn't been hot.

No. They were cold. Dead. "Hang on, okay?"

A streak of light shot out of the distance, and suddenly

Cage was kneeling beside us with what looked like a test tube of water in his hand. I lifted Imani's head and Cage held the water to her lips. She gulped it greedily, making a murmur of protest when he pulled it away. "Not too fast," he urged, making her wait a minute before offering another sip.

"Where'd you find water?" I asked.

"In one of the storage rooms. It took a while. Their taps don't exactly operate like ours."

"You're certain it's water, right?"

Cage nodded. "Tried it to make sure. If it's not, it's close enough that I couldn't tell the difference."

That wasn't the most reassuring thing I'd ever heard, but Cage didn't look any worse for drinking it. And Imani sat up, the water seeming to strengthen her. She still clutched my hand. "Thanks," she whispered, almost growled.

"Don't mention it." Cage settled on his haunches. "Imani, right? You want to tell us what happened?"

She blinked. "What's wrong with my voice?" We exchanged helpless glances, but before we had to answer, she pressed on: "I can't see very well."

I winced, not wanting to mention her eyes, either. "What *can* you see?" I asked cautiously.

"Shadows. My eyes hurt."

She reached up to rub them, but I stopped her before she could claw herself. "They were doing something to you," I said, ignoring Cage's look of warning. I didn't want to panic her, but she had a right to know. "I'm not sure what. We're going to help you if we can, but first we need to know how you got here."

Imani nodded, drawing a deep breath. "Right. Well. I was in sector four. The cells opened, and no one knew what to do. I was sitting on the couch with my sister. . . ." She paused. "Aliya. Where is she?"

"I don't know." I glanced at Cage, signaling him to check the walls for anyone who looked like Imani's sister. For once, he obeyed without argument or question, stalking off with the light. "Cage is looking for her."

"I was on the couch with Aliya," she repeated, sinking against the wall. Again she reached for her face. This time I took her hands in mine and held them. "I don't remember much after that. An alarm went off. Everyone jumped up, ran for the cells in case we were going into lockdown. Suddenly all the air seemed to disappear from the room. I went flying and hit my head. I guess I blacked out." She grimaced. "I woke up and . . ." Her breathing increased rapidly, her fingers clenching over mine. "It was a dream. It must have been a dream."

"Imani. Imani, it's okay. Listen to me." I squeezed her hands, bringing my face close to hers, speaking in a low, reassuring tone. Somehow, her panic was easing my own grief and terror. Having someone else to focus on let me bury the thought of Mom even deeper. "Everything's okay. We're not going to let anything hurt you. Tell me what happened."

"I woke up in . . . some sort of tub. Covered in liquid.

But I could breathe. Every breath I drew, the liquid filled my lungs and I thought I'd drown, but . . . I didn't. My head throbbed. My arms hurt. Everything hurt. And these *things* staring at me . . . Oh God . . ."

"I know," I said quickly. "I've seen them too."

"Then it wasn't a dream?" Her voice caught. "It can't be . . ."

Cage returned. He angled the light toward his own face and nodded down the hall, but his expression didn't fill me with hope. I got the sense he'd found her, but not in a state he wanted to describe. "Imani," he said, his tone gentle. "What's your power?"

"My power?" She shook her head. "Healing. I heal fast. But . . . not with the chip."

Cage angled the light to her arm, revealing a faint scar. "I think your chip is gone. If your power is healing, that might explain why you're awake."

"What else do you remember?" I asked. Cage crouched beside me and I instinctively shifted closer, needing the reassurance. My stomach had tied itself into permanent knots, my heart hammered a thousand beats a minute. I wanted to stay calm for Imani's sake, but I was pretty damn close to losing it.

Cage must have known, because he smoothed his hands down my arms, steadying me. I drew a deep breath, forcing myself to focus on Imani as she continued. She seemed to have forgotten her sister for the moment, which was probably a blessing, all things considered. I'd just lost my mom, and I was barely holding it together. I didn't know how she'd react if she lost her sister the same way. "They stared at me," she said, "but I don't think they saw me. Their eyes were *white*, this horrible, creepy . . . Still, somehow, they knew I was awake. They seemed surprised. One of them . . ." She shuddered. "It poked a claw into my arm. I screamed, got a mouthful of gel, and two more of them came over, but I passed out before I saw anything else. The next thing I knew, I woke up here."

Cage cupped her face in his hand, tilting her head to examine her eyes more closely. "How quickly do you usually heal?"

Her face contorted as she adapted to the change in questioning. Whatever the creatures had done to her, she hadn't recovered completely. "I don't know. Fast. Um. I broke my leg once, and that took about twenty-four hours to get back to normal."

I followed his gaze. No change in her eyes or her nails, but she sounded stronger. As I watched, though, her eyelids drooped, her body going slack. "Imani?" I said, frantic. "Imani!"

She pulled herself awake. "Need . . . rest . . . ," she managed. "For the healing to take effect. My chip . . . it's gone?"

Cage helped her stretch out on the floor, careful to keep her from hitting the legs of the prisoners dangling on either side. "It's gone," he said. "For good."

A slight smile touched her lips as her eyes drifted shut again. I held her hands until they went loose, then found her pulse. It was strong and steady. "Is she okay?" I asked.

"I think so." Cage helped me to my feet. "She should be all right here while we check out the rest of the area." He hesitated. "Kenz . . . there are more of them. All down the walls in this area, every prisoner from Sanctuary."

"Are they . . . ?" I swallowed.

Cage shook his head. "I only checked a few, but they all have a pulse."

So why did Mom and Rita die? Age? Or . . .

The answer hit me with the force of a brick wall. "I have to get back to the computer consoles."

I don't know why I expected an argument, but I didn't get one. "Let's go," he said, tucking his arm around my shoulders. Without knowing I was going to do it, I turned into him, burying my face in his chest. He hugged me tightly, silently, with no demands, no questions.

Just one moment, I told myself. I just needed one moment to gather my strength, and then I could do this. I could, because I had to.

I still had people to save.

But walking away from my mother's body was the hardest thing I'd ever done. So I did what I always did: forced myself to consider the problem at hand. I stepped back from Cage and he released me without a struggle, although I felt the loss of his warmth like a physical blow. "Are we okay to leave Imani?" I asked, and was pleased at the steadiness of my voice.

"Do you want me to stay with her?"

Hell no. I wanted him with me. But . . . "Walk me to the consoles," I said. I didn't want to stumble along in the darkness. "Then, yeah. You'd better stay with her. I think I might be able to decipher their language if I focus, and you can't help me with that. I mostly need time to concentrate."

Cage must have been following my thoughts, because he evinced no surprise at the statement. "All right. I'll try to keep watch and check in with both of you."

"Did you find her sister?"

"I think so. She's just like all the others. I'll watch over all of them in case there's a change."

I fiddled with the edge of his shirt, staring at his chest, and then pushed the words out in a rush. "And keep an eye on Mom and Rita, okay?"

"Kenzie . . ." The one word spoke volumes.

I cut him off. "I know they're dead. I *know*. But I don't want the creatures doing anything else to their . . . their bodies. Just watch them. Okay? Please."

He nodded, and the understanding in his expression cracked something in my heart. I turned away from it before I could break further.

We retraced our steps to the exit from this nightmare room of half-dead and comatose people, and a rush of relief made my knees weak as we regained the dim light from the consoles. "Come find me if you hear anything," Cage said.

I glanced at him in alarm. "You don't think those things will wake up, do you?"

"No," he said, too quickly. "I just don't want to take chances."

I nodded, pretending to believe him. "I'll be as quick as I can."

Was I dreaming, thinking I could do this? The symbols swirled around, nothing but gibberish. I touched the screen, and the liquid re-formed into raised letters. I stared at them, desperately seeking some sort of meaning. They remained nothing but symbols: lines, dots, the occasional curve.

My head throbbed, and I rubbed my eyes. What was I doing wrong? It hadn't been this hard to pick up Cage's Mandarin. So far when I'd used my power, the language just came to me, sliding over me like a comfortable sweater.

Then it hit me. These creatures didn't read with their eyes.

I closed mine and traced the symbols, letting my hands wander. Raised bumps, slightly warm to the touch, brushed my skin. I half stroked them, struggling to absorb their meaning.

After a while, I heaved a sigh and opened my eyes. Cage was in the doorway. "Thought you were with Imani?"

"Told you, I'm wandering. Nothing?"

"Not yet. Any change with the prisoners?"

He shook his head, and I spun on the console in frustration. "This is a waste of time. I don't even know if my powers work on an alien language."

"You don't know they won't. It took you a while to catch what I was saying before. Don't put so much pressure on yourself."

I nodded, stretching out the stiff muscles in my neck. "You're right. I'll keep trying. Just . . . give me some space, okay? It's harder with you watching me."

He looked like he wanted to say something, but in the end he only nodded and retreated into the corridor. I drew a deep breath and replaced my fingers on the screen.

What was I doing when Cage's tattoo started to make sense? I hadn't tried to read it, that was for sure. I needed something to distract me from the impossibility of this endeavor. Cage came instantly to mind, the strength of his embrace, the cute quirk of his lips when he smiled, the rush of wind when he carried me away from danger. Hard to believe that only a day ago I'd considered him a dangerous criminal. But then, my whole life I'd feared anomalies. I'd been taught that a few lived peacefully and incongruously among us but that most were criminals and murderers. Cage had shown me the opposite was true. I was beginning to suspect that whenever Omnistellar found an anomaly—no matter whether they'd committed a crime or not—they arrested them and tossed them in prison.

Somehow, my parents had avoided that fate for me, although how or why, I didn't know. They chipped me, yeah, and kept it a secret, but maybe it wasn't the betrayal I imagined. Maybe, in their way, they were protecting me. Maybe their position in the company allowed them to circumvent normal procedures. If so . . . could that explain Mom's slavish devotion to Omnistellar policies? Perhaps her single-minded dedication to her career came from a desire to keep me safe. And perhaps a lifetime of near-maniacal patriotism, of total devotion to the corporation she believed saved her daughter—not to mention utter terror of the havoc she thought the prisoners would wreak if they got loose—led to her pushing that button.

I'd never get to ask her, of course. My throat caught, and I turned my thoughts to Dad. But that didn't help, because someone had to tell him about Mom. What would he say? Did he still love her? Would he still love me once he realized what I'd done?

I leaned against the console, clenching my jaw against tears. I still didn't dare cry. I wanted to, more than anything, but if I started, I wouldn't stop, and I'd wind up huddled on the floor incapable of saving anyone, including myself. My parents would want me to fight through this with the values they'd instilled in me, however twisted those values might be.

Forget it. I didn't owe anything to my parents. I owed it to *myself*.

Suddenly, I realized my fingers were moving with purpose, sliding over words and letters I recognized—distantly, but recognized all the same. This method of reading was unfamiliar, but my ability had picked it up without my noticing.

And the word beneath my fingers right now?

Assimilate.

THIRTY

CONQUER.

Genetic.

Probe.

Every word came with agonizing effort. My initial understanding of the language required letting my mind wander; now, it called for my whole attention. Words rose to my fingers unbidden, as if I'd subconsciously summoned the information. It came faster and faster—too fast for me to keep up, but as the speed increased, so did my understanding. I stopped trying to translate each word, instead letting the language itself wash over me. As soon as I made that switch, everything became easier, less fractured.

It bore no resemblance to English. This was more like knowledge dumped straight into my brain, and I reeled in an effort to control it. I trembled on the precipice of consciousness, overwhelmed not only by the rush of data—like clutching onto a roller coaster when your seat belt has come loose—but by what I was seeing.

This *couldn't* be right. But the alien ship had no reason to lie. And something deep inside me was taking the information and twisting it into neat packages, aligning it so it made sense. The ship itself, working with my mind? Or was there a more insidious explanation, like something within *myself* recognizing the ship and instinctively responding to what I was learning?

The probes . . . all those years ago. They were *terraforming*. Actually, no. They weren't forming the Earth. It was more like . . . *people-forming*.

My stomach gave a sickening lurch. I needed space and time to process the data, but unlike my tablet, the alien console didn't have a pause button. It seemed to know I'd grasped the core concept, how the probes had altered human DNA, and it lurched onward, forcing me to the next idea, and the next, before my terrified brain had time to cope or react. Images flashed before my eyes—the aliens superimposed on other species, other creatures, screaming and blood and terror combined with a deep primal satisfaction until I didn't know where one feeling began and the other ended.

At last I gasped, physically wrenching myself from the console and straight into Cage's arms. I shoved him away in an instinctive recoil, but he caught my wrists and held tight. "Take it easy," he said. "It's me."

"God." I closed my eyes, leaning against his shoulder.

"You okay?"

"Yeah. No." I shook my head. "Cage, I know what's going on. The probes they sent all those years ago—it's how the aliens reproduce. They find hosts, inject them with their DNA, and then take them over. That's why the prisoners are all alive but Mom and Rita aren't. Their DNA was pure human. Ours is part alien."

He stared at me, realization slowly dawning. "So everyone with powers . . ."

"We're alien incubators," I replied, my voice shaky to my own ears. "They set us up, altered our DNA in preparation. And we went and stashed everyone affected in a nice convenient prison. They didn't even have to hunt us down—they just *descended*. And I don't think we're the only ones they've done this to either."

"Wait." He dropped my hands and retreated a step, raking his hands through his hair. "So you're saying not only are there other aliens, but this race drifts through the galaxy stealing their bodies? Which means that the aliens attacking right now might have been just like us. Innocent creatures from another planet, transformed into . . ."

I nodded. "They release the probes, keep track of where they end up. People initially exposed to the probe won't do. It has to be their children, or their children's children. So a couple of decades later, they launch a reproductive cycle, descending on the planet and harvesting everyone exposed to their DNA." I shuddered. It sounded so clinical, like I was delivering my own history lecture. But the alien satisfaction, their sense of accomplishment, still washed through me. A wave of nausea threatened, and I tasted bile at the back of my throat. "Then, before they leave, they drop another probe, leaving the planet readying for another harvest a few generations down the road. Total asexual reproduction. They're like a virus."

"And the . . ." His face twisted in disgust as he swiped his fingers on his pants leg, probably not even aware he was doing it. "The junk they're soaking everyone in?"

I shook my head helplessly. "Something to ease the transition? To keep us asleep? I'd need a lot more time with the computers to figure out the details."

Cage's gaze traveled toward the cargo area, where maybe fifty kids hung from the walls, slowly transforming into aliens. "How do we stop it?"

"I don't know. The aliens weren't exactly looking for ways to *stop* it."

"We can't let them . . ." He swallowed hard. "Okay. First step: let's get them off the walls and clean them up. Maybe that'll arrest the procedure."

I hesitated. Cage read my reluctance, and his eyes flashed dangerously. "Kenzie, I'm not leaving them here."

"I'm not saying that," I shot back, irritation swelling in my gut. I pushed it down, forcing my voice calm. I was the one who'd just lost her mother. Why was it also my responsibility to be the one thinking straight? "But it's going to take us hours to accomplish that—hours in which the creatures on Sanctuary could get to your sister."

Cage winced, guilt instantly suffusing his face. Obviously, he'd forgotten Rune entirely. I understood—confronted as he was with something like the horror in the other room, who could blame him for a second of distraction? But I didn't think he'd thank me for saying so, and I pressed on. "We need to get everyone off Sanctuary."

"Off Sanctuary?" He arched an eyebrow. "What do you have in mind?"

I struggled to remain calm. This was a chance, nothing more. A glimmer of a sliver of a hope to survive. But it was more than we'd had a few minutes ago. And somehow I felt like if I managed to save the others, well . . . it might give some meaning to Mom's death. To Rita's death. At any rate, it would give me purpose.

"Kenzie?" asked Cage.

Oxygen, check. Water, ditto. We could bring supplies from Sanctuary. "Cage," I said. "What if we came *here*?"

"What?"

"Instead of destroying this ship, what if we . . . take it over? If all the aliens are asleep, if we get everyone in XE suits and bring them here . . ." Could we survive this disaster after all?

A spark of optimism lit his face, then instantly disappeared under his normal cocky mask. "It's possible," he allowed. "We could get off Sanctuary, destroy it—with the aliens inside—and find a way to communicate with Earth. Preferably from a distance so we don't all immediately get arrested."

"Between me and Rune, we can operate this ship. I know we can."

He frowned. "Are we really doing this?"

"I think so. Even if something goes wrong, well, we can't survive on Sanctuary much longer. It's not much of a chance, but it's something, isn't it?"

"It's something. Better than anything else we've come up with." I could almost see him planning and scheming, his eyes dancing in the light. I was starting to get why Cage had been the one to lead the prison break. It wasn't just his charisma, the way people followed him. He *couldn't stop* planning.

Then he grabbed me and gave me a quick kiss, and I stopped thinking at all. "You're a genius. You know that?"

I half smiled in spite of myself, my cheeks growing hot in the darkness. "But that means we need to get back to Sanctuary as soon as possible."

"Then we'd better get started."

A few more minutes spent with the ship's consoles yielded a ton of data. The creatures we'd passed were all in a state of suspended animation. They traveled this way. The mission commanders awakened to conduct the harvest, waking others as necessary. Once they completed the mission, all the creatures on the ship rose to tend the newborn aliens, and then they were on their way to wherever they went next—I had trouble gleaning that information.

In the short term, we were pretty safe on the alien ship. I didn't think the creatures woke without outside intervention. And I remained almost certain I could pilot this ship with Rune's help. The computer system didn't work the same as human technology; the AI instantly tried to forge what seemed like a psychic bond with me. Fighting it reminded me of battling Tyler's intrusion into my brain, a memory that still set my teeth rattling. But in this case, the intrusion was beneficial, making it a matter of thought to direct the ship. I'd need practice, but the ship didn't seem to care about my human brain. It simply wanted to forge its bond.

And if I was wrong, well, we probably wouldn't survive long enough to find out. Or at least *I* wouldn't, because Mia would strangle the life out of me.

There was only one flaw in our plan: Imani. We couldn't take her to Sanctuary with us—we didn't have a spare XE suit, and frankly, she was probably safer here. But I didn't want her waking up alone and terrified, thinking we abandoned her.

We rejoined her, hoping to wake her long enough to explain things. We drew up short when we found her sitting against the wall, her breathing regular and normal. I angled the light at her face and she blinked, shielding her eyes. They remained coated in cataracts, but hints of dark irises peered out from beneath. And her nails had retracted several centimeters. I breathed a sigh of relief. Imani, at least, would be fine.

To my surprise, she didn't complain about staying on the ship by herself. She only had one request: that we leave her the light and the backup screwdriver. "I'll make a start on cutting everyone down," she said. "As soon as I can see again. I'm half-way there already."

Cage gave her a crash course in opening the cuffs, using Aliya as his example, and she nodded, her face a mask of deter-mination.

We still needed a way to transport the prisoners to the alien ship, though. "Do you remember how the creatures brought you here?" I asked Imani.

She shook her head. "I don't remember anything between the prison and the slime pit."

I nodded, my mind racing. "As for the aliens themselves," I said, "I think—I'm not sure, but I *think* they can survive for a limited time in space. Don't ask me what I'm basing that on. The absence of XE suits and shuttles, maybe, or the way they tore into sector four."

"Well, that sucks," Cage replied grimly. "So what do we do? Take turns with the XE suits? Lead the prisoners over here one at a time?"

"There are more suits," I said, "but they're in the shuttle bay. If we get in there, we can take more people. One at a time won't work. We'll run out of air, and that's if the creatures don't guess what we're doing. With more suits, we can evacuate in groups. It should buy us enough time to get across."

"Then we have a plan: get back to Sanctuary, collect the XE suits, grab everyone else, and evacuate."

"Fantastic." This plan sucked. "I don't suppose any of them have zero g experience?"

"Rune does, but she's not great. I can't say for the others. I'd guess not many."

"Awesome." I rubbed my forehead. Neither of us mentioned the obvious—what exactly to do with the hundred slumbering aliens on the ship. If we managed to escape, we sure didn't want them waking and attacking us. Three was bad enough; ten would obliterate us in seconds. But what could we do? Pry open each chamber and stab them as they slept?

We'd cross that bridge when we came to it. "All right. Let's get moving."

Unbidden, my head turned toward where I'd left my mother's body. I wanted so badly to go back, say one last good-bye—but she was beyond caring, and the prisoners on Sanctuary weren't. If we managed to pull this off, I'd have plenty of time to mourn. Until then, I was going to have to be Mecha Dream Girl and set my feelings aside, become an emotionless machine capable of feats I'd never imagine doing under normal circumstances.

I passed Imani the screwdriver and the light. This left us to find the airlock in the dark. No big deal, right? It was more or less a straight shot, and Cage had already done it once. We locked hands and stayed within a step of one another, advancing into the shadows.

But every second, I expected a hiss or a growl or one of those god-awful screams that meant the creatures had woken and found us. The worst moment came in the second-to-last chamber. We'd found the previous exits by feeling along the walls until we hit the knobs, but we missed this one. We spent at least fifteen minutes groping along in the dark, all too aware of the slumbering creatures nearby. When at last I found a knob, I almost sobbed in relief. We fumbled with it until it popped open. I released Cage, staggered to my XE suit, and stabbed my helmet light to life.

Illumination obliterated the darkness, and my hands trembled on the helmet. "Let's not do that again," I suggested.

Cage laughed, although he too sounded strained. "No. Add a step to our plan: find more light."

We suited up and brought our displays to life. Returning to Sanctuary cost a bit of thruster fuel, but it wasn't enough to worry me. We still had plenty left to get us and our companions to the ship. Matt released the airlock from the command center, and we waited the agonizing few minutes while it repressurized. We slid out of our suits, opting to leave them and return later rather than having to drag them along with us. "Matt," I said into my comm unit as we left the airlock, "tell Rune to get everyone ready to leave the station."

His reply almost shattered my eardrum. "*What?* And go where?"

"I'll explain when we're all together. Just get them ready.

Anya's too small to fit any of the suits properly. We can make it work but . . ."

When we emerged into the corridor, I cast a quick glance in both directions, making sure the coast was clear before setting off at a near jog, barking orders into my comm as forcefully as possible without raising my voice above a whisper. ". . . we'll need to move quickly. Is everyone safe?"

Mercifully, Matt seemed to have bowed to my authority. "Yeah, they were all ready and waiting. Should I rejoin them?"

"Yes. Call me once you're there, okay?"

"Got it."

Matt signed off, and I turned to Cage. "We're good to go. Let's find your sister and get out of here."

He nodded, relief clear in his expression. "I can't say I'm sorry to—"

The claw shot out of nowhere, piercing Cage's back.

For a second that felt like an eternity, we both stared at the claw sticking out of his chest. Then one of the aliens hoisted him in the air and whipped him violently across the hall, its reptilian features creased in something like a snarl. Cage skidded across the floor and collided with the wall, landing limp in a puddle of blood.

The creature turned to me and hissed. I twirled, just as another blocked the hall, its fangs bared, saliva dripping to pool on the ground.

Trapped.

THIRTY-ONE

WITH NO OTHER OPTIONS, I REVERTED TO standard scared animal behavior: I froze in place and stood stock-still.

Luckily for me, I also swallowed my whimper of terror. The creatures twitched, sniffing the air. Even though I hadn't made a sound, they seemed to know I was there.

My gaze traveled to Cage's limp form. I couldn't see his face, but the extent of the damage on his back was staggering: two jagged claw marks oozing a mess of blood, fusing his shirt to his body. I couldn't tell if his chest was rising and falling.

And I couldn't leave him here. Which meant I not only had to evade these creatures—I had to get rid of them altogether. Then came the simple task of dragging a hundred-and-seventy-pound boy to safety. My fingers drifted to the pistol at my belt.

One of the creatures screamed its piercing howl, and a third alien dropped through the ceiling, landing with a clatter of claws. I clamped my jaw and refused to let a sound escape. I also released the pistol. It didn't matter how good a shot I was—and marksmanship was *not* my best subject. I'd never hit all three of them before they gored me.

There *had* to be another way out of this.

One creature skittered forward, sweeping its tail behind, jerking its head in either direction.

The second followed suit. Almost across the hall from me, the third took a careful step, closing the triangle, fencing me in.

I shifted toward the airlock. I wasn't sure what I had in mind. By the time the door opened, the creatures would have ripped me to shreds. Besides, it would make a god-awful racket opening, and it was slow—too slow, given how fast these things moved. But I could hardly stand in the corridor waiting for them to attack.

I reached the wall and sidled toward the control panel. The aliens continued to advance, pausing between steps, their clawed arms snapping at the air and their heads tilted for any sound, any suspicious movement. If the corridor hadn't been so narrow, I might have ducked beneath them . . . but those sweeping tails covered four feet with every swish. No escape. I'd have to come up with something else.

And I *would* come up with something else. There was no way in hell I'd made it this far—through Mom's death, discovering my own chip, jetting through space to explore an alien ship—only to die in the halls of Sanctuary because I couldn't find a way past three alien creatures entirely dependent on sound to find me.

Sound . . . Could it be that simple? I fumbled for something, anything, to throw. The gold band on my right index finger brushed my palm—a simple gold affair with *daughter* inscribed inside, a sixteenth-birthday gift from my parents. I hesitated, but in this instance, I thought they would approve. I pried the ring off my finger and tossed it over the shoulder of the far alien.

It clinked softly in the hall. All three creatures froze, then pivoted in that direction. I waited with bated breath and, apparently, so did they, listening for any repeat of the sound.

None came.

And they resumed their march toward me.

I made a face. Well, it always worked for the robo mechs. Time for Plan B. *Fall down seven times* . . .

My back brushed against the inner airlock door—the loudest, slowest door on the entire station aside from the shuttle doors and the outer airlock itself. Nonetheless, I pressed my thumb to the control panel. It leaped to life with a series of whirrs and beeps. The creatures stiffened. One shrieked.

The airlock door unsealed itself with a hiss and began the slow, laborious process of sliding open.

The aliens charged.

I leaped, diving beneath a creature's outstretched claws and over its tail, landing heavily on the ground behind it. One of them pivoted in my direction, hesitating, but the continued draw of the opening door reclaimed its attention. The aliens lunged inside.

I threw myself at the control panel and aborted the procedure halfway through opening. The door changed tracks and began sliding shut. Inside, the aliens paid no heed to the slight change in sound, screeching to one another as they tore through the airlock. The door sealed behind them, and I allowed a small smile of satisfaction to touch my face.

"Matt," I said into my comm unit, "are you in the command center?"

"No, I'm halfway to the prison."

I swore loudly.

"I'm still in contact with the computer," Rune's voice cut in. "I can do almost anything from here. What's up, Kenz?"

"Blow the primary airlock."

She hesitated. "But . . . why?"

Through the airlock window, the creatures faced me, sheer malevolence twisting their features as they recognized the ruse. "I don't have time to explain. Just blow the damn airlock!"

"Emergency depressurization initiated," chimed in Sanctuary's voice. *Rune, you're amazing.* The creatures twisted, their heads perking at the sound. Whether or not they understood the words, they obviously recognized trouble, because they screeched to one another. They swung around the room, frantically searching for something—I didn't know what and hoped I wouldn't find out.

Both outer airlock doors gave way. Within seconds, everything in the room not bolted down—tools, storage kits, and the three aliens—whipped into space, vanishing from sight.

Unfortunately, that included our two XE suits. But better them than me. "So long, suckers," I murmured, and reactivated my comm. "Good work, Rune. Matt, detour to my location. Rune can direct you."

"Why?" she demanded. "Kenzie, what's going on?"

I hesitated, not sure how much to tell her. "Cage is hurt," I settled on at last, praying it wasn't worse. As I spoke, I bolted to his side, then rolled him over and examined him for signs of life. "I need Matt's help."

Rune replied in Mandarin, a rush of terrified cursing. I muted her so as not to distract myself and bent over Cage. He was breathing but unconscious, the claws having gored all the way through his body. "You are *not* going to die on me," I snarled at him. "Do you understand?"

He didn't reply. I took his silence as agreement.

I shot to my feet and raced to the airlock door, then stabbed at the control panel. The room had resealed itself, but from this angle, I couldn't see if the emergency med kit remained on the wall. I waited an impatient thirty seconds for the room to pressurize, then entered. Luck held for once: the kit was still in place, tightly sealed. I broke the hinges to get it down and dragged it into the hall.

There wasn't much to work with in the med kit, but I

cleaned and bandaged his wound, my hand surprisingly steady in spite of the pooling blood. Matt showed up when I was half-way done and plunked himself beside me without a word. He held bandages out of the way and lifted Cage so I could wrap the wound more tightly. "You think he'll be okay?" I asked when I was finished.

Matt shrugged. "I feel his life as strongly as I feel yours, if that means anything. I'm not sure it does."

I glared at him. "We need to get him to the prison. Grab his arm." Before helping Matt, I darted down the corridor and retrieved my ring. A sense of peace settled over me after I slipped it onto my finger. I'd worn it every day for a year and a half, and being without it felt as strange as being without my wrist comm. Besides, it was the only thing I had remaining of Mom.

We hoisted Cage, propping him upright between us, and I tore the stun gun free from his holster and held it out to Matt. He hesitated, but I pressed it on him. "Cage isn't going to be able to use this if an alien comes back. You can." *You can,* I repeated silently, my gaze locked on his.

After a moment, he nodded, accepting the stun gun. He tucked it into his waistband—gingerly, like he was afraid it might go off any minute. Before I could start second-guessing my decision, he tugged on Cage's arm and got us moving. "Please tell me you have a plan," he grunted.

"Actually, I do," I gasped, pausing to catch my breath. "I'll explain later." As an afterthought, I reactivated my comm unit.

Rune's angry voice flooded all channels, panic and fear underlying her fury. "Sorry, Rune," I interrupted, a wave of guilt overtaking me. This was her twin brother, after all. "I think Cage is all right. He got clawed by one of the creatures and he's unconscious, but I stopped the bleeding. We're heading to you now."

"Can I deactivate the emergency lockdown?"

I hesitated. Just because we hadn't seen more than three aliens didn't mean more weren't lurking around. Still, I needed the prisoners ready to move. "Yeah, it should be okay. We'll be there in a few minutes. Prep everyone to head out."

That news pacified her somewhat, although I had to endure a full five minutes of lecturing before we reached the prison entrance. That was when Cage opened his eyes. "Hey," I said, a physical rush of relief tearing through me. "You all right?"

He swallowed and shook his head. "Ow," he complained. "Rune, stop yelling. You're giving me a headache."

That triggered another bout of screaming. All three of us stopped to rest against the wall until she calmed down, and then Cage said, "I'll see you soon, *meimei*," and slapped my wrist to cut the connection.

"I think I can walk by myself," he said at last. "You two ready?"

I examined his wound dubiously. "You sure about that, tough guy?"

"It looks worse than it feels." He gave me a wink, his

old humor resurfacing, and shouldered away from the wall. Instantly, his knees gave out, and he toppled to the floor.

I rolled my eyes. "My hero."

Over Cage's protests, Matt and I slipped our arms around him again. It was much easier with Cage moving under his own power, even though he leaned on us heavily. Every step he took gave me another burst of hope. I might have lost Mom and Rita, but I'd be damned if I lost Cage too.

We made it through the door and down the first flight of stairs before something clanged in the distance.

All three of us froze. "Rune?" I called.

Silence.

"Probably nothing," Matt said at last. "The station makes noises all the time, right?"

No. Not like that. "Let's be careful," I replied. Even if we only had three aliens on Sanctuary, more might awake and approach from the ship. Or the three I'd blown into space—if my theory about their ability to survive in a vacuum was correct—could find a way back to Sanctuary, in which case they'd hunt us with a vengeance. There could be aliens around every corner.

Or, it could be nothing. Just a bang.

"Hurry," I murmured. We increased our speed, ignoring Cage's gasps of pain, and made it down another flight of stairs before one of the creatures exploded from the door to sector 2.

THIRTY-TWO

IT TORE THROUGH THE DOOR, SENDING CHUNKS of jagged metal flying in every direction. "Run!" I shouted. Cage toppled, grabbing a railing for support. He managed to take his own weight long enough to vanish down the stairwell. A thud at the bottom told us of the predictable result. Matt and I raced after him.

We rounded the corner and Cage grabbed me. He was on his feet somehow, presumably through pure adrenaline, but his hands trembled and his face was a mask of terror. "We can't lead them to four," he gasped.

I cursed myself. If only I hadn't told them to deactivate emergency lockdown! "Rune!" I shouted as I frantically worked the door controls for sector 3. Above us, the creature howled. Why hadn't it attacked already? Trouble with the narrow stairways?

"Kenzie?" Rune's voice was frantic. "Is Cage okay?"

"He is for now." I plugged in the last few numbers and pressed my thumb to the scanner. Almost before the scan registered, I pulled the pistol and spun into the hall, holding it at the ready. "Reactivate emergency lockdown in sector four and get it prepped for three, but for the love of God, don't activate it unless I tell you."

She didn't ask questions or demand explanations, just shouted, "Mia, get everyone back in position for lockdown." A loud string of Mia cursing followed. Then Rune returned. "Kenz, there's a ten-second countdown before the electrical panels activate. Keep that in mind when giving me your cue."

The door slid open. I grabbed Cage and scanned for Matt. He stood at the foot of the stairs, staring up. "Matt!" I whispered. "Come on!"

He shook his head. "It's not there."

"What do you mean?"

He crept halfway up the staircase, ignoring our frantic hisses. "There's nothing there. I don't know why, but I think it—"

The creature dropped through the stairwell in what would have been an eerily beautiful display from anything else. It fell without noise, landing feetfirst on Matt's shoulders, and bore him to the ground in a clatter of screams and claws. Matt roared in pain, and the creature slashed again. His cry became a gurgling moan. "Matt!" I shouted.

"Kenzie, shoot it!" Cage roared.

I targeted the creature with shaking hands. It was moving so *fast* and . . .

I pulled the trigger.

The bullet caught it in the shoulder. It howled, pivoting in our direction. I squeezed off another shot as it charged, but the shot went wide, missing the creature entirely.

Matt screamed as the alien tossed him aside. "Matt!" Cage lunged in his direction, and the alien tensed.

I grabbed Cage and bolted for sector 3. "Rune!" I cried. "Activate the lockdown! Now!"

Almost instantly, Sanctuary's voice broadcast over the loudspeaker: *"Emergency lockdown is now in effect. All prisoners return to your cells. Emergency lockdown in ten . . . nine . . ."*

I dragged Cage past the first few cells. We had to time this precisely. The creature was hot on our tail, and if we simply leaped into the first bed, it would attack before the floor electrified. Take too long, and we'd electrocute ourselves. And I sure as hell didn't have time to line up another shot.

But adrenaline would carry Cage only so far. He stumbled, caught himself on my arm, and almost tripped us both. The creature screeched, its hand raking so close behind us the wind of its passing brushed my skin. *"Five . . . four . . . three . . ."*

We weren't going to make it. The creature would string us up on the alien ship before harvesting the others. I closed my eyes, tensing in anticipation of claws tearing my flesh.

Cage's arms closed around me. There was a sudden burst of speed, and I hit a cot face-first, his body crashing heavily on top of mine, as Sanctuary announced, *"One. Emergency lockdown mode is active. Please remain in position until further notice."*

A hideous scream engulfed the room. Something sizzled and crackled. I kept waiting for it to end but it went on and on, the creature howling as electricity rifled through its body.

I pushed at Cage, gasping for air beneath his weight, but that last burst of energy had finished him and he was unconscious again. I maneuvered him off me, taking care he stayed on the cot—I didn't think I could lift him if he fell on the floor, even if I found a way to do it without getting electrocuted. Blood seeped through his bandages, but I ignored it. Instead, I stood on the mattress, craning my neck in search of the alien.

The screams stopped, but the sizzle remained. The creature was on the floor directly outside our cell, its limbs spasming with each electrical jolt. Its eyes were open and staring—not that *that* was much of a change—and its jaw hung slack. Electricity had coursed through it for a solid minute now. I decided to give it a minute more.

Cage groaned. I dropped beside him and tightened the bandages as best I could. "No, don't try to sit up," I growled. "What the hell were you thinking?"

He groaned again. "You're welcome." He hesitated. "Matt?"

I remembered the other boy's scream. Had I shot fast enough? "I don't know." I stared at the twitching monster before reactivating my comm. "Rune, we're clear to power down sector three."

"Copy that."

The lights briefly dimmed, then illuminated, and the creature stilled. *"Emergency lockdown has been lifted,"* Sanctuary announced. *"Thank you for your cooperation in this matter."*

"Oh, shut up," I muttered. "Cage, can you walk?"

He nodded, although judging by his set jaw, he wasn't so sure. I looped his arm over my shoulders and helped him to his feet. We climbed over the creature as carefully as we could. If that many volts hadn't killed it, nothing would, but I'd learned my lesson about making assumptions. I briefly considered pumping a few bullets into its head, but I'd already wasted two shots and didn't want to expend any more.

We found Matt where we'd left him in the corridor. "Matt," I called as we approached.

Cage slumped against the stairs, eyes closed, breathing heavy. "He won't answer you. I have a theory," he said.

"Great. Good time for it."

He ignored my sarcasm, gesturing toward Matt without opening his eyes. "The aliens inject their victims with a sedative," he said. "Matt's unconscious. Mia and I both passed out after the creatures' attacks. Imani described the same thing."

"Like a mosquito."

"What?"

I glanced at him. "Mosquitoes inject a local anesthetic when they feed. It keeps you from feeling the bite."

"Something like that, then, yeah."

I nodded and bent over Matt. Cage was probably right, and . . .

"Oh my God," I whispered.

"What?" Cage appeared at my side, tottered, and fell. His gaze followed mine, and his jaw dropped.

Blood soaked Matt's shirt, but it wasn't from gashes made by the alien's claws. It was from the bullet wound in his chest. My last shot had missed the alien—but it had struck home just the same.

We stared at him a moment longer, and then I fumbled for his neck. "Come on, come on," I whispered, applying pressure on the wound with one hand, searching for a pulse with the other.

Nothing.

Cage gently pushed me aside and inspected his friend. When he sat back, his face was pale and drawn. "He's . . . he's dead."

My heart and lungs gave out at the same moment. I collapsed on the floor, the world spinning around me, because when Cage said *he's dead*, what he meant was *you killed him*.

"Kenzie," said Cage sharply. "Kenzie!" He grabbed my shoulders and shook me.

At the same instant, Rune's semi-hysterical voice cut through the fog. "Kenzie? What's going on? I'm sending Mia and Alexei to you right now!"

Cage's head shot up and he grabbed my wrist, applying pressure to the comm unit. "No, don't do that. We're okay, but . . . the alien got Matt."

I winced when Rune's startled cry echoed through the hall. "We'll be right there," he continued, his expression fierce, and cut the feed. "Come on. Help me."

"Help you what?"

"Move him into sector three." Our eyes locked in challenge, and Cage broke first, turning his gaze to Matt's body. "I wasn't lying. The alien did get him. This wasn't your fault. You were trying to save him, and for all we know, he was already dying. But if the others find out . . . Come on, Kenz. I can't do this by myself."

I swallowed hard, grinding my fists into my eyes, forcing myself to focus. Cage was right. It had been an *accident*. I hadn't meant to kill him.

Try explaining that to Mia. Somehow I wasn't sure Rune would be entirely logical where Matt was concerned either.

Steeling myself, I got to my feet and grabbed one of Matt's arms. Together, we pulled him into sector 3. I folded his hands over his chest and dropped a kiss on his forehead. "I'm sorry, Matt," I whispered. "I'm so sorry."

I hated to leave him like that, next to the alien body, as if they were the same and deserved the same treatment. "Maybe we should . . ."

"Kenzie."

I closed my eyes against the sight of Matt's lifeless face. Cage took my elbow and pulled me to my feet. "Let's go," he said, a hard, unnatural edge in his voice.

Almost on autopilot, I followed his orders. He pulled me along and, judging from the way he collapsed against the stairwell, used the last of his strength to get me out of sector 3.

"Okay," Cage said. "Signal Rune and get the others. Let's move."

I glanced at him, not sure about his tone, but I did as he asked. Was he angry? On some level did he blame me for what just happened? Or was he just physically and mentally exhausted? I would understand if he did blame me. I pulled the trigger. My lousy aim took a boy's life—the first boy who'd offered me any kindness in the prison. I remembered the wry smile on Matt's face when he sank down beside me after we removed Alexei's chip. The resulting wash of self-loathing and guilt almost knocked me off my feet.

There was plenty of blame for Matt's death to go around, between Sanctuary and Omnistellar and the aliens, but a big chunk of it landed right on my shoulders.

Cage caught me watching him and forced a smile, reaching out to touch the side of my face. I nodded in return, sinking my nails into my palms to stop my hands from trembling. We had to concentrate on escaping Sanctuary now. Grief, guilt, conversation—all of that could wait until later.

But oh my God, what had I done? It felt like someone was squeezing my throat so tightly I couldn't draw in a breath. My stomach lurched sickeningly, and my knees trembled, threatening to give out. I closed my eyes to focus and instead saw Matt's pallid face, the life drained away.

A loud clatter of voices and footsteps jerked me awake. I swallowed what felt like a mouthful of sand. *Get yourself under control. You still have people alive on this station, and your first duty is to them.* I abandoned Cage and raced down the stairs, meeting the prisoners halfway. "Quiet!" I shouted. "All of you, shut up, right now!"

The prisoners, led by Rune, staggered to a halt. Rune took a shaky step forward. Shadows of tears stained her cheeks, but a look of resolve settled over her features. "We're ready to go," she said, her voice surprisingly controlled. She glanced around and lowered her voice. "Kenzie . . . where is he?"

I hesitated, not sure how to answer. I didn't want to lie to Rune. Not about Matt. But if she saw the body . . .

Behind me, Cage sighed. "Come here, *meimei*."

Rune let out a cry when she saw him and raced to his side, babbling in Mandarin. I understood most of it, which wasn't much comfort at this stage in the game. Cage caught her before she could throw her arms around him and maneuvered her into a gentler hug, kissing the top of her forehead. "I'm fine," he murmured. "I promise. I've had worse injuries."

She hugged him again, collapsing in on him as if the sight of his wounds had drained her courage.

With Cage and Rune occupied, every eye turned to me. I looked over the faces, each and every prisoner staring at me expectantly—or maybe at Cage behind me. "All right," I said. "It's time we got the hell off Sanctuary."

THIRTY-THREE

SHEPHERDING THE PRISONERS THROUGH Sanctuary's halls was like herding a bunch of cats. We'd warned them about the aliens, told them the truth about what was going on, but fear and inexpérience made them impossible. There were even a few nervous whispers and giggles at first. Cage and I snapped on that at the same time, though, and everyone shut up.

That didn't mean they were quiet. Mia went invisible— I wasn't sure why; the aliens couldn't see her anyway—and scouted ahead, her footfalls all but inaudible. Alexei's face tightened in annoyance at that, but he couldn't stop her, so he brought up the rear, bracing the stun gun in one hand and pulling Anya along with the other. Rune moved quietly, supporting Cage's weight, but Tyler and Kristen both had a heavy stride, as did a couple of the other kids.

All in all, it would probably have been quieter leading a trumpeting elephant. I bit my tongue over and over to keep from telling them to shut up. They were only kids; they didn't know any better. But every heavy step, every scrape of a boot against the floor, set my nerves jangling and tightened my finger on the trigger of a gun I wasn't sure I had the nerve to fire again.

All at once, I realized we'd left the second stun gun with Matt. I winced. It wasn't like I could suggest returning for it. No one besides Rune had so much as mentioned him yet, accepting the loss as they accepted all the others. I quickly forced the thought of him away before it could overwhelm me again. If I could just pretend it hadn't happened long enough to escape Sanctuary and reach the alien ship . . .

Miraculously, we made it to the shuttle bay without incident. Maybe we'd finally killed the last alien—or maybe they'd retreated to their own ship, and even now waited for us with three dozen more. *Don't get cocky,* I reminded myself. We tried that once. It didn't work. I gestured for everyone to stay back and examined the bay as best I could through the window. There was no sign of the alien who'd destroyed the shuttle.

Cage limped to my side, clutching his torn stomach. "Where'd it go?" he murmured.

Hopefully it wasn't hiding around a corner. I signaled the others to wait, tightened my grip on the gun, and popped the door. A quick, terrified search of the bay revealed nothing—

another mystery I didn't have time to solve. I called the others, holstered my gun, and began laying out emergency XE suits.

The prisoners stared at the suits nervously, which might explain the lack of argument when Cage divided everyone into groups—although Alexei standing at his back with his arms folded, glowering at the crowd, also quelled any dissent. I'd expected more argument when we told them we were headed to the alien ship, but they hardly responded at all, aside from a few unhappy grumbles. The prisoners had been somewhat sheltered from the terror of the last few hours, but they sensed enough to know we had to get out while we could. That was one small blessing, at least. One of the kids, Reed, had a power that allowed him to heal others, so even though they hadn't removed his chip yet, we put him in the first group. He might be needed on the ship.

It took way too long to help everyone into their XE suits— including Cage, who could barely move. I remembered playing with fashion dolls with my cousins on one of our rare family visits. My life was training camps and junior guard clubs, and there I was, awkwardly forcing a doll's arm into a sweater while my cousin yelled at me not to bend it *that way*. Of course, I hadn't really cared if I broke the *doll*. I preferred not to snap Cage's arm.

We managed it at last, though. I hesitated for a moment, then offered my pistol to Mia. She snatched it from my hand and thumbed the safety in a way that gave me confidence. If I never fired that thing again, it would be too soon. Let Mia carry the burden. "Careful," I said. "I shot one of them and it didn't seem to have much effect."

"You target the head?"

"No," I muttered, not bothering to mention that what I targeted and what I hit weren't necessarily one and the same.

"You've never seen a zombie movie? *Always* target the head." She offered me a half smile. "Careful. And hurry."

Then, before I could reply, she disappeared.

I shook my head and turned to Tyler. "The room next door is the ship's primary storage," I told him. "Gather up anything that might be useful. The only things we know for sure the aliens have are water and oxygen. Food, light, clothing— anything you can find, stack it up and we'll drag it along in the last load." I glanced around. "Maybe put it in the shuttle, just in case the aliens show up. Might as well use it for something." If it couldn't get us off the ship, it could at least be a protective locker until we returned.

Tyler nodded, looking faintly alarmed at being entrusted with anything at all, but I knew Mia was listening nearby. For a moment I contemplated giving her the order directly, and I almost laughed out loud at the thought. She'd take the hint anyway.

It took a while to reach the alien ship with four kids in tow. Interestingly, Alexei seemed to have quite a bit of experience with zero g, so having him aiding Anya at the rear helped. But

Reed was useless, Cage more so, and Rune was worse. Alexei and I half pushed, half dragged them along, and we used a lot more thruster fuel than I wanted getting to the ship. In a way I was grateful for the occupation. It kept me from picturing Mom's empty stare, Matt's blood-soaked chest. My own breathing echoed loudly in the suit's chambers—an attack of claustrophobia threatened to overwhelm me. I fought it down. The others were depending on me.

Once inside, I double-checked the corridors. The aliens remained in their slumber, and I didn't hear anything disturbing. Breathing a sigh of relief, I returned to the prisoners.

Each of these suits had an emergency tool kit, meaning plenty of screwdrivers and flashlights. Alexei still had one of the stun guns, and he passed it to Cage. Meanwhile, I showed Rune how the doors worked, cautioning her against using them. "Stay here," I instructed, indicating the corridor with the depressed areas. "Get inside the holes, if you can. You can use the lights, but keep quiet. I'll be back as soon as I can."

"*We'll* be back as soon as we can," Alexei corrected.

I glared at him. "I need you here."

"No, you need me with you. You'll never keep them organized by yourself."

I hated to admit it, but he had a point. And I didn't have time to argue. "Fine. Let's go."

Dragging the empty suits through space was almost harder than guiding them with bodies—at least the prisoners directed their thrusters when you told them to. I didn't want to admit it, but Alexei's help proved invaluable. Still, by the time we reached Sanctuary, I'd burned through so much thruster fuel I had to switch to one of the other suits. I checked them all and frowned. At this rate, we'd have enough to guide everyone over, but just barely. "Try to conserve," I murmured to Alexei, and he nodded.

Mia had not been idle in our absence. In addition to guarding the shuttle bay door, she'd set the kids to foraging the area for anything useful and had accumulated a small pile of emergency med kits, tools, flashlights, and rations, which she'd stacked in the middle of the room. I nodded my appreciation, but she didn't look up from sorting the pile. A moment later, she disappeared.

Once we'd gathered the second group, we discovered that only Mia and Tyler would be left behind, much to Tyler's dismay. "Come on, Kenzie," he complained, following me around as I checked XE suits for seals. "Don't leave me on this station. . . ." His voice dropped to a whisper. "Especially with *her*."

"Look, Mia will keep you safe. Just do as she says. We won't be long."

He groaned audibly and glared at the doorway where Mia, presumably, lurked. "You have no idea how creepy it is hanging out with an invisible person!"

I grinned. "Well, there's your challenge: sharpen your mental skills by finding her."

"Right, invade Mia's mind. That'll go well."

"You invaded mine with no problems."

Tyler blanched, and I sighed. At the time the invasion had felt vicious, unprovoked, and unnecessary . . . but I'd come to see it was desperation, not malice, that motivated their actions. If my own parents refused me answers, well . . . I couldn't guarantee I wouldn't ask Tyler to find them.

Besides, who was I to talk? At least Tyler hadn't killed anyone. Suddenly I regarded him with suspicion. How much did he see? Did he know what I was thinking right now? If Tyler realized I'd killed Matt, he might . . .

Oh, for God's sake. What was I going to do about it? Kill him too? Semi-hysterical laughter bubbled inside me, and I turned away before it could escape. For a moment that sickening sense of vertigo threatened again, and I took a moment to fight it off. God, I needed rest. I needed to stop, to think.

Behind me Tyler let out a shuddering breath that sounded like a sob. "Kenzie, I am so sorry."

Great. He thought my reaction was at the memory of his mind invasion. Well, that ought to keep him out of my thoughts. "Forget I said anything."

"No. You're right. It was a lousy thing to do."

"Then I guess you're lucky I'm such a forgiving person." I didn't quite keep the sarcasm out of my voice. Slapping Tyler on the shoulder, I sealed my own helmet. I felt like I was watching myself from the outside, but the other Kenzie, the one who didn't seem bothered that she'd just killed one of her friends, that her mother had just died, put on a pretty good show. "Suck it up," I said, my voice tinny and mechanical through the speaker. "We won't be long."

And take your own advice, Kenzie.

The second group reached the ship a little faster, but much to my annoyance, there was no sign of the first group in the corridor where we'd left them. "Great," I muttered to Alexei as we stood with our helmets off, the kids behind us clumsily removing their suits. "Did they wander off or were they taken? Do we waste time hunting for them or return to the station? If something did happen, this group is sitting ducks, but the longer it takes to escape Sanctuary . . ."

Alexei swore in Russian. I was pleased to note I understood most of it, and went so far as to hesitantly reply in the same language, "This has Cage written all over it."

He blinked at me in surprise. "You speak . . . no, of course you don't. Rune told me. Your power."

He added something in Russian, and I shook my head. "Too fast." I'd gotten the gist of it, but . . .

He grinned and switched to English. "You're not wrong. Even injured, Cage isn't the type to wait around, and the others will follow him anywhere."

I threw my hands up in disgust. "What do we tell everyone?"

Sure enough, Kristin popped up between us. "Where's Cage?" she demanded.

Alexei and I exchanged speaking glances. "We sent him on

ahead," I lied, a sick feeling in my stomach. I'd tried so hard to set my fear and grief aside, but they kept clawing their way back up. Finding the others missing triggered the emotions all over again. Were they really just following Cage? Or were they lying in a pool of blood?

I went through the same spiel I'd gone through with the others, emphasizing they should stay where we left them, and prayed I wasn't abandoning them to be discovered by a prowling group of creatures. I really wanted to go after Cage, but common sense won out. He'd probably gotten worried about Imani and dragged the others off to check on her. But to be safe, I poked my head into the next chamber to ascertain that all the aliens were still asleep. They were, which meant that the group here was probably safe; and Mia and Tyler awaited us back on Sanctuary, where it was definitely *not* safe. So with that in mind, Alexei and I returned to the station to make one last trip.

Only to find that Mia and Tyler had disappeared too.

THIRTY-FOUR

THIS TIME, ALEXEI'S RUSSIAN SWEARING CAME too fast to follow. "What now?" I groaned, running to the door. I glanced up and down the hall, even whispered, "Mia!" in case she was nearby but invisible.

Nothing.

I found the supplies neatly stacked inside the shuttle. Tyler and Mia had used the shuttle's XE tethers to bind everything together in a way that would be easy to transport. "Okay," I said. "They can't have gone far." I glanced at Alexei and, having caught a moment of sheer terror on his face, grabbed his arms and forced him to meet my gaze. "Alexei. *They can't have gone far.* Mia would have shot anything trying to get in here, and she wouldn't just wander off. Something must have gotten too close for comfort, and she moved to a safer place." They were okay because they had to be okay. I refused to let anyone else die on my watch.

Alexei nodded, but although I'd staved off his hysteria, I knew it wouldn't take much to tip him over the edge. I pictured Alexei having a full-fledged panic attack and nearly had one of my own, so I dumped the XE suits beside the supplies in the shuttle and put him to work helping me push everything to the back, out of range of any curious invaders. "Let's try the storage room," I said once we'd finished, trying to cover up the hopeless tinge to my voice. What looked like all of Sanctuary's emergency supplies were currently sitting in the shuttle. I didn't know why Mia would be back in storage, but we had to start somewhere.

Halfway to the door, something caught my attention. "Wait," I said. It was a torn strip of red cloth I recognized as the shuttle's emergency landing parachute. The creature had done a number on that shuttle, but had it tossed pieces all the way over here? The cloth's arrangement on the ground seemed purposeful, almost like . . .

"Is it a signal?" Alexei asked.

"Let's find out." I followed the cloth behind a stack of emergency supplies and discovered a loose access vent. I frowned. "The shuttle bay's a sealed room, like the airlock. This vent can't actually go anywhere."

"It must go somewhere," Alexei replied shortly. "It's not a hatch to nowhere, Kenzie."

Obviously it wasn't a hatch to nowhere. I'd been thinking out loud. I bit off an irritated reply and examined Alexei's broad shoulders. "I think you're going to have to let me check this one out on my own."

He scowled but stepped aside. It was going to be a tight squeeze for me to get through that vent—Alexei didn't have a hope.

I returned to our stash of tools for an emergency belt, thus gaining a few screwdrivers and a flashlight. If only I hadn't left the stun gun with Cage's group. At this point, I needed it a lot more than they did. I shook that thought aside and clasped the penlight between my teeth, then squirmed headfirst into the vent. "What do you see?" Alexei demanded at once.

I made an inarticulate sound around the flashlight. The metal vent scraped my elbows as I dragged myself forward. It was a tight fit, doable for an average-size human. But why did it exist in the first place?

I got my answer about thirty feet in. The vent widened to a maintenance corridor providing access to the circuitry in the shuttle bay. A ladder stretched up, and there was a hatch above my head. I climbed the ladder and tucked the flashlight into my armpit. "There's a hatch," I called to Alexei. "I'll be right back."

He said something in return, but his voice faded into echoes and murmurs.

The maintenance hatch didn't require any codes, just the leverage to twist it open. I'd never seen anything like it on the station. Incredible how much I was learning about Sanctuary—a station I'd thought I knew inside and out.

Just like I'd thought I knew my mother, my father. Omnistellar. Myself, for that matter. My hands shook at the memory of the gun's recoil, and I tightened them on the wheel, giving it a particularly vicious twist.

The hatch gave way with a hiss, revealing it to be sealed in case of depressurization, which made sense, given it connected to the shuttle bay. I climbed the ladder to find myself in a short tunnel extending up, another hatch over my head. This one had a red seal around it. I reached down and pulled the first hatch shut. When its seal turned red, the one above my head changed to green.

This had better not go on much longer. I put my weight on the first hatch and used both hands to twist the one above my head.

It popped open with a hiss, and something closed around my wrist. I swallowed my scream, jerking involuntarily, only to be met with a familiar string of curses.

I stopped fighting. "Mia?" I called.

She shimmered into existence above me, her face a taut mask of fear or anger or both. "Oh, you're back," she said irritably. "That's nice."

"What the hell happened?" I hauled myself up to find a small maintenance tunnel. Tyler trembled against a wall, his face pale. "Are you okay?" I asked.

He managed a nod and, to his credit, a slight smile. "Thanks to Mia," he said. "She was kind of brilliant."

Mia snorted. "I shoved your ass into a vent. But if you want to call it brilliant, that's fine by me." She glanced over my shoulder. "Are they dead?"

"Are what dead?"

She stared at me like I'd lost my mind. "Did you think we hid in this shaft for our entertainment? *The creatures.*"

At least five seconds of dead silence followed in which my lips moved but no sound came out. "How many?" I managed at last. "What happened?"

"It was a few minutes after you left. Something didn't feel right. I couldn't put my finger on what. And Tyler here was even jumpier than usual—kept saying he sensed something."

Tyler shot to his feet, smashed his head against the ceiling, and sank back to his knees. "I *did* sense something," he muttered, rubbing his head. "I can't read their minds— they're too . . . well, alien. But I'm starting to get a sense for them. Not a good sense. Just enough."

"So you sensed creatures," I prompted. "And?"

"And," Mia snapped, "they came out of the metalwork. I mean that literally. One second everything was calm, and the next we were surrounded by the things. I'm guessing they have some sort of camouflage. That, or they're learning."

"Learning?"

Mia shrugged. "I've turned invisible in front of them a few times. I know they can't see, but they might have other senses we don't know about."

Oh God, I really did not want to consider *that* possibility. "How did they get in?" I demanded, my voice verging on hysterical. "How long were they there?"

"How the hell should I know? You think I stuck around to ask? Four of them surrounded us. No way to shoot them all, so I grabbed this infant before he could scream"—she indicated Tyler with a jerk of her thumb, ignoring his scowl—"and looked for another way out. We found the vent, and I grabbed the cloth and hoped you'd be bright enough to spot it. So I'll ask you again: Are they dead?"

"No," I said. "No, they're not dead. We didn't see them at all."

"We?" Mia stared at me a moment, and her face took on a deadly set. "Where's Alexei?"

"He's . . ." Oh God. My throat tightened. "He's in the shuttle bay."

With the creatures.

THIRTY-FIVE

I SCRAMBLED DOWN THE LADDER, ALL TOO aware of Mia at my back, pistol clutched in her hand. Anger radiated off her like a physical force. For once, I didn't blame her. I cursed myself for leaving Alexei behind. I knew he wouldn't have fit in the vent, but I should have . . . what? Made him hide in the shuttle? Something. I'd lost Mom and Rita today. Matt was dead because of my own stupidity and carelessness. Had I left Alexei to die too?

But then, the creatures didn't really want to kill him. They wanted to assimilate him. I clung to that hope, but I didn't say it out loud. It wouldn't comfort Mia and might earn me a shot in the back—especially since I didn't know if there was any way to return from assimilation without Imani's very specific set of powers.

As soon as we opened the second hatch, Tyler sucked in a breath. "They're still there," he confirmed in a whisper. I glanced over my shoulder to find his face twisted in what might be pain, fear, or concentration. Probably a combination of the three. "Their . . . signatures. They're getting stronger."

I nodded and took the ladder at an agonizing but silent crawl. Mia's breath came in short, livid gasps. I knew this pace must be killing her. Part of me was even on her side, wanted to get to Alexei as fast as possible. But for once I was going to think before I acted. Yet again I fought back a sickening wash of grief and anger—at myself, at the creatures, at Omnistellar, even at Mom, as if she'd somehow died to spite me. I knew that wasn't true, but the crumbling cage around my grief didn't seem to respond to logic.

Focus, I reminded myself. *Quiet. Strong. Keep moving.*

Of course, crawling through a metal vent on my elbows and trying to do it soundlessly felt nearly impossible. By the time I reached the exit, I'd made enough noise to wake the dead. Somehow Mia managed to stay quiet—except for the occasional whispered command to shut up—but Tyler was even louder than me.

I paused, still inside the vent, and peered out. I couldn't see anything—no Alexei, and no creatures. A wall of metal supply boxes blocked my vision. I took my time prying myself loose of the opening, just in case they'd somehow managed to miss our approach, and crouched behind the boxes. Mia slithered free without a sound and turned to drag Tyler through, ignoring his resistance. The muscles in her arms stood out in sharp relief as she half lifted, half guided him down, far more silently than he could have managed on his own. She shoved him into a corner and held a finger to her lips.

I gestured for Tyler to stay put while Mia and I crept behind the boxes. She held the pistol at the ready, and I had a moment of gratitude that it was in her hands, not mine. Mia was half a step ahead of me, and when she rounded the boxes, she sucked in a breath. I slipped out beside her and froze.

Alexei stood stock-still, his back against the shuttle. Four creatures circled the shuttle like a group of playground bullies. They tossed their heads, sniffed, occasionally let loose one of those barking screams.

They obviously knew he was there. They were just as obviously toying with him.

But we had one hope: in their obsession with Alexei, they didn't seem to have noticed us.

Alexei, on the other hand, did. His face relaxed with relief when he caught sight of Mia. He lifted a finger to his lips, another unnecessary warning, and twisted his wrist. A spark of flame emerged between his fingers, and he glanced at me for confirmation.

Fire. I scanned the shuttle bay. Fire in a contained environment like a space station was always a bad idea. The idea became exponentially worse when there was highly volatile shuttle fuel nearby. But what else could we do? Alexei had said that Mia was a crack shot—and there wasn't a single part of me that doubted that—but I didn't think even Mia's aim would stand up to shooting four aliens before they attacked us. As for powers, Mia's invisibility and Tyler's mind reading wouldn't do us much good here, and me, well . . .

I frowned. What about me? I beckoned to Alexei to hold off, and he lowered his hand, letting the flame die down. The creatures alternated between shouting to one another and sniffing the air.

Mia's lips almost touched my ear. "Shouldn't they be attacking him?" she whispered. She slurred the *S* in "shouldn't" slightly, impressing me—she knew it was the most likely sound to carry.

I shook my head. "Not sure," I said, mimicking her intonation. "It might be a trap. They know you're nearby, and they're waiting for you to charge to the rescue."

Her eyes widened slightly. I sympathized. We routinely underestimated the aliens' intelligence.

No more.

"Give me a second," I whispered, closing my eyes and leaning on the boxes, trying to forget my surroundings.

My power had helped me read the aliens' language before. Wouldn't it help me hear it?

A creature screamed again, and another snorted in response. It wasn't a language, exactly—but I was starting to get the gist of it. Not words. More like directions. *Go this way. Wait here.*

I opened my eyes and took a deep breath. I wasn't sure I

had the vocal cords to mimic these particular sounds. I thought I knew the call meaning "Over here—I've found something," but that didn't mean I could reproduce it.

Come up with something else, Kenzie. Quickly.

"Where are the XE suits?" Mia murmured in my ear.

"In the shuttle."

We both glanced at the ruined hull. Still, if we got inside, it would provide temporary protection from the creatures until we came up with something better.

Or . . . did it have to be so temporary? I looked at the shuttle more closely. The hull was beyond damaged. The creature's claws had torn it to shreds, leaving huge gaping holes everywhere. But did that matter if we had XE suits? Not as long as the engine still functioned.

"Tyler," I whispered, beckoning him forward. He got up and stumbled over his own feet, and one creature's head shot up. We all froze, and no one needed to hear her to know Mia was internally cursing Tyler with great inventiveness. After a moment of silence, though, the alien returned to circling Alexei.

I grabbed Tyler before he advanced any farther. "You can read minds. Can you talk to them? Can you tell Alexei something for me?"

He looked hesitant. "I've never tried that at such a distance," he said. Mia groaned softly and moved a few steps away, as if distancing herself from the noise. I shot them both a warning look, but luckily the aliens seemed too preoccupied with

Alexei to notice us. Occasionally their heads twitched toward the door. I wondered if they expected us from that direction. If so, coming through the vent might actually catch them off guard. As long as we kept reasonably quiet, they might not realize we were here.

I gave Tyler a slight shake. "Try now," I ordered. "Focus on Alexei. Tell him when these boxes go down, he needs to get inside the shuttle and get ready to slam the door."

Tyler's eyes went wide. "When the boxes go down? But . . ."

Mia's hand slammed over his mouth, her eyes glistening inches from his. *"Shut. Up."*

"Tyler, please. Try."

He nodded, glared at Mia, and pushed her hand aside. Wherever the sudden burst of courage came from, I gave him a tight-lipped smile of approval.

Tyler closed his eyes. His jaw set in a hard line, becoming sharper and more pronounced with every second. I divided my attention between him and Alexei, biting my cheek in frustration. No sign of anything but tension and fear from Alexei. "This won't work," Mia murmured at last.

I rolled my eyes and bit off an annoyed response. Fear and worry drove her, the same as they drove the rest of us. "Make yourself useful," I returned. "Rig that length of parachute you pirated into something we can use to topple these boxes from a distance."

Her eyes narrowed dangerously, and for a second I thought

I'd gone too far. But then Mia set to work. Watching her move deftly around the area, I knew I'd guessed right—she had prior experience with sabotage. It made sense. Just as Cage's and Rune's powers made them invaluable to a street gang in Taipei, a lot of businesses and governments wouldn't mind using Mia's invisibility. Cage had said Mia claimed she'd been set up for her act of terrorism. That might be true, but there was more to the story.

Suddenly, Alexei frowned. He glanced at me, his mouth set in confusion, and I gestured behind me at Tyler. Alexei's eyes widened. He tilted his head and closed his eyes.

Then he opened them, pointed at the shuttle, and nodded.

At the same moment, Mia appeared behind me holding a length of parachute that she'd wrapped around the crates. "It's done," she said. "But we'll have to stand a bit close for my comfort."

"How close is 'a bit'?"

She held up the parachute, revealing maybe ten feet of extra cloth. "I needed the rest to secure the boxes. One tug and Humpty Dumpty will fall, making a huge racket in the process."

But someone needed to stay pretty close to do the pulling. Cage would be ideal—he could yank the boxes down and zip across the shuttle bay before anyone knew what happened.

Except Cage wasn't here.

I gave Mia a quick smile. "Well," I said, "it's my brilliant plan. I guess that means it's up to me."

THIRTY-SIX

I EXTENDED THE SCRAP OF CLOTH, MY HANDS shaking so badly that waves rippled along its length. With no chance of a test run, I hoped Mia had set the trap properly. If she hadn't, the boxes wouldn't make enough noise to cover our retreat, and the aliens would tear into us before we reached the shuttle.

I sent Mia and Tyler across the room. If the trap failed, they could still escape while the creatures tore me to pieces or injected me with venom or whatever they did. It wasn't bravery. I wanted someone to have a chance of getting off Sanctuary and launching a rescue if the creatures put *me* in chains. Of course, I had the pistol—Mia had returned it to me without a word before retreating with Tyler. So if I could just plug four bullets into four alien eyes before they were on me, that would be fine. At least this time, I didn't have to worry about hitting anyone but myself.

I took a deep breath. The aliens continued circling Alexei, who stood like a statue, ignoring the claws inches from his face with a lot more stoicism than I could have mustered. He locked his gaze on Mia. In the far corner of the room, she stood stock-still, one hand pressing Tyler behind her. He clutched her arm, his eyes wide. I wasn't sure if he was more frightened of the creatures or Mia, but either way, his fear kept him silent. Mia met my gaze and nodded.

She was ready. Alexei was ready. The trap was ready. But my hand clenched on the fabric, resisting that final tug. I closed my eyes, clamping my jaw so tightly that my grinding teeth echoed in my ears. Every second brought an increasing chance one of us would make a noise, drawing the aliens' attention. I opened my eyes and focused on the boxes. *Pull, damn it!* I ordered myself.

I put every ounce of strength behind my grip, yanking on the makeshift rope. The shock of the pull reverberated through me as the foundation gave way. Before the boxes even hit the ground, I spun and raced in the opposite direction.

The crates tumbled down in a clatter. The creatures shrieked at the top of their lungs, and again I caught glimmers of meaning—*There! Attack! Watch! Wait!*—before they lunged for the debris. Using the commotion as cover, I darted straight through the falling boxes, throwing my hands over my head for protection. One struck my elbow, and the pain of the impact spread through my arm and almost toppled me, but I made it out the other side before the aliens leaped onto the pile.

Alexei lunged for the shuttle, the rest of us racing up behind him. I leaped for the door and he hauled me inside. Mia shot across the bay, dragging Tyler behind her. He stumbled, eyes fixed on the creatures across the room.

"Tyler, come on!" I shouted, throwing caution to the wind. I risked leaning around the shuttle. The creatures spun in our direction, howling in rage.

Mia swore loudly and shoved Tyler in front of her. The creatures leaped, and one of them landed within inches of Mia and Tyler. Its claws grazed Mia's arm, and she shrieked but didn't stop. If anything, she ran faster, pushing Tyler along. He tripped, but Alexei grabbed him and dragged him inside. I slammed the control panel. The door began its descent as Mia lunged for Alexei's outstretched arms.

His hand closed around her wrist as one of the creatures sank its claws into her calf. Mia screamed again, her face twisted in agony.

I pulled the gun but hesitated. "Kenzie, shoot!" Alexei shouted. The aliens yanked on Mia, the force jerking Alexei to the ground, the top half of his body outside the shuttle.

My hands trembled on the gun. What if I missed? Hit Mia? Forget the aliens. Alexei would break my neck. Matt's lifeless face flashed in front of my eyes.

But I couldn't just let them take her. I dropped to my knees, whispered a silent prayer to anyone who might be listening, and pulled the trigger.

The bullet hit the creature in the eye, passing inches over Mia's head. It screamed in agony and collapsed, releasing her. She slid halfway into the shuttle before two other aliens sank their claws into her legs. Mia went limp.

"Tyler, help us!" I shouted. I squeezed off another shot, but the alien must have heard it coming, because it ducked beneath the bullet.

Tyler caught Mia's arms below the elbow. He and Alexei pulled, their faces red from effort. The claws tore through Mia's muscle but that was the least of our problems right now. I forced my breathing steady and fired again. This time I caught one of the creatures in the neck. It flew back, claws pressed to the wound, which wasn't bleeding so much as oozing a strange, clear fluid, reminding me of the gunk on the alien ship.

Tyler snatched the nearest object—a fire extinguisher—and flew across Mia's body, then slammed the canister into the creature's face. It barely staggered, but it did scream, its claws slipping loose from Mia's leg. Alexei hauled her inside, inches below the descending door. I grabbed Tyler's arm to pull him after . . .

And his face went blank.

He stared up at me, shocked and bewildered, his grip going slack around my elbow. For a moment I didn't know what had happened.

Then his body heaved against me. Taken off guard, my hands slick with sweat, I lost my grip. Tyler slid beneath the shuttle door. It actually bumped his arm as it settled into place.

"No!" I screamed, lunging for the door, and then I saw it. One of the aliens still had its claws buried deep in Tyler's abdomen. It hoisted him in the air, howling, and this time I understood every nuance of that vocalization, every note of triumph and mockery and rage.

"Tyler!" Alexei banged his fists on the door. The aliens stared at us, unseeing but unerring, daring us to open the door.

It was too late. Blood seeped from the sides of Tyler's mouth, his eyes wide and gaping.

The aliens had given up on assimilation. Because there wasn't a doubt in my mind that Tyler was dead.

THIRTY-SEVEN

WE COLLAPSED EXHAUSTED ON THE FLOOR of the shuttle. I squeezed my eyes shut against tears, but as soon as I did, Tyler's lifeless body superimposed over my vision. Mom. Matt. Rita. Tyler. How many more on the ship? My hands trembled, and the long-fought fatigue threatened to overcome me, besieging me with tears and terror.

Beside me, Alexei stroked Mia's face with a trembling hand. "She's okay," I promised him, forcing myself calm, forcing the tears back. No time to grieve. Not yet. "We think the creatures have some sort of sedative in their—"

"She is *not* okay." He cut me off with short, sharp syllables. "She's bleeding all over the place. We need to get her out of here."

At that instant, a creature shrieked. Something struck the side of the shuttle. With the sickening rend of tearing metal, one of the gaps widened.

I shot to my feet, scrambling for the XE suits. "Get Mia dressed," I ordered, tossing one at Alexei. He obeyed without question. For just a moment agony overwhelmed me again and I collapsed against the seat, jamming my fist into my mouth to hold back my sob. Tyler had been such a . . . child. Younger than his years. So afraid. And yet he'd overcome that fear to help Mia.

Look what it had earned him. Just like what Matt had gotten for his kindness, for daring to help me.

As if to punctuate that thought, another screech resounded. I glimpsed light through a tear in the metal, and an alien claw scrabbled in the gap. "Kenzie," snapped Alexei.

I pushed Tyler and Matt into the depths of my mind—not letting them go, not letting Mom go, just setting them aside for the time with a promise to come back. They would not be forgotten.

I groped for my own XE suit, and fumbled with the clasps. Alexei had stuffed Mia into hers and fastened her in place. After finishing with his own, he sealed me in. My heart raced, leaping each time a creature screamed, or struck the shuttle, or scratched the hull. "Do you really think this is going to work?" Alexei murmured in Russian as he secured my helmet. As far as I could see, he had no reaction whatsoever to Tyler's death.

I returned the favor, checking him over. "No idea," I whispered, heading for the pilot seat. I was careful to avoid looking out the shuttle porthole. Whatever they were doing to Tyler, I didn't want to see it.

The shuttle was not meant to be operated in an XE suit. Fortunately an emergency mode allowed for it, meaning I could manage the controls through my gloves. The old touch screens only responded to skin contact, and on another station a couple of decades ago, that had spelled disaster when the guards couldn't access any station systems without breaching their suits. Since then, all space vehicles and dwellings had included emergency buttons operable without electrical impulses.

I powered up the shuttle, relieved to find everything in order. Of course, alarms instantly blared, warning me we didn't have pressurization or life support. I silenced them with a jab of my finger. Outside, everything was strangely calm. I didn't miss the aliens battering the shuttle, but I wasn't sure I liked their silence, either.

I engaged the engines, overriding controls that really didn't want me lifting off without life support. "What can I do?" demanded Alexei over the comms.

"Nothing," I returned, my attention focused on the console. "Sit down and strap in. It'll be a rough ride."

As if the aliens could hear me, something struck the shuttle so hard it rocked, almost tipping. I exchanged worried glances with Alexei. If the creatures built up enough force to move the shuttle, we might hit the bay doors and damage the engines, not to mention ourselves. The aliens could rip through the shuttle hull—I knew that already. That they hadn't yet meant they were too angry to think about it logically, or maybe that they needed more time. Either way, we were in a hurry.

I triggered the launch doors, but the system fought me, determined not to engage without a proper seal on the shuttle. I swore in a combination of Russian, Mandarin, and English, earning an approving nod from Alexei, and pulled up the visual code. "This is going to take a minute," I announced.

The shuttle rocked and a sickening screech reverberated through the small space. Alexei winced. "You don't have a minute."

"Shut up, shut up," I muttered, focusing on the code. I rearranged a few pieces and isolated a safety segment, deleting it entirely before retriggering the launch.

A satisfying alarm ricocheted through the room. *"Depressurizing,"* announced Sanctuary, and the creatures' screams filled the air. I ducked my head below a crack in the windshield to watch the shuttle bay doors slide open, inch by agonizing inch.

I kept expecting the creatures to bullet past us. Piles of crates did, loose supplies—but not the creatures, and not Tyler. The vacuum should have pulled them into space, or at least trapped them against the door. I checked the rear porthole, found nothing, and cursed the shuttle's design. Why did we only have one window and two tiny portholes?

But as the doors slid wider, two of the creatures whipped

past, their tails flailing before they vanished into space—and Tyler went with them. Alexei made a choking sound that belied his indifference, his hands clamping on the arms of his chair. For just a moment bile rose in my throat, but I swallowed the grief. That left two in the bay, probably clinging to something against the vacuum. I didn't have time to worry about them. I fired up the shuttle's engines and lurched into space.

Piloting the shuttle was almost impossible with all the damage. The controls responded like a comm device stuttering through the last of its battery. Of course, we didn't need the shuttle to reach the ship. We'd only needed it to escape Sanctuary. With our XE suits, we could abandon it anytime, but that also meant abandoning Mia's supplies.

Alexei's voice cut into my comms. "Any weapons on this thing?"

"What? No. It's a station-to-Earth transit, not some sort of warship." I hesitated, cold foreboding clutching my heart. "Why?"

Alexei nodded at the back window. The last two creatures were on our tail. "How?" I shrieked. "How are they alive?" I had no idea how they maneuvered without thrusters, but they did, making course adjustments, aiming at the ship. Then again, the ship's AI had seemed totally foreign to me. It was completely possible the aliens had technology I didn't understand. More importantly . . . "Alexei, they're heading straight for us."

THIRTY-EIGHT

I SWORE, JAMMING THE SHUTTLE'S CONTROLS, veering left. Instead of responding, the controls cut out completely, leaving us drifting through space. I slammed my fist into the panel in frustration.

The creatures grew steadily in the porthole. I unstrapped from my seat and floated to the rear of the shuttle. Alexei joined me. The creatures moved through space like fish in water—graceful, their tails lashing, their course clear. "Well," I said, "we now know they can survive without oxygen."

Alexei's expression turned thoughtful. "But for how long? Their ship, it's pressurized and oxygenated."

"Maybe that's only to keep us alive until we complete the transformation?"

"Maybe," he echoed, but he continued to stare at the creatures, frowning.

"What are they doing?" I demanded as the aliens floundered around. My voice seemed shrill. I drew a deep breath, bringing it under control. "They should be on us by now."

Comprehension dawned on Alexei's face. "Of course. They can't hear us. There's nothing *to* hear in space."

We stared at one another. "Then . . . how do they navigate between their ship and the station? How do they . . . ?" The words caught in my throat. I flew to the control panel, banging on it until it flickered reluctantly to life. "Radio signals," I muttered, altering the sensors. Sure enough, I found what I was looking for on an incredibly low frequency. "Here!" I exclaimed. "The ship emits a signal. That's what jammed our comms before. The creatures—they're not following us. They're going home."

Alexei bent over me as best he could in his bulky XE suit. "Can you block it?"

"Maybe." I pulled up the shuttle's visual code. "We don't have weapons, but if I find the location, I can get out there and yank it off manually." I scanned the system until I found a small device affixed to the bottom of the alien ship. "Can you pilot this shuttle, Alexei?"

I couldn't see his face, but suspicion laced his voice. "I've flown personal aircraft back on Earth. This looks similar enough to manage. Why?"

"I need you to try to reactivate the shuttle's controls while I'm gone."

A long silence, and then his voice, tinged with danger: "Where are you going?"

I pulled a wrench out of the tool kit and tucked it into my utility belt. Nothing in my standard tool belt would stand up to what I intended. "To dismantle that thing before the creatures get there."

"No. I should do it. I'm stronger."

"I have more experience maneuvering in zero g," I returned sharply. This was not the time for some testosterone-driven battle. "Stay with Mia," I added, playing my trump card, and his expression told me I'd won. "I'll be back soon."

I hoped.

I checked the thruster levels on my suit. I'd grabbed one at random, and fortunately it was a new suit, with almost full charges. Before Alexei could talk me out of my own suicide, I popped the shuttle door and pushed off, directing myself at the ship.

The creatures drifted behind me. They *were* drifting, at least, and not likely to catch the shuttle any time soon. And I didn't have to worry about them hearing me. I aimed myself at the ship and accelerated. The temptation, of course, was to go too far too fast. Adrenaline coursed through my system, leaving me in full fight-or-flight mode. But if I hurried, I might overshoot the ship, wasting time and fuel turning around, so I forced myself to keep a steady pace. I fixed my gaze on my goal, but in my peripheral vision I could still see the two dead aliens in the distance . . .

and Tyler's body tumbling between them, frozen and hollow. I hoped we were right about the sedatives in the aliens' claws. I hoped he'd died quick and hadn't felt a thing. It was the best I *could* hope for, and more than I'd given Matt.

Had Matt died in terror, bleeding out, his last sight Cage and me running away from him at top speed? I allowed myself a broken sob at the memory. I couldn't afford to lose it, not here, not now. But my hands shook and my stomach lurched and I swore to myself that even if I couldn't ever tell anyone what had really happened, I would find a way to honor his memory—not to mention my mother's. *She* wouldn't get much sympathy from the prisoners, I knew. It would only be me who mourned her—and maybe Dad. I didn't know. I didn't know what to think.

At last I reached the ship. I grabbed its blocky exterior and clambered hand over hand to the small box fastened underneath. I stared at it dubiously. It looked like any other chunk of the ship. I'd examined the readings pretty carefully before I took off. But what if I was wrong? What if I hacked off something essential—or something completely useless? "Alexei?" I asked, hoping the comms worked. Only static greeted me. This close to the radio signal, our comms were fried.

Seven falls. Time to get up again. I steeled myself and grabbed the ship with one hand. With the other, I swung the wrench. The impact jarred all the way up my arm, shaking my grip loose. The wrench broke free and spiraled into space.

A cry of dismay escaped my lips. I could chase after it, but it was already a distant glimmer, and my fuel only went so far. The shuttle drew steadily closer—Alexei must have the controls working—and the creatures were not far behind. I clutched a protrusion with both hands and swung myself around, kicking the device with all my might. Without gravity, though, that didn't go far. I cursed myself for not letting Alexei do this. Maybe his increased strength would have made the difference. But I doubted it. The angle, the lack of gravity, made it impossible to build enough force.

Except . . . I still had nearly half a tank of thruster fuel.

I realigned myself, angling my feet toward the device. For an instant I drifted loose, surrounded by infinite space, about to do something incredibly stupid. If I gave myself too much time to think, my resolve would falter, so I didn't think. I triggered the thrusters, driving myself forward with half the remaining fuel behind me.

I collided with the device. It snapped—and so did something in my foot. I cried in pain, the sound echoing in my helmet. But the device dangled loose, hanging from the ship by a single solid shard. I tugged at it, but it stuck fast. Gritting my teeth, I angled myself again, positioned so my good foot would hit the device, my bad foot tucked beneath me. I expended the rest of my fuel. This time I didn't hurt myself, although the impact jarred my leg. The device came free and hurtled into space—and me behind it. Frantic, I scrambled for a hold on the ship as it flashed by. At the last second my fingers closed around a protrusion. I clutched it, wrenching my shoulders, and managed to hold on. Pain reverberated through my leg, and my shoulder throbbed. Something wet trickled down my arm—I'd torn Cage's stitches.

The thought of Cage got me moving. I climbed the ship, awkwardly, my right leg almost useless. Tears pricked my eyelids, but I bit my lip, holding them back. Hurt later, cry later. Move now.

At last I rounded the far side of the ship. In the distance, the aliens drifted toward the device as it floated away. Was it my imagination, or were they already moving more slowly—as if they wouldn't last much longer without atmosphere?

I climbed a bit further, my limbs trembling with exhaustion, and paused to rest, clinging to the side of the ship. That turned out to be a mistake. My sore foot throbbed in agony, and any attempt to move it sent pain rifling through my whole leg. After a few tries I gave up and let it lie limp, tugging myself forward with my hands and my good leg, leaving the injured one dangling behind me.

I wouldn't last much longer. I summoned the last of my reserves, a final push of adrenaline forcing me to the top of the ship.

And then my straining grasp fumbled over a handhold and slid loose. Instinctively I activated my jets, but I'd burned through the last of my fuel. Panicked, I grabbed for the ship, my fingers brushing its bumps and crannies as I spun in space, my own struggles propelling me into the void.

Suddenly, a gloved hand clamped over my wrist, and Alexei hauled me forward. He dragged me the last few feet to where he'd magnetically locked the shuttle to the ship's exterior. The rational part of me realized the ship must contain some form of metal for that to work, meaning it wasn't plastic after all. The rest of me just shivered in exhaustion. "You made it," I managed. "You landed the shuttle."

"*Da*. Are you all right, *dorogaya moya*?"

I almost laughed at the endearment. Less than thirty-six hours ago, Alexei had argued in favor of punching me in the face and hurling me into a prison cell. Now . . . "My leg," I managed. "Can you help me inside? Where's Mia?"

"I already got her in." And he'd left her to come after me? Something twisted in my heart. I wondered if he'd be as concerned if he knew the truth. After losing three people in as many hours, after losing the mother I'd thought loved me more than anything, I suddenly felt that Alexei's friendship was the most important thing in the solar system.

Alexei half lifted, half pushed me into the ship, then pulled the hatch shut behind us. The second that pressurization returned—and with it, gravity—I collapsed, groaning in pain at the pressure on my leg. Alexei stripped off his gloves, but pulled me free of my suit before escaping his own.

After a few minutes gasping for air, I struggled to my feet, ignoring Alexei's protests. The pain wasn't as bad now. I'd maybe broken a toe, sprained my ankle. It hurt, but a few deep breaths brought it under control, as long as I didn't try to stand on it. "Where are Cage and the others?"

He snorted. "When did you think I had time to look for them?"

I examined Mia as Alexei freed her from her suit. She was bleeding badly, but her wounds didn't look life threatening. I worried about the condition of her legs, though—the creatures had sunk their claws deep. "Will she be okay by herself?" Alexei asked. I blinked at him in surprise, and he shrugged. "The best thing I can do for her right now is find Reed. He can help her."

I nodded. "She's stable. She should be fine." As long as she didn't wake up. Of course if she did, I suspected we'd hear her swearing from anywhere in the ship.

A quick glance into the next room's chambers revealed the creatures, peaceful in their slumber. When we opened the last set of doors, voices reached our ears, arguing in Mandarin. "Cage!" I cried.

He appeared in front of me, a wide grin splitting his face, and he threw his arms around me. I screeched in protest. "Careful! What about your . . . ?"

He twirled, showing off his bandages. "Feeling much better now that I'm pumped full of painkillers."

"Painkillers?" I asked, stumbling as he stepped away and I lost his support.

"Yeah. We found them in the emergency kits on our tool belts." He inspected my limp. "You hurt?"

"My foot," I said. "It's a long story. Mia's down too. And Tyler . . ." For about the hundredth time that day, my eyes swam with tears. I swallowed hard, blinking them back. "He was trying to help Mia."

Cage's face fell. He tugged me against him, a slight tremor racking his limbs. "He was just a kid," he whispered. "I dragged him into this mess."

Alexei cleared his throat softly, and we pulled away. "Later," he reminded us, not unkindly.

"Kenzie, is that you?" Rune demanded from around the corner. "Come help me with this, please."

Alexei nudged me. "Don't tell her. Not yet. I'm going to get Mia."

I nodded. I leaned on Cage as we walked into the command center, wincing with every step. His warmth suffused me. I'd missed having him by my side. Rune waited, her face creased with worry. "What's going on?" I demanded.

Rune gestured to the consoles. "I managed to interact with the system, at least on some level. It's . . . complicated. It doesn't operate with the same logic as the computers I'm used to."

I rested against one of the consoles since the aliens didn't appear to believe in chairs. "And?"

Cage blew out his breath in frustration. "And, we have a simple solution to our problem, but Rune has a moral objection." He gestured around the ship. "We don't have to return to Earth, not for quite a while. Rune says the shuttle's outside, so I'm assuming we have supplies. We have life support, and between you and Rune, we can keep the ship running, go wherever we want."

I stared at him like he'd lost his mind. "Yeah, no problem at all, except for the hundred-odd aliens sleeping in the next room."

"And that's the solution. Rune's found a way to blow them into space. We can vent the circles individually—just like the prison sectors back on Sanctuary."

She stomped her foot. "Right. And kill a hundred sentient creatures in their *sleep*."

"Is that worse than what they planned to do to us?"

"We aren't *them*, though." Her voice took on a pleading note. "*Cage.* Exterminate an entire race of aliens? If we do this, we're as bad as they are."

"I doubt this is their entire race." Cage sighed in exasperation. "Rune, this is about survival. There's no time for sentiment!"

"This isn't our only option! We can turn ourselves in and let the Earth authorities take over."

"And what do you think they're going to do with the aliens, serve them milk and cookies?" Cage threw his hands up in disgust. I got the feeling this wasn't the first time they'd had this conversation. He pointed at me. "*You* know this is the only choice."

Rune shot me a look of appeal. "They might be unfriendly, but they're *alive*—thinking, feeling beings. We can't simply murder them in their sleep."

The two of them stared at me. Not for the first time, I wished this was all some dream, maybe a *really* messed-up episode of *RMDG5* I was watching, huddled under a blanket in a bed at camp. "You two started this. You fight it out." I struggled to disguise the tremor in my voice.

"Fight what out?" Alexei returned, carrying Mia in his arms.

Mia shook her head, slowly regaining consciousness. Both Cage and Rune gaped at the sight of her. "God, Mia," Cage said. "Those things did a number on you."

"Tell me about it," she choked. Cage vanished and reappeared with barely a flicker, holding what looked like a beaker of water and a couple of pills, presumably painkillers. She didn't protest when he dropped them straight into her mouth and brought the beaker to her lips. "Thanks," she said. "Put me down, Lex."

His jaw tightened, and Mia's eyes narrowed. They had some sort of intense silent confrontation, ending when Alexei carefully set Mia on her feet, keeping one arm looped around her waist. She wobbled and he tensed, ready to catch her, but she managed to stay upright. "What's going on?" she asked.

Rune blinked. "Where's Tyler?"

Cage and I exchanged glances. "There's another reason to get rid of them," he said at last, and proceeded to fill both Rune and Mia in on the details they'd missed. I expected tears from Rune, but she only closed her eyes, as if she'd become numb to loss and death.

But for just a second, utter rage glinted in Mia's eyes. "How is this even a debate? Vent the damn things into space."

"It's not that simple," I said. "Rune's right. If we do this, aren't we as bad as them?" I hesitated. "For the sake of argument, how difficult is it to vent the chambers?"

Rune shrugged. "The chambers are sealed. They connect directly to the exterior. There's no danger to us."

"Then there's no argument," Mia snapped. Alexei shifted, and her eyes slanted in his direction. "What?"

"So far, these haven't done anything but sleep." Alexei shrugged apologetically. "Do we really have to kill them?"

Mia gaped at him. "You have got to be kidding me."

"I'm fine with killing something that's trying to kill me. I'm less fine with murder."

"*It isn't murder!*" Mia shouted so loudly we all jumped. "They killed Tyler. They killed Matt. *They are trying to* exterminate *us!*"

"Kenzie?" Cage interrupted.

"What?"

"We have two against, two for. What do you think?"

"Oh, no." I shook my head frantically. "I am not going to be your tie breaker. Not on this one."

He exchanged speaking glances with Mia. "Leave it to me, then. Rune, how do I do it?"

She folded her arms. "Kenzie's right. We can't make this decision. We . . ."

"Hu Lin, show me how to vent the damn chambers."

"No!"

He turned, towering over her, and grabbed her arm. "Right now you are standing between me and the safety of everyone on this ship," he snarled. Rune flinched, her eyes round and huge, as if she couldn't believe this was her brother yelling in her face. "If you're not going to do what I say, then show me a *gaisi de* button and I'll do it myself!"

"Cage," said Alexei quietly.

He blinked, as if realizing what he was doing, and released her. Tears spilled over Rune's lashes. After scrubbing them away with her fists, she glared at Cage and spun on the console. Her fingers dipped below the surface. A moment later a large red circle rose on one of the screens. "There," she said, her voice unsteady. "There's your damn button!"

"Rune . . ." Cage reached for her, but she leaped back, her eyes flashing rage.

"Enough!" I stepped between them. I'd never seen Rune and Cage at odds like this, and the betrayal sketched across her face reminded me painfully of how my mother had turned her back on me. "There's a better solution here. Let's get all the survivors together and vote on this. Where are they now?"

Cage ran both hands through his hair and dragged them across his face. "Imani got almost everyone down, and Reed's doing his best. He has anyone who can move bandaging and stitching. Survival seems to depend on how long people have been in stasis, and how susceptible they were to begin with. Some people died as soon as we disconnected them. Some are going to pull through. For most, it's too soon to tell."

"We should vote on this," I insisted.

"Are you serious? Have you tried getting these people to agree on anything? They've spent half their lives on an orbital prison. They aren't exactly open to dialogue."

"Kenzie's right!" Rune interjected, her hands clenched into fists. "This isn't a decision we can make on our own."

A shrill beep cut through our argument. We spun to find Mia hunched over the console, barely on her feet. "Mia," I gasped. "What did you do?"

She twisted to glare at me, one hand holding her abdomen closed, the other still clamped over Rune's button. "What needed to be done."

I ran for the console, Rune at my side. She closed her eyes and plunged in while I frantically fumbled through the alien text. Even the short time that had passed since I'd interacted with the system had eroded my hard-won familiarity with the language, though—before I began to grasp the meaning of each scrolling symbol, Rune was already stepping back, shaking her head. "It's done," she said, her gaze drilling through Mia. Her voice caught. "We just sent a hundred sleeping creatures to their deaths."

Mia shrugged. "Not you, sweetheart. Me. Let me worry about the consequences." She tried to straighten up, grimaced, and collapsed to her knees.

Alexei swooped in, lifting her again. "Where did you say Reed was?"

"Through there," said Cage.

Without another word, Alexei carried Mia away.

Cage reached for Rune. *"Meimei . . ."*

She recoiled from his touch. "Don't even talk to me." Shoving away from the console, she ran for the exit. I chased after her as best I could on my injured foot, catching up as she entered the aliens' stasis chamber.

We shone a flashlight into the nearest cubicle. Empty. The creature who'd slept there was gone. We made our way through both rings, but they were completely deserted. I checked cubicles randomly, finding only traces of slimy gel, empty coffins.

Once we reached the inner airlock, we stood in silence, staring at one another. And it *was* silent. I hadn't realized it before, but the chambers used to emit a slight hum. Now . . .

"It might be for the best," I acknowledged at last. "Cage had a point. What were we going to do with them?"

Rune shook her head. "I don't know. But I can't shake the feeling this is going to come back to haunt us."

Maybe she was right. But a tiny part of me—maybe the Omnistellar guard, the one who understood my parents' actions—breathed a silent thanks to Mia for doing what I couldn't.

THIRTY-NINE

RUNE AND I HUDDLED ALONE IN THE CONSOLE room a few hours later, working out the computer. We had a difficult task in front of us: find the weapons on this ship and destroy Sanctuary. Because if we didn't, if there were any more aliens, we might not have saved Earth at all, and the next people to visit the station would get a nasty surprise.

And the next people would probably be Dad and my friends. Besides, the station was a vivid clue regarding our whereabouts—the missing prisoners, the empty shuttle bay, the cameras.

We managed to pull up a viewscreen, which gave me an immense sense of relief, alleviating some of the alien ship's claustrophobia. The computer hadn't been designed to show us anything outside—after all, the aliens couldn't see. But between us, Rune and I were finding it easier and easier to manipulate the AI into doing exactly what we wanted.

I stared at Sanctuary. It seemed so peaceful, drifting in space. You couldn't see any of the damage on the screen, smell the blood, hear the screams. If any aliens remained, they prowled in silence, making no further effort to return home. Maybe they didn't realize we'd gone—or maybe there really weren't any left. I choked on unshed tears and, stupidly, thought of freeze-dried strawberries and my poster of Yumiko. Those were about to disappear forever. Stupid things to worry about, given everything that had happened, but there it was. "Okay," I whispered to Rune, my hands trembling on the console. "I'm ready. Let's . . ."

Something shimmered on the screen, and Sanctuary exploded in a silent but vivid display of fireworks. My jaw dropped as it burst in on itself, flames and lights and debris winking in and out of existence in a heartbeat. "Rune, did you . . . ?"

"I didn't do anything! I barely found the ship's weapons, let alone figured out how to work them." She joined me at the screen and we watched pieces of my home drift away. "Maybe there were aliens left on board?" she suggested dubiously. "Maybe they triggered something?"

"Maybe." Or maybe enough damage had been done and Sanctuary couldn't sustain itself anymore under the pressure. I didn't know. Either way, its destruction left a gaping hole in my heart, as if I'd lost another friend.

And yet . . . part of me felt something like relief. Destroying Sanctuary meant—at least in my mind, if not in reality—that I was really and truly done as a guard. I couldn't go back.

And of course, it meant no questions about the gaping wound in Matt's chest.

Matt. The aliens. How many deaths would land on my conscience? "Rune," I said softly. "When Cage was yelling at you—why'd you give him the button? Mia couldn't have vented the ship if you hadn't."

I spoke hesitantly, afraid of hurting Rune's feelings. But she looked more angry than sad. "Believe me, I've thought of that," she said, her gaze fixed on the console. "In a lot of ways, what happened was my fault. I didn't think Cage would really do it, though. And I was . . . I don't know. Overwhelmed. He was yelling at me." She blinked at me, a bewildered expression in her wide eyes. "Cage never yells at me. I've never seen him so angry. I just didn't know what to do." A bitter laugh escaped her throat. "I wish I was strong like you, Kenzie. I wish I knew the right thing to do and just *did* it. Things would be so much simpler."

There was so much wrong with her perception of me, I didn't even know where to begin correcting her. Instead I took her hand, and she squeezed before turning to the console and saying with obviously forced cheer, "So, what should we work on next?"

I let the moment pass. After all, Rune didn't deserve me trying to unload my own guilt on her shoulders. I had to live with what I'd done.

By the time we separated the dead from the wounded, twenty-three prisoners survived Sanctuary. Imani's sister, Aliya, was not one of them, and Imani's grief—so raw in its power and fury—ripped my own heart to pieces. Mom. Rita. Tyler. And God help me, Matt. So many deaths to carry.

We buried the bodies at space, so to speak. We tried to find something to say about each person, but it wasn't easy. None of the prisoners from sectors 2 through 4 had survived, obviously excepting Imani and Anya, meaning I was the only person with a chance of recognizing their faces and names from distantly remembered files. I spent hours chewing my lip, racking my memory for any tidbit of information to turn them from nameless prisoners into people. Most of the time, I failed. Some of the time, I lied. Names and stories seemed to bring everyone comfort, and if I could give them that, I would.

We held a private service for Tyler and Matt, just the prisoners from sector 5 and me. I hadn't wanted to attend, but Cage insisted. Matt had been Catholic, and Rune said Tyler was Jewish, so we said a few prayers before committing their spirits to wherever they had gone.

Of course, everything we said about Matt's death was a lie.

Rune stood beside me through Matt's service, her chin held high and her lips trembling, her eyes wet but resolute. Halfway through, she reached out and took my hand, clinging to me like a lifeline. I squeezed back, remembering Matt's rueful grin, the blank look on his face when he died. What would she say if she knew the truth? I hadn't wanted to lie about it. I hadn't meant any of this to happen. But now the lie was out there, and I didn't dare tell anyone the truth. Even if they didn't blame me for Matt's death—and how could they not, given the circumstances?—they would hate me for lying.

At last, a few tears spilled over Rune's cheeks. She wiped them away almost angrily, and I squeezed her hand more tightly. Cage stared at both of us, his expression a mask of misery. He alone knew what I was going through, and I could see the urge to comfort his sister like an itch he just couldn't scratch. But he knew she'd only push him away.

I lingered after the service, where Cage stood against the airlock, his body taut, one arm propped against the wall. "We didn't even have a body to launch," he said shortly. I couldn't read his expression with his forehead resting on his arm, and I didn't know if I dared reach out to him. Would he even want my comfort? "I just wish we'd . . ."

"I'm sorry," I said softly. It felt miserably inadequate, but what else could I say?

At last he looked at me, his eyes bright with unshed tears, his face pale and drawn. "No one's blaming you. You were trying to save his life. I know that."

"Yeah, well, that's not how it worked out, is it?"

"No," he said flatly, and my heart sank. "I guess it isn't." He stared at the wall another moment, then seemed to shake off his grief. I sighed, raising my hand and tracing the lines of his face. Cage always wore a mask. I guess I was grateful he trusted me enough to let it down for even a short time, but I wished he'd give himself time to grieve properly.

"Look who's talking," he said dryly, and I realized I'd murmured the thought out loud. I blushed. I was more exhausted than I'd imagined. But then Cage drew me into his arms and gripped me a little tighter than usual. I pulled him in as close as I could and held him there. He didn't speak or cry or tremble, but he clung to me like I was a life preserver, and for a long time we just stood like that, two people afloat in the midst of an ocean of grief.

I buried Mom and Rita separately too, not wanting it to become a spectacle. Alexei and Cage carried their bodies, wrapped in some loose tarps we'd taken from Sanctuary, and laid them carefully in the airlock. Rune stood by my side, clutching my hand again, this time offering support instead of seeking it. "You want to say anything, Kenz?" Cage asked.

I hesitated. I'd never attended a funeral. My family wasn't religious, and I couldn't just list names and powers as I had for the prisoners. I glanced helplessly between them—Cage crouched by the bodies, Alexei on my left, Rune on my right, as far from Cage as she could get.

She stepped forward, careful to avoid her brother's eyes. "What's your mom's name?"

I blinked. "Angela. Angela Cord." The words twisted in my throat, threatening to choke me. Cage appeared at my side and took my arm, steadying me.

Rune smiled. "Angela Cord," she said, "and Rita . . .

Hernandez?" I nodded, and she continued: ". . . were officers on board Sanctuary. They were hard-working, loyal, brave women. They weren't always perfect. They made mistakes. But when it came down to it, they met their end with courage and strength. And they had this in common: they loved Kenzie, and she loved them. We didn't know these women, but we see a piece of them every time we look at Kenzie, reflected in her determination and conviction. We may have been on opposite sides while they lived, but I think that if we'd known each other better, we would have liked each other. Because in the end, what side you're on doesn't really matter. All that matters is who you are *inside*—and we know, *I* know, that if Kenzie loved someone, they must have been good at their core."

Tears stung my eyes. I reached for Rune, pulling her into my arms, and we hugged tightly.

Someone cleared their throat. I swiped at my tears and turned to see Mia lurking in the corridor. She inclined her head at me and limped to stand beside Alexei, awkward and uncomfortable, never holding the same position for longer than a couple of seconds, until he laid his hands on her shoulders, stilling her. In a moment of insanity or grief or something, I almost reached out to her. Somewhere along the way, I'd come to value Mia. It meant a lot that she'd dragged herself here— stumbling, in pain, uncertain, but still, she'd come.

"Kenz?" Cage asked again, his voice so gentle it almost retriggered my tears.

I closed my eyes, tensed my muscles, and nodded, stepping back from the airlock. He followed, allowing it to seal. Rune crossed to a console, plunged her arms inside, and gave the computer a command. The thick walls prevented us from hearing anything, but a moment later the door slid open to reveal . . . nothing.

Mom and Rita were truly gone.

I stumbled blindly from the room, terrified with every step that someone would call my name and my composure would break before I could escape and find the privacy I so desperately needed. No one did, though. They had the good sense to let me go. I barely cleared the room before the tears started, a deluge of the agonizing grief that had clawed at me from the moment I saw my mother's body. I wedged myself into a crevice in an abandoned area of the ship, wrapped my arms around my legs, and buried my face in my knees, the tears flowing freely now and soaking through the legs of my uniform.

Everything was so wrong. Omnistellar was at best misguided and at worst evil. My mom had tried to kill me, and she'd died before I could so much as ask for an explanation. Hundreds of prisoners had died, including Tyler and, of course, Matt. And the stain of that blood wouldn't be fading from my hands or my heart any time soon.

I huddled in the darkness, alone and silent, and cried for what felt like hours, until everything inside me was drained and exhausted and dull. Then I wiped my face with the back of my hand, rearranged my hair, and set my mask back in place.

There was still work to be done.

We gathered in the control room: Cage, Rune, Mia, Alexei, Imani, Reed, and me. Reed looked almost as exhausted as I felt—he'd been run off his feet getting everyone healthy and mobile, and his brown skin seemed ashy and sallow under the emergency lights. Imani had found a scrap of cloth somewhere and fashioned it into a hijab. She lounged against a console, shadows of grief still lining her face.

Reed had done what he could, but Mia, Cage, and I still bore our own injuries. My ankle throbbed whenever I moved too quickly, and I caught Alexei threatening to tie Mia down after she tore her stitches a second time running around the ship, barking orders.

The seven of us had become the ship's de facto leaders. The other kids brought us their problems—and they had problems all the time, ranging from "this food is gross" (*so don't eat it*) to "where should we go to the bathroom?" (We found a drainage room at the end of the hall where the kids had been chained. It seemed to function as a large shower and waste recycling system, so for now, everyone used that. No one was happy about it.)

"What now?" Rune asked the question on everyone's minds. She stayed on the opposite side of the room from Cage and Mia, and I knew Cage felt it from the way he kept glancing to her, his jaw working as though considering and rejecting explanations. I'd overheard a conversation between them outside the command center the night before, and I'd picked up enough Mandarin to understand it.

"Would you give me a chance to explain?" Cage had demanded.

"Explain what?" Rune's voice had been high and shrill, on the edge of hysterics. "You *killed* those creatures!"

"*I* didn't—" He'd sputtered, sucking in a deep breath. "You know, it's not the first time I've had to kill someone to keep you safe. It's just the first time you had to see it."

"Is that supposed to make me feel better?"

I wondered that myself. Who had Cage killed—and why? I stared at my folded hands. Maybe that was why he wasn't blaming me for Matt's death. Had Cage killed similarly, by mistake? Or was it something more? I realized again how little I knew about these people I'd been thrown in with. If I transferred blind trust from Omnistellar to the prisoners, had I really made any progress?

Cage's angry voice countered, "You rely on me to protect you, but only if I keep you in the dark, is that it?"

"So stop protecting me!" she shouted. "Just leave me alone!"

Cage's voice dropped dangerously. "That's not going to happen."

"It will if I have anything to say about it." She'd stormed

into the command center so quickly I'd stumbled over a console, frantic to look busy. Guilt had assailed me—I'd really had no right to eavesdrop on their conversation—but Rune had been too furious to notice. And after a moment, Cage had sighed and stomped away.

Now, I casually stepped between them, breaking the angry tension. "The way I see it, we have two options. We can contact Earth and head home. If we're lucky, we might get some leniency from Omnistellar—and yes, I mean *we*," I added, catching Mia's glare. "*I* helped you escape. *I* had that chip cut out of my arm. I'm one of you. Whatever happens to you, I'm in the same boat."

"Or," said Cage, "we can see where this ship takes us. Rune and Kenzie figure they can keep us afloat for a few months at least. That's enough time to consider our next step. The area is dotted with space station merchant colonies, and there are mining colonies nearby on Mars. We should be able to avoid them as long as we want to, but it's not like we're drifting aimlessly through space. If we need to dock, we can."

An uncomfortable silence met that suggestion as everyone weighed the options. Return to Earth, almost certainly to prison? Or head into the unknown on a dark alien ship meant to serve as our destruction? "Both ideas have merit," I said with forced cheer.

I got a hollow smile from Imani. Mia rolled her eyes. "Why are we even talking about this?" she demanded. "You guys can do what you want. I'm not going back to prison. Not now, not ever." She pointed at me. "If you were *really* one of us—if you'd ever spent a day not living in privilege and luxury—you'd agree."

"Take it easy," Reed replied. "I spent three years on Sanctuary, and I'm not sure I prefer this ship."

"It's trading one prison for another," Cage admitted. "But at least we're in charge of this one."

That seemed to sum things up. No one voted for a return to Earth—not even me, although as the vote passed, I closed my eyes against the memory of my father. I'd blocked him from my mind for the last day, but soon enough he'd learn about Sanctuary and go wild with worry. I'd find a way to contact him, I vowed, without compromising everyone on the ship. I still hadn't read his messages—or Mom's. I was sure there was a stockpile by now. Part of me was afraid to look. But Dad had to know the truth about what happened to me. And what happened to Mom.

My dad had some questions to answer too.

Six days after Sanctuary's destruction, I finally walked the ship's corridors, taking in the excited buzz of laughter and conversation. The thrill of freedom hadn't let up. Kids were sad, frightened, missing their friends, but also hopeful. They didn't know where we were going, and they didn't care. They trusted us—or more accurately, Cage, who could talk his way up one side of the ship and down the other, leaving everyone encouraged and excited, even if he was chastising them. And of course they were happy not to have their every minute structured and book-ended by the prison's routine.

I discovered a private spot in the inner ring and sank against the wall, staring at the empty chambers where the creatures had slept. It didn't take long before Cage found me. "Hey," he said, dropping beside me. "You finally escaped the control room."

I cleared my throat. Why did things feel so awkward between us now? I still hadn't been able to tell him what I'd overheard, to ask him who he'd killed, and when, and why. Maybe that was the unspoken barrier. Or maybe it was some-thing else. "Yeah," I replied. "Rune and I have things running pretty smoothly at this point. The ship's on autopilot, but it'll alert us if something unexpected happens."

"I'm impressed. You two figured out an alien spaceship in an alien language in less than a week." His arm brushed mine. He was still wearing the bottom half of the prison jumpsuit and Dad's T-shirt, but he'd washed them at some point recently. They were faintly damp and smelled clean. I imagined what I probably smelled like and surreptitiously put a bit more space between us.

"What can I say? We're gifted." I meant it as a joke, but it came out hollow.

Cage nodded, picking at a loose spot on the hem of his shirt. "Has Rune . . . ?" He cleared his throat. "She's still pretty mad at me, huh?"

Mad wasn't the word. She didn't talk about it much, but every time Cage's name came up, hurt and confusion glinted in her eyes. Cage shielded her from the darker side of their time in Taipei, and she'd never had to confront what he was willing to do to protect her. Now that she had, it threw everything into question—the foundation of her family, her life. I understood the feeling. "Give her time," I said.

"Yeah." He glanced aside, then back at me. "I'd better tell you. I found this." He reached into his pocket and produced Mom's missing pistol.

I gaped at it, and at him. "You . . . what? Where?"

"In one of the storerooms. Either it fell from her uniform when they took her, or . . . well. Or they knew what it was and grabbed it."

"That's a comforting thought." We had two guns again. Problem was, I'd been looking for a way to get rid of mine. I never wanted to shoot anything again, and certainly not anyone.

Cage hesitated. "And us?" he asked. "Are *we* okay?"

I examined him. Did I really blame him for wanting to kill the aliens, or was that Rune's voice in my head? I wasn't so sure he'd been wrong. But what about the other deaths? What had Cage done?

The worry in his eyes softened my heart. Whatever he'd done in the past, we could come to terms with it later. I might not know everything about his life, but I *knew* Cage. I'd seen the core of him, and that core was good. I didn't have to trust him blindly, but I would trust him, and not just because I didn't have any other options. I smiled and tipped my head onto his shoulder. "Yeah," I said softly. "Yeah, we're good."

His arm encircled my shoulders, his lips brushing my dirty hair. I closed my eyes and nestled closer, absorbing his warmth. We stayed there a long time, the ship drifting slowly on its path to nowhere, the other kids' voices a soft buzzing in the distance.

I didn't know where we were going. I did know we couldn't run forever. At some point I had to contact Dad, warn Earth about the aliens, find some answers.

But for now . . . for now, I was content to rest against Cage, our fingers entwined, letting the silence wash over us. He'd fought for this freedom. The other prisoners went along with him—some willingly, some reluctantly, some dragged kicking and screaming in his wake. And although I hadn't realized it, I'd fought for the same thing. For the first time in my life, I *was* free: free of my parents' expectations, Omnistellar Concepts, the chip surreptitiously controlling me.

After everything that had happened, I deserved a few days to experience that feeling.

ACKNOWLEDGMENTS

I AM ONE OF THOSE RARE INDIVIDUALS WHO actually reads acknowledgments. So if you're like me, welcome. I acknowledge you as you acknowledge me, acknowledging the many people who brought this book to life! And thanks for being here.

Sanctuary is the result of tireless work by so many people. First and foremost, they include my family (Audrey, Lanny, Chris, Kim, and Emmett), as well as my amazing family-by-marriage (Brian, Elizabeth, and Erin) and my incredibly supportive husband, Dan, who has never been anything but there for me. They also include my cousin Sarah, whose life goal is apparently to be mentioned in a book's acknowledgments. Glad I could help.

They include the bewilderingly supportive friends who have stood by me through thick and thin, the teachers who have encouraged me through the years—particularly Mrs. Rochester, Mr. Feschuk, and Mr. Montalbetti, all of whom put a pen in my hand and said, "WRITE." They include the teachers I work with now, more like family than colleagues, who have been my cheering squad since day one.

In a special way, they include my students. Your smiles when I read to you, your excitement when we talk about writing, the way you embrace every day as a challenge—you are the people I think of whenever I sit down to write.

Of course, in a more practical sense, there are many, many people who had a direct hand in this book. I never could have written a word (sometimes literally) without the support of my critique partner, Timanda J. Wertz, an amazing writer herself, and all of the other writers who have supported me through the years. My agent, Caitie Flum, and #TeamCaitie, as well as all the staff at Liza Dawson Associates, have been amazing from the start.

My editor, Sarah McCabe, and the fantastic staff on the Pulse team at Simon & Schuster, as well as all the other people who had a hand in putting this book on paper (or, as the case may be, on your device)—thank you. You never realize the people who go into making a book until you try to make one: Tricia Lin, Mara Anastas, Liesa Abrams, Rebecca Vitkus, Catherine Hayden, Amy Hendricks, Katharine Wiencke, Mike Rosamilia, Tom Finnegan, and Samantha Benson all deserve a huge shout-out. And of course, there's Sarah Creech, who designed the beautiful cover art that I hope blew your mind as much as it did mine!

And then, above all, there is you. Yes, you. You know who

you are. You're the person I forgot to mention by name, but without whom this book never would have been written. You're the one who supported me tirelessly and gave me all the love and encouragement I ever could have needed, and, wouldn't you know it, I've gone and forgotten you. But I haven't. Not really. Because if you think this statement refers to you, I'm going to tell you a secret: it most certainly does.

Last but not least—writers write so readers can read. If you read this book and enjoyed it even a little bit, and especially if you've come this far with me: THANK YOU. From the bottom of my heart. Thanks.